ISBN 978-1-333-01878-8
PIBN 10452129

English
Français
Deutsche
Italiano
Español
Português

www.forgottenbooks.com

Mythology Photography **Fiction**
Fishing Christianity **Art** Cooking
Essays Buddhism Freemasonry
Medicine **Biology** Music **Ancient
Egypt** Evolution Carpentry Physics
Dance Geology **Mathematics** Fitness
Shakespeare **Folklore** Yoga Marketing
Confidence Immortality Biographies
Poetry **Psychology** Witchcraft
Electronics Chemistry History **Law**
Accounting **Philosophy** Anthropology
Alchemy Drama Quantum Mechanics
Atheism Sexual Health **Ancient History**
Entrepreneurship Languages Sport
Paleontology Needlework Islam
Metaphysics Investment Archaeology
Parenting Statistics Criminology
Motivational

IN TWO VOLUMES

SCOTT'S LAST EXPEDITION THE JOURNALS

CAPTAIN R. F. SCOTT R.N., C.V.O

II. BEING THE REPORTS OF THE JOURNEYS
AND THE SCIENTIFIC WORK UNDERTAKEN BY DR. E. A. WILSON
AND THE SURVIVING MEMBERS OF THE EXPEDITION

ARRANGED BY

LEONARD HUXLEY

WITH A PREFACE BY

SIR CLEMENTS R. MARKHAM, K.C.B., F.R.S.

With Photogravure Frontispieces, 6 Original Sketches in Photogravure by
Dr. E. A. Wilson, 18 Coloured Plates (16 from Drawings by Dr. Wilson),
and Full-Page and smaller Illustrations, from Photographs taken by Herbert
G. Ponting, and other Members of the Expedition ; Panoramas and Maps

VOLUME II.

LONDON

Edward A. Wilson

from a photograph by D. R. J. Wilson

IN TWO VOLUMES

BEING THE JOURNALS OF

CAPTAIN R. F. SCOTT, R.N., C.V.O

BEING THE REPORTS OF THE JOURNEYS
& THE SCIENTIFIC WORK UNDERTAKEN BY DR. E. A. WILSON
AND THE SURVIVING MEMBERS OF THE EXPEDITION

ARRANGED BY

LEONARD HUXLEY

WITH A PREFACE BY

SIR CLEMENTS R. MARKHAM, K.C.B., F.R.S.

With Photogravure Frontispieces, 6 Original Sketches in Photogravure by
Dr. E. A. Wilson, 18 Coloured Plates (16 from Drawings by Dr. Wilson),
260 Full-Page and smaller Illustrations, from Photographs taken by Herbert
G. Ponting, and other Members of the Expedition ; Panoramas and Maps

VOLUME II.

LONDON

1914

CONTENTS

OF

THE SECOND VOLUME

THE WESTERN JOURNEYS

By GRIFFITH TAYLOR, B.A., B.Sc., B.E., F.G.S.

CHAPTER I

KOETTLITZ, FERRAR, AND TAYLOR GLACIERS

CHAPTER II

THE GEOLOGICAL EXPEDITION TO GRANITE HARBOUR

ILLUSTRATIONS

IN

THE SECOND VOLUME

FULL PAGE PLATES

*The Full Page Plates are from Photographs by Herbert G. Ponting,
except where otherwise stated*

MAPS

THE BARRIER SILENCE

THE Silence was deep with a breath like sleep
    As our sledge runners slid on the snow,
And the fate-full fall of our fur-clad feet
    Struck mute like a silent blow
On a questioning 'Hush?' as the settling crust
    Shrank shivering over the floe.
And the sledge in its track sent a whisper back
    Which was lost in a white fog-bow

And this was the thought that the Silence wrought,
    As it scorched and froze us through,
For the secrets hidden are all forbidden
    Till God means man to know.'
We might be the men God meant should know
    The heart of the Barrier snow,
In the heat of the sun, and the glow
    And the glare from the glistening floe,
As it scorched and froze us through and through
    With the bite of the drifting snow.

These verses were written by Dr. Wilson for the *South Polar Times*. It was characteristic of the man that he sent them in typewritten, lest the editor should recognise his hand and judge them on personal rather than literary grounds. Many of their readers confess that they felt in these lines Wilson's own premonition of the event. The version now given is the final form, as it appeared in the *South Polar Times*.

SCOTT'S LAST EXPEDITION

THE WINTER JOURNEY TO CAPE CROZIER

By Dr. Edward A. Wilson, Lieut. H. R. Bowers, R.N., and Apsley Cherry-Garrard

June 27, 1911, to August 1, 1911

THE object of this expedition to the Emperor penguin rookery in the darkness and cold of an Antarctic winter was set forth years before in Dr. Wilson's Report of the Zoology of the *Discovery* Voyage. It was to secure eggs at such a stage as could furnish a series of early embryos by which alone the particular points of interest in the development of the bird could be worked out; for it seemed probable 'that we have in the Emperor penguin the nearest approach to a primitive form not only of a penguin, but of a bird.' These points could not be investigated in the deserted eggs and chicks which had been obtained in *Discovery* days. Such a journey 'entailed the risks of sledge travelling in midwinter with an almost total absence of light,' for the Emperor is singular in nesting at the coldest season of the year, and 'the party would have to be on the scene at any

rate early in July. . . . It would at any time require
that a party of three at least, with full camp equipment,
should traverse about a hundred miles of the Barrier
surface and should, by moonlight, cross over with rope
and axe the immense pressure ridges which form a chaos
of crevasses at Cape Crozier . . . which have taken a
party as much as two hours of careful work to cross by
daylight.

Furthermore, it afforded an opportunity of obtaining
an exact knowledge of the winter conditions on the
Barrier at its western end, and throughout its dangers
and difficulties Bowers kept a most remarkable meteorological record (given at the end of this volume), the
substance of which is embodied in this Report. The
three travellers also experimented with their sledging
rations, each for some time taking a different proportion
of pemmican and biscuit, the results of which were used
in order to make up the rations for future use.

The journey was planned to last six weeks, with a
stay of several days near the rookery, but was shortened
by the extreme cold and consequent consumption of
their store of fuel, and the tempest which drove the
party back from Cape Crozier.

To the report written by Dr. Wilson various
notes and details are added in square brackets from
Mr. Cherry-Garrard's diary. This diary, be it said,
was never written for publication. It was a private
record, for private remembrance. It tells of incidents
and impressions in their personal bearing, and so telling,
incidentally preserves the fuller human colouring that

BOWERS   WILSON,   AND

ABOUT   TO   LEAVE   FOR   CAPE   CROZIER

has been sedulously stripped away from Dr. Wilson's objective record, written with a more strictly scientific outlook.

Such notes have a manifold value. Every personality receives its own impression of the same incidents, recalls a different aspect, throws sidelights from a different angle. The young traveller records for himself a fresh and vivid personal impression, undiminished by reshaping into the perhaps necessary reticence of an official report. Not least, also, he gives us details about his chief which Dr. Wilson could not or would not have set down.

His own share in the expedition is the more remarkable because, short-sighted as he was, he could not wear his spectacles under such conditions.

With the help of these notes, the reader can fill in somewhat of those lights and shades which the official report, addressed to a Polar explorer, needed not to add. Now that the other two comrades in the adventure are no more, Mr. Cherry-Garrard has been prevailed upon to let his diary be used as it is used here. Let him be assured that his chief fear is groundless—the fear that in allowing such very personal jottings to be quoted, he should be imagined to magnify his own share in the expedition, instead of insisting, as he would have insisted in a public report, on the wonderful work of his friends: the strength, the steadfastness, and the serenity with which they carried it through. There was never an angry word from beginning to end, even in the most trying times. These unpremeditated notes help to make Wilson and Bowers stand out in their true colours.

Tuesday, June 27, 1911.—Leaving the hut at Cape Evans shortly before 11 A.M., Bowers, Cherry-Garrard and I started for our first march, accompanied by Simpson, Meares, Griffith Taylor, Nelson and Gran, who all helped us to drag our two sledges, and by a number of others who came to see us round the Cape.

We made for the western extremity of Big Razorback Island, and halted when it had just closed and covered the Little Razorback. We were then not 100 yards from the actual end of the rock and the sledgemeter read 3 miles 700 yards. Nelson and Taylor left us here and we continued with the other three.

We could now just distinguish the rock patches of Castle Rock and Harbour Heights and we made in a bit to pass as close as possible to the end of Glacier Tongue, where pressure lines were said to be less numerous in the sea ice than farther out. It was so dark, however, that we never saw the end of this Glacier Tongue, and we only knew we had passed it when the lower two-thirds of the Turk's Head Cliffs were suddenly cut off.

We then ran into some very difficult hummocky sea ice with steep-cut drifts, and our rear sledge capsized. It was too dark to avoid them, so Meares, Simpson and Gran remained with us and helped us until we had cleared them. We were then about three-quarters of a mile beyond Glacier Tongue and the sledgemeter read 5 m. 250 yds.

The wind, light southerly airs alternating with calm all the forenoon, now began to blow with some force from the east, and the sky became more and more overcast in the south [a half blizzard, in fact]; so we per-

THE **TIDE-CRACK AT RAZORBACK ISLAND**

A WEDDELL SEAL GETTING ON TO THE ICE

suaded the three helpers to return from here. After this we had very little trouble with rough ice, and though the loads (about 250 lbs. each) were heavy enough to make us slow, we had a good surface to go on.

We camped for lunch at 2.30 P.M., having made six and one-third miles from Cape Evans. The double tent was easy to pitch, and we began a routine of brushing down the inside, after removing all the contents, every time we broke camp. This routine we continued the whole way to Cape Crozier, and it made a great difference to the collection of ice on the upper two-thirds of the tent. It was the duty of the cook for the day to see to this, and we were each of us cook for one day in turn. The lower third of the tent skirt lining gradually got more and more iced up by trickles from above during the running of the primus, and nothing short of melting it out would have enabled us to keep it clear of ice. We gave up the brushing-down routine on the journey home from Cape Crozier, for we had to burn oil so sparingly that we tied up the ventilator permanently and kept in all the steam and heat we could, to thaw out our finnesko, which we hung in the roof at night. We were so iced up as to our clothes and sleeping-bags that nothing outside made any difference, and the omission of brushing down saved time in getting off.

After lunch we got away at 4 P.M. and made for what we believed to be Hut Point, but in the dark we got a good deal too close in towards Castle Rock, much more than was necessary. Our pace was slow owing to the weights, but the surface was not bad. It was chiefly crusty rough sea ice, salt to the taste still ; or it had an inch or two of white crusty snow on the rough, darker sea ice, alternating with broader drifts of hard wind-swept snow, making long, low mounds over which the sledges ran easily. These seemed here to result from an E.N.E. wind coming from the neck on the promontory, the wind which we caught just after passing the Glacier Tongue, and again off the ridge along Castle Rock, where it blew to force 5, up to 8 P.M., when we camped for the night, having made 9¾ miles from Cape Evans. [Setting this tent in dark is difficult, but not too bad even in that wind. Bill warns me seriously against running risk of frostbite. I find no specs. very hard in setting tent—must be sure not to let any inability arising from this get on my nerves—41 more days we hope.] Castle Rock was here nearly abeam. The wind dropped soon after and we had a clear starlit night.

The temperature for the day ranged from − 14·5° to − 15°, and the minimum temperature for the night was 26°.

Wednesday, June 28, 1911.—Turned out at 7.30 A.M. The going became very heavy with the two sledges, and we made very little more than a mile an hour over a surface which was all rough, rubbly salt sea ice with no snow on it. Bowers thinks that we were on definitely younger ice than that which we were on farther out yesterday and on our return. He thinks there was a large open lead along the shore which was the last to freeze up, and that this resulted from off-shore winds.

We reached Hut Point at 1.30 P.M., having crossed

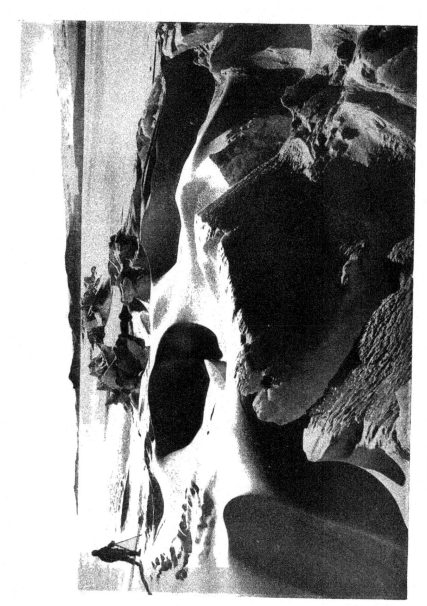

A PRESSURE RIDGE IN THE SEA-ICE RUNNING TOWARDS CAPE BARNE

three or four cracks and lines of pressure chiefly radiating from Hut Point itself. The sledgemeter showed 13 m. 1500 yds., but we had not come in a direct line from Cape Evans. We lunched in the hut and had no difficulty with the door, as there was hardly any snowdrift against it.

After lunch we made better going to Cape Armitage, though there was still no snow here on the rough, rubbly ice, but it was not so bad as what we had been on during the forenoon, where the sea ice was still salt and crunchy, with humps everywhere, formed from the old weathered ice and salt flowers, none bigger than one's fist, allowing the feet to crush between them every step at a different angle. After Cape Armitage the surface became hard and snow-covered; and with the best going we met with the whole journey for a short two miles, we quickly reached the edge of the Barrier, finding a good slope of snowdrift where we struck it, and having no difficulty in drawing our sledges up one at a time. There was a snow-covered crack as usual at the top of the drift, not a working crack, and invisible until broken into.

Unfortunately, both in going out and in coming back, we reached the Barrier edge in too bad a light to see whether these snowdrifts were quite continuous all along the edge, but from the fact that they were so at the two different points at which we struck the edge in the dark, I think it is probable that the slope is now continuous pretty well everywhere. We rose about 12 ft. off the sea ice.

Coming down the snow slope off the Barrier was a stream of very cold air which we felt first when we were only a few yards from the foot, and lost very soon after reaching the top. [Got both hands bitten going up Barrier—all ten fingers.]

It was now 6.30 P.M., and we camped at 7, the last half-hour on the Barrier surface being uphill, and very heavy compared with the easy going on the snow-covered sea ice from Cape Armitage. There was no doubt as to the existence of this slope up; we confirmed it on our return, and I take it to be a proof that the Barrier at this point has in recent years broken back at any rate half a mile or a mile farther than it did this year—for the previous broken edges can be supposed to fill up suc cessively in this way and so to produce a gradient without steps.

We had nothing but light variable airs all day with a clear sky. The temp. ranged from − 24·5° in the morning by Castle Rock to − 26·5° at Hut Point and − 47° at the edge of the Barrier.

Thursday, June 29, 1911.—We spent a cold night with temp. down to − 56·5° [Frightful cold last night— bad night. Bill has hardly slept for two nights—clothes beginning to get bad], and it was − 49° when we turned out at 9 A.M.; but the day was fine and calm on the whole, with occasional light easterly airs only.

Curtains of aurora covered a great part of the sky to the east both morning and evening, and it was one of the chief pleasures of our journey out that we were facing east, where almost all the aurora occurred, and so we could watch its changes as we marched, almost the whole time. Nine-tenths of the aurora we saw was in the east and S.E. of the sky, often well up to the zenith, but always starting from below the Barrier horizon. We never saw any that appeared close at hand.

The temp. remained at − 50° all day, and Cherry and I both felt the cold of the snow very much in our feet on the march, he getting his big toes blistered by frostbite, and I my heel and the sole of my foot. A good many of Cherry's finger-tips also went last night at the edge of the Barrier and are bulbous to-day; but he takes them as a matter of course and says nothing, and he never once allowed them to interfere with his usefulness.

The surface to-day was firm, generally; hard and windswept in some places, and soft and sandy in others. The sledges to-day went heaviest on the harder areas for some reason, which was quite exceptional. I think there was a fixed deposit of gritty crystals on the apparently smooth surface. Always after this it was the soft sandy drifts which held us up more than anything else.

We made two or three long sloping gradients to-day in our march going eastward. These also we confirmed on our return journey, when we recrossed three long low waves on about the same line, and I believe them to be the continuation of a series of extensive waves which run out from the point at which the glacier flow from Mt. Terra Nova runs into the Barrier. These waves curve gradually south-westward from the south-easterly direction in which they first join the Barrier. Hodgson and I followed up and roughly charted one of this group of waves in our journey in 1903 when we were examining the tide crack along the south side of Ross Island. They are very long and definite disturbances, and in our march were taken so diagonally that they seemed much longer. The difference of surface was quite noticeable, harder on the ridge summits and softer in the hollows. We have never met with anything like a crevasse on them.

Friday, June 30, 1911.—The surface to-day proved too heavy for us—we were unable to drag both sledges together, so we relayed one at a time, by daylight from 11 A.M. to 3 P.M.—and by candle-lamp from 4.30 P.M. to 7.45 P.M. We made only 3¼ miles in the day. The surface was soft and sandy, and though always crusted, always let one through an inch or two, as well as the sledge runners.

Heavy subsidences were continual all day, and the surface seemed to give way more when we were on the edges of the softer sandy patches. They were not extensive as a rule as far as one could judge, but they were exceptionally frequent—much more so than I have known them in the summer. There was no reason to think they dropped more than ¼ to ½ inch. The temp. to-day ranged from −55° in the morning to −61·6° at lunch and −66° on camping for the night. We had calm weather all day, and some aurora to watch in the E. and from N.E. to S. during the march.

[*June* 30.—Relaying all day—surface awful. It does not look as if we could pull this off. Last night was record sledging temperature −75° on sledge, −69° under sledge.* I was in big bag and most of night shivered till back seemed to break, then warm for half minute

---

* Wilson gives this under July 1 for the night of June 30. For the lowest temperature met, see under July 6.

and then on again the same thing : turned right over, froze in and got a little sleep. Feet liable to go. One big toe went and I don't know for how long.]

Saturday, July 1, 1911.—We turned out at 7.30 A.M. No dawn was visible, but at 10.45 A.M., when we got away, we were able to relay by daylight, and continued so until 3 P.M. After lunch we relayed by candle lamp from 4.15 P.M. to 7.45 P.M. The surface was like sand, and so heavy that we could only slowly move one sledge along. Subsidences very frequent all day. We made only 2¼ miles in all. [Bill and Birdie very unselfish and helpful—impossible to wear glasses and so I am handi capped.]

Between 5 P.M. and 7 P.M. there was a very fine aurora, large beams making very extensive curtains from E. to S. up to an altitude of 45°, and with characteristic black sky beneath the arches. The colour was a very orange yellow.

Erebus smoke has been difficult to see, no long stream of smoke, but very small puffs apparently going eastward each day.

The min. temp. last night was − 69°, and to-day we had − 66·6° in the morning and − 60·5° at 10 P.M. Light south-easterly airs and north-easterly airs during the march, at these temperatures, forced us all to adjust our noseguards.

Note.—All the temperatures and weather notes in this Report are taken directly from Bowers' record. Bowers also made himself responsible for the sledgemeter records, and for notes on the condition of the ice on Ross Sea when we were at Cape Crozier. He also kept full

notes of the auroræ, and did so much generally throughout the journey and with so much persistence notwithstanding the difficulties that beset us, that this Report
must be considered as much his as mine. He has moreover read it all through and has materially helped me in
making it complete. What I think of him and of Cherry-
Garrard as companions for a sledge journey of this kind
I have already made known to you, sir, in conversation.
It would be impossible to say too much about either of
them. I think their patience and persistence from
beginning to end was what made five weeks of discomfort
not only bearable but much more than pleasant. I have
added this note since his revision of the Report.

Sunday, July 2, 1911.—Min. temp. for the night was
− 65·2°, and this notwithstanding a breeze of force 3
from the S.S.E. with slight drift. The temp. during the
day ranged from − 60° to − 65° with calm, and light airs
which again made us adjust nose nips. After their use
this day and yesterday, however, they were unnecessary,
and some of us never again used them.

A fog bank formed along the Promontory ridge during
the afternoon, but rose, and later dispersed to the westward. We all noticed that our frozen fur mits thawed
out on our hands while it lasted.

Sunday, July 2, 1911 (continued).—We were again
relaying to-day by daylight from 11 A.M. to 3 P.M., and
by moonlight instead of candle-lamp from 4.30 to 8 P.M.
This was the first we had seen of the new moon. As it
passed exactly behind the summit of Erebus it gave us
an extraordinary picture of an eruption.

We had a fine aurora in the south low on the horizon as a low curtain and arch, with a very striking orange colour all over.

We made only 2½ miles in the day. [A terrible day. I felt absolutely done up at lunch—three frostbitten toes on one foot—and heel and one toe on the other— burning oil is all that keeps us going now—better night however. We are getting into the swing of doing every- thing slowly and in mits.

I have pricked six or seven blisters on fingers to-night.] *Monday, July* 3, 1911.—The min. temp. for the night was – 65°. The weather was calm to begin with and clear, but became gradually overcast all round, starting with a few curve-backed storm clouds over Terror. After lunch however the sky cleared again completely, and we were able to relay by moonlight in the afternoon. We had made only 1½ miles by daylight in the forenoon march, and in the whole day only 2½ miles.

The temp. ranged from – 52° to – 58·2°.

We had a magnificent display of auroral curtains between 7.30 P.M. and 8 P.M., during which four-fifths of the eastern half of the sky was covered by waving curtains right up to the zenith, where they were all swinging round from left to right in foreshortened, swaying curtains forming a rapidly moving whirl, constantly altering its formation. Some of the lower curtains were very brilliant and showed bands of orange and green and again orange fading into lemon yellow upwards. Bowers noted it as follows : ' Remarkably brilliant aurora working from the N.E. to the zenith and spreading over two-thirds of the sky. Curtain form in interwoven arcs, curtains being propelled along as if by wind ; the whole finally forming a vast mushroom overhead and moving towards the S.E. Colours, lemon yellow, green and orange.'

It was such a striking display that we all three halted and lay on our backs for a long time watching its evolutions.

Our sleeping-bags are beginning to show the effect of these low temperatures notwithstanding every care to keep them and our clothing dry. We left Cape Evans with three reindeer-skin bags for use to begin with, and a down bag each as a reserve lining. Cherry's fur bag was a very large one, much too large for warmth at these temperatures. My own was a good fit for warmth, but became so small when wet and frozen up that it broke in every direction. Bowers' bag was the right size for him, but also broke in more than one place later on when wet and frozen. All were as good as could be wished as regards the skins. Cherry has been so cold in his large bag with the hair inside that to-day he has turned it to hair outside, and bent his down bag as a lining to decrease the space.

Bowers' bag, begun with hair outside, is still so in use. My own, begun with hair inside, is still so in use. All are already rather wet and stiff when frozen, but we sleep in them well enough, and have no difficulty in rolling them up and unrolling them at night. [Bill having cold bad nights—feels it a bit I think—I have been half falling asleep at halts, Birdie ditto—surface a little better —foreshortening the mountains. Clothes for day have been so stiff we have to stop in position we just stand in when we get out of tent.]

Tuesday, July 4, 1911.—The min. temp. for the night was – 65·4°, but on turning out at 7.20 A.M. we found the sky completely overcast and snow falling, with occasional gusts from E.N.E. to S. and S.S.E. At 9.30 A.M. the temp. had risen to – 27·5°, with a wind force of 4 from the N.E.

Nothing was visible anywhere by which to make a course, so we had breakfast and turned in again. We were warm and comfortable all day, but though there were signs of clearing by night time we had to do without a march.

The min. temp. for the day was – 44·5°, and during the following night – 54·6°.

Everything was obscured round Erebus and Terror by clouds, though later it became possible to see Terror Point, and we knew that we were still out of the direct path of the southerly blizzards which sweep round Cape Crozier.

This lie-in has saturated our clothing through, and our Burberries stiffen outside the tent so much that it becomes almost difficult to get in again through the door. Our feet so far have been almost constantly warm, except on the march when plodding slowly on soft snow. We had then to keep a watchful eye on them to avoid getting frostbitten toes or heels. I regretted having left my puttees behind, as the additional wrapping round the ankles would have been a great protection to the feet.

We are using oil in the double tent now, after cooking is done, to dry and thaw out socks and finnesko before putting them on in the morning. It has seemed to us an almost necessary precaution at these temperatures unless one is prepared to take the damp socks into the sleeping-bag every night, and this with so many weeks ahead of us we are loath to do, as we are trying our best to keep the bags dry in many ways—for instance, we kept our pyjama trousers and pyjama jackets only for night wear to begin with, until they became so wet and stiff that in order to wear them at all they had to be kept on permanently. From the day of the blizzard incident at Cape Crozier back to Cape Evans, neither Bowers nor I made use of our jackets, however, at all—they were stowed away, stiff, in the tank, and so returned home.

Wednesday, July 5, 1911.—At 3 A.M. the whole sky was clearing and at 7 A.M. we turned out. The surface was now worse than we had as yet experienced, and we moved dreadfully slowly with one sledge load at a time. In 7½ hours hauling we only made 1½ miles good.

The min. temp. last night was − 54·6°, and by the evening the temp. had dropped to − 61·1°. We were then surrounded by a white fog, but could see Erebus and Terror. The cirro-stratus gave a white-looking sky in the moonlight and a fair halo with mock moons and vertical beams and a particularly well-defined mock moon beneath on the horizon.

All day we had been hauling up hill, and we hoped it was Terror Point we were crossing. Settlements of the crust occurred regularly again at short intervals. The surface still shows no sign of windcut sastrugi, and though much of it is wind-hardened and smooth, it appears to be the result of variable winds of no great force, and it is also covered to a very great extent by deep sheets of soft snow, on which the sledges hang up exactly as though they were going over sand. There is no surface marking on this snow except marks resembling horses' hoofs, with edges that have a peculiar planed-off appearance.

Whether harder or softer, the whole surface is crusted and lets one's feet in for a couple of inches, spoiling one's pull on the sticky-runnered sledges.

Thursday, July 6, 1911.—Again a calm day and clear, though a heavy bank of fog lies over the pressure ridges ahead of us, and over the seaward area to the east.

We had relay work again on a very heavy surface, which, however, improved slightly in the afternoon. But the result of $7\frac{1}{2}$ hours' hauling was a forward move of $1\frac{1}{2}$ miles only.

The min. temp. for the night had been $-75\cdot3°$. At starting in the morning it was $-70\cdot2°$ and at noon $-76\cdot8°$. At 5.15 P.M., when we camped for lunch, it was $-77°$ exactly, and at midnight it had risen again to $-69°$, when there was some low-lying white fog and mist to the N. and N.N.W. The butter, when stabbed with a knife, 'flew' like very brittle toffee. Our paraffin at these temperatures was perfectly easy to pour, though there was just a trace of opalescent milkiness in its appearance.

Friday, July 7, 1911.—We got away late, at noon, in a thick white fog, in which it was impossible to see where we were going. We still had to relay, though the surface had distinctly improved. There was no sign of wind sastrugi yet.

After lunch, which we finished about 6.30 P.M., we got an indistinct view of the mountains, and saw we were beginning to close Mt. Terra Nova with Mt. Terror, but the fog came down again at once, and at 9.45 P.M. we camped, as we were unable to guess at all what direction we had been making. We only made one and two-thirds miles good in the day.

The min. temp. for the night from 12 to 2 P.M. had been − 75·8. At 2 P.M. it was − 58·3°, and at 7 P.M. had risen to − 55·4°, a change which we felt as a grateful one both in our hands and feet on the march. [There is something after all rather good in doing something never done before—these temperatures must be world's record.]

Saturday, July 8, 1911.—A day of white fog and high moonlight but without a trace of landmark to guide us. We relayed as usual, four hours in the forenoon, for 1¼ miles, and three hours in the afternoon for one mile only. We were on a better surface, either more windswept or else improved by the rise in temperature, but still deep and soft to walk in, though often with harder crusted areas. Here and there were really hard and slippery windswept snow surfaces occurring under a covering of some inches of quite soft snow, showing the peculiar planed-off appearance which was always associated with horse-shoe impressions and very heavy dragging. We made our course to-day by compass.

The min. temp. for the night was − 59·8° and at 10.30 A.M. − 52·3°, with south-easterly airs, and − 47° at 7.15 P.M.

Sunday, July 9, 1911.—Dense mist, and white fog [the fourth day of fog], and snow falling all day. made relaying impossible, but we found we could manage the two sledges together again on the improving surface.

Our chief difficulty was to avoid gradually and unwittingly mounting the slopes of Mt. Terror to our left, where there are any number of crevassed patches of ice, and running into the pressure ridges on our right. Between these two lay an area of more or less level land ice which was safe going—but in two or three places I knew it was necessary to cross long snow capes running across our path from Mt. Terror—and here, if one wished to avoid very long uphill drags one had to approach the pressure ridges fairly closely—a thing quite easy with daylight, but affording us constant trouble in the dark and fog which hampered us all along this part of our journey.

To-day no landmarks were visible at all. We made a little over one mile in the forenoon and $\frac{3}{4}$ mile more in the afternoon. It was a great relief to have done so without relaying. The moon was invisible [only a glow where she is] and everything was obscured by fog, but the surface was improving every hour. In the afternoon we ran into crevassed ground, after having suspected we were pulling the sledges up and down several rises of moderate gradient. As we expected this, however, before reaching the second long snow cape, we went on. The surface was again hard and icy in places, with sometimes six inches of snow loose upon it. Our feet went through this snow and slipped upon the ivory-hard surface underneath. This was often near the top of the ridges. In the hollows the surface was deep and soft and crusted. One could judge much of the nature of the surface, and of the chance of finding crevasses, by the sound and by the feel of one's feet on the snow, without seeing anything at all of the surface one was covering. Occasionally the moonlit fog allowed an edge to be lit up here and there, but the surface is so extraordinarily uniform and feature-less that we believe we are still well out of the windswept line of southerly blizzard and still in an area of eddying winds, heavy snowfall, and constant fogs formed by the meeting of cold Barrier air with the warmer, moister air which comes up from the sea ice, and especially from the innumerable fissures of the pressure ridges. We called this Fog Bay.

The moon had again become visible almost overhead, but nothing else, until just as we found ourselves going up a longer rise and a steeper one than usual we saw a grey, irregular, mountainous-looking horizon confronting us close ahead. So here we unhitched from the sledges, and tying our lanyards together into a central knot, we walked up about 50 yards of icy slope interspersed with cracks, and having reached the top found we had another similar broken and irregular horizon ahead of us and another on our left. These were obviously the pressure ridges, and when we stood still we could hear a creaking and groaning of the ice underneath and around us, which convinced us, and later led us to think that the tidal action of the coast here was taken up in part at any rate by the pressure ridges without forming any definite tide crack.

This excursion from our sledges gave us, as we thought, our right direction for the safer land ice, but on turning

ourselves with them in that direction, we found we were
still running into the same crevassed mounds and ridges,
so, finding a hollow with deeper snow in it, we camped
for the night, and decided to wait until we could see
exactly where we had got to.

The absence of a well-marked tide crack—which had
rather puzzled us in the *Discovery* days—in the crossing
of land-ice slopes such as Terror Point (Cape McKay)
and the 'second snowcape,' both of which come straight
down from Terror and run into the pressure ridges, was
a question which we had in our minds all these days.
We assuredly did cross several small cracks on these slopes
which had the appearance of a certain amount of working,
but their breadth was a matter of a couple of inches only,
and if tidal they must take up only an insignificant
fraction of the movement. They are so small that
they may easily have been obscured by snowfall in the
old days. Bowers is convinced they are to be considered
tidal cracks. I am not so sure myself, and hope to have
a better view of them by daylight before deciding whether
there is anything to take up tidal movement besides the
pressure ridges, which seem to me more than sufficient.

This day the temp. ranged from $-36.7°$ up to $-27°$,
with light airs northerly and southerly.

Some hours after midnight it began to blow and to
snow more heavily.

The min. temp. for the night was $-24.5°$ up to noon
the next day.

Monday, July 10, 1911.—By noon a blizzard was
blowing from the S.S.W., of force 6 to 8, and the air was

as thick as could be with snow. This continued all day, and we lay wet and warm in our bags, listening to the periodic movements of the ice pressure, apparently tidal to some extent, beneath and about us.

Tuesday, July 11, 1911.—The temp. at 10 A.M. went up to +7·8° ['a rise of over 80°' from the record minimum], and at 8 P.M. was still +6·8°, with a minimum for the day of +3·2°. The wind came from S.W., force 5 to 9, and very squally. This continued all day with a very considerable snowfall which packed our tent in 1½ to 2 feet all round, as well as all our sledge gear. Cherry is still in his down bag inside the reindeer with fur outside. Bowers still as he started, with fur outside. I turned my bag yesterday from fur inside to fur outside. The rise in temperature and the long lie-in during this blizzard have steamed us and our clothes into a very sodden wet condition, and one wondered what a return to low temperatures would effect.

We have been discussing our respective rations, and they have been somewhat revised as follows :

On July 6 Cherry felt the need for more food, and would have chosen fat, either butter or pemmican, had he not been experimenting on a large biscuit allowance. So he increased his biscuits to twelve a day, and found that it did away to some extent with his desire for more food and fat. But he occasionally had heartburn, and has certainly felt the cold more than Bowers and I have, and has had more frostbite in hands, feet, and face than we have.

I have altogether failed to eat anything approaching

my allowance of 8 ozs. of butter a day. The most I have managed has been about 2 or 3 ozs.

Bowers has also found it impossible to eat his extra allowance of pemmican for lunch.

So yesterday—that is, a fortnight out—we decided that Cherry and I should both alter our dietary, he to take 4 ozs. a day of my butter and I to take two of his biscuits, i.e. 4 ozs., in exchange.

This brought Cherry's diet and mine to the same. Bowers continued his diet, taking his extra pemmican when he felt it possible—but this became increasingly less frequent and all the way home he went without it.

Cherry's diet and mine was now, *per diem* ·

Pemmican   .   .   . 12 ozs.
Biscuit   .   .   . 16 ozs.
Butter   .   4 ozs. (we rarely eat
                                        more than 2 ozs.)

Bowers' diet was now ·

Pemmican   .   12 ozs.
Biscuit   .   .   . 16 ozs.
Extra pemmican   4 ozs. (rarely eaten).

Our daily routine was, for breakfast, to have first tea, then pemmican and biscuit ; for lunch, tea and biscuit (and butter for Cherry and myself) ; for supper, hot water and pemmican and biscuit.

We none of us missed sugar or cocoa, or any of the other foods we have been used to on sledge journeys, and we all found we were amply satisfied on this diet. Cocoa would have been pleasanter at night than plain hot water, but the hot water with biscuit soaked in it was very good.

We still carry out the brush routine every time we break camp, to clear away all the rime formed on the inner tent lining. The outer tent is extraordinarily free from frost—and remained so to the day we returned to Cape Evans. The lower skirts of the inner tent, however, are solid with ice.

Towards evening the wind abated considerably, and parts of Mt. Terror came into view, but during the night the wind came on again with much snow and violent gusts, increasing at times to force 10. We were unable to march. The min. temp. for the night was – 7·6°.

Wednesday, July 12, 1911.—We were compelled to remain in our bags again all day. Wind from S.W., force 10, and squally up to force 9 all the afternoon, with much drift. Temp. up to + 2·9° again in the morning. Towards night there were lulls, and at 3 A.M. the wind ceased. Bowers turned his bag from hair outside to hair inside, his first change since starting.

Thursday, July 13, 1911.—After digging out our sledges and tent, which were pretty deeply buried in drift, we had a really good day's march, making 7½ miles in 7½ hours with both sledges. [Seems a marvellous run.] During our march, in our effort to avoid the pressure ridges on our right, we got imperceptibly somehow too high up on to the slopes of Terror and were held up by a very wide crevasse with an unsafe-looking sunken lid, which we caught sight of in a momentary break of moonlight just in time to avoid it. We turned down its side and found it was one of a number that marked a low mound in the land ice slopes. We made out east again to get once more into the safety limit of land ice on the flat, which seemed very narrow in the dark.

We camped about 8 P.M. Min. temp. for last night was – 22·2° and by the evening the temperature had dropped to – 28·6°, but there was still a lot of cirro-stratus about, which the blizzard doesn't seem to have cleared away. There were also windy-looking clouds about, with lunar coronæ and occasional halos. During the daylight there was a very striking rosy glow all over the northern sky even up to the summit of Mt. Terror. The whole sky was a rich rosy purple, due to a thin cirro-stratus or alti-stratus I think.

The new surface was very flat, and very windswept, but not cut into sastrugi at all. Most of the new areas are low, flat, soft drifts, or low mounds, slightly rounded at the top and of large area. The softer areas have still the shaved or planed-off appearance with none but the horse-hoof shaped impressions on the surface.

Friday, July 14, 1911.—We made five and one-third miles in all to-day by a good morning march, but an afternoon march cut short by a complete loss of all light. After lunch we once more found we had overdone our easting and had run again into one of the higher pressure ridges. We turned north from it and encountered more crevasses, but by zig-zagging and sounding in advance on a longer trace we succeeded in getting clear of them. We had the Knoll before us at the time while there was light enough to see it. Our moonlight was, however, all but spent, so much of it had been lost in fogs and blizzard and bad weather. We were making for rather east of the

Knoll to-day in our endeavour to keep within the flat area of land ice. Sastrugi were increasing rapidly here, and we were now entering the true path of the southerly blizzard.

The min. temp. for the night had been − 35°. At 8.30 A.M. it was − 17·4°, and in the afternoon and evening it was − 24·6°. [The experiences so lightly passed over in the official account were sufficiently thrilling in themselves. The other diary records :

Rather a hair-raising day—very bad night—by hard slogging 2¾ miles this morning—then on in thick gloom which suddenly lifted and we found ourselves under a huge great mountain of pressure ridge looking black in shadow—we went on bending to left when Bill fell and put his arm into a crevasse—we went over this and another and some time after got somewhere up to left, and both Bill and I put a foot into a crevasse—we sounded all about and everywhere was hollow, and so we ran the sledge down over it and all was well. My nerves were about on edge at end of day.]

AT THE KNOLL

Saturday, July 15, 1911.—The min. temp. for the night was − 34·5°, but at 10.30 A.M. it was − 19·2°, with a breeze of force 3 from the S.S.W. We got a clear view this morning, however, and could see the moraine shelf facing the Knoll, where we had decided to build our stone hut. We had a short, steep, uphill three miles' pull over very hard and deep-cut sastrugi to this spot, and then, rounding the lower end of the moraine, we found ourselves in the Knoll gap and pitched our last outward camp in a large

open smooth snow hollow, hard and windswept as to surface, but in places not cut up by sastrugi. This camp lay
about 150 yards below the ridge where we proposed to
build our stone hut. [Here we are after a real slog—
700 feet up, camped on very hard snow with our hut site
chosen off to W. on some moraine—we have been discussing what to call the hut which we hope to build
under a big boulder on the slope, walling one side of it—
Terra Igloo I expect. It seems too good to be true—
19 days out, this is our 15th camp—four days' blizzard.
Surely seldom has anyone been so wet—our bags hardly
possible to get into—our windclothes just frozen boxes.
Birdie's patent balaclava is like iron—it is wonderful
how our cares have vanished.] We had originally intended building on the Adélie penguin rookery, but so
much of our time has been taken up in getting here, and
our oil was already so short, that we decided to build as
close as we could to our work with the Emperor penguins,
and take the chance of doing so in the blizzard area.
In the Adélie penguin rookery we should have been out
of the blizzards, but five miles from our principal work.
We hoped, however, to find something of a lee for our
hut, and to put up with the blizzards.

On the ridge top above the snow hollow where we were
camped was a low, rough mass of rock *in situ* with a
quantity of loose rock masses of erratics of various kinds,
some granite, some hard basalt, and some crumbly volcanic
lava lying around. There was also a lot of rough gravel
and plenty of hard snow which could be cut into paving-
stone slabs. So here we had all the material we wanted,

and as the corner under the rock *in situ* [which, it was hoped, would make a large part of one of the walls] was too solidly iced up with ice and gravel to clear out, we chose a spot [a moderately level piece of moraine] some 6 or 8 yards on the lee side of the actual ridge, a position which we thought would be out of the wind's force itself, but which we eventually found was all the more dangerous for that reason, as it was right in the spot where the upward suction was to be at its greatest. At lunch time, 4.15 P.M., we still had a southerly wind of force 4, with the temp. at − 13°, and this wind we found to be due to a more or less constant flow of cold air down from the slopes of Terror.

We had a magnificent outlook from this spot where we were building our hut. To the east we looked out over the Great Barrier with the whole range of pressure ridges laid out at our feet, about 800 feet below [looking as if giants had been ploughing up with ploughs which made furrows 40 or 50 feet high]. To the north and N.E. we had the Knoll, and beyond it a clear open view over the ice of the Ross Sea. And to the south we looked along the path we had come along the slopes of Terror, stretching away towards the Bluff, while on our right these slopes climbed up to the summit of Mt. Terror, which was plainly visible against the sky.

We saw that Ross Sea was completely frozen over. No open leads were to be seen, but much of the ice appeared to be young and thin, with little snow on it. These and the following notes on the ice of Ross Sea were kept by Bowers.

I began the use of my eiderdown bag to-day inside the reindeer bag with the fur outside, and after this made no change till the day we reached Cape Evans again.

Sunday, July 16, 1911.—To-day looking over Ross Sea we saw a cloud of frost smoke drifting eastward along the Cape Crozier cliffs, evidently from an open lead along the coast. Otherwise the sea was covered by an unbroken sheet of ice.

The temp. varied to-day between $-20\cdot8°$ and $-28\cdot5°$, and we again had the south-westerly breeze of force 3 to 5 coming down our snow slope from Mt. Terror. The weather was clear in the morning, but became hazy with cirro-stratus and fog soon after noon from the south.

We worked at the stone hut all the daylight and as long as we could see by the waning moonlight, and while Cherry built up the walls, Bowers and I collected rocks and piled up the outside of the walls with snow slabs and gravel. We had a pick and a shovel to work with.

[It was quite a question what it was to be called in his Diary Bill called it 'Oriana Hut,' and the ridge the Oriana ridge : we discussed 'Terra Igloo,' 'Bleak House,' 'The House on the Hill.'

Birdie gathered rocks from over the hill; nothing was too big for him. Bill did the banking up outside. The stones were good; the snow, however, was blown so hard as to be practically ice : a pick made little impression upon it, and the only way was to chip out big blocks gradually by the small shovel.

There was now little moonlight or daylight, but for the next two days we used both to their utmost, being up

at all times by day and night, and often working on
when there was great difficulty to see anything : one day
Birdie was digging with the hurricane lamp by his side.]

The hut was placed so as to escape the force of the
southerly wind under the moraine ridge. We were about
800 feet above sea level. Our method of construction
was to build four walls of solid rock, leaving a small gap
for a door in the lee end. The weather wall was highest,
and the breadth of the hut was $7\frac{1}{2}$ to 8 ft., so that the
9-foot sledge rested across from wall to wall as a cross
rafter to support the canvas roof. The two side walls
were built up to the height of the weather wall at the
weather end, but were not so high by a couple of feet at
the door end. The length of the hut was about 10 ft.

Against the outer side of the rock-walls were laid
large slabs of hard snow like paving stones, each having
its icy windswept surface outside. Between the slabs
of snow and the rock walls we shovelled moraine gravel.
Over all this fell the canvas roof, anchored by lanyards
to heavy rocks all round, and battened down to its outer
side again by a double banking of ice slabs and gravel ;
finally, every crevice was packed in by hand with soft
snow until the whole wall was uniformly tight all round.
The work took us all the light we had of three days to
finish. The canvas roof was made so ample in size that
it came right down to the ground on the weather side
and more than half-way down all the other sides. This,
we thought, could not fail to make the walls tight when
packed in and over as explained above, but it completely
failed to keep out either snow drift or gravel dust when

the wind began to blow in earnest later on, for both drift and dust poured in through every crack between the stones of the weather walls and lee walls without shifting any of the more bulky packing at all.

Monday, July 17, 1911.—We continued with the hut and spent the whole of available daylight and moonlight in getting on with the walls, which were all but finished for placing the roof and door.   For this we want a calm if possible.

We began work to-day in a light air, but it was blowing again with force 3 from the S.W. from noon onwards, and the temp. all day varied between – 19·5° and – 23·3°. The sky was overcast. [Birdie was very disappointed that we could not finish the whole thing that day, but there was a lot to do yet, and we were tired out. We turned out early the next day to try and get the roof on, but it was blowing hard. (*Tuesday*, 18*th*.) When we got to the top we did some digging, &c., but it was quite impossible to try and get the roof on, and we had to leave it.   We realised this day that it blew much harder at the top of the slope than where our tent was pitched.   It was bitterly cold up there that morning.]

Over Ross Sea are now two open leads of water like broad irregular streets extending from the Cape Crozier cliffs away to the N.E. and lying more or less parallel to one another.

Tuesday, July 18, 1911.—No leads or open water were visible to-day over Ross Sea. The temp., – 26·5° to 27·3°, with S.S.W. wind of force 4 to 5 all day, made work almost impossible at the hut.   We got everything ready for placing and fixing the roof, but couldn't do it in the wind. We left the work at noon and turned in to spend a very cold night, a thing which we generally found was the consequence of not having done any hard work or marching during the day. [During this time our bags were getting worse and worse, but were still very possible, and we always looked forward to the days of the 'Stone Age' when the blubber stove should be going and we were to dry everything. When we arrived we had begun our fifth out of six tins of oil, and we were economising oil as much as possible, often only having two hot meals a day.

It was curious how the estimate of how much oil was necessary to our return, diminished as our stock decreased : at first we said we must have at least two gallons to go back with : then about Terror Point a tin and two full primus lamps ; until it came down to one full gallon tin, and this is what we actually did use.]

Wednesday, July 19, 1911.—As it was a fine, calm day we decided to use it in an effort to reach the Emperor rookery and get some blubber, as our last can of oil but one was already running low and we had determined to keep the last can untouched for the journey home. We started down at 9.30 A.M., just as dawn appeared on the horizon in the east. We took an empty sledge, with a couple of ice axes, Alpine rope, harnesses, and skinning tools. We had about a mile to go down snow slopes to the edge of the first pressure ridge, and our intention was to keep close in under the land ice cliffs which are very much more extensive now than they were ten years

... . the roof, but couldn't
... ... at noon and turned
... ... night, ... thing which we generally
... ... of not having done any hard
... the day. [During this time
... getting worse and worse, but were still
... looked forward to the
... the blubber stove should
... everything. When we
... our last ... of six tins of oil, and
... as much as possible, often only

... ... the estimate of how much oil was
... ... , diminished as our stock decreased
... must have at least two gallons to go
... with then about Terror Point a tin and two full
private lamps; until it came down to one full gallon tin,
and this is what we actually did use.]

Wednesday, July ... As it was a fine, calm day
we decided to set to to an effort to reach the Emperor
... ... Stubben, as our last can of oil but
we had determined to
keep the ... ... untouched for the journey home. We
started down at 9.30 a.m., just as dawn appeared on the
horizon in the ... We took an empty sledge, with a
couple of ice axes, Alpine rope, harnesses, and skinning
... We had about a mile to go down snow slopes to
the edge of the first pressure ridge, and our intention
was to keep close in under the land ice cliffs which are
... much more extensive now than they were ten years

CAVE IN THE BARRIER, CAPE CROZIER, JAN. 4TH, 1911.

ago. Then we hoped to get in under the actual rock
cliffs which had always been the best way down to the
rookery in the *Discovery* days. But somehow we got
down by a slope which led us into a valley between the
first two pressure ridges, and we found it impossible
to get back in under the land ice cliffs. Nor had we
then seen any other way down from the land ice except
by the slope we followed. The rest was apparently all
ice cliff about 80 to 100 ft. high. We tried again and
again to work our way in to the left where the land ice
cliffs joined the rock cliffs, but though we made considerable headway now and then along snow slopes and drift
ridges by crossing the least tumbled parts of the intervening pressure lines, we yet came time after time to
impossible places [with too great a drop], and had to
turn back and try another way. [Bill led on a length
of Alpine rope on the toggle of the sledge. Birdie was
in his harness on the toggle, and I was in my harness
on the rear of the sledge. Two or three times we tried
to get down the ice slopes to the comparatively level
road under the cliff, but it was always too great a drop.
In that dim light every proportion was distorted, and
some of the places we actually did manage to negotiate
with ice axes and Alpine rope looked absolute precipices,
and there were always crevasses at the bottom if you
slipped. This day I went into various crevasses at
least six times, once when we were close to the sea
going right in to my waist, rolling out and then down
a steep slope until brought up by Birdie and Bill
on the rope.] We tried one possible opening after

another, and all led to further impasses until the daylight was two-thirds gone, and we found ourselves faced
in a large snow hollow by a chaotic pile of ice blocks and
snowdrifts standing almost vertically in our path and all
round us, to a height of some sixty feet, and completely
stopping all chance of progress forward [a great *cul-de-sac*
which probably formed the end of the two ridges, where
they butted on to the sea ice]. Here we had the
mortification of hearing the cries of Emperor penguins
echoed to us by the rock cliffs on our left. We
were still, however, out of sight of the rookery and
we had still a quarter of a mile of chaotic pressure
to cross [to be caught in the night there was a
horrible idea], so we reluctantly gave up the attempt
for the day and with great caution and much difficulty
owing to the failing light retraced the steps it had taken
us about three hours to make. We had been roped
together the whole time and had used the sledge continually over soft and rotten-looking snow bridges. It
was dark by the time we reached safe ground after
clambering about five hours to no purpose. [Birdie was
very good at picking the tracks up again. At last we lost
them altogether and settled we must go ahead. As a matter
of fact we picked them up again, and by then were out
of the worst ; but we were glad to see the tent again.]

During the day a light southerly breeze had been
blowing with a clear sky. The temp. had varied from
− 30° with south-westerly wind of force 2 at 4 P.M. to
37°, which had been the minimum in the early morning
between 3 A.M. and 9.30 A.M.

There was again some frost smoke over the sea ice under the Cape Cliffs and a small shining open lead of water in the offing.

Thursday, July 20, 1911.—We turned out at 3 A.M. in order to get our hut roof fixed on and made safe in calm weather, and we had decided to make another attempt when day came at 9.30 A.M. to reach the Emperor rookery and get the blubber which we now really began to need. We got the roof on the hut and made it all safe. [Little did we think what that roof had in store for us as we packed it in with snow blocks, stretching it over our second 8-ft. sledge which we put athwartships in the middle of the wall. The windward end came right down to the ground, and we tied it down securely to rocks before packing it in. To do this we had a good two feet or more of slack all round, and in every case we tied it to rocks by lanyards at intervals of every two feet. The door was the difficulty, and for the present we left the cloth arching over the stones, forming a kind of portico. The whole was well packed over with slabs of hard snow, but there was no soft snow with which to fill up the gaps between the blocks.] We then had breakfast and got away in good time for the pressure ridges before day broke. We had the same equipment as yesterday, and crampons of the new canvas pattern which Cherry and I found most reliable and comfortable, though Bowers preferred the old pattern used at Hut Point. Going down to-day we made for a different and rather narrow slope leading much more directly down to the foot of the land ice cliffs. We had missed it yesterday in the

bad light when walking along the cliff tops looking for a
way down, but we had seen it from below [at a place
where there was a break in the big ice cliff] and had
decided to try for it to-day. It took us down the right
direction [twice we crept up to the edge of the cliff
with no success, but the third time we found the ridge
down], and we got down directly in under the old land
ice cliffs which still cover the more southern portions of
the basalt cliffs of the Knoll. These ice cliffs are a monu-
ment to what wind can do; they are more than a hundred
feet high in places and are deeply scooped out into vast
grooved and concave hollows as though by a colossal
gouge. By following along the foot of these weather-
worn and dirty-banded old relics of glaciation one comes
by a series of slides and climbs and scrambles to quite
recent exposures of dark rock cliffs which were not exposed
when I was here ten years ago.

Then, passing along the foot of these, one comes to
more and loftier ice cliffs and more and still loftier rock
cliffs, and along the very foot of these, in among rock
débris and snow drifts and frozen thaw pools, and boulders
which have fallen into the trough, we had to walk and
climb and slide and crawl in the direction of the sea ice
rookery. [We got along till finally we climbed along the
top of a snow ridge with a razor-back edge. On our
right was a drop of great depth with crevasses at the
bottom : on our left was a smaller drop, also crevassed.
We crawled along : it was exciting work in the half darkness. At the end was a series of slopes full of crevasses,
and finally we got right in under the rock on to moraine.]

At one spot we appeared again to have come to an impasse, for one of the largest and most chaotic pressure ridges had actually come up against the rock face of the Crozier cliffs, but we found a man-hole in the space between the ice and the rock which was big enough, and only just big enough, for us to crawl through one by one. [Bill disappeared into the hole, and we followed and managed to wriggle through, working ourselves over a gully the other side by jamming our bodies against one side with our legs against the cliff on the other. In another place we got up another hole between two jams of pressure, rather like an enlarged rabbit-hole. The place was strewn with fallen ice blocks and rocks, and if one fell on us we should have finished, also if the Barrier had just then chosen to give a squeeze.] We had to leave the sledge here. Once past this we were in an enclosed snow pit with an almost vertical wall which required about fifteen steps to be cut to get out of it. From here we had again a series of drift troughs between the rock cliffs and the pressure ridges until at last we got out on to the actual ice foot, overhanging the sea ice by a small overhanging cliff of 10 or 12 feet. This was the lowest point of the ice foot and there was no snow drift running down from it on to the sea ice anywhere. This rather suggests that even this bay ice was not at all old as yet—possibly not even a month old. Farther on round the foot of the Crozier rock cliffs the ice foot cliff was very considerably higher, 20 to 30 feet.

The light was rapidly failing when we at last reached the sea ice, and we had to be very quick in doing what we had to do here. We saw there was no seal in sight. We saw also that there were only about 100 Emperor penguins instead of a couple of thousand as in 1902 and 1903. They were all standing in one compact group under the ice cliffs of the Barrier a few hundred yards from where we had emerged. We decided to get three penguin skins with their blubber and a few eggs. We therefore left Cherry on the ice foot with the Alpine rope to help us up again from the sea ice. Bowers and I jumped down and went off to the Emperors. We saw at once that some of them were crouching with eggs on their feet, as they tried to shuffle away with them without losing their hold. As we hustled them, however, a good many eggs were dropped and left lying on the ice, or were picked up again by the unemployed birds that saw and took their opportunity to seize an egg. We collected six eggs and killed and skinned three birds, and went back to the ice foot where Cherry was waiting to help us up with the rope. We passed the eggs and skins up, and then by climbing on Bowers' back I also got up; but no amount of combined pulling would lift Bowers, as the rope only cut and jammed into the overhanging cliff of ice. He, however, hunted round till he found a place where he helped himself up by cutting steps while we hauled at the same time. It took a little time, but at last we were all up, and at once started back by the way we had come in a very failing light. Bowers had unfortunately got one leg into a crack in the sea ice, and his crampon, finnesko and socks became frozen into a solid mass. Had we been able to bring the sledge

EMPEROR PENGUINS

along to this point the ice foot would have given us no difficulty at all, but we had left it behind at the man-hole. [A whole procession of Emperors came round just as they were coming back from the floe.]

The small number of Emperor penguins collected here at this time is surprising. There were not more than 100 birds, and without forcing all of them to abandon their eggs it was impossible to guess how many had laid or were incubating. It looked to me as though every fourth or fifth bird had an egg, but this is only a guess and may be quite wrong, though I am certain that there were more birds without eggs than with eggs. Why there should be so few birds here this July, when there were so many more here in September and October ten years ago, is difficult to understand. The examination of the three eggs we have brought back with us may throw some light on the question. They may have only just begun to lay, and these may have been the earliest arrivals. Others may yet arrive in numbers and lay this year.

Another possible explanation is that the ice has not remained in, and that the rookery has been dissipated lately; and some support is lent to this possibility by the absence of all snowdrifts on to the sea ice from the ice foot.

I see no way of deciding this question except by another visit to the rookery—either this year in September or October—or next year, preferably in August. The most valuable work probably could be done in August, and a visit would be much facilitated if by any possibility some supply of oil and food could be left at the Adélie penguin rookery by the ship during the coming summer. But I am not blind to the difficulties there may be in her doing this.

A very interesting fact we saw at the rookery this time was that these birds are so anxious to incubate an egg that they will incubate a rounded lump of ice instead, just as before we noticed them incubate a dead and frozen chick, if they were unable to secure a living one. Both Bowers and I, in the failing light, mistook these rounded dirty lumps of ice for eggs, and picked them up as eggs before we realised what they were. One of them I distinctly saw dropped by a bird, and it was roughly egg-shaped and of the right size—hard, dirty and semi-translucent ice. Another was, as I thought, a deformed egg, and as such I picked it up. It was shaped thus ·

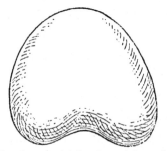

Ice 'nest-egg' mistaken for a deformed egg.

I also saw one of the birds return and tuck one of these ice 'nest-eggs' on to its feet, under the abdominal flap. I had a real egg in my hand, so I put it down on the ice close to this bird, and the bird at once left the lump of ice and shuffled to the real egg and pushed it in under its flap on to the feet. It apparently knew the difference, and it shows how strong is the desire to brood over something.

EMPEROR PENGUINS' EGGS FROM CAPE CROZIER

FROST-SMOKE

The three birds that we killed and skinned were very thickly blubbered, and the oil we got from them burnt very well indeed—and much more fiercely than the seal oil. There was about ¾ inch of pure fat under the skin. The birds were in excellent plumage. Bowers noticed there was very little soiled sea ice where they were standing, which also supports the idea of a very recent arrival, or recent freezing of the bay ice, or both.

There was another small group of Emperors wandering by the ice foot down which we came, but none of them had eggs. We saw no others.

The sea was frozen over as far as the horizon. There was a little evidence of pressure in cracks of the sea ice in the bay. Our visit was a very hurried one, unfortunately, owing to the shortness of the light and the risk of getting benighted in the pressure ridges. Subsequent events unfortunately made another visit impossible.

[We legged it back as hard as we could go, two eggs each in our fur mits; Birdie with two skins tied on behind, and myself with one. We were roped up, and climbing the ridges and getting through the holes was very difficult. In one place where there was a steep rubble and snow slope down I left the ice-axe half-way up; in another it was too dark to see our former ice-axe footsteps, and I could see nothing, and so just let myself go and trusted to luck. Bill said with infinite patience, ' Cherry, you must learn how to use an ice-axe.' For the rest of the trip my windclothes were in rags.

We found the sledge, and none too soon. We had four eggs left, more or less whole. Both mine had burst in my mits : the first I emptied out, the second I left

in my mit to put in the cooker; it never got there, but
on the return journey I had my mits far more easily
thawed out than Birdie's (Bill had none), and I believe
the grease in the egg did them good. When we got into
the hollows under the ridge where we had to cross, it
was too dark to do anything but feel our way—which we
did over many crevasses, found the ridge and crept over it.
Higher up we could see more, but to follow our tracks
soon became impossible, and we plugged straight ahead
and luckily found the slope down which we had come.

It began to blow, and as we were going up the slope
to the tent, blew up to 4; it was such a bad light that
we missed our way entirely and got right up above our
knoll, and only found it after a good deal of search;
meanwhile the weather was getting thick.]

On returning to the stone hut we flenced one of the
penguin skins and cooked our supper on the blubber stove,
which burnt furiously. I was incapacitated for the time
being by a sputter of the hot oil catching me in one eye.
We slept in the hut for the first time.

[We moved into the igloo and began a wretched night.
The wind was coming in all round. It began to drift,
and the drift came in by a back draught under the door
and covered everything—bags, socks, and all our gear.
Bill started up the blubber stove with the blubber ready
in it. The first thing it did was to spurt a blob of boiling
blubber into his eye: for the rest of the night he lay,
quite unable to stifle his groans, in obviously very great
pain—and he told us afterwards that he thought his eye
was gone. We managed to cook a meal somehow, and
Birdie got the stove going afterwards; but it was quite

useless to try and warm the place. The wind was working in through the cracks in the snow blocks which we had used for baulking outside, and there was no possibility of stopping these cracks. I got out and cut up a triangular piece outside the door so as to get the roof cloth in under the stones, and then packed it down as best I could with snow and so blocked most of the drift coming in. Bill said the next evening, ' At any rate things look better. to-night—I think we reached bedrock last night '—as a matter of fact we hadn't by some long way. The igloo was naturally very cold, and it blizzed all that night, blowing 6.

The greater part of the next day the wind had fallen, and we got all the drift we could find from the last night—it wasn't much—and packed in the sides of the igloo.]

The temperature to-day had not been below – 28·3°. There had been a southerly wind all day which we had felt at all the more exposed parts of the way down to the sea ice and in the hollows under the cliffs. It gradually freshened in the afternoon and stratus came up from the south. At 8 P.M. it was blowing force 6 from the S.S.W., but the sky was clear to the N.E.

Friday, July 21, 1911.—Our first night in the hut was comfortable enough, though the breeze freshened during the night and increased to force 8, but fell to 5 in the morning. The only thing we did not quite like was the tendency the wind had to lift the canvas roof off its supporting sledge—so we piled large slabs of icy snow on the canvas top to steady it down and prevent this.

The temp. ranged from – 20·4° to – 23·7°, and though

the wind dropped to light airs the weather looked thick and unsettled, with stratus moving up rapidly from the south.

We spent the whole of our daylight in packing our hut with soft snow, until not a crack or a crevice remained visible anywhere on the outside.

Then we brought up our tent from the hollow below, and pitched it, for the sake of convenience, under the lee end of our hut, quite close to the door. My idea in doing this was to get more efficient heat for drying socks and other gear than was possible in the hut. The large open canvas roof of the hut allowed all the heat to escape at once, but in the double tent the intense heat of the blubber stove dried anything hung in the apex in a very short time.

We cooked our supper in the tent, nearly stifling ourselves with the smoke, but the heating effect was immense. [The blubber stove heated the oil so much that we expected every minute that the whole would flare up. It took a lot of primus to start it. We took our finnesko in to try and dry them there with the rest of the gear when we left. Bill and I, however, took our private bags back into the igloo. After dinner we flenced one of the Emperor skins as hard as we could and boiled down the blubber in the inner cooker—very good stuff—nearly filling the stove up.] We then moved to the hut to sleep, believing it to be as safe and as comfortable as it could be made until we got some covering for the roof, such as sealskins. When we turned in there was practically no wind at all, but the sky was overcast. When I turned out three or four hours later there was still no wind; but it came on to blow suddenly soon after 3 A.M., and blew heavily from the S. with little drift at first.

Saturday, July 22, 1911.—By 6.30 A.M. it was blowing force 9 to 10 from the S.S.W., with heavy drift and wind in strong gusts, and when Bowers turned out he found the tent had disappeared, legs, lining, cover and all, leaving the cooker and all the gear we had left in it overnight on the ground. The drift was now very thick and there was nothing to be done but to collect the gear, which Bowers and Cherry did and passed it in to me in the hut. Very little of the gear was lost. All our finnesko were there and were recovered, as well as a quantity of smaller gear. The only losses were the two flat parts of the cooker, which we never found afterwards.

[We were woken up by Birdie shouting through the door, 'Bill, Bill, the tent has gone.' I got out, helped Birdie, and passed the gear which had been in the tent into the igloo, where Bill took it. It was impossible to stand against the wind : Birdie was blown right over; each time we got something it was a fight to get the three or four yards to the igloo door : if the wind had started us down the slope nothing would have stopped us. The place where the tent had been was littered with gear. When we came to reckon up afterwards we had every-thing except the bottom piece of the cooker and the top of the outer cooker. The former was left on the top of the cooker, the latter was in its groove. We never regained them. The most wonderful thing of all was

that all our finnesko were lying where they were left,
which happened to be on the ground in the part of the
tent which was under the lee of the igloo. Also Birdie's
private bag was there, and a tin of sweets.

Birdie brought two tins of sweets away with him
as a luxury, for we had no sugar in our ration :
one we had on our arrival at the Knoll; this was the
second, of which we knew nothing, and which was for
Bill's birthday, the next day. We started eating them
on Saturday, however, and the tin came in useful to Bill
afterwards.

The roar of the wind in the igloo sounded just like the
rush of an express train through a tunnel. As it topped
the rise it sucked our roof cloth upwards, letting it down
with tremendous bangs. We could only talk in shouts,
and began to get seriously alarmed about our roof.]

Inside the hut we were now being buried by fine snow
drift, which was coming through the cracks of the walls
in fine spouts, especially through the weather wall and
over the door in the lee wall. We tried to plug the inlets
with socks, but as fast as we closed one the drift came in
by another, and heaps of soft drift gradually piled up to
6 and 8 inches on everything. It seems that the strong
wind blowing over the roof of the hut sucked it upwards
and tried hard to lift it off, producing so much suction
into the interior of the hut that the fine drift came in
everywhere notwithstanding our day spent in packing
every crack and cranny. When there was no more snow
drift to come in, fine black moraine dust came in and
blackened everything like coal dust. The canvas roof,

upon which we had put heavy slabs of icy snow, was lifted clean off and was stretched upwards and outwards like a tight dome and as taut as a drum. There was no chafe or friction anywhere except along the lee end wall top, and there we plugged every space between the canvas and the wall stones with pyjama jackets, fur mits, socks, &c. So long as the ice slabs remained on the top, more-over, there was no flapping and everything seemed fairly secure. Our only fear was that to allow of the admission of so much drift and dust through the weather wall there must have been openings in our packing—and we thought it possible that by degrees the upward tension might draw the canvas roof out. We could not be quite certain that the ice-slabs were not being eaten away. This, however, proved not to be our danger; the slabs remained sound to the end and the canvas buried in the walls did not draw anywhere at all, even for an inch.

The storm continued unabated all day, and we decided to cook a meal on the blubber stove. We felt a great satisfaction in having three penguin skins to cook with for some days, so that we could last out any length of blizzard without coming to our last can of oil.

We got the blubber stove going once or twice, but it insisted on suddenly going out for no apparent reason. And before we had boiled any water, in trying to restart it with the spirit lamp provided for the purpose, the feed-pipe suddenly dropped off, unsoldered, rendering the whole stove useless. [That was the end of the stove; very lucky it ended when it did, for it was obviously a most dangerous thing.] We therefore poured the melted oil into tins and lamps for the journey home in case our candles ran out, and for drying or thawing out socks and mits.

We then considered matters in the light of a shortage of oil and absence of tent. We decided first to go as long as we could without a hot meal so long as the blizzard kept us inactive. We also saw that we could not afford to start our last can of oil with the vague chance of getting a seal and improvising a blubber stove and so staying on here. We still had a fill of oil in our fifth can. As for the tent, we believed we should at any rate find part of it, if only the legs, and we saw no impossibility in improvising a tent cover of some sort from the canvas roof of our hut, even if the tent and lining were both lost.

Lying in our bags in the hut we were very wet, and got wetter from the fine drift every time we moved in or out of them. Everything was buried in a pile of soft, fine drift. But we were not cold. We finished our breakfast on the primus when the blubber stove gave out, and this was our last meal for a good many hours as it happened. [At intervals during the next 24 hours Birdie, who was absolutely magnificent, was up and about, stopping up every crevice where wind or drift was working in with socks, mits, and anything handy. A drift hole was especially bad in the middle of the windward wall, drifting us all up lightly, and putting a lot in Birdie's corner. The only possible thing to do for the roof would have been lashings over it outside, and in that wind that was out of the question. Our position, with the tent gone, was bad.]

We could not understand quite how the tent had been blown away, for we had taken extra precautions in setting it, and had got as nearly perfect a spread as possible. Moreover, it was in the lee of the hut, and we had buried the valance not only with heaps of snow, but with 4 or 5 rocks on the snow in each bay, and to make things quite secure, the last thing before turning in Bowers and I had hoisted the heavy canvas tank, full of gear, almost more than one could lift alone, on to the weather skirt.

We could only think that the same sucking action which lifted our roof also lifted the tent, or that it was twisted off its legs by getting caught sideways by a squall which came partly round the end of the hut corner. Anyhow, as it was gone, we decided to take the earliest opportunity of any light to go and look for it.

Other things happened before this opportunity arrived.

Sunday, July 23, 1911.—Bowers estimated the wind at force 11 and noted it as blowing with almost continuous storm force, with very slight lulls followed by squalls of great violence.

About noon the canvas roof of the hut was carried away, and the storm continued unabated all day, but latterly without much drift.

It happened that this was my birthday—and we spent it lying in our bags without a roof or a meal, wishing the wind would drop, while the snow drifted over us.

The roof went as follows. We saw, as soon as light showed through the canvas in the early morning, that the snow blocks on the top had all been blown off, and that the upward strain was now as bad as ever, with a greater tendency to flap at the lee end wall. And where the canvas was fixed in over the door it began to work on the heavy stones which held it down, jerking and shaking them so that it threatened to throw them down. Bowers was trying all he could to jam them tight with pyjama jackets and bamboos, and in this I was helping him when the canvas suddenly ripped, and in a moment I saw about six rents all along the lee wall top, and in another moment we were under the open sky with the greater part of the roof flapped to shreds. The noise was terrific, and rocks began to tumble in off the walls on to Bowers and Cherry, happily without hurting them, and in a smother of drift Bowers and I bolted into our bags, and in them the three of us lay listening to the flap of the ragged ends of canvas over our heads, which sounded like a volley of pistol shots going on for hour after hour. As we lay there I think we were all revolving plans for making a tent now to get back to Hut Point with, out of the floorcloth on which we lay—the only piece of canvas now left us, except for the pieces still firmly embedded in the hut walls. We were all warm enough, though wet, as we had carried a great deal of snow into the bags with us, and every time we looked out more drift which was accumulating over us would fall in. I hoped myself that this would not prove to be one of the five- or eight-day blizzards which we had experienced at Cape Crozier in days gone by.

Monday, July 24, 1911.—The storm continued unabated until midnight, and then dropped to force 9 with squalls interspersed by short lulls. At 6.30 A.M. the wind had dropped to force 2. At 10 A.M. it was about force 3, and we awaited the moment when there would be light enough for us to look for our tent. Meanwhile Bowers suggested an *al fresco* meal under the floorcloth as we sat in our bags. We lit the primus and got the cooker going and had a good hot meal, the first for 48 hours, the tent floorcloth resting on our heads.

As it was still dark when we had finished we lay in our bags again for a bit. Daylight appeared, and we at once turned out, and it was by no means reassuring to find that the weather in the south still looked as bad and thick as it possibly could. We therefore lost no time at all in getting away down wind to look for the tent. Everywhere we found shreds of green canvas roof the size of a pocket-handkerchief, but not a sign of the tent, until a loud shout from Bowers, who had gone more east to the top of a ridge than Cherry and I, told us he had seen it. He hurried down, and slid about a hundred yards down a hard snow slope, sitting in his haste, and there we joined him where he had found the whole tent hardly damaged at all, a quarter of a mile from where we had pitched it. One of the poles had been twisted right out of the cap, and the lower stops of the tent lining had all carried away more or less, but the tent itself was intact and untorn.

We brought it back, pitched it in the old spot in the snow hollow below our hut, and then brought down our bags and cooker and all essential gear, momentarily expecting the weather to break on us again. It looked as thick as could be and close at hand in the south.

We discussed the position, and came to the conclusion that as our oil had now run down to one can only, and as we couldn't afford to spend time trying to fix up an improvised blubber stove in a roofless hut, we ought to return to Cape Evans.

It was disappointing to have seen so very little of the Emperor penguins, but it seemed to me unavoidable, and that we had attempted too difficult an undertaking without light in the winter.

I had also some doubt as to whether our bags were not already in such a state as might make them quite unusable should we meet with really low temperatures again in our journey home.

I therefore decided to start for Hut Point the next day. To this end we sorted out all our gear, and made a depôt in a corner of the stone hut of all that we could usefully leave there for use on a future occasion. This depôt I fixed up finally with Cherry the next morning while Bowers packed up the sledge at our tent. We put rocks on our depôt and the nine-foot sledge, and the pick, with a matchbox containing a note tied to the handle, where it could not be missed. We also fixed up bamboos round the walls to attract attention to the spot.

[Mr. Cherry-Garrard's account of this episode must be quoted in full :

All that day and night *it blew* 11, with absolutely no real lull ; what the wind was in the gusts we shall never know—it was something appalling. We quite lost count of time, but Sunday morning it was just the same. This was Bill's birthday.

About now we began to realise that the roof must go. The stones holding the door end (leeward) of the roof began to work : drift was coming in, and the place where I had slit up the roof to fold it in over the door was obviously weak : the foodbags did something to remedy this. Bill told us he thought that to turn over, flaps under, would give us our best chance. We could do nothing, and lay in our bags until Birdie told us that the roof was flapping more : he was out of his bag trying to hold the rocks firm, and I and Bill were sitting up in ours pressing against them with a bamboo. Suddenly the roof went—first, I believe, over the door, splitting into seven or eight strips along the leeward end, and then ripping into hundreds of pieces in about half a minute.

We got into our bags as best we could. I remember trying to get Bill into his, as he was farther out than I was ; he wouldn't let me—'Please get into your bag, Cherry.' Both Birdie's hands went in getting back to his. We turned our bags over, flaps under, as much as possible, and were gradually drifted up.

It was a most appalling position. I knew that Peary had once come through a blizzard lying in the open in his bag in the summer. I had no idea that human beings could do so in winter in the state in which we were already. I wondered whether it was really worth trying to keep warm. I confess that I considered that we were now come to the end. If we got out of the blizzard and had, as we decided, to try and get back by digging ourselves into the snow for the night, I meant to

ask Bill to let us have enough morphia to deaden the
pain when, as I think still it must have come, the cold
became too much to live. With a steep icy slope below
us, ending in an ice-cliff which itself led into the pressure,
I don't know whether any of us had much hope of finding the tent—though afterwards as the wind went down
we said we had. Without the tent I think we must have
died.

I suppose at times all through this blizzard we must
have dozed—I remember waking once after this to hear
Bill singing hymns—every now and then I could hear a
little, and Bill says Birdie was doing the same : I chimed
in a bit, but not very much. Early Monday morning
there were decided lulls in the wind, and the blizzard
had practically blown itself out. Before daylight, while
it was still blowing, we turned out and went down the
slope to try and find the tent. We could see nothing,
and were forced to return. It was now 48 hours since
we had had a meal, and we managed about the weirdest
meal ever eaten N. or South. We got the floorcloth
under the heads of our bags, then got into our bags and
drew the floorcloth over our heads and got the primus
going in this shelter, and the cooker held by hand over
the primus. In time we got both tea and pemmican—
the blubber left in the cooker burnt and gave the tea
a burnt taste—none of us will ever forget that meal.
I enjoyed it as much as such a meal ever could be enjoyed,
and that burnt taste will always bring back that memory.

A little glow of light began to come up and we turned
out to have a further search for the tent. Birdie went off

before Bill and me. I dragged my eiderdown out on my feet all sopping wet; it was impossible to get it back, and I let it freeze—it was soon just like a rock. I followed Bill down the slope when we heard a shout on our right and made for it with hope. We got on a slope, slipped, and went sliding down, quite unable to stop ourselves, and came to Birdie with the tent, outer lining still on the bamboos. We were so thankful we said nothing. The tent was over the ridge to the N.E. of the igloo at the bottom of the steep slope about half of a mile away. I believe that it blew away because part of it was in the wind, and part in the lee of the igloo.

It looked as if it would start blowing again at any moment and was getting thick, and we hurried back with the tent, slithering up and down, and pitched it where we had pitched it on our arrival. Never was tent so firmly dug in, by Bill, while Birdie and I got our gear, such as we could find, down from the igloo. Luckily the wind from the S. and the back-draught from the N. had blown everything inwards when the roof went, and we managed to find or dig out almost everything except Bill's fur mits. These were packed into a hole in rocks to prevent drift coming in. We had a meal in the tent; searched for the parts of the cooker down the slope, but only found a track of small bits of roof cloth. We were very weak. We packed the tank ready for a start back in the morning and turned in, utterly worn out. It was only $-12°$ that night, but my left big toe was frostbitten in my bag, which I was trying to use without an eiderdown lining.]

Tuesday, July 25, 1911.—There was a stiff cold breeze
of force 4 and temp. – 15·3° which came down our slope
from S.S.W., with thick weather and heavy clouds moving
up from the Barrier in the south. We quickly finished
all our final arrangements and got away down into the
gut by the pressure ridges, where we found ourselves
pulling against a gale rapidly freshening from the S.W.
[My job, writes Cherry-Garrard, was to balance the sledge
behind : I was so utterly done I don't believe I could
have pulled effectively. Birdie was much the strongest
of us. The strain and want of sleep was getting me in
the neck, and Bill looked very bad.]

This wind became so strong after we had gone a mile
that we camped, much against our inclinations, in amongst
ice-hard, wind-swept sastrugi [our hands going one after
the other], and the gale continued and freshened to force
9 and lasted all night. Bowers here determined that
the tent should not go off alone, and arranged a line
by which he fastened the cap of the tent to himself as
he lay in his bag. The temp. during the day was from
15·3° to – 17°, and the whole sky was overcast.

Bowers to-day turned his bag to hair outside. Cherry
had a sound sleep in his bag, which he badly wanted.

[I, writes C.-G., was feeling as if I should crack, and
accepted Birdie's eiderdown, which he had not used and
had for many days been asking me to use. It was
wonderfully self-sacrificing of him, more than I can write.
I felt a brute to take it, but I was getting useless, unless
I got some sleep, which my big bag would not allow. The
day we got down to the Emperors I felt so done that I

did not much care whether I went down a crevasse or not. We had gone through a great deal since then. Bill and Birdie kept on assuring me that I was doing more than my share of the work, but I think that I was getting more and more weak. Birdie kept wonderfully strong · he slept most of the night; the difficulty was for him to get into his bag without going to sleep. He kept the meteorological log untiringly, but some of these nights he had to give it up for the time because he could not keep awake. He used to fall asleep with his pannikin in his hand and let it fall, and once he had the lighted primus.

Bill's bag was getting hopeless : it was really too small for an eiderdown and was splitting all over the place— great long holes. He never consciously slept for nights— he did sleep a bit, for we heard him. Except for this night and the next, when Birdie's eiderdown was fairly dry, I never consciously slept ; except that I used to wake for five or six nights running with the same nightmare— that we were drifted up and that Bill and Birdie were passing the gear into my bag, cutting it open to do so— or some other variation, I did not know that I had been asleep at all.]

All our bags were by this time so saturated with water that they froze too stiff to bend with safety, so from now onwards to Cape Evans we never rolled them up, but packed them one on the other full length, like coffins, on the sledge. Even so, they were breaking or broken in several places in the efforts we made to get into them in the evenings. We always took the pre-caution to stow our personal kit bags and sleeping fur

boots and socks in such parts as would give us an entry
to start getting in by. They were all very uncomfortable
and our whole journey home was done on a very limited
allowance of conscious sleep, while one or other of the
party almost invariably dozed off and had a sleep over
the cooker in the comparative comfort of sitting on a
bag instead of lying inside it.

Wednesday, July 26, 1911.—We got in only half a
day's march, as the wind continued until nearly all the
daylight had gone. Leaving at about 2 P.M., we made
4½ miles in 3½ hours, and once more found ourselves on
a very suspicious surface in the darkness, where we
several times stepped into rotten lidded crevasses in
smooth, wind-swept ice. We continued, however, feeling
our way along by keeping always off hard ice-slopes
and on the crustier deeper snow which characterises the
hollows of the pressure ridges, which I believed we had
once more fouled in the dark. We had no light, and
no landmarks to guide us, except vague and indistinct
silhouetted slopes ahead, which were always altering and
whose distance and character it was impossible to judge.
We never knew whether we were approaching a steep
slope at close quarters or a long slope of Terror, miles
away, and eventually we travelled on by the ear, and by
the feel of the snow under our feet, for both the sound
and the touch told one much of the chances of crevasses
or of safe going. We continued thus in the dark
in the hope that we were at any rate in the right
direction.

The sky cleared when the wind fell, and the temperature

dropped from $-21 \cdot 5°$ at 11 A.M. to $-45°$ at 9 P.M. We then made our night camp amongst the pressure ridges off the Terror moraine, on snow that felt soft and deep enough to be safe in what we believed to be one of the hollows [and when we camped after getting into a bunch of crevasses and being completely lost, 'At any rate,' Bill said, as we camped that night, 'I think we are well clear of the pressure.' There were pressure pops all night, just as though someone was whacking an empty tank.]

Thursday, July 27, 1911.—We got away with the coming of daylight and found that our suspicions over-night had been true. We were right in amongst the larger pressure ridges and had come for a considerable distance between two of them without actually crossing any but very insignificant ones. Ahead of us was a safe and clear road to the open Barrier to the south, but we wanted to go to the S.W. And as the pressure ridges were invariably crevassed on the summits we hoped that by continuing along this valley we might find some low spot where we could cross the ridge on our right, and again get on the safer land ice. We, however, found no such dip, and after some time decided we must cross the ridge on our right [an enormous pressure ridge, blotting out the moraine and half Terror, rising like a great hill]. In doing so we managed to negotiate several rottenly bridged narrow crevasses [both Bill and I putting a leg down] and one broad one which we only discovered when we were all on it with the sledge, and then Bowers dropped suddenly into one and hung up in his harness out of sight and out of reach from the surface. It was a crevasse I had just put my foot in, but Bowers went in even as I shouted a warning. We were too close to one another in our harness and the sledge followed us and bridged the crevasse. I had hold of Bowers' harness, while Cherry lowered a bowline on the end of the Alpine rope into which Bowers got his foot, and then by alternately hauling on one and the other we got him up again. After this, for the next few days while we were on doubtful ground, I went ahead with 12 or 15 feet of rope on my trace, and so was able to give good warning and to change the course easily if I found we were getting on to bad ground.

[C.-G. gives a fuller account

Just over the top Birdie went right down a crevasse, which was about wide enough to take him—he went down slowly, his head disappearing quite slowly—and he went down till his head was four feet below the surface a little of his harness catching up on something. Bill went for his harness, I went for the bow of the sledge. Bill told me to get the Alpine rope and Birdie directed from below what we could do : we could not possibly haul him up as he was, for the sides of the crevasse were soft and he could not help himself. I put a bowline on the Alpine rope, and lying down over him gave him the loop, which he got under his leg. We then pulled him up inch by inch: first by drawing up his leg he could give one some slack, then raising himself on his leg he could give Bill some slack on the harness, and so we gradually got him up. It was a near go for Birdie : the

crevasse was probably about 100 feet deep, and did not
narrow as it went down.

It was a wonderful piece of presence of mind that
Birdie in such a position could direct us how to get
him up—by a way which, as far as we know, he invented
on the spur of the moment, a way which we have used
since on the Beardmore.

In front of us we could see another ridge, and we did
not know how many lay beyond that. Things looked
pretty bad. Bill took a long lead on the Alpine rope and
we got down our present difficulty all right. From this
moment our luck changed and everything went for us
to the end. This method of the leader being on a long
trace in front we all agreed to be very useful. When
we went out on the sea ice the whole experience was over
in a few days and Hut Point was always in sight—and
there was daylight. I always had the feeling that the
whole series of events had been brought about by an
extraordinary run of accidents, and after a certain stage
it was quite beyond our power to guide the course of
events. When, on the way to C. Crozier, the moon
suddenly came out of the cloud to show us a great crevasse
which would have taken us all with our sledge without
any difficulty, I felt that we were not to go under on this
trip after such a deliverance. When we had lost our
tent—and there was a very great balance of probability,
to me, that we should never find it again,—and were
lying out the blizzard in our bags, I believe we were
face to face with a long fight against cold which we could
not have survived. I cannot put down in writing

how helpless I believe we were to help ourselves, and how we were brought out of a very terrible series of experiences.

When we started back I had a feeling that things might change for the better—and this day I had a distinct idea that we were to have one more bad experience and that after that we could hope for better things. Bill, I know, has much the same feeling about a divine providence which was looking after us.]

We then got on well and soon reached safe land ice, having sounded for and found all the cracks in our path in time to avoid or cross them safely.

We next got on to a very long upward incline, and made good going till we had to camp, having covered $7\frac{1}{4}$ miles in the day.

The temp. varied from $-45°$ to $-47°$ during the day, but the weather was calm and clear enough later on for us to see something of where we were going.

Friday, July 28, 1911.—We were away before daylight and found ourselves still on the upward slope of a very long gradient facing a gentle breeze, which as usual was flowing down the slope. The Bastion Crater was on our right with the Conical Hill surmounting it, a landmark visible from Observation Hill.

We went on and on up this slope until at last we found ourselves in a calm on the divide with a magnificent view of the Western Range, Mt. Discovery and the Hut Point Peninsula and all the other familiar landmarks showing very clearly in the dim daylight. [I cannot describe what a relief the light was to us.] We then knew we

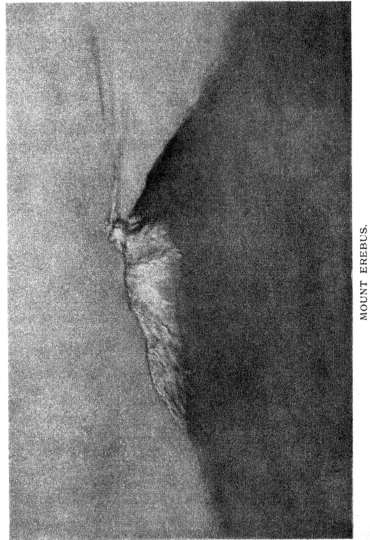

MOUNT EREBUS.

were over Terror P... ...

The surface all up this slope ... hard but smooth, hardened however ... ... great ..., with but few ...

... are the heavy ... ...

... ..., the ... it...f, with trifling ... and heavier pulling, a surface into which the sledge runners and the feet sank a couple of inches. Sub-sidences again began and soon became frequent. Bright fine weather, and Terror peak visible all day, as well as Erebus from the time when we first caught sight of it over ... slope. One of the features of Erebus during the ... of this march was the outstanding old Northern ..., which stood out boldly against the skyline part ... down the slope. We lost it, however, at the ... march

Bowers turned his bag again to-day from fur outside to fur inside, and so it remained till we reached Cape Evans. The temperature ranged from $-47 \cdot 2°$ in the morning to $-38°$ in the evening. At our lunch camp it was $-40 \cdot 3°$. We made $6\frac{3}{4}$ miles in the day.

We were now travelling with a view to getting in all the daylight we could and at the same time with a view to reducing our nights to the shortest possible, for we got but little sleep and were often uncomfortably cold all night. We therefore turned out generally at 5.30 A.M., lunched at 2.30 P.M., and camped at 6 P.M., to turn in between 9 P.M. and 10 P.M. ...

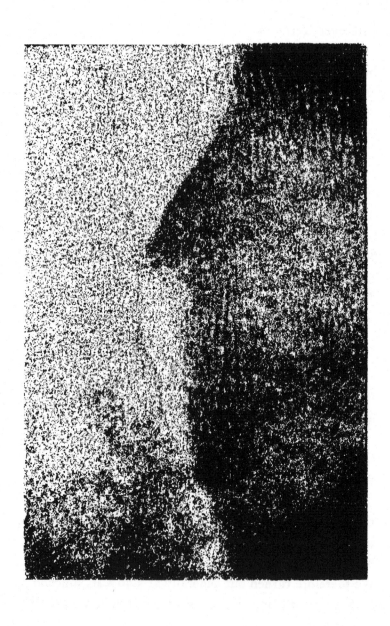

were over Terror Point and almost out of the blizzard area. The surface all up this slope was good going, hard but smooth, hardened however by variable winds of no great force, with but few areas of the softer sandy drifts which are the heavy ones to drag over.

Across the divide we went downhill with the air-stream on our backs, and very soon we were once more on the old softer crusty surface of the Barrier itself, with trifling sastrugi and heavier pulling, a surface into which the sledge runners and the feet sank a couple of inches. Subsidences again began and soon became frequent. Bright fine weather, and Terror peak visible all day, as well as Erebus from the time when we first caught sight of it over Terror slope. One of the features of Erebus during the whole of this march was the outstanding old Northern Crater, which stood out boldly against the skyline part of the way down the slope. We lost it, however, at the end of to-day's march.

Bowers turned his bag again to-day from fur outside to fur inside, and so it remained till we reached Cape Evans.

The temperature ranged from $-47\cdot2°$ in the morning to $-38°$ in the evening. At our lunch camp it was $-40\cdot3°$. We made $6\frac{3}{4}$ miles in the day.

We were now travelling with a view to getting in all the daylight we could and at the same time with a view to reducing our nights to the shortest possible, for we got but little sleep and were often uncomfortably cold all night. We therefore turned out generally at 5.30 A.M., lunched at 2.30 P.M., and camped at 6 P.M., to turn in between 9 P.M. and 10 P.M.

[Though our sledge, which we called the Pantechnicon, was a mountain, and of a considerable weight, we started to do good marches. We dare not roll up our bags since the blizzard in case they should break. For two nights I got a fair sleep in the new eiderdown, nights which would have been nightmares under ordinary circumstances, but which now put some new life into me. Bill was now having the worst nights—never sleeping as far as he knew. We were not much better. My new eiderdown was already sopping and as hard as iron : I never thawed out the greater part of my big bag. Even Birdie began to shiver in his bag. Sometimes we would have done a great deal not to stop marching and turn in : but we had to turn in each night for six or seven hours, rising about 5 A.M.]

Our hands gave us more pain with cold than any other part, and this we all found to be the case. In the bags the hands, and half-mits and any other covering we liked to use, got soaking wet, and the skin sodden like washer-women's hands. The result, on turning out, was that they were ready to freeze at once, and even the tying of the tent door became a real difficulty, the more so as the tie had become stiff as wire. Another difficulty in the bags was the freezing of the lanyards after one had tied them inside the bag. Nothing would loosen them save thawing, in one's already painfully cold hands, and this was often awkward if one wished to turn out quickly. I believe the only satisfactory covering for the hands in these conditions would be a bag of dry saennegras, but we had only sufficient for our feet and it was not tried.

Our feet gave us very little trouble indeed, except on the march, when they were often too cold for safety during slow and heavy plodding in soft snow. We always changed our footgear before eating our supper, and to this we attribute the fact that we seldom had cold feet at night, even at the worst.

Saturday, July 29, 1911.—We got away before daylight and marched a good soft plod all day, making 6½ miles. Subsidences were frequent, and at lunch the whole tent and contents, myself included, as I was cook for the day, dropped suddenly with a perceptible bump, and with so long and loud a reverberation all round that we all stood and listened for some minutes. Cherry said it started when his foot went through some snow under the top crust, not when he was digging through this crust. The central subsidence set off innumerable others all round and these others in continually widening circles, and the noise took quite two or three minutes to die away.

We had no wind to-day, calm and southerly airs only, and a temp. ranging from − 42° A.M. to − 45·3° P.M.

There was an aurora all night, and at 3 A.M. Bowers noted a brilliant variegated curtain, altitude 30° to 60°, extending from the N.E. to about S.S.W., with much motion in the rays, and with orange and green well defined.

Sunday, July 30, 1911.—We had a day of perfect weather and good travelling and covered 7½ miles. The amount of daylight during this and the preceding two days has been surprisingly great, and enabled us to see a tremendous amount of detail in the hills and snow

slopes of the promontory on our right, all of which looked
very much nearer than they actually were. The dawn
on the eastern horizon was also exceptionally fine in
colour, almost pure carmine in a very broad band, changing imperceptibly, but without any intermediate orange
or yellow, into green and blue above. The peaks of the
Western Range all caught pink lights reflected from
the sky, and these shone up against the greyer pink fore-
glow behind them. None of them caught the actual
sunlight yet.

The temp. was low, $-55.3°$ in the morning, $-63.2°$
to $-61.8°$ in the afternoon, and on to the evening, with
light easterly and north-easterly airs from time to time.
[*Apropos* of the cold : we now got low temperatures
once more, but $-60°$ now hardly called for comment ; in
fact some nights of $-60°$ we never even inquired the
temperature.]

Once we saw a drift swirl suddenly spring into the
air about 100 ft. high and sweep along the surface for
a long way before it disappeared.

After lunch we had interesting views of the formation
and dispersal of fog banks which formed from time to
time all along the Hut Point promontory. There appeared
to be a line along which the cold Barrier air met the
warmer sea ice air of the north side. Fog resulted, which
gradually rose and spread, and blotted out all the land
ahead of us, and then as rapidly dispersed to the south,
leaving the whole sky and air as clear and bright as
before. This happened again and again with no
formation of cloud south of the ridge.

Eventually, however, the northerly wind came over, rising, and forming a complete overcast beneath which one could see the Western and Southern Mountains and horizon all perfectly clear.

We saw to-day and yesterday, hanging round the summits of Erebus and Terror, some very unusually delicate spider-web-like cirrus cloudlets, coloured dark reddish, and looking like tangled thread or like unravelled silk—they were slight and thin, but very well defined, and they changed very slowly.

Monday, July 31, 1911.—We turned out soon after 5 A.M. and had calm clear weather again ahead of us, though Terror was apparently again in trouble, for it was covered in a cap cloud.

We had good going and had covered $5\frac{1}{2}$ miles in $5\frac{1}{2}$ hours by the time we reached the edge of the Barrier about $1\frac{1}{2}$ miles off the Pram Point ridges.

The surface of the Barrier during this march had to-day become very much harder and more windswept. It was not cut into sastrugi, but polished into low, flatly rounded areas, with only occasional drifts of sandy snow, which dragged heavily and allowed the feet to sink in through a thin crust. The difference this walking on a hard surface made to the warmth of our feet was very noticeable, notwithstanding that the temperature was still $-57°$.

At the Barrier edge we simply ran down a drift slope on to the sea ice, which had only a few inches of snow covering, six inches at the most as noted by Bowers, and hard and wind-swept. Here again we felt the flow of cold air pouring from the Barrier on to the sea ice, so we camped about 100 yards away to be out of it and had lunch. The temp. here was – 43°. The sledge-meter now showed 38 miles from our camp in the Knoll gap at Cape Crozier. From this point to Hut Point was 3 miles, and it was again an excellent hardened smooth snow surface all the way to Cape Armitage, and rather the same rough, crunchy sea ice, with very few snow-covered patches, from Cape Armitage to Hut Point.

By the time we reached the hut the sky had become completely overcast and the temp. had gone up to – 27°. It was still quite calm, and the sky cleared again during the night. We camped at the hut. [The last day we had been using our oil to warm ourselves, since we had a half-tin left, having used the first half very sparingly. Birdie made a bottom for the cooker out of an empty biscuit-tin, which was most successful. We cooked on Bill's bag in the middle, generally one of us steadying the cooker with his hands.

It used to be quite a common experience to spill some water or hoosh on to our bags as they lay on the floor-cloth. This did not worry us, since it was practically impossible for our bags to be wetter than they were.

During the last four days Birdie quite often fell asleep as he was marching; I do not know that Bill ever did this. I never did so till the last day, when for about an hour I was falling asleep constantly as we marched along—waking when I came up against Bill or Birdie.]

Tuesday, August 1, 1911.—In the hut we pitched

HUT POINT FROM OBSERVATION HILL.

of cold air pouring from the Barrier on to the sea, so we camped about 100 yards away to be out of it and had lunch. The temp. here was −43°. The sledge-meter now showed 38 miles from our camp in the Knoll

From this point to Hut Point was 3 miles, and it was again an excellent hardened smooth snow surface all the way to Cape Armitage, and rather the same rough, crunchy sea ice, with very few snow-covered patches, from Cape Armitage   Hut

By the time we reached the hut the sky had become completely overcast and the temp. had gone up to −27°. It was still quite calm, and the sky cleared again during the night. We camped at the hut. [The last day we **had been using our oil to warm ourselves, since we had a half-tin left, having used the first half very sparingly. Birdie made a bottom** for the cooker out of an empty biscuit-tin, which was most successful. We cooked on Bill's bag in the middle, generally one of us steadying the cooker with his hands.

It used to be quite a common experience to spill some water or hoosh on to our bags as they lay on the floor-cloth. This did not worry us, since it was practically for our bags to be wetter than they were.

During the last four days Birdie quite often fell asleep as he was marching; I do not know that Bill ever did this. I never did so till the last day, when for about an hour I was falling asleep constantly as we marched along, waking when I came up against Bill or Birdie.]

Tuesday, August 1, 1911.—In the hut we pitched

HUT POINT FROM OBSERVATION HILL.

the dome tent and lit a primus to warm it while we cooked
our supper. We had thus a much more comfortable night
than the blubber stove could have given us.

[The hut struck us as fairly warm ; we could almost
feel it getting warmer as we went round C. Armitage.
We managed to haul the sledge up the ice foot. We
pitched the dome tent in the place where Crean used to
sleep and got both primus going in it—for there was
plenty of oil there, and we got it really warm, and drank
cocoa without sugar so thick that next morning we were
gorged with it. We were very happy, falling asleep
between each mouthful. After some hours of this we
discussed several schemes of not getting into our bags
at all, but settled it was best to do so.]

We had three hours in our bags and turned out at
3 A.M., hoping to make an early start to get into Cape
Evans before dinner-time. But a strong easterly wind
got up and prevented our start, so we continued to doze
in the tent as we sat there, in preference to being in our
bags.

At 9.30 A.M. the wind dropped, and we got away at
11, but met with a very cold breeze off the land on rounding Hut Point. We walked out of it, however, in a mile
or so by getting into the open, and then made a straight
course all the way for Cape Evans, deciding not to camp
for lunch until we had passed the broken ice off the end
of Glacier Tongue by daylight. This took us 5½ hours,
and we camped at 4.30 P.M., exactly 8 miles from Hut
Point.

The surface was varied, and we were a mile or so

farther out all the way on this our return journey than on our outward journey, so it differed rather from the surface we had then.

After leaving Hut Point we had very rough, rubbly sea ice with no snow worth mentioning for two or three miles. What indications there were of wind came from the land and showed north-easterly winds off shore. Their direction, however, very gradually altered till we were crossing them exactly at right angles, indicating due easterly winds from the ridge. Later still and farther on towards the Glacier Tongue and Cape Evans the indications gradually turned to show south-easterly winds. These are the winds which seem chiefly to affect the surface of the strait ice during the winter, and as we got on towards the Glacier Tongue the snow-covering became increasingly greater, as well as the evidence of stronger easterly winds. Extensive flatly rounded, hard-surfaced drifts became more abundant and afforded excellent going, so that when we were about 6 miles from Hut Point we were doing about 2 miles an hour. After this, and especially during the 8th mile from Hut Point, we met with a lot of hummocky cracks where the ice had been pressed up into long ridges and subsequently had been drifted up, forming very difficult sastrugi and providing much trouble for a sledge. We still had sufficient daylight, and after lunch, moonlight, to negotiate these, though it was easy to see how much trouble they might give one in the dark, as they did on our way out.

All the day we were watching the changes in some iridescent clouds which hung low on the northern horizon.

The edges were brilliant with pale yellow sunlight, while inside this was a broad band of orange yellow, and inside this again a narrow band of grey surrounding a large and vivid patch of emerald green. There was no trace of the violet and rose pink which characterises the opalescent cirrus clouds one sees later on when the sun is higher in the sky.

On the actual horizon was a band of rich red with purple streaks of cloud on it, giving it a very unusual magenta colour.

After lunch we had good moonlight and a good wind-swept, snow-covered surface—and though there were more of these pressure ridges abreast of Tent Island we had plenty of light to negotiate them.

We had had no wind to-day. The temp. had ranged from $-27\cdot3°$ at Hut Point to $-31°$ off Glacier Tongue.

Off Inaccessible Island at 9.30 P.M. we were met by a northerly breeze of force 3, which continued until our arrival at Cape Evans. [I well remember when we got into the hut here, and we were very keen to get in without any fuss. We got right up to the door before anyone saw us, and then I simply could not get out of my harness.

As we came round the Point, Bill asked us to spread out if anyone came out of the Hut, to show we were all there —a very useful idea.]

This was the thirty-sixth day of our absence.

E. A. WILSON.

So ends the official Report of the Cape Crozier Party, simple and reticent to the last. But again the reader,

eager for more colour, will welcome the fuller description
of the last march home, the welcome at Cape Evans, and
general impressions of travel, which we owe to Mr. Cherry-
Garrard's pen.

We just pulled for all we were worth and did nearly two
miles an hour ; for two miles a baddish salt surface, then
big, undulating, hard sastrugi and good going. Several
times I fell asleep as we were marching. We had done
eight miles by 4 P.M. and were past Glacier Tongue. Then
half a mile of bad pressure ice running from Glacier Tongue
to Tent Island, and then rather worse going past Inaccessible, where we met a strong northerly wind. Up to now
the light from the moon had been good, but now the light
was worse and we were very done. At last we rounded
the Cape and gradually pulled in and right up to the door,
without disturbing anything. As we were getting out of
our harness, always a big business in our frozen state,
Hooper came out, suddenly said ' By Jove ! ' and rushed
back, and then there was pandemonium.

It was 9.30 P.M., and a good many had turned out of
their beds. Everybody hung on to some part of us and
got our clothes off : mine next morning weighed 24 lbs.
As they heard our story or bits of it they became more
and more astonished. We were set down to cocoa and
bread and butter and jam : we did not want anything else.
Scott I heard say, ' But, look here, you know, this is the
hardest journey that has ever been made.' They told us
afterwards that we had a look in our faces as if we were
at our last gasp, a look which had quite gone next morning.

WILSON, B WERS, AND CHERRY-GARRARD ON THEIR RETURN FROM CAPE CROZIER

Ponting said he had seen the same look on some Russian prisoners' faces at Mukden. I just tumbled into my dry, warm blankets. I expect it was as near an approach to bliss as a man can get on this earth.

Sleeping-bags. (Written August 3, 1912).—The life of a man on such a journey as this depends mainly upon the life of his sleeping-bag. We all three of us took eiderdown linings. Bill's bag proved really too small to take his eiderdown, and on the return journey his bag split down the seams to an alarming extent, letting in the cold air. Latterly in this journey it was by no means an uncommon experience for us to take over an hour in getting into our bags. One night I especially remember when Bill had practically given up all hope of getting his head into his. He finally cut off the flaps of his eiderdown, and with Birdie on one side and myself on the other we managed to lever the lid of the head of the bag open and gradually he got his head into it. I made a great mistake in taking a ' large-sized ' bag—though it was a small one. What a man really wants is a large ' middle-sized ' bag. The last fortnight, whenever the temperature was very low, I never thawed out the parts of my bag which were not pressing tight up against my body. I have forgotten what Bill's and Birdie's bags weighed when we got in. Mine (bag and eiderdown) was 45 lbs., personal gear 10 lbs. When we started that bag was about 18 lbs. : *the accumulation of ice was therefore 27 lbs.*

Birdie's bag just fitted him beautifully, though perhaps it would have been a little small with an eiderdown inside. As I understand from Atkinson, Birdie had undoubtedly a greater heat supply than other men ordinarily have. He never had serious trouble with his feet, while ours were constantly frostbitten. He slept I should be afraid to say how much longer than we did, even in the last days. It was a pleasure to lie awake, practically at any rate all night, and hear his snores. Largely owing to the arrangement of toggles, also not having shipped his eiderdown bag, but mainly due to his extraordinary energy, he many times turned his bag during the journey, and thus he got rid of a lot of the moisture in his bag, which came out as snow or actual knobs of ice. When we did turn our bags, the only way was directly we turned out, and even then you had to be quick before the bag froze. Getting out of the tent at night, it was quite a race to get back to your bag, before it began to get hard again. Of course this was in the lowest temperatures.

On the return journey we never rolled our bags up, but let them freeze out straight—arranging them carefully so that they should freeze in the best shape for getting into them again. On the Barrier they were literally as hard as boards, but coming back down the Sound they never got so hard that they would not bend. I cannot say what a self-sacrifice I consider it to have been that Birdie handed over his dry eiderdown to me when we were coming back. At the time a dry sleeping-bag would have been of more value to any of us than untold wealth.

Our bags were of course much worse after lying out a blizzard in them.

Clothes.—The details of our clothes were all taken down by Scott after we got in, and I will not repeat. We

all agreed that we could not have bettered our clothing.
I was foolish in starting with a vest which I had worn
some time and which had stretched. A close-fitting vest
would have been much warmer. As it was, on the march
on the stillest day there seemed to be a draught blowing
straight up my back.

Before we had been many days in these very cold
temperatures our clothes used to freeze so stiff in a few
seconds after stepping outside the tent, that from our
waists upwards we could never move our body or heads
from that position until they were thawed out again at
the next meal. We therefore got into the way of getting
frozen in a position which would be most comfortable. Our
arms we moved with a good deal of straining, and getting
into our harness was always a long job, all three doing
one set of harness at a time. We got into the way of
doing everything with mits on and very slowly, stopping
immediately our hands were going, and restoring the
circulation.

Routine.—We used to turn in for at least seven hours.
This was the worst part of the day, and breakfast to
me became in consequence quite the best meal. Sometimes I used to feel like shouting that it must be time to
get up. Getting under weigh in the morning used to
take generally a little under four hours, $3\frac{1}{2}$ hours as far
as I can remember was good. Going out we had the primus
going a large part of the time, though we turned it low after
the meal was cooked. In the worst times we used to light
the primus while we were in our bags in the morning
and keep it going until we were just getting or had got

the mouth of our bags levered open in the evening. We also tried getting the primus into our bags to thaw them out, but it was not very successful. Cooking coming back was a much longer process, since we had to hold the cooker up, having lost its proper stand and the top of the outer cooker—though Birdie's substitute was very good.

After breakfast we would be pretty warm, and having loaded the sledge the next job was to get a bearing on to some star or the moon if anything was visible. This meant lighting matches, always a big business. To light the candle in the tent we used sometimes to have to try three or even four boxes before one would light. Steering was very haphazard generally

Then into our harness—and then four hours' march or relaying, if possible. The possibility depended on whether our feet got too cold, but the difficulty was to know when they were frostbitten.

Relaying was at first by naked candle—later by hurricane lamp—following back our tracks in the snow for the second sledge. We never could decide which was the heavier. We camped for lunch if possible before we got too cold, since this was always a cold job.

We cooked alternately day by day. The worst part was lighting up. The weekly bag was very cold to handle. Generally (often) we had to take off our finnesko or one of them to examine our feet and nurse them back if they were gone.

Then four hours' march more if possible.

Footgear on as soon as possible on camping. Our night footgear was very good.

It is also difficult already, after two nights' rest, with a dozen men all round anticipating your every wish, and with the new comfortable life of the hut all round you, to realise completely how bad the last few weeks have been, how at times one hardly cared whether we got through or not, so long as (I speak for myself) if I was to go under it would not take very long. Although our weights are not very different, I am only 1lb. and Bill and Birdie 3½ lbs. lighter than when we started, we were very done when we got in, falling asleep on the march, and unable to get into our finnesko or eat our meals without falling asleep. Although we were doing good marches up to the end, we were pulling slow and weak, and the cold was getting at us in a way in which it had never touched us before. Our fingers were positive agony immediately we took them out of our mits, and to undo a lashing took a very long time. The night we got in Scott said he thought it was the hardest journey which had ever been made. Bill says it was infinitely worse than the Southern Journey in 1902–3.

I would like to put it on record that Captain Scott considered this journey to be the hardest which had ever been done. This was a well-considered judgment.

A. CHERRY-GARRARD.

MEMBERS OF THE NORTHERN PARTY

Lieut. Victor L. A. Campbell, R.N.

Surgeon G. Murray Levick, R.N.

Raymond E. Priestley (Geologist)

Petty Officer G. P. Abbott, R.N.

Petty Officer F. V. Browning, R.N.

Seaman H. Dickason, R.N.

THE LAST BOAT LEAVES FOR THE SHIP

NARRATIVE OF THE NORTHERN PARTY

Between January 25, 1911, and January 18, 1913

By Commander Victor L. A. Campbell, R.N.

Wednesday, January 25, 1911.—We said good-bye to Captain Scott and the Southern Depôt Party, and at 9 the following morning left Glacier Tongue for Butter Point, to land the Western Geological Party. A light southerly wind had cleared the loose ice out of the bay, and we had no difficulty in getting the ship alongside the ice foot, so that by 6 the same evening we had landed the party, laid out a depôt, and left on our cruise to the eastward, where I hoped to effect a landing, if not on King Edward's Land itself, at least in some inlet near the eastern end of the Barrier.

I had received the following instructions from Captain Scott, and they explain our subsequent movements :

'Winter Quarters, Cape Evans,
'23rd January, 1911.

'*Instructions to Leader of Eastern Party*

'Directions as to the landing of your party are contained in the instructions to the Commanding Officer of the *Terra Nova* handed to you herewith.

'Whilst I hope that you may be able to land in King Edward's Land, I fully realise the possibility of the conditions being unfavourable and the difficulty of the task which has been set you.

'I do not think you should attempt a landing unless the Ship can remain in security near you for at least three days, unless all your stores can be placed in a position of safety in a shorter time.

'The Ship will give you all possible help in erecting your hut, &c., but I hope you will not find it necessary to keep her by you for any length of time.

'Should you succeed in landing, the object you will hold in view is to discover the nature and extent of King Edward's Land. The possibilities of your situation are so various that it must be left to you entirely to determine how this object may best be achieved.

'In this connexion it remains only to say that you should be at your winter station and ready to embark on February 1, 1912.

'If the Ship should not arrive by February 15, and your circumstances permit, you should commence to retreat across the Barrier, keeping at first near the edge in order to see the Ship should she pass.

'It would be a wise precaution to lay out a depôt in this direction at an earlier date, and I trust that a further depôt will be provided in some inlet as you go east in the Ship.

'When I hear that you have been safely landed in King Edward's Land I shall take steps to ensure that a third depôt is laid out. This will be placed by the

Western Party one mile from the Barrier Edge and thirty miles from Cape Crozier.

'You will of course travel light on such a journey, and remember that fresh food can be obtained at Cape Crozier. A sledge sail should help you.

'From Cape Crozier you should make for Hut Point, where shelter and food will be found pending the freezing over of the bays to the north.

'Should you be unable to land in the region of King Edward's Land you will be at liberty to go to the region of Robertson Bay after communicating with Cape Evans.

'I think it very possible that a suitable wintering spot may be found in the vicinity of Smith's Inlet, but the Ship must be handled with care as I have reason to believe that the pack sometimes presses on this coast.

'Should you be landed in or near Robertson Bay you will not expect to be relieved until March in the following year, but you should be in readiness to embark on February 25.

'The main object of your exploration in this region would naturally be the coast westward of Cape North.

'Should the Ship have not returned by March 25 it will be necessary for you to prepare for a second winter.

'In no case would it be advisable for you to attempt to retreat along the coast. Seals and penguins should be plentiful and possibly some useful stores may remain at Cape Adare, but the existence of stores should not be regarded as more than a possibility.

VOL. II

'In conclusion I wish you all possible good luck, feeling assured that you will deserve it.

(Signed) R. Scott.

By 9 A.M. on the 27th we were off Cape Crozier and commenced our survey of the Barrier to see what changes had taken place since 1901.

About 9 A.M. on January 30 we passed an inlet opening N. by W., 1100 yards long, 250 wide, having perpendicular sides about 90 feet high.

This evening about seven we saw a large piece of the Barrier break off. We were at the time within 900 yards of the cliff, when we heard a noise like thunder and saw a cloud of spray rise up about half a mile ahead of us. The cloud of spray completely hid the Barrier at that place, and as this cleared we saw that a large piece had broken off, while débris of ice was forced out across our bows, making us alter course to avoid it.

January 31.—While steaming up a bay this afternoon another large piece of the Barrier broke away. It must have been five miles away, but we heard the noise like a peal of thunder and through our glasses saw a cloud of spray hanging over the place like a fog.

Soon after 3 P.M. we were up at the head of the bay, when we found new ice had formed. The Barrier here runs down nearly to the water's edge, and were it only farther to the eastward would not be a bad place to winter.

A number of Sibbald whales were blowing in the bay, and on the ice we saw several seals, and some Emperor

A BERG CALVING FROM A GLACIER AT CAPE CROZIER

penguins. Time and coal were precious; so we did not wait, but turned, and steamed out of the bay.

On getting outside we found a strong S.E. wind, and as we had the current against us as well, we decided not to work along the Barrier, but to shape course direct for Cape Colbeck, in which case we could carry fore and aft sail. We encountered strong S.E. wind but no pack, until 3 o'clock on the morning of the 2nd, when we made heavy pack with a number of small bergs in it right ahead.

The sea was breaking heavily on the pack edge, so we altered course to the southward, and after a few hours' steaming against a nasty head sea we got round it. About eight o'clock the wind fell, and shortly afterwards we sighted what was apparently ice-covered land on the starboard bow—soundings gave 208 fathoms. The day was lovely, and we had a good view of the land, which proved to be Cape Colbeck, a long convex ice dome without a rock showing. Sextant angles made the summit 750 feet high, while the ice face averaged 100 feet. Some heavy pack and a large number of bergs were lying off the cliff, but working our way slowly through we found open water under the cliff. Our prospects were now bright; open water ahead and a perfect day. However, in the afternoon our hopes were blighted; about 10 miles east of Cape Colbeck we came on a line of solid unbroken pack, into which a number of bergs were frozen, stretching from the ice cliffs of King Edward's Land out to the N.W. as far as we could see from the crow's nest. We steamed up to the edge of the ice, stopped, and sounded, getting bottom at 169 fathoms.

Several seals, one of which looked like a sea leopard, and some Adélie and Emperor penguins were on the ice, while large flocks of Antarctic petrels were flying about everywhere.

The ice cliffs, stretching as far as we could see, gave us no hope of finding a landing-place.

There is evidence of a great deal of pressure here and the upper edge of the cliff near us, 100 feet high, showed a pressure ridge, where evidently a large berg had been forced against it.

At 5.0 P.M. we reluctantly turned and retraced our steps, the only chance of a landing-place being Balloon Bight or some inlet at the east end of the Barrier. Soundings off Cape Colbeck gave us 89 fathoms. During the night we sailed as close as possible to the ice face but passed nothing but high cliffs. About 3 o'clock on the morning of the 3rd a strong S.E. wind sprang up, bringing a low mist, but not thick enough to prevent us keeping close to the coast. Soon after the cliff dipped a little and appeared on both bows, showing we were running into a bay; this was the place where I had had great hopes of effecting a landing, but we were unable to do so.

It was interesting to note that while the eastern side of the bay was clean cut, the western side was much weather-worn and honeycombed with caves, evidently worn by the strong westerly current which sweeps along the Barrier. We saw two narrow inlets opening N.E. but not wide enough to trust the ship in; moreover, as they open in this direction they are more liable to be blocked by any loose ice drifting in.

In the afternoon the weather cleared and we were able to get sights, showing we were still to the eastward of Balloon Bight. By 9 A.M. we were off the place where Balloon Bight should have been, and our sights put us south of the old Barrier edge. There was no doubt about it; Balloon Bight had gone. By midnight we were off Shackleton's Bay of Whales. On rounding the eastern point our surprise can be imagined when we saw a ship, which I recognised as the *Fram*, made fast alongside the sea ice.

Standing in, we made fast a little way ahead of her and hoisted our colours, she answering with the Norwegian ensign. There was no doubt it was Captain Amundsen.

Pennell and I immediately went on board and saw Lieutenant Neilsen, who was in command. He told us Amundsen was up at the camp about three miles in, over the sea ice, but would be down about 9 o'clock, and accordingly soon after 9 I returned on board and saw Amundsen, who told me his plans. He had been here since January 4, after a good passage, having been held only four days in the pack. He had intended wintering at Balloon Bight, but on finding that had gone, had fixed on the Bay of Whales as the best place.

He asked me to come up and see his camp, so Pennell, Levick and I went up, and found he had erected his hut on the Barrier, about 3 miles from the coast. The camp presented a very workmanlike appearance, with a good-sized hut containing a kitchen and living-room with a double tier of bunks round the walls, while outside several tents were up and 116 fine Greenland dogs picketed round.

His party, besides himself, consisted of Johansen, who was with Dr. Nansen in his famous sledge journey of '97, and seven others. After coffee and a walk round the camp Amundsen and two others returned with us and had lunch in the *Terra Nova*.

We left early in the afternoon, and after sounding and dredging in the bay, proceeded west along the Barrier, of which there still remained nearly 100 miles we had not seen.

Outside the bay we were unlucky enough to pick up a S.W. wind, but with clear weather we kept close along the Barrier edge to long. 170° W., where we had left it on our way east, without seeing any inlet or possible place to land. This was a great disappointment to us all, but there was nothing for it but to return to McMurdo Sound to communicate with the main party and then try and effect a landing in the vicinity of Smith's Inlet or as far to the westward as possible on the north coast of Victoria Land, and if possible to explore the unknown coast west of Cape North.

We therefore made the best of our way to Cape Evans, and in spite of a moderate S.W. gale arrived on the evening of the 8th.

Here I decided to land the two ponies, as they would be very little use to us on the mountainous coast of Victoria Land, and in view of the Norwegian expedition I felt the Southern Party would require all the transport available.

After landing the ponies we steamed up to the sea ice by Glacier Tongue, and from there, taking Priestley and Abbott, I went with letters to leave at Hut Point, where the Depôt Party would call on their way back. The surface was good and we got back to the ship about 3 A.M., and then proceeded to water ship at Glacier Tongue. While watering ship an accident occurred which might have been serious. The ship was secured alongside, and Abbott was just stepping ashore when a large piece of ice broke away with him on it and fell between the ship and the ice edge. Luckily he was not hurt, and was soon pulled on board again, none the worse, except for a ducking.

By 8 o'clock in the evening of the 9th we were all ready, and proceeded north with a fair S.E. wind, but thick snow.

During the afternoon of February 12th the wind freshened into a gale with heavy snow, and not wanting to close Cape Adare in such thick weather we hove to under main lower topsail with Cape Adare bearing N.W., distant 20 miles.

During the night the wind increased, and continued blowing a very heavy gale until the evening of the 15th. In spite of the very heavy sea the ship was fairly dry, but being so light we took a lot of ice water, washing away the bulwarks we had repaired since the previous gale.

The coal question was becoming serious; if this went on much longer it looked as if we should not be able to land, as Pennell had to keep enough coal to get back to New Zealand.

On the evening of the 15th the wind eased a little, and by 10 A.M. on the 16th we raised steam and shaped

course for Cape Adare, which was now 110 miles to the
S.W. It came on to blow hard again from the S.E.
in the afternoon, but we were able nearly to lay our
course under lower topsails; the snow squalls were
very thick, but luckily not much ice was sighted. Late
in the afternoon the weather cleared and we sighted the
mountainous coast of Victoria Land. During the night
we got among a lot of weathered bergs and loose pack,
which had the effect of smoothing the sea.

At 4 A.M. on the 17th we were within about 2 miles
of the coast just east of Smith's Inlet.

The land here was heavily glaciated, hardly a rock
showing, except some high cliffs and the Lyall Islands
to the westward.

Heavy pack lay to the west of us, so we had to
work along to the eastward, where the sea was fairly
clear of ice.

Some large floes lay close in under the cliffs, grinding
up against them in the heavy swell that was running.
I was very much disappointed at seeing no piedmont
to work along on the western sledge journey. The
cliffs were several hundred feet high except where the
glaciers ran down, the front of these being from 50 to
180 feet high.

We worked along to the eastward, keeping as close
as we could, and keeping a good lookout for a possible
landing.

The scenery was magnificent. In the afternoon we
entered Robertson Bay and found we had a strong tide
with us, which was fortunate as the wind had freshened

FACE OF A GLACIER IN VICTORIA LAND

DUGDALE GLACIER

again from the S.S.E.   The scenery here was even wilder, the Admiralty Range towering over our heads and so steep that, except in the valleys, no snow or ice was able to lodge, and bare rock showed everywhere.

Large glaciers filled all the valleys, but the gradient was so steep that they were heavily crevassed from top to bottom.

By 5 o'clock we were off the Dugdale Glacier, which runs out in three long tongues, in places only 10 feet high.

It appeared to have altered considerably since Borchgrevink's time, as he charts only one long tongue. It was not a good place for wintering, the surface being crevassed and the sides too steep to be climbed; the ice tongue would have been a good place to lie alongside and land stores, but as some of this broke away and drifted out to sea a week later, it was as well we did not try.

After having a look at Duke of York Island we steamed up to the head of the bay, but with no better success.   So about midnight we turned and made for Ridley Beach, a triangular beach on the west side of Cape Adare, the place where the Southern Cross Party wintered in 1900.

I was very much against wintering here, as until the ice forms in Robertson Bay one is quite cut off from any sledging operations on the mainland, for the cliffs of the peninsula descend sheer into the sea.

Pennell, however, had only just enough coal as it was to get back to New Zealand, so at 3 A.M. on the 18th we anchored off the south shore of the beach and commenced landing stores.   A cold, wet job it was.   A lot of loose

ice round the shore and a surf made it difficult for the
boats to get in ; the water shoaled some way out, which
meant wading backwards and forwards with the stores,
while several times the boats broached to as they touched
and half swamped. We worked from 3 A.M. till midnight,
and started again at 4 A.M. on Sunday.

The way everyone behaved was splendid, Davies the
carpenter in particular working at the hut for 48 hours
on end. Communication with the ship was twice cut
off by heavy pack setting into the bay.

By 4 A.M. Monday everything was landed, the ship
party re-embarked, and the ship proceeded north, while
we of the shore party, who were all dead tired, turned
in for a few hours' sleep. One of Borchgrevink's huts
was standing, but was half full of snow ; the other one
had no roof and had evidently been used as a nesting
place by generations of penguins. After clearing out the
snow of the former we had quite comfortable quarters
while we built our own hut. With the exception of the
21st, when we had a mild blizzard, we had fine weather
for building the hut, for which we were very thankful,
as that, and carrying up all the stores, proved a long job
for a small party. We used to start work every morning
at 6, and knock off between 8 and 9 every evening, by
which time we were pretty tired.

By an oversight only two hammers had been landed,
so four unfortunates had to use Priestley's geological
hammers. These are heavy, square-headed implements,
designed to chip, and judging by our mangled fingers
the man who made them knew his business. We had

PENGUINS PROMENADE

rather a shock on Friday, when on examining the fifteen carcases of frozen mutton left by the ship we found them to be covered with green mould.

They must have been in this condition on board, as we buried them in the ice as soon as they were landed; anyhow we had to condemn them, to the great delight of the skua gulls; but penguins and seals are plentiful, so we shall not be short of fresh meat.

While at work on the Saturday we heard a loud report up at the head of the bay, and through our glasses we could see that a large piece of the Dugdale Glacier tongue had broken off.

By working late Saturday night we had the outside of the hut ready and the guys set up, so on Sunday we had a wash and change of clothes, church in the forenoon and a day off, which gave us an opportunity for a look round.

The view is magnificent: to the southward we see the Admiralty Range of mountains, with Mts. Sabine, Minto, and Adam rising to over 10,000 feet; away to the west the mountains are not so high, but completely snow-covered, and slope gradually down to Cape North; behind us are the black basalt cliffs of the Cape Adare Peninsula, and in one place there is quite an easy way to the top. When we landed we found Borchgrevink's hut inhabited by a solitary moulting penguin. He was very indignant at being turned out and stood all day at the door scolding us. He also did showman to the crowds of sightseers who came to watch us. I am afraid many of the sight-seers got knocked on the head and put in the ice-house. It is brutal work, for they are such friendly little beasts, and take such an interest in us; but they and the seals are our only fresh meat.

Sunday, March 5.—-We have put in a good week's work, thanks to fine weather. The hut was ready and we moved in last night, and celebrated the occasion with a great house-warming. We have also had time to put up the meteorological screen and dig a beautiful ice-house in a small stranded berg on the south shore. Unfortunately, the day after the larder was filled a big surf came rolling in and the berg began to break up. We had only just time to rescue the forty penguins with which we had stocked it, and carry the little corpses to a near ice-house built of empty cases filled with ice and well out of reach of the sea. The whole beach we are on is a penguin rookery in summer, and has been so for generations. We are constantly reminded of it—in fact so forcibly is this so inside the hut, that before putting down the floor Levick dressed the ground with bleaching-powder. He did this so thoroughly, and inhaled so much of the gas, that he had to retire to his bunk blind in both eyes, with a bad sore throat and all the symptoms of a heavy cold in his head.

This afternoon Abbott, Priestley, Levick, and I climbed to the top of Cape Adare, and certainly the view over the bay was lovely, the east side of the peninsula descending in a sheer cliff to the Ross Sea. We collected some fine bits of quartz and erratic boulders about 1000 feet up, and Levick got some good photographs of the Admiralty Range. On the way down I found some green alga on the rocks.

SKUA GULLS FIGHTING OVER SOME BLUBBER

PENGUINS JUMPING ON TO THE ICE-FOOT

Monday, March 6.—We set to work on the coal and stores and carried everything up to the hut, stacking them on the weather side.

We have now settled down into a regular routine ; we turn out at 7 A.M., have breakfast at 8 A.M., dinner at 1 P.M., and supper at 7 P.M.

The weather is fairly fine, the temperature keeping between 18° and 20° F., but with a cold east wind. Loose pack sets into the bay with the flood and drifts out with the ebb tide.

March 9.—We had a most magnificent surf breaking on the western shore over a fringe of grounded pack, throwing spray and bits of ice 30 or 40 feet into the air.

On the 11th and 12th we had our first blizzard with heavy drift, and the hut shook a little, but nothing gave way. The remaining penguins began gathering in parties on the sea shore, which looked as though they were going to leave us for the winter ; we had now 120 penguins and 4 seals in the ice-house, whic   ⁀ be sufficient for the winter. All manner of bergs drift past our beach, and it is interesting to note the difference in the buoyancy between the two types of berg —the glacier-formed iceberg and the barrier berg composed chiefly or wholly of névé. In one instance a glacier berg about 70 or 80 feet high grounded off our beach in 36 fathoms, and a few days after a barrier berg of similar height drifted past well inside the former.

March 19.—A week of snow and drift, with very little sun.

This morning about seven o'clock it came on to blow

from the S.E., with lots of drift. Our anemometer registered wind at 84 miles an hour and then broke ; some of the squalls after this must have been of hurricane force. The dome tent which I had up for magnetic observations was blown away, and we never saw a sign of it again. The wind eased in the evening, but blew a gale all night.

A very big sea was breaking on the south shore, the spray being carried right across the peninsula, coating our hut with ice. During the heavier squalls it was impossible to stand. The hut shook a great deal, but beyond a few things being shaken off the shelves no damage was done.

The following day was lovely, and we had a fine aurora in the evening. An arc of yellow stretched from N.W. to N.E., while a green and red curtain extended from the N.W. horizon to the zenith.

On March 27 we launched the ' pram,' which is a Norwegian skiff, and tried trawling off the south shore, but did not do very well, our total catch being one sea louse, one sea slug, and one spider ; certainly the fishermen, Priestley, Browning, and Dickason, had plenty of difficulties to contend with, as the sea ice was forming so fast that they were compelled to spend most of their time breaking a passage through it.

March 30.—We had another wonderful aurora display this evening. It was like a great curtain of light shaken by a wind, the lower edges being a red colour.

April 9.—The last week has been calm and snowy, and young ice is forming very quickly on the south shore, but on the north shore where there is more swell the sea

LAUNCH OF THE PRAM

CAMPBELL AND PRIESTLEY AFLOAT ON PANCAKE ICE

keeps fairly open. The whole shore since the last gale is piled with enormous blocks of ice, 15 to 20 feet square, and as many of them are glacier ice we find them most useful for our drinking water.

One of the problems of our spring journey along the coast is how we are going to get back if the ice goes out, or even get over the big lanes that are sure to open in the spring, so I have decided to build two kayaks, by making canvas boats to fit round the sledges ; these can be carried on the sledges when travelling over the ice and the sledge fitted in them when crossing open water.

April 17.—The first kayak was finished last Thursday and the canvas dressed with hot blubber, but owing to a week of winds we had not been able to try her until to-day. She proved a great success. I made the first cruise in her along the north shore, using a bamboo as a paddle ; she was not at all crank and carried me easily. We will build another, so that by lashing the two together we should have a very seaworthy craft.

May 2.—A lovely day, and as the second kayak was ready we tried her. I have given her more freeboard than the last, and she is, if anything, more seaworthy.

The temperature, which had been steadily dropping all last month, is now at about $-7°$ F., very pleasant in calm weather, but in the winds most of us have had our faces frostbitten.

It is wonderful how quickly the time is passing. I suppose it is our regular routine, and the fact of all having plenty to do.

Levick is photographer, microbiologist, and stores

officer. His medical duties have been nil, with the exception of stopping one of my teeth, a most successful operation ; but as he had been flensing a seal a few days before, his fingers tasted strongly of blubber !

Priestley's geology keeps him wandering on the top or on the slopes of Cape Adare, and he certainly gets more exercise than any of us.

He is also meteorologist, and when he does have any spare moments is out with the trawl or fish trap.

I am doing a survey of Cape Adare and the magnetic observations.

Abbott is carpenter and has the building of the kayaks.

Browning is assistant meteorologist and his special care is the acetylene gas plant, a thankless task, as any escape of gas or bad light brings a certain amount of criticism.

Dickason has proved himself a most excellent cook and baker, while the ' galley ' is a model of neatness.

The following was our daily routine during the winter :

At 7 A.M. we turned out, one hand going down to the ice foot to get ice for cooking purposes. A number of empty cases were kept full of ice in the ' lean to ' outside the hut for use during blizzards when we could not get down to the ice foot. Breakfast was at 8 A.M., and consisted of porridge, seal steak or bacon, and tea. After breakfast we would turn to at our various jobs and worked till 1 P.M., when we had a cold lunch, bread and cheese and sometimes sardines, then work again until 4 P.M., when we had tea. After tea we cleared up decks, and then the rest of the day everyone had to himself.

CAMPBELL AFLOAT IN A KAYAK

THE TWO KAYAKS ASHORE

Dinner was at 7 P.M., and was usually seal or penguin, pudding, and dessert. After dinner hardly a night passed without a gramophone concert.

Saturday morning was devoted to a good soap-and-water scrub of the whole hut, everyone piling their belongings on their beds, Saturday afternoon being ' make and mend.

Sunday breakfast was at 9 A.M. to give the cook a lie-in, and every week church was held at 10.30 A.M.

In fine weather Sunday was a great day for a long walk, either over the sea ice or up Cape Adare.

During the week everyone had a washing day, when he had a bath and washed his clothes, clothes lines being rigged across the hut.

Of the two huts left by Sir George Newnes' expedition in 1899, one hut was standing in fairly good condition, the other was roofless. The former we repaired, and it made a very good workshop, while the latter, after clearing out and roofing with a tarpaulin, we turned into a store house. Taking it all round we were a very happy and contented little community, but as a wintering station Cape Adare is not good, being cut off from the mainland until June, when the sea ice can be trusted not to go out in a blizzard.

The sea ice has been forming in Robertson Bay for the last week, and now we are able to walk several miles to the southward. To the northward of our beach is a lot of open water, owing to the strong tidal streams off Cape Adare.

On May 5 began our longest and hardest blow

lasting with occasional lulls until the 14th. The morning was overcast, with a cold southerly wind, and when I was out for a walk with Levick we both got our noses frost-bitten. In the evening a strong gale blew with drift, and between 1 and 4 A.M. on the 6th the squalls were of hurricane force.

The hut shook and creaked, but stood up to it all right, though some of the ruberoid on the roof was ripped off, a heavy ladder blown some way to leeward, and the outer wall of our porch, made of cases and boards, blown in. In the forenoon the wind eased a little and we were able to get out and secure what we could. The squalls were still so fierce it was impossible to stand in them, and one had to ' heave to' on hands and knees until they passed.

All the sea ice had gone out, although it was over 2 feet thick, and on the 8th the gale freshened again, and during the night the squalls were as hard as any we had had, stones and pebbles rattling against the hut. On the 9th it eased a little, but blew a whole gale until Saturday 13th, when the wind dropped. The peninsula had been swept bare of snow, but the beach and huts were covered with frozen spray. On the 19th the sun left us, but the weather improved, being clear and cold, while the temperature dropped to below zero F. By May 28 the sea ice seemed pretty solid all round us, the temperature being − 30° F., and we walked out to the ' Sisters,' two pillar rocks lying off Cape Adare. The ice here showed heavy pressure. There are a good number of bergs frozen in to the northward of us.

HANSEN'S GRAVE ON CAPE ADARE

CLEARING DRIFT FROM WINDOW OF HUT AT CAPE ADARE

Now the winter cold had set in we were obliged to rig our second stove in the hut, finding it impossible to keep the temperature of the hut above − 25° F.

On June 1 we had a twenty-four hours' blizzard, but I am thankful to say the sea ice held, except off the north shore, where it was driven out for about 100 yards along the beach.

June 11.—We have had a week of the most glorious calm and clear weather, the temperature to-day being 25° F.

We have been out to most of the neighbouring bergs, and one in Robertson Bay has the most wonderful caves. Levick got some very good photographs of these with flashlight. Unfortunately Priestley, who was working the flash, got his face badly burnt.

We have felt the want of an alarm clock, as in such a small party it seems undesirable that anyone should have to remain awake the whole night to take the 2–4 A.M. observations, but Browning has come to the rescue with a wonderful contrivance. It consists of a bamboo spring held back by a piece of cotton rove through a candle which is marked off in hours. The other end of the cotton is attached to the trigger of the gramophone, and whoever takes the midnight observations winds the gramophone, ' sets ' the cotton, lights the candle, and turns the trumpet towards Priestley, who has to turn out for the 2 A.M., and then turns in himself. At ten minutes to two the candle burns the thread and releases the bamboo spring, which being attached to the trigger starts the gramophone in the sleeper's ear, and he turns out and stops the tune. This arrangement works beautifully, and can be timed to five minutes.

Other things we should have brought are fencing masks and foils. As it is, Abbott has manufactured some helmets out of old flour-tins and also some bamboo sabres, and there have been desperate encounters out on the snow.

The prismatic skies we get during the day now are perfectly lovely, and last night we had, I think, the best coloured aurora we have seen. It was a great curtain across the northern sky, the colours being red, green, and yellow.

This spell of fine weather continued until June 18, when the glaciers were obscured with drift, and we could hear the rumbling of pressure on the other side of Cape Adare, a sure sign of wind, although with us it was still quite calm.

We counted twenty-six seals along the tide crack to-day, whereas for some weeks before we had not seen any.

June 19.—Last night about 8 it came on to blow a full gale, with heavy drift and squalls of hurricane force. The hut worked a good deal and some of the outer planking was ripped off. It was my turn for the midnight rounds, and I got my nose rather badly frostbitten, so to-day it is one big blister.

On the morning of the 20th the wind went down and we were able to repair the hut. The sea ice stood the blizzard well, but again it had been forced back about a hundred yards from the north shore.

On June 22 we celebrated Midwinter Day with the usual festivities.

July 10.—The days are already a little lighter, and we are making ready our sledging equipment, for on the 28th of this month I propose making an expedition into Robertson Bay for a week to see what sort of surface to expect up the coast, the pressure all round our beach and Cape Adare being very bad.

We have seen several Antarctic petrels, and it is hard to account for these birds down here in the middle of winter, unless there is open water a little north of us.

July 29.—Priestley, Abbott, and I left the hut for our short expedition into Robertson Bay.

Taking provisions for a fortnight, we left about 8 A.M., when it was beginning to get light. The surface was appalling, and in spite of our light sledge (400 lbs.) it took us three days to reach Duke of York Island, a distance of 22 miles by the route we took to avoid the bad pressure. The salt-flecked smooth ice, being very sticky, was much heavier going even than the pressure ice.

We spent a day at Duke of York Island collecting, and started back at daybreak, August 2. During the day the weather looked so threatening I made for the cliffs just south of Warning Glacier to get some shelter in case of a blizzard. We got some heavy squalls and drift in the afternoon, which nearly made us camp, but keeping on we reached land about 5.30, camping between two high pressure ridges under the cliffs. The noise of the wind in the bay was terrific, and we were thankful to have got some shelter. After supper we

turned in, and being tired after our hard pull were soon
asleep. I was awakened about 9 P.M. by a tremendous
din, and found the lee skirting of the tent had blown
out from under the heavy ice blocks we had piled on it,
and the tent poles were bending under the weight of wind.
We just had time to roll out of our bags and hang on to
the skirting or the tent would have gone. Taking advantage of a lull we got out and piled more ice on the skirting,
but even that was not enough, and we spent a miserable
night hanging on to the skirting of the tent. The blizzard
dropped by noon the next day, and by one o'clock we
were off again, camping at 5.30, when it was too dark
to go on.

Starting again just before daybreak on the 4th, we
reached the hut the same evening. The temperatures
we experienced were not low, the lowest being − 26·8° F.

The chief result of this journey was to show that we
must expect very bad travelling surfaces up the coast
and that I must alter my original plan, which was to
start about August 20 with two units of three. I now
saw that it would take a party of four to get along over
the pressure ice we must expect, so I decided to take
Priestley, Abbott, and Dickason with six weeks' provisions
and do without a supporting party, leaving Levick and
Browning to carry on the work at Cape Adare.

August 8.—Levick, Priestley, Browning, and Dickason left this morning for Warning Glacier to do geology.
We had depôted our outfit about 10 miles down the
coast, only packing our sleeping-bags, so they were able
to go without a sledge, taking their sleeping-bags on their

'THE WARNING.' AN ONCOMING BLIZZARD

SLOPE OF THE WARNING GLACIER

backs. I remained at the hut with Abbott, who was laid up with water on the knee, and I was kept busy by the combined duties of cook and bottle-washer, meteorologist, etc.

August 10.—Levick's party returned at 4 P.M., bringing in all our equipment. They had had overcast weather and high temperatures, and Levick had only been able to get six photographs, which were not good.

August 16.—We woke up this morning to find the ice had gone out in the night. This was a bitter disappointment and a blow to all my hopes of a western journey over the sea ice—the only comfort is that it came when it did, as had it come a fortnight later, we should have gone out with it. Yesterday a strong blizzard began to blow from the S.E., with lots of drift, and the gale continued very hard all day. About 8 P.M. it lulled a little, only to come on again with redoubled violence between 10 P.M. and midnight.

The squalls were terrific, harder than anything we had yet experienced, shaking the hut so that several things fell off the shelves. The roof of our store house was torn off, and the two gable ends which took all six of us to lift were slung about 20 yards away.

This morning the water extended from our beach to the coast of the mainland a little west of the Dugdale Glacier, and as far as we could see to the westward.

Three Antarctic and two snowy petrels, attracted no doubt by the open water, were flying about the beach.

On the 17th, Levick, Priestley, and I climbed Cape Adare to see the ice conditions in the Ross Sea after the gale.   Large stretches of open water lay to the S.E. and east, while small pools and lanes were very numerous on the northern horizon, and a heavy bank of fog or mist seemed to indicate a lot of open water there.   To the S.W. across Robertson Bay the open water appeared to reach right up to the cliffs of the mainland, but the day was not very clear, and it was hard to make out distinctly if there was a strip of fast ice along the coast.

August 21.—A lovely clear day.   We went up Cape Adare again to see the ice conditions to the westward. Owing to the young ice over the open water it was hard to make out if there was an ice foot along the cliffs of the mainland.   If the ice remains in I shall go into Robertson Bay early in September to see if the coast journey is feasible, for our only other alternative is to find glaciers leading on to the plateau.

To get a better idea of the gradient of these I climbed about 2500 feet up the slopes of Cape Adare, and the result was not very encouraging.   I doubt if the glaciers in Robertson Bay lead directly to the plateau, as the Admiralty Range rises in a series of unbroken ridges of bare rock from the sea to apparently far inland.

Altogether the outlook made me wish more than ever that the ship had had sufficient coal to take us back to Wood Bay.

The spell of fine weather lasted till the 30th, allowing thin ice to form over the open water, except in some pools near Cape Adare which the current seemed to keep open.   The night of the 30th a blizzard began, with heavy drift, some of the squalls being very heavy indeed, but it moderated towards the morning. The new ice had not gone out, but a large sheet of open water was visible to the north, while along the northern horizon an open water sky was visible. A decided swell along the beach makes me certain open water is not far distant.

September 7.—September came in with blizzards which prevented our getting away as early as we wished. Yesterday and to-day, however, we have been getting sledges and outfit over the bad pressure ice which lies to the southward of the beach.

We are taking a 12-ft. and a 10-ft. sledge, the latter being on iron runners, as no wooden runners would stand the sharp edges of the pressure ice for long. We also find the iron runners, in spite of the 40 lbs. extra weight, run much better over the salt-flecked ice. Once over the pressure we packed the 12-ft. sledge and secured it on the 10-ft.

Our total weight including sledges amounts to 1163 lbs

The sledging ration we are taking is based on Shackle ton's ration adapted for coast sledging.

We are convoying Levick and Browning as far as Warning Glacier, where the former is going to take photographs.

September 22.—On this journey the surfaces were so bad that we only managed to reach Cape Barrow, the western limit of Robertson Bay.

After our return we experienced a spell of bad weather until the 22nd, when it cleared, so Levick started off again for Warning Glacier to get the photographs he had been unable to take before.

Priestley, Browning, and Dickason went with him, and the party took provisions for a week.

September 27.—Levick and his party returned to-day and reported bad weather and blizzards nearly the whole time. They managed, however, to get a few photographs. I am arranging to start on our western journey October 1. Levick and Browning will come as far as Cape Wood to take photographs.

October 3.—Weather-bound until to-day, when, the weather clearing in the afternoon, we transported our sledges and gear over the pressure ice lying round the beach and left them three miles south.

October 4.—A fine morning, so after a 5.30 breakfast we started away with our sleeping-bags on our backs, and picking up our sledges made pretty good progress over salt-flecked ice with occasional belts of pressure.

To show the superiority of our iron runners over salt-flecked ice, I may mention that two of us pulled the iron-runner sledge weighing 1000 lbs. and kept ahead of Levick's sledge with only 200 lbs. and four men in the traces. About 12 miles out we came to a lot of pressure, so I took my party, consisting of Priestley, Abbott, and Dickason, and steered for Relay Bay, telling Levick and Browning to go their own pace and make the best of their way to the cave.

We camped that night in the middle of Relay Bay and after supper pulled the iron-runner sledge and depôt to a cave discovered on the north side of Point Penelope on a former journey, where we left it, as this sledge is no use in deep snow. We found Levick had just arrived all right, so picking up our ski and a few things we had left there, we returned to camp. The temperature remains – 15° F.

A lovely morning with the temperature – 21° F.; we were on the march by 8.30 over a fairly good surface.

In the afternoon we got into deep snow again and had to put on ski; we had fitted each ski with a detachable strip of sealskin which made pulling on them much easier. We camped that night 4 miles south of Cape Wood, after picking up our 12-ft. sledge and depôt at Birthday Point. Temperature – 28° F.

October 6.—The morning was overcast but warmer, the temperature being – 3° F. To-day we reached a little bay north of Cape Barrow.

After supper we heard an extraordinary noise like a ship's siren, which I suppose must have been a seal, but none of us had heard anything like it before. During the night we were awakened by an avalanche falling near us, but we were not near enough to the cliff to be in danger.

October 7.—We made a depôt in Siren Bay, leaving one sledge and taking on the 12-ft. sledge and four weeks' provisions. We had an early lunch and started. By keeping some way from the coast we got into fairly good surface, but I noticed round some of the pressure ridges pools of very new ice, while some large areas of flat ice appeared to have been recently flooded, the ice being dark and slushy.

We camped at 6.30, having done five miles since noon. In clearing away the snow for the tent we found the ice brownish in colour and quite salt. While we were turning in, Priestley, who was in his bag, heard a seal gnawing the ice just under his head and remarked to me that it seemed very close, so I sung out to Abbott to take an ice-axe and test the ice. After a few blows he was through and reported the ice only eight inches thick and very soft and sodden. .

We turned out and tried several places, with the same result.

Then Priestley and I went about a quarter of a mile towards the land and tried again, with no better result. Finally we found a small patch where the ice was about 15 inches thick and we shifted camp.

Things looked serious, for the season was becoming advanced and the summer thaw approaching, while we had to advance along a straight coast line with steep cliffs as far as we could see.   After talking over the situation with Priestley we decided that unless we could find thicker ice near the land we should have to turn, as this ice might break up any time.

It was a bitter disappointment, for I had expected at least to be able to get beyond Cape North this way.   It came on to blow with drift in the night, but fortunately the wind did not last, and to our delight on turning out we found the sun breaking through.

After breakfast, taking ski and a spade, I went in towards the land, trying a lot of places and always finding thin sodden ice ; in places the under layers of snow were so wet and soft it seemed as though the ice was depressed below the surface of the sea.

After taking a round of angles we returned, making

Siren Bay the same night. On our way back we sounded the ice several times, finding thin ice until we reached the tide crack at the mouth of the bay.

October 9 and 10.—We went north along the coast on ski, collecting and examining the face of the glacier, but we found no place where it was possible to climb up. The snow along the coast was very soft and deep, making progress difficult even on ski. We saw a good number of snow and Antarctic petrels circling about the cliffs as if they nested here.

October 11.—The temperature when we turned out was – 22·8° F.

Our only chance of doing anything now was to try and get up on one of the glaciers, and although we had seen no accessible place on our outward march, we decided to follow round each bay and examine the coast closely. To-day we returned to Birthday Point.

October 12.—A fine morning; I got a round of angles while Priestley went round the bay on ski. We saw a seal near the camp which had just given birth.

Our noses are frostbitten and sunburnt and are a curious sight. They have swollen very much; Abbott's is the worst, being one great blister. I had an attack of snow blindness in the afternoon.

October 13.—Temperature – 1° F., weather thick, with snow. We pulled out after breakfast and made for Sphinx Rock, where we camped at 1.30, just in time, as it came on to blow hard, with heavy drift. We saw several seals up along the side crack.

October 14.—Weather-bound all day in the tent,

blowing a blizzard, with heavy drift, impossible to see five yards.

October 15.—The wind dropped in the morning, but the weather remained overcast. Priestley went collecting and taking photographs, while the rest of us took one sledge half-way over to Point Penelope, as our load was very big after picking up the depôts.

October 16.—Weather overcast and snowing, but much warmer; we went round the bay collecting. It is impossible to get on to any of the glaciers from the sea ice, as they are all wall-faced.

October 17.—After getting some photographs of icebergs we started for Point Penelope. The forenoon was fine, but during our halt for lunch a heavy bank of cloud worked up from the N., and soon after resuming our march a S.E. wind sprang up, bringing snow and drift. The weather got so bad we had to leave one sledge about a mile out, and got into camp in the cave with the others just as the blizzard came on. In the cave we were as snug as could be, and finding some seal meat Levick had left, put it in the hoosh and had a great feed.

October 19.—Temperature zero. Weather very thick. We laid out a depôt off the Dugdale ice tongue which will do for our next trip into Robertson Bay.

October 20.—Weather very thick; land on the other side of the bay being obscured, we had to shape course by compass to Cape Adare. Starting about 9, we pulled through the fog, getting into rather troublesome pack, till one o'clock, when we halted for lunch. During lunch the fog lifted, and by climbing a berg I was able to see

CAMP IN THE CAVE UNDER PENELOPE POINT

LEVICK OUTSIDE CAMP AT PENELOPE POINT

a lead of smooth ice about half a mile to the northward.
Getting on to this we made good progress, arriving back
at the hut at 5 P.M. A good many seals were up, and
about two miles from home we came on the first party
of penguins.

After our return from this second coast trip the sea
ice became too rotten to be trustworthy, even in Robertson
Bay, while to the north of the beach, where the sweep of
the current was exceptionally strong, the various open
water patches which had been present since August
rapidly widened and coalesced, and in December the ice
both east and west of the cape broke out with great
rapidity.

Our work, therefore, was now restricted to the immediate confines of the beach and the peninsula of Cape
Adare, and this time was principally occupied in taking
routine observations and adding to our biological
collections.

Amongst the specimens collected at this time were
several fine sea leopards, which I was fortunate enough
to shoot near the rookery. As most of them were
shot in the water, we had some difficulty in securing the
bodies, and it was here that our kayaks were very useful.

We could carry these light and yet seaworthy craft
down to the ice foot and launch them, and from them slip
a noose round the body as it lay on the bottom in two
or three fathoms of water. The line was then passed
ashore and the united strength of the party just sufficed
to land the quarry.

After Christmas a permanent camp was established on Cape Adare and we were divided into three watches, one of which was always stationed on top of the cape to look out for the ship. During one of these watches Priestley and Dickason walked ten miles south along the cape, to find out whether, in the event of the ship not picking us up, it was possible for us to make our way south this way. They report the cape to reach a height of 4200 feet at its highest point, and from there they were able to get a good view of Warning Glacier and consider that it would be impossible to make an extended journey in this direction.

On the morning of January 4 Browning sighted the ship and signalled us on the beach below by hoisting a flag as arranged, and two days later all our gear was aboard and we were on our way to try our fortune two or three hundred miles farther south along the coast.

January 8, 1912. P.M.—This evening Pennell and I from the crow's nest saw open water behind the heavy pack we had been working through all day. I had given up hope of being able to land at Evans Coves, and talking it over with Pennell had just decided to come down in the ship and pick up Debenham first, when we saw the open water, and by 9 the same evening we were secured alongside the sea ice about 1½ miles from the piedmont, north of Evans Coves. It was a lovely evening, and with the help of the ship's people we soon had our outfit on the piedmont by a big moraine, where we had arranged to make our depôt, and be picked up by the ship on February 18.

THE HUT AT CAPE ADARE

THE NORTHERN PARTY AT CAPE ADARE
Left to right, top—Abbott, Dickason, Browning
„ *bottom*—Priestley, Campbell, Levick

Our stores were six weeks' sledging rations, one 12-ft. sledge (Priestley, Dickason, and myself), and one 10-ft. sledge (Levick, Abbott, and Browning). In addition to this I landed a depôt consisting of seven boxes of biscuits, one box of cocoa (24 tins), one box of chocolate (36 lbs.), one box of sugar (56 lbs.), 4 weekly bags of pemmican (14 lbs. each), 2 weekly bags of raisins, 2 cheeses, 1 bag of onions, 14 tins of oil, a little spare clothing, a spare sleeping-bag, and a spare tent and poles. Also my small primus stove, and two spare sledges, one of which was fitted with iron runners. By midnight we were camped, and saw the last of the ship steaming out of the bay.

January 9.—Turned out at 6 A.M., but we did not get away until 10.30, shaping course N.W. for some foothills between us and Mt. Melbourne. Hard rough ice and a strong S.W. breeze made our sledges skid and did the runners no good. Crossed many thaw pools and channels covered with thin ice, through which we broke. After about an hour's pulling, however, we got on to a snow surface, which was better going. We camped early to try and repair the sledgemeter. Got a good round of angles after hoosh. Night calm but overcast. Lengthened the traces as we may expect crevasses.

January 10.—Overslept ourselves, not turning out until 7. It was 9 o'clock before we were under way. Our course lay over the piedmont ice, close under the northern foothills which lay between us and Mt. Melbourne. Some way ahead it looked as if a glacier from Mt. Melbourne came out on the piedmont, thereby giving

us a road to the north.   Soon after starting snow began
to fall, and that, combined with a slight up-grade.
made our sledges very heavy.   About noon we rounded
a point (Cape Mossyface), on which we found a quantity
of lichen, and came on to a smooth glacier, of easy gradient,
and snow-covered, which I hoped came from Mt. Melbourne; but the weather was so thick with snow we could
see nothing, so camped for lunch in the hope of its clearing,
as I had no wish to pull the heavy sledges up a *cul-de-sac*.
This evening so much snow fell that we had to remain in
camp, being unable to see ten yards.   Snowing all night.

January 11.—Still snowing as hard as ever at 5.30 A.M.,
but by 7.30 the clouds began to break, and by 9 we were
on the march.   Snow very soft and deep, making pulling
very heavy, so that we had to relay.   All six of us had
difficulty in getting one sledge along.   We then all put
on ski, and were able to get along better as we broke
a regular trail along which the sledge ran.

The snow and mist cleared away about 10 A.M., giving
us a magnificent view up a large glacier, the main body of
which seemed to flow past the west slope of Mt. Melbourne.
A few miles south of Mt. Melbourne and on the west side of
the main glacier, a tributary glacier, which we named from
its shape the Boomerang, flows in.   In the afternoon a
S.W. wind improved the surface and each team was able
to manage its own sledge.   A lovely night, but all hands
very tired.

January 12.—Woke at 3 A.M. to find strong wind, with
drift.   The snow ceased a little while we had breakfast,
only to come down harder than ever afterwards, and as

Dickason and I were suffering from snow-blindness we did not march till 3, when the wind eased. Camped at the entrance of the Boomerang Glacier, which I think may be a possible way through to Wood Bay.

January 13.—Turned out at 6. A lovely morning, so leaving camp standing we went a little way up the Boomerang Glacier to see if it would be possible to get the sledges up. The route looked feasible but probably difficult for sledges, so I decided to try the main glacier first. Returning to camp about 1 o'clock we pulled north, camping for the night north of the Boomerang and under some steep ice slopes.

January 14.—Another fine day. Dickason and I were snow-blind, so the others climbed the ice slope to see if they could find a way for the sledge. They returned to camp about 3.30, and said that after climbing several ice undulations, more or less crevassed, they came to a steep ice slope leading to a rocky ridge.

Owing to the nails having come out of Browning's boots he kept losing his balance and nearly dragging the party down with him, and as there were several large crevasses at the bottom of the slope, Priestley very wisely decided to return. The icefalls we see from our present camp apparently connect with the ridge. It was worth going on to see, however, so we got under weigh and marched till 7 P.M., when we camped at the foot of the first ice falls on snow, the weather having come over very thick in the afternoon.

January 15.—Still and very thick when we turned out at 6 A.M., so there was nothing for it but to turn in again after breakfast.   The Antarctic teaches one patience if nothing else.

We are fairly sheltered, but can hear the wind roaring in the crags on the side of the glacier, and the snow and drift are so thick that we can only see a few yards.   Occasionally in the lulls we can see the blue icefalls looming up through the drift, and then everything shuts down again.

The conditions remained the same until breakfast on January 19, when it began to clear from the southward. We started away after breakfast with the surface awful, and the snow so deep I doubt if we should have got the sledges along at all if we had not had ski, which enabled us to break a trail.   As soon as it was clear to the northward, Priestley and I climbed the slopes on our left on ski, leaving the remainder halted at the bottom.   The view from the ridge was not promising.   The icefalls reached right up to the ridge, a mass of séracs and crevasses as far as we could see, and I decided to return and try the Boomerang Glacier, which lay a few miles south of us. The sun now came out, and in the deep sticky surface it took all six of us to pull one sledge.   We had to relay all the way, and it was six o'clock before we reached the N. lateral moraine of the Boomerang Glacier, where we camped.

January 20.—After breakfast we divided into two parties.   I, taking Levick and Dickason, climbed the mountain on the N. side of the glacier.   Priestley, taking Abbott and Browning, went up the glacier on the moraine, where Priestley wanted to collect.

ICE STRUCTURE

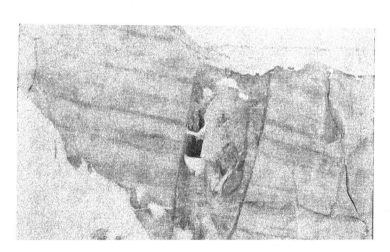

At the first possible place my party left the glacier, and, after about an hour's climb, came out on a snow field, where we roped up and ploughed through deep snow lying over ice, along the foot of a steep slope, which we attempted to climb by cutting steps in order to reach a rocky spur several hundred feet above us. Half-way up, however, we had to retrace our steps, the snow being inclined to avalanche, and continue our way along the foot of the slope for about an hour, when we were able to get on another rocky spur and climb.

Some of the granite boulders were hollowed out in a wonderful way by the action of sand-carrying wind. We crawled right inside some, and found room for five or six men.

The view from where we were was very fine in every direction but N.W., where a higher ridge bounded our horizon. Looking down on the Mt. Melbourne neck we had first proposed crossing, I saw, to my surprise, that the flat ice on top of the neck was heavily crevassed.

We got back to camp about 6.30, and found the others had not yet arrived. They turned up a little before 9, all very tired. Priestley reported very heavy going, soft snow up to their thighs, which completely hid the crevasses, and they dropped down a good many.

They reached a height of 3680 feet above the camp, but could not see whether the glacier would form a good route over into Wood Bay.

As far as they went it would be possible to get sledges, but progress would be very slow indeed, so considering our limited time we decided to work along more to the

westward in the hope of finding a larger and easier glacier.
Even if unsuccessful we should be breaking new ground,
and Priestley could put in some good collecting from
the different moraines, while I surveyed.

January 21.—A fine morning, but wind in the
mountains. After getting a round of angles, we started,
my party crossing the Boomerang Glacier and working
down the west side of the Melbourne Glacier, while I
sent Levick's party back the way we came, down the
east side of the Melbourne Glacier, with orders to collect
from the different exposures, and join us at the S.W.
entrance of the main glacier.

The surface was better, and we camped that evening
on the south moraine of the Boomerang and well down
the Melbourne Glacier.

We had been unable to wear our glasses yesterday
climbing, and were now paying the penalty, for we were
all snow-blind, so we dressed each other's eyes with
Hemisine, and turned in very sorry for ourselves.

January 22.—Only one eye among the three of us,
and that belongs to Dickason. He tells me that it is a
lovely morning, and that he can see to cook hoosh. After
hoosh our last hope goes and we do no more cooking
that day. We have all had snow-blindness before, but
never anything like so bad as this, and are in great pain.
Priestley's eyes and mine are quite closed up, and I think
Dickason's are nearly as bad.

January 23.—Eyes better, but still very painful.
Started after breakfast. Surface a little soft, but good
pulling on ski.

After 6 P.M. the surface got so bad, owing to undercut sastrugi, that we had to relay half our load at a time, and even then had frequent upsets. We camped at 9.30 P.M. about 1 mile E. of a cape we named Cape 'Sastrugi.'

January 24.—A fine morning, but no sign of Levick's party, so after getting a true bearing and round of angles, I joined Priestley and Dickason collecting, on Cape Sastrugi. I made some sketches. This piedmont we are on extends west to the Mt. Nansen Range, and seems quite flat, except where glaciers run in, where there are undulations and crevasses.

January 25.—Overcast. Levick has not turned up yet, which is very annoying. It is useless going to look for him, as the undulations at the mouth of the Melbourne Glacier would completely hide a party, unless both happened on the same route. Collecting to-day on some moraines south of us, Priestley fell through a snow bridge of a crevasse up to his arms. He was not roped at the time, so it was lucky he did not go through altogether.

January 26.—A clear morning, but blowing hard, with drift. Climbed the hills to the N.W., taking the theodolite and sketch-book, and got a true bearing and good round of angles.

I also made out the truant party calmly camped on the east side of the Melbourne Glacier. So returning to camp we packed food for eighteen days, and depôted the remainder, together with the specimens, and a note to Levick telling him my proposed plans, which were to try the two glaciers which came in at the N.W. corner of the piedmont, for a route into Wood Bay, and directing him not to attempt them unless he caught me up, but to photograph and collect on the shores of the piedmont.

January 27.—Overcast. Tops of mountains obscured. Strong wind in squalls. Started after breakfast, and with our light load made good progress. We made a big sweep round Cape Sastrugi to try and avoid the crevasses, but without success.

The afternoon was hot and muggy, and when we camped that night we were wet with perspiration. After supper I went out with Priestley to collect, and the sun being hot I took off my vest, and, turning it inside out, put it over my sweater, where it dried beautifully. I remarked to Priestley at the time that this ought to bring me luck, and sure enough, immediately afterwards I found a sandstone rock containing fossil wood, the best specimen as yet secured by the party.

January 28.—Blowing hard from the N.W., with drift, but clear sky. The temperature being warm, the drift made everything very wet. After breakfast Priestley hunted for fossils, while I got another round of angles. We then marched, edging over to the northern moraines, on which we camped that night.

January 29.—A beautiful day, but no sign of the other party. After breakfast we started, and crossing moraine, steered for what we called 'Corner Glacier,' a small steep glacier whose course lay more on our route for Wood Bay. The going was easy, and we camped that evening on the north lateral moraine, which lies at the foot of a steep scree descending from the mountains. The moraine was a very large one, with a number of

CREVASSED ICE AT ENTRANCE TO PRIESTLEY GLACIER

CREVASSED ICE AT ENTRANCE TO PRIESTLEY GLACIER

conical heaps and with lakes in all the little valleys. The noise of running water from a lot of streams sounded very odd after the usual Antarctic silence. Occasionally an enormous boulder would come crashing down from the heights above, making jumps of from 50 to 100 feet at a time.

January 30.—Another fine morning, so after breakfast we started for the south end of 'Black Ridge,' from which place we could get a view up the Priestley Glacier. Arriving there about 1 o'clock we found we were cut off from the moraine by a barranca from 40 to 50 feet deep. The glacier itself seemed an important one, judging by the disturbance it made in the piedmont where it flowed in, large undulations and big crevasses extending many miles out.

Although not so steep as Corner Glacier, it was much more crevassed, but what decided us to try Corner Glacier was that the Priestley Glacier curved from a S.W. direction, which would have taken us off our course. Accordingly, after I had secured a round of angles, we steered for the foot of the icefalls of the Corner Glacier, getting there about 5 P.M. After hoosh we left camp standing and climbed the glacier, which proved a very easy job, as, although steep and broken, the séracs are worn smooth and many of the crevasses filled in, which looks as if there was very little movement now.

Arriving at the top of the first icefall we found ourselves on rather a steep broken surface, the valley running in a north-westerly direction for a few miles, where it was fed by several steep glaciers or ice cascades from

the heights. It would have been interesting to follow
this glacier up, but the route was quite impossible
for a sledge and we returned to camp footsore and
disappointed.

January 31.—Fog, snow, and then drift kept us in
our tent till one o'clock, when, the snow easing up a
little, we marched for the moraines of the Priestley Glacier.
I had now given up all hope of getting through to Wood
Bay this year, our time being too short to get over
by the Boomerang Glacier, which I consider the only
practicable route for a sledge, so we turned our attention
to the Priestley Glacier, on whose moraines Priestley
hoped to find some more fossil wood.

We camped about 6 on the southern moraine. While
so doing Dickason caught sight of Levick and his party
heading for the Corner Glacier. After some difficulty
we managed to attract their attention and they pulled
over and camped near us. Levick had apparently
misunderstood my instructions, and waited for me at
Cape Mossyface, then seeing his mistake he headed for
Cape Sastrugi across the mouth of the Melbourne Glacier
and crossed a maze of crevasses. He says, ' Getting
under way about 10, we marched till 12.30 over fairly
good surface. After that we got into a perfect net-work
of crevasses. They were mostly snow-bridged, and had
we not had ski on we could never have got over, as we
could break holes in them in places with our ice-axes. It
was 7.30 before we found a place where there was a small
space sufficiently free from crevasses to enable us to
camp. One of the snow bridges we had to cross broke

INSIDE DOOR OF IGLOO BY LIGHT OF BLUBBER LAMPS

LEVICK'S CAMP AMONG CREVASSES

under the weight of the sledge, but only just under the
bows. Had she gone down altogether the result might
have been serious. After that we relayed, taking half
our load at a time.'

February 1.—We decided to put in the rest of our time
collecting from the moraines and foot-hills north of where
we had landed, as we knew we should have no time to get
far enough up the Boomerang to survey any new ground.
During the day I found one large piece of sandstone with
the impression of part of a fossil tree.

February 2.—We spent the forenoon breaking up a
big boulder, a longer job than we expected, as the lower
half was embedded in the frozen soil. After digging it
out and rolling it over, Priestley split it open. Inside
we found a beautiful specimen of wood. Levick photographed it before we proceeded to break it up, as we knew
we could never get it out whole.

February 3.—The weather, which had been perfect
up till now, changed, and we woke to find it overcast, with
a cold N.W. wind blowing

We started away after breakfast and made good way,
passing Cape Sastrugi before we camped.

February 4.—Fine day. We crossed the Campbell
Glacier. The surface was very good for pulling on ski,
but too soft without.

We camped to-night about 6 miles off the main depôt.
My eyes rather bad.

February 5.—Priestley and Dickason went over to
collect on Lichen Island, while Levick and Abbott did the
slopes north of us.

Priestley found an extraordinary quantity of lichens on the island.

February 6.—Fine morning, but a strange south-westerly wind.

Getting under way after breakfast, we reached the main depôt about 3 o'clock, and found to our surprise Debenham's party had never landed, our letters to him being still in the ' post box ' we had fixed up.

February 7.—The wind, which had fallen yesterday evening, freshened up between 1 and 2 A.M., and, when we turned out, was blowing a whole gale, but with a clear sky. An ex-meridian altitude gave the latitude of this place 74° 55′ S. In the afternoon Levick, Priestley, Dickason, and I climbed to the top of what we afterwards called Inexpressible Island to see if we could make out the Nansen Moraine, which Priestley wanted to visit. I told him to take Abbott and Dickason to-morrow, while I carry the theodolite up here and get a round of angles.

February 8.—Both parties started directly after breakfast ; Priestley, taking Abbott and Dickason and a week's provisions, went round west of the island, keeping on the piedmont ice, and I climbed the island with the theodolite, taking Levick and Browning with me.

It was a clear day but blowing a regular gale from the west, the wind from the plateau feeling very cold—an unpleasant day for theodolite work. By aneroid I made the height of the island 1320 feet. We returned to camp about 7 P.M.

February 9.—It came on to blow very hard in the morning, and we had to secure the tents with big stones

PENGUINS ON ICE-FOOT

on the skirting, the snow being all blown off. In the evening Browning got two penguins for the pot.

February 10.—Still blowing very hard, too hard in fact to set up the theodolite. Priestley and party pulled in about 2 P.M. He said they had had a gale of wind the whole time, the wind only dropping for two hours. The moraine we saw from the top of the island appears to be the Priestley Glacier moraine. They found some sandstone with fossil wood inclusions, but not such good specimens as we got inland.

In the afternoon Priestley and I found a lot of shells, worm casts, and sponge spicules in little holes on the piedmont.

February 11.—The wind dropped after breakfast, so Priestley, Dickason, and I sledged over to the hills north of us and camped by a lake on the southern slopes. Levick, Abbott, and Browning, leaving their camp standing, examined Evans Coves on the S. Island. They found a small penguin rookery and a large number of seals on the ice foot.

They also found a large number of old dead seals on the beach, one or two of the largest measuring 12 feet in length.

February 12.—Heavy snow, wind, and drift all day. Levick and his party pulled in about 3 P.M. and camped near us.

February 13.—Snowing all night, and although it eased this morning, it kept on all day, stopping our survey completely. In the evening we killed three penguins for food. Levick and party returned to the main depôt.

February 14 *and* 15.—Priestley and I spent the two days collecting and surveying. On the night of the 15th it began to snow, and, a strong plateau wind getting up, we spent the 16th in our tent, the drift being too thick to do anything.

February 17.—Still blowing hard, with drift, but clear overhead. In the afternoon we packed up, and pulled over to the main depôt, as the ship was due the following day. We camped late in the evening in our old place under the moraine. Blowing a heavy gale all night.

February 18 *to* 29.—Most of this time while we were waiting for the *Terra Nova* the wind blew with uninterrupted violence and the tents suffered considerably. Our own tent split near the cap, but after several failures we managed to tie a lashing round the top and so saved the split from spreading to the body of the canvas.

Levick's tent also split near the opening, and Abbott was obliged to sew the rent up in spite of the coldness of the blizzard.

On February 24 the blizzard lulled for a short time and we were enabled to get a little exercise, but the whole of this time was occupied with a not too cheerful discussion about food.

Our sledging provisions were due to give out on the 27th and it was necessary to reserve at least half of the depôt food for the sledge journey down the coast in the spring which would become inevitable should the ship not relieve us. It was therefore necessary to reduce the ration at once, and I asked Priestley to take charge of all food

THIS PENGUIN HAS AN INDUSTRIOUS MATE

from now on till the time we were relieved or relieved ourselves.

We decided to reduce the biscuit to half ration and cut out everything else for the time being except seal meat and a small portion of pemmican for flavouring. This same day we were fortunate enough to kill a small crab-eater seal. I tasted a small piece of raw blubber and rather liked it, while Abbott and Browning declared that it had a very strong flavour of melon.

It was some time, however, before the blubber was added to our diet as a regular ration. During this short period of calm several times one or other of the party thought they saw smoke off the end of the Drygalski, but there seems no doubt that what they saw was only what is known as frost smoke, the vapour from the leads of open water on pack ice, though the ship certainly was at one time within 25 miles of us.

On the 27th further discomfort was added to our condition as the gale was accompanied by blinding drift, so that we had all the unpleasantness of a barrier blizzard with no adequate shelter; for the tents were threadbare and torn in several places. The snow was soon so thick that the sledge was completely buried with drift and the tent three-quarters hidden.

During most of this fortnight we were living on one meal a day, and on this day we were unable even to get this, so that by the 29th, when the wind eased for a day or two, we were in no wise in a condition to look forward with equanimity to the chance of a winter without sufficient food or decent shelter; in fact so weak were we that a walk of a mile or two tired us far more than a hard day's sledging had done a month before.

Perhaps the worst feature in our present position, however, is the absence of any news from our comrades, and the fear which is naturally growing within us lest the ship should have got into some trouble during this heavy weather.

February 29.—The wind dropped in the morning, and we had our first fine day since the 15th. In the afternoon we pulled over and camped on the island south of the moraine, which we have named Inexpressible Island. In the evening after hoosh we climbed 'Look-out' Hill, and saw what we thought was smoke on the horizon, and under it a small black speck. Unfortunately, it turned out to be only an iceberg with a cloud behind it, showing dark under a snow-squall.

Soon after the wind and snow recommenced.

March 1.—The weather cleared at 10 A.M. I had decided to start killing seals for the winter to-day if there was no sign of the ship, so after seeing no sign of anything from Look-out Hill, we killed and cut up two seals and eighteen penguins.

There are very few of the former up, and seals hate wind, so we must pray for fine weather to stock our larder, as the animals seldom leave the water in the winter.

March 2 *to* 4.—It came on to blow hard in the night of the 1st, and continued blowing steadily for the next three days.

The gale reached its height on the 3rd, when the tent split and we had to shift camp on to a snowdrift, where we

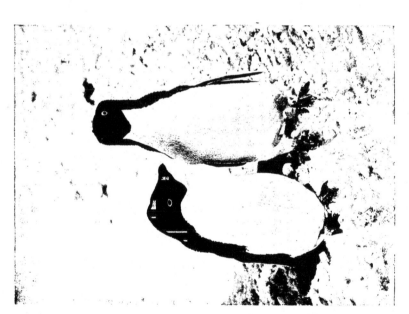

A PAIR OF ADÉLIE PENGUINS

could raise a bit of a snow wall. These last three days we have been lying in our wet bags, watching the tent poles bend and quiver as each squall strikes the tent, and speculating as to what can have happened to the ship.

We also feel having only two biscuits a day and an insufficient supply of seal meat. We are hungry both for news of the Southern Party and for more food.

March 5 to 15.—The conditions are gradually but surely becoming more unbearable, and we cannot hope for improvement until we are settled in some permanent home for the winter. The tents we are living in at present are more threadbare than ever, and are pierced with innumerable holes both large and small, so that during the whole time we are inside them we are living in a young gale.

To-day, March 15, is the last that I expect the ship, and from now on I shall conclude something has happened and that she is not coming.

For some days we have been preparing in every way possible for the winter, and our position may be summed up as follows : We landed, besides our sledging rations, six boxes of biscuits with 45 lbs. in each box. The sledging biscuits were finished on March 1, and of the others we have to keep two boxes intact for our journey down the coast.

We have also enough cocoa to give us a mug of very thin cocoa five nights of the week ; enough tea for a mug of equally thin tea once a week ; and the remaining day we must reboil the tea leaves or drink hot water *solus.* Our only luxuries are a very small amount of chocolate and sugar, sufficient to give us a stick of chocolate every

Saturday and every other Wednesday, and eight lumps of sugar every Sunday. A bag of raisins we are keeping to allow twenty-five raisins per man on birthdays and red-letter days, and I can see that one of Priestley's difficulties in the future is going to be preventing each man from having a birthday once a month. We have decided to open up neither the chocolate nor the sugar till we are settled in our winter quarters, and, at present, breakfast and supper each consist of a mug of weak seal hoosh and one of weak cocoa, with one biscuit.

To eke out these provisions we have eleven seals and 120 penguins already killed, but to get through the whole winter, even on half rations, we shall require several more seals, and the infrequency of their appearance is causing us all great anxiety.

The wind is incessant, but although strong and very cold, it at least has the merit of being usually free from drift, so that on most days we can work even if under very disadvantageous conditions.

There is plenty of work for all hands, for besides collecting the seals and penguins we have had to carry over our equipment, such as it is, and the provisions from our depôt at Hell's Gate to the site of the snow cave on Inexpressible Island, while three or four of us are usually at work there with pick and shovel.

We have selected a hard drift under the lee of a small hill and have commenced burrowing into it, using two short-handled ice-axes of Priestley's. It is slow work, but after a few hours we had a sheltered place to work in and made better progress.

We have also been experimenting on a blubber reading-lamp and are, I think, on a fair way to success.

March 16.—Blowing hard all day, very cold. Our bags and all gear are covered with drift. The outlook is not very cheerful. We are evidently in for a winter here, under very hard conditions. When we can be out and working things are not so bad, but lying in our bags covered with drift, with nothing to do but speculate as to what has happened to the ship, is depressing. We are using salt water in our hoosh and some bleached and decayed sea-weed from a raised beach, which we try to imagine is like cabbage. Priestley says he would not object to fresh seaweed, but cannot induce himself to include prehistoric seaweed in our regular ration.

March 17.—Still blowing, but clear, so after breakfast we struck camp, and started carrying our gear to the hut. The distance is only 1 mile, but over a chaos of big boulders which are the cause of many falls. Our boots have given out and finnesko would not last a day on such surface. Before we had got all our gear over, it came on to blow harder than ever, the squalls bringing small pebbles along with them, and we were several times taken off our feet and blown down.

Luckily no one was damaged, although we all got pretty well frostbitten. It was a great relief to get into our finished hut out of the wind.

We were all dead tired, and turned in directly after hoosh.

March 18.—Our first night in the hut was cold, as we have no door yet and no insulation ; in fact, it will take at least two days' more work to make it big enough for us, but it is a shelter from the wind, which we can hear roaring outside.   We spent the day chipping away at the ice walls and floor.   As a matter of fact our ' hut ' is only a cave dug into the snow drift, and our roof is of hard snow about 3 feet thick, while the walls and floor are of ice.   As snow is a better insulator than ice, we shall line the walls with snow blocks and pack the space between the snow and ice with seaweed.   The floor will be of a layer of small pebbles on the ice, with seaweed on top of that ; then our tent cloths are spread on the seaweed.

March 19.—A very heavy gale is blowing, but this no longer interferes with our work, and the hut has grown to quite a respectable size.

Our craving for biscuit is growing awful.   We do not like this meat diet.   In the afternoon the wind moderated a little, but the squalls were still heavy.   About 6 P.M. we heard voices outside, and Levick and his party arrived without sleeping-bags and all pretty well frostbitten. They had had a bad time, their tent poles having been broken in a squall, and their tent blown to rags.   They had piled rocks on the rest of their gear and then came over to look for us.   After reviving them with hoosh, we spent a most uncomfortable night, sleeping two in each bag.

Levick was my partner.   My bag was, luckily, a good one, and nothing split, but I should not care to repeat the experience.

March 20.—Luckily the weather had improved enough for Levick's party to get their bags and gear over.   The rest of us worked at the hut.

BROWNING AT THE IGLOO DOOR

EXTERIOR OF IGLOO

(The dark heap on the left consists of old seal bones and refuse thrown out by the party below)

March 21.—A cold wind, but fine. Priestley, Levick, and Dickason worked at the hut, while Abbott, Browning, and I went over to the main depôt to bring some more gear over. On the way over we saw a seal come up several times and try to get on the ice foot. Leaving Browning to watch the seal, Abbott and I went over for the load, and on our way to our great joy we saw Browning cutting up the seal. But a still greater treat was in store for us. The seal's stomach was full of fish, thirty-six of which were nearly whole. We took these up to the hut, fried them in blubber, and found them excellent. In future we shall always look for fish as soon as we kill a seal.

March 22.—Spent the day bringing up what stores we had left, while some worked at the hut, which is already beginning to look more habitable. The weather is clear and cold, but these strong plateau winds continue, and we get our noses frostbitten every time we go out. My nose is one great blister.

The sea was freezing over in the bay, but the wind kept the ice from forming permanently.

March 23.—We put in another good day's work at the hut. Abbott and I killed and cut up a seal. We have now 13.

March 24, 25, 26.—Blowing a gale, with drift. We worked at insulating the hut.

March 27.—It lulled a little in the forenoon, so three of us managed to get as far as the ice foot to bring up blubber, which we pack on our backs, and which, in spite of being frozen, makes our clothes in an awful mess.

In fact we are saturated to the skin with blubber, and our clothes in consequence feel very cold.

When we kill a seal, we cut out the heart, liver, and kidneys; then cut the meat up into convenient joints and the blubber and skin into pieces about 2 feet square, which we can carry up on our backs and flense in the hut. We also preserve the head, as besides its meat it contains the greatest delicacy of all, the brain. The gale came on harder than ever in the afternoon.

Browning and I are suffering from dysentery.

March 29 *to April* 5.—High wind and bitterly cold. We all get frostbitten constantly while working at the hut, and most of us are suffering from dysentery.

April 5.—A great improvement in the weather, and we got on well with the hut. We also carried up a lot of our things from the depôt. In the evening just as we were stopping work I saw three seals up on the ice, so we turned out again and killed and butchered them. This makes sixteen seals, and if we can march early should put us out of danger with regard to food. To celebrate the occasion Priestley allowed us an extra biscuit each.

April 7.—Northerly gales and drift since the 5th. The way from the hut to the ice foot is strewn with huge boulders, and it is a difficult job walking over these in a gale of wind without a load, while when one is staggering up under a load of meat or blubber, it is particularly maddening. When a squall catches you, over you go between two boulders, with your legs in the air and the load of blubber holding you down firmly. Our boots

are all giving out with this rough walking, and we dare
not use our finnesko, but must keep them for spring
sledging. Our feet are getting very frequently frostbitten and are beginning to feel as if the circulation
might become permanently injured.

April 9.—Warmer to-day. We saw a small seal on
a floe but were unable to reach him. The bay remains
open still. On the still days a thin film of ice forms,
but blows out as soon as the wind comes up. In these
early days, before we had perfected our cooking and
messing arrangements, a great part of our day was taken
up with cooking and preparing the food, but later on
we got used to the ways of a blubber stove, and things
went more smoothly. We had landed all our spare
paraffin from the ship, and this gave us enough oil to use
the primus for breakfast, provided we melted the ice
over the blubber fire the day before. The blubber stove
was made of an old oil-tin cut down. In this we put
some old seal-bones taken from the carcases we found
on the beach. A piece of blubber skewered on to a
marline spike and held over the flame dripped oil on the
bones and fed the fire. In this way we could cook hoosh
nearly as quickly as we could on the primus. Of course
the stove took several weeks of experimenting before it
reached this satisfactory state. With certain winds we
were nearly choked with a black oily smoke that hurt
our eyes and brought on much the same symptoms as
accompany snow-blindness.

We take it in turns to be cook and messman, working
in pairs: Abbott and I, Levick and Browning, Priestley

and Dickason, and thus each has one day on in three. The duties of the cooks are to turn out at 7 and cook and serve out the breakfast, the others remaining in their bags for the meal. Then we all have a siesta till 10.30, when we turn out for the day's work. The cook starts the blubber stove and melts blubber for the lamps. The messman takes an ice-axe and chips frozen seal meat in the passage by the light of a blubber lamp. A cold job this and trying to the temper, as scraps of meat fly in all directions and have to be carefully collected afterwards. The remainder carry up the meat and blubber or look for seals. By 5 P.M. all except the cooks are in their bags, and we have supper. After supper the cooks melt ice for the morning, prepare breakfast, and clear up. Our rations at this time were as follows :—Breakfast, 1 mug of penguin and seal hoosh and 1 biscuit. Supper 1½ mugs of seal, 1 biscuit and ¾ pint of thin cocoa, tea, or hot water. We were always hungry on this, and to swell the hoosh we used occasionally to try putting in seaweed, but most of it had deteriorated owing to the heat of the sun and the attentions of the penguins.

The cocoa we could only afford to have five days a week and then very thin, but as we had a little tea we had weak tea on Sunday and reboiled the leaves for Monday. As already stated we had a little chocolate (2 ounces per man a week), and 8 lumps of sugar every Sunday. Our tobacco soon ran out, even with the most rigid economy, and we were reduced to smoking the much-boiled tea and wood shavings—a poor substitute. About the middle of this month we found we were getting through our seal meat too fast, so had to come down to half the above ration, and it was not until the middle of July, when we got some more seals, that we were able to go back to the old ration.

There is no doubt that during this period we were all miserably hungry, even directly after the meals. Towards the end of June we had to cut down still more, and have only one biscuit per day, and after July to stop the biscuit ration altogether until September, when we started one biscuit a day again. By this means we were able to save enough biscuits for a month at half ration for our journey down the coast. I am sure seals have never been so thoroughly eaten as ours were. There was absolutely no waste. The brain was our greatest luxury; then the liver, kidneys, and heart, which we used to save for Sundays. The bones, after we had picked all the meat off them, we put on one side, so that if the worst came to the worst we could pound them up for soup. The best of the undercut was saved for sledging. After our experience in March, when we got thirty-nine fish out of a seal's stomach, we always cut them open directly we killed them in the hope of finding more, but we never again found anything fit to eat. One of our greatest troubles was a lack of variety in the flavouring of our meals. Two attempts were made by Levick to relieve this want from the medicine chest, but both were failures. Once we dissolved several ginger tabloids in the hoosh without any effect at all, and on the historic occasion when we used a mustard plaster, there was a general decision that the correct term would have been linseed plaster, as the mustard could not be tasted at all and the flavour of linseed was most distinct.

For lighting purposes the blubber lamps we made were very satisfactory. We had some little tins, which had contained ' Oxo.' These, filled with melted blubber and a strand of rope for a wick, gave quite a good light. A tin bridge was pierced to hold the wick and laid across the top of the Oxo tin. We luckily had one or two books —' David Copperfield,' ' The Life of R. L. Stevenson,' and ' Simon the Jester ' being the favourites—and after hoosh Levick used to read a chapter of one of them. Saturday evenings, we each had a stick of chocolate, and usually had a concert, and Sunday evening at supper twelve lumps of sugar were served out and we had church, which consisted of my reading a chapter of the Bible, followed by hymns. We had no hymn-book, but Priestley remembered several hymns, while Abbott, Browning, and Dickason had all been, at some time or other, in a choir, and were responsible for one or two of the better-known psalms. When our library was exhausted we started lectures, Levick's on anatomy being especially interesting.

April 12.—A calm day. Priestley and I went over to the main depôt to get some oil we had left there on the sledges, and in the afternoon I went into the cove south of us to look for seals. I saw one lying on some new ice, but I could not reach him. I found an old penguin egg. It was four months old if it had been laid this year, so I brought it back on the chance of its having been frozen all the time, but no such luck. It was hopelessly bad.

IGLOO PASSAGE

DOWN WHICH THE LIGHT IS SHININ

April 13–17.—Strong westerly wind, bitterly cold.

April 20.—The same wind continues, but slightly warmer. A large piece had calved off the Drygalski ice tongue. I think this northern face must be altering very fast, as its appearance does not tally with the last survey.

April 23.—Another calm day. Browning and Dickason saw two seals on floes, but were unable to reach them. The sea is still open. On calm days a thin film of ice forms, but disappears as soon as the wind gets up. The current also plays an important part, I am sure, as in Arrival Bay, where there is no current, the ice has formed, and is several feet thick, although the winds are just as strong.

April 24, 25, 26.—Blowing a hard blizzard. On the 25th Dickason dropped ' Y ' deck watch and broke the glass, but ' R ' and ' C ' are going strong, and with sticking-plaster and ' new skin ' we have mended Y's glass. We are very snug in our den, and hardly hear the wind.

From *April* 27 *to May* 5 the weather prevented much outside work and we spent most of our time in our bags, or working at the improvement of the long tunnel which led to our home. We are roofing this with sealskins on a framework of bamboos, trusting to the drift to increase the thickness of the roof and so insulate us more thoroughly against the cold. We have also dug out one or two alcoves in which to keep meat, blubber, and miscellaneous stores.

We lost the sun to-day and shall not get him back till August 12.

May 6.—About three times a week we have to bring up salt water ice for the hoosh, as we have run out of salt. This morning Priestley and I went down for sea ice, and as usual were walking round Look-out Point to see if any seals were up, when coming across the sea ice in Arrival Bay we saw figures. We had often talked of the possibility of the ship being caught in Wood Bay and relieving us from that direction.

We both got rather a thrill on sighting them, though they were so close to the open water as to make it improbable that they should be anything but penguins. Still I ran back to the hut for my glasses, as through the low drift they seemed tall enough to be men.

Abbott followed me down with an ice-axe, since, if they were not men, they were food. They turned out to be four Emperor penguins heading into Arrival Bay, so we jumped the tide crack, all getting wet, and made off to intercept them. We came up with them after a long chase, and bagged the lot, Levick coming up just too late for the kill. They were in fine condition, and it was all we could do to carry them back to the hut, each taking a bird. There is no doubt our low diet is making us rather weak. We had a full hoosh and an extra biscuit in honour of the occasion.

May 7.—A blizzard with heavy drift has been blowing all day, so it was a good job we got the penguins. We have got the roof on the shaft now, but in these blizzards the entrance is buried in snow, and we have a job to keep the shaft clear. Priestley has found his last year's journal, and reads some to us every evening.

From now till the end of the month strong gales again reduced our outside work to a minimum, and most of our energies were directed to improving our domestic routine.

We have now a much better method for cutting up the meat for the hoosh. Until now we had to take the frozen joints and hack them in pieces with an ice-axe. We have now fixed up an empty biscuit tin on a bamboo tripod over the blubber fire. The small pieces of meat we put in this to thaw; the larger joints hang from the bamboo. In this way they thaw sufficiently in the twenty-four hours to cut up with a knife, and we find this cleaner and more economical.

We celebrated two special occasions on this month, my wedding-day on the 10th, and the anniversary, to use a paradox, of the commissioning of the hut on the 17th, and each time the commissariat officer relaxed his hold to the extent of ten raisins each.

Levick is saving his biscuit to see how it feels to go without cereals for a week. He also wants to have one real good feed at the end of the week. His idea is that by eating more blubber he will not feel the want of the biscuits very much.

On May 25 we had an unpleasant experience that might have been serious. Drift had blocked the funnel and shaft so that the smoke from the blubber stove became unbearable and we made up our minds to put it out. As a matter of fact it went out, and we had the greatest difficulty in keeping the lamps alight. This ought to have warned us the air was bad.

In spite of this we lit the primus stove to cook the

evening hoosh, though we•had the greatest difficulty in making it burn.   Just before hoosh was ready it went out, and all the lamps followed suit.

Three matches struck in succession did the same before we realised there was no air.   I groped for a spade, and crawling along the shaft drove it through the drift, when a match burned immediately, the primus stove gave us no trouble, and all went well; but it was a lesson to us, and in future I kept a long bamboo stuck through the chimney, and the wind keeping it shaking maintained an air-hole. When I fetched the bamboo it was only about 10 yards from the entrance of the shaft, yet the drift was so smothering and the night so dark, it was with the greatest difficulty I could find it.

Towards the end of the month the shaft was so frequently blocked with snow that we dug it out altogether, and then made a hatch with a sack and some bamboos, the coamings being of snow blocks, and the effect of this was at once to be seen in the improvement of the ventilation.

In spite of frequent frostbites during our few trips outside, they have one good point, for they make us appreciate the shelter of the hut and allow us to forget the dirt and grease of everything.

June 1.—Still blowing hard, but clear.   Open water in the bay; but when the moon is in the east we can see the blink of ice in the Ross Sea, so I hope the bay will soon freeze over.   We have been discussing our best route down, whether to go round the Drygalski on the sea ice or over the tongue.   I do not myself think the ice can be

depended on round the Drygalski.   It runs out so far into
the Ross Sea, and even in winter I believe there is a lot of
movement far out.

On the other hand, Professor David speaks of the
Drygalski ice tongue as a bad place to cross owing to
rough ice, barrancas, and crevasses.   I think that unless
the sea ice looks very good I shall choose the ice
tongue.

June 2.—A still, fine day, and we are able to lay in
a good stock of sea ice, blubber, and meat from our depôts.

One of the seal meat depôts being on the south side of
the cove, about a mile away, it is only on fine days we can
reach it now we get no daylight.

June 7.—The wind came up again on the night of the
2nd, and has been blowing hard ever since.   Levick some
days ago designed a new stove, which we call the ' Complex ' in opposition to our old one, the ' Simplex.'   The
reason the ' Complex ' did not catch on with the rest of
us he put down to professional jealousy, but to-day I came
in to find the designer using the old ' Simplex,' while a
much battered ' Complex ' lay outside on the drift, where
it remained for the rest of the winter.

June 10.—The last two days have been calm, and
with thick snow, but to-day the old wind came back again,
and now it is blowing a gale and the drift is smothering.
Levick searched his medicine case for luxuries, and found
bottles of ginger, limejuice, and citron tabloids.

The limejuice we keep for sledging, but the two others
we serve out from time to time.   Our new hatch works
well, and although it gets covered up, it keeps the shaft

from getting blocked with snow, while the bamboo in the chimney keeps us an air hole.

June 12.—The wind moderated to-day, and we were able to get out for sea ice and meat, and also a fresh store of bones from the old carcases of seals which we make use of in our blubber stoves.

June 16.—Being Sunday we get twelve lumps of sugar and have two tabloids of ginger each. These chewed up with sugar and a little imagination give us preserved ginger. The weather during the week has been thick with snow when it has not been blowing, but we have given up hoping for good weather, and if we can get a lull every few days to bring up sea ice and blubber, we shall not worry.

June 20.—The wind eased a little to-day, and I got out for a walk, but soon came in with a frostbitten nose. Our wind clothes are torn and so rotten with blubber that we have to be constantly mending them. The grease makes any snow or drift stick to them, and brushing them when we come in from a walk is a long business. We are feeling very excited about the feast on Midwinter Day, and have been discussing the menu for some time. It will consist of liver hoosh and biscuits, four sticks of chocolate, twenty-five raisins, and a sip of Wincarnis each.

June 22.—Midwinter Day. The weather was seasonable : pitch dark, with wind and a smothering drift outside. We woke up early, and being too impatient to wait longer, turned out, and for breakfast had our first full hoosh. In the evening we had another followed by cocoa with sugar in it, then four citric acid and two ginger tabloids, finishing up the evening with a sing-song and a little tobacco, which had been saved for the occasion. In addition four biscuits and four sticks of chocolate were served out, so that we retired to bed with full stomachs once again, and some of us have even saved a bite or two for to-morrow.

After Midwinter Day time passed more quickly, and the knowledge that every day the sun was approaching us cheered us immensely. During the next month we have to celebrate no less than three birthdays, and each with its accompanying slight increase of ration gives us something to look forward to and so helps to pass the intervening days.

The only occurrence which was worthy of note before the end of June was an unpleasant one involving much extra work.

On June 29 we found our seal carcases nearly buried in salt ice, although they were some 200 yards back from the seaward edge of the icefoot. Evidently the spring tides had been the cause of this, and we had a lot of trouble digging the bodies out.

July 4.—Southerly wind, with snow, noise of pressure at sea and the ice in the bay breaking up. Evidently there is wind coming, and the sea ice which has recently formed will go again like the rest. It is getting rather a serious question as to whether there will be any sea ice for us to get down the coast on. I only hope that to the south of the Drygalski ice tongue, where the south-easterlies are the prevailing winds, we shall find the

ice has held. Otherwise it will mean that we shall have
to go over the plateau, climbing up by Mount Larsen,
and coming down the Ferrar Glacier, and if so we cannot
start until November, and the food will be a problem.

We made a terrible discovery in the hoosh to-night:
a penguin's flipper. Abbott and I prepared the hoosh.
I can remember using a flipper to clean the pot with, and
in the dark Abbott cannot have seen it when he filled
the pot. However, I assured everyone it was a fairly
clean flipper, and certainly the hoosh was a good one.

July 5.—A heavy snowstorm from the S.E., the
first one we have had from that quarter since the hut
was ready. It blocked the entrance completely. Consequently the air got pretty bad. The primus went out
and the lamps burnt dimly until we dug through the
drift and let in fresh air. Priestley and I cleared the
door, but it was so thick with snow it soon drifted up again.
It felt wonderfully warm out and we got quite hot digging.
During the night we kept night watch two hours each,
the watchman's duty being to keep the entrance from
being blocked, as it was useless trying to keep the chimney
clear—in fact, snow came down so fast it put the
blubber fire out, and the smoke rendered the hut almost
untenable, so that we had to cook the evening hoosh
with the primus and use most of our precious oil.

July 7.—Blew hard all night, drifting up the outer
door completely. We cleared the shaft, but as our
chimney was buried in drift, we could get no draught
for the blubber fire, so we had to build the chimney up
with seal skin and snow blocks. All this time the drift

was perfectly blinding, although the stars were showing overhead.

That evening we had another 'no air' scare, the primus going out and lamps burning dimly until we had made air-holes with bamboos. I see we shall have to be careful in these snowstorms.

July 8.—Still blowing hard, but not so much drift. We had an awful job digging out, as the drift over our door was packed quite hard. This storm has added 2 or 3 feet of hard snow to our drift. It has made the hut much warmer, but has buried our outside meat depôt, and Priestley and I have been trying all day to find it without success.

July 10.—A 'Red Letter' day. As I was walking down to Look Out Point I saw a seal up. It was getting late, so I returned for the knives, and taking Abbott and Browning with me, we ran down and found 2 fat seals.

Abbott had only a short-handled ice-axe with him and had a job to stun his seal. He made several mis-hits, and finally, as the seal was making for the edge, he jumped on its back and gave it a blow on the nose that stunned it. Abbott then got out his knife and tried to stick the seal, but the handle was greasy, and his hands cold, and they slipped up the blade, cutting three fingers badly, so that I had to send him back to the hut, where he arrived feeling very faint from loss of blood. It was quite dark when Browning and I finished cutting up the seals. They were in good condition, the blubber being very thick. It was quite late by the time we got back, but we were able to have a big hoosh, and we shall no longer have to be on half-rations of seal meat. We were running things uncomfortably close before. We had six lumps of sugar in honour of the occasion.

July 12.—Abbott's fingers are badly hurt. Levick is afraid the tendons are cut and that he will not be able to bend them again.

Browning and Dickason went for a walk to-day and killed 2 fat seals they found, so we had another double hoosh. The rest of us spent to-day and yesterday depôting the meat from the first two seals.

July 13.—A lovely morning. The sky orange and saffron in the north about noon. Spent the day carrying meat up. The wind got back to its old quarter in the afternoon, and came on to blow hard and very cold, punishing us badly as we struggled up with the meat.

The thin ice that had formed over the bay during the last few days blew out. I do not think this bay will ever be safe to travel on, so we shall have to take the Drygalski ice tongue route and march later.

July 20.—It has been blowing since the 14th, but being clear we have been able to get out every day. To-day being Priestley's birthday we allowed him to do no work and served out six lumps of sugar, a stick of chocolate, and twenty raisins. A sing-song followed in the evening. Altogether a most successful day.

July 24.—The wind got round to the southward yesterday and came on to blow really hard, and is blowing great guns now.

July 26.—The wind dropped suddenly, after blowing a hard gale since the 24th. Priestley and I got down to

our last kill and found the bay ice had broken away to
within 3 or 4 feet of the carcases, but none of the meat
had gone, for which we were very thankful. In the
afternoon it was blowing very hard again, and we all got
frostbitten carrying up the meat.

July 31st.—After two days of warm snowy weather
with a moderate S.E. breeze the wind has again swung
to the west and is blowing a gale. Signs and tracks of
seals are numerous and we have seen several swimming
near the ice foot. I think our lean days are over.

August 3.—It has been blowing the same hard
westerly wind, clear and cold. Browning got his hand
badly frostbitten getting sea ice. It ' went ' right up
to the wrist and he was a long time bringing it round.

I walked over to the piedmont in the afternoon to look
for some penguins we had depôted there. The bay ice
had held well. On the piedmont it was blowing hard,
with drift, but evidently a low level wind, as half-way
up the hills at an altitude of about 1000 feet lay a thin
stratus cloud, above which there was no drift off the hills.
The sky was very fine to the north.

August 7.—To-day and yesterday have been very
warm, the weather overcast, with snow and drift, and
our door continually drifting up. Abbott and Browning
improved the entrance by building a torpedo-boat hatch
out of ski sticks and snow blocks. We felt the increased
draught for the blubber stove immediately. The heavy
snow of the last month has buried our whole hut about
3 ft. deeper and made it much warmer. Our trouble
now is the water that drips from the roof whenever we

light the blubber stove. We lost our depôt of sledging meat under the new snow, and although we knew its position to within a few yards it took us a week's digging before we found it.

August 10.—To-day we celebrated the return of the sun, but needless to say we did not see him, owing to a heavy gale. We made merry to-night over brain and liver hoosh, two biscuits, six lumps of sugar, and a stick of chocolate, finishing up with sweet cocoa.

We have built up a high chimney, using snow blocks, seal skins, and an old biscuit tin, and we get much less smoke inside now.

August 13.—The wind, which had eased in the early morning, began to freshen about 10. In spite of the gale, Abbott, Browning, and myself started over to the depôt sledge in Arrival Bay. Before we got half-way across the bay the wind and drift came down, shutting out everything; but we kept on and reached the depôt, leaving a note in case a relief party came up. Each of us carried back a load of oil, or of mending material for repairing sledging gear.

On our way back we saw the rays of the sun over the tops of the hills, and this made us feel very cheerful.

August 14.—Blowing hard all night, but eased in the forenoon. Priestley managed to pick the brain out of one of the frozen seal carcases. I walked up the ridge at the back of the hut and had the first view of the sun. He was shining through a pink haze of drift and looked lovely. We stood blinking at each other for some time and then a frozen nose sent me home.

August 15.—Being a fine morning we decided to bring the iron runner sledge over from Arrival Bay. Of course as soon as we started the wind came down on us again, but the drift was not so thick as before. I foolishly did not put on a helmet, and my cheeks, nose, and chin ' went ' rather badly, taking a long time to come round, though Priestley and Abbott helped to thaw it out for me. This evening our other sledge is completely buried.

August 20.—My birthday, and as it was my day on as cook, the others relieved me and I spent a lazy day.

It has been blowing for the last two days, with open water, but last night the wind eased for a few hours, and immediately ice formed all over the bay.

Our birthday ration to-night consists of two biscuits, twenty raisins, six lumps of sugar each, strong tea, and liver hoosh. As usual we finished up with a sing-song.

August 28.—The wind dropped last night after blowing hard since the 20th, and we put in a good day carrying blubber and meat up from the ice foot. There was a cold breeze and I got my nose and feet frozen. We are all suffering much from frostbitten feet, as our ski boots are pretty well worn out and their soles are full of holes.

In the evening Abbott came running in for my glasses as he saw something that looked like a sledge party on the piedmont, but as usual this proved a false alarm.

August 31.—Calm and very cold since the 28th. We had our last stick of chocolate till we start sledging, but to-morrow we start one biscuit a day each. We have been all this month without biscuit and have felt none the worse, so evidently a seal meat and blubber diet is healthy enough.   Strangely enough we do not get tired of it.

From the top of the hill I could see sea ice on the horizon, but the bay remains open.

September 5.—A very heavy gale has been blowing since the first, keeping all hands inside the hut.   We have had an epidemic of enteritis which is hard to account for, as we are eating seal meat that has never seen the sun, but I think the ' oven ' or tin we thaw the meat out in may have had something to do with it, so we have condemned it.

It is a great pity getting this a few weeks before starting sledging, as it is making us all so weak.

September 6.—A great improvement in the public health due to Levick's wisely curtailing the hoosh.   I have been the least affected, but Browning and Dickason are still very bad.   I hope this may be the end of it, as we are still all weak, and for the first time in the winter there has been a general gloom.   The weather has been vile, but improved to-day.

September 11.—The best day we have had yet, bright and clear with a light westerly wind.   Priestley and I went over to the depôt moraine to look at the geological specimens and put them round the bamboo mark, but found they had been buried in a drift, and after digging all day had to come away without them.   On our way back we dug out the sledges, which had been nearly buried. When we got back we found Abbott and Dickason had been all round the coves after seals, but without success. We are still short of sledging meat, having only five bags of cut-up meat, and we shall require eight. The allowance will be two mugs per day for each man, and each bag contains forty-two mugs, or one week's meat for each tent.

A thin scum of ice formed over the bay, but even if the sea ice did form now I should not trust it for sledging.

September 12. — Overcast and low drift. I am repairing Levick's sleeping-bag and putting a new flap on my own ; a slow job when one has to work by the light of a blubber lamp.

September 13.—Browning and Dickason saw a seal with a fish in its mouth, but he would not come up on the ice. These two are still very bad with diarrhœa, and we are giving them fresh-water hoosh to see if that does any good.

September 14.—Browning was very bad in the night. I wish we had a change of diet to give him. He has been ill, off and on, for five months now and has been very cheerful through it all. Priestley and Dickason are also down with enteritis but are not so bad. We have some Oxo and I shall try Browning on this before sledging. The rest of us are feeling fairly fit. At the beginning of this month we started Swedish exercises, and will keep it up until we start sledging, as our leg muscles have shrunk to nothing. As the hut is not nearly 6 feet high we are obliged to do these exercises and all our other work without standing upright, and this has given rise to what we called the ' Igloo Back,' which is caused by the stretching of the ligaments round the spine and is very painful.

September 17.—A fine morning. Priestley and Abbott went over to the moraine depôt to dig for the specimens, while Dickason and I dug out the sledges, which had been buried again. After a hard day's work we got our sledges clear, and brought up the tent poles to shorten and repair for sledging. Getting back late we heard that Priestley had found a seal, which he and Browning killed and cut up. There has been great rejoicing to-night, for this will complete our sledging provisions. We served out an extra biscuit for supper. The fine day has made us all impatient to start.

September 19.—Snowing all day, but we had plenty of work to do in the hut, sewing bags and repairing sledge gear. The sea is freezing over again.

September 20.—Priestley and Abbott went over to the depôt moraine to dig for the precious specimens, the rest of us sewing or cutting up meat for the journey. In the afternoon I walked over and joined Priestley. I found them very disappointed, having been digging all day without success. I thought they were digging too far to the westward, so I tried sinking pits at the east end of the drift, and after about half an hour's work, found the specimens. We carried them all to the moraine and stacked them round the bamboo mark. We got back late and found the others cutting up the last bag of sledging meat.

Served out one biscuit and six lumps of sugar each and had seal's brain in the hoosh.

September 21.—A fine morning; Levick and Abbott dug out the last sledge, but had to come back in the afternoon, as it came on to snow and blow hard. I got noon sights for time and found my watch had kept a fairly even rate, which was satisfactory.

September 24.—We were able to start carrying meat, &c., down to the sledges to-day as it was fine. The weather the two previous days had been very bad. Browning has had another acute attack of dysentery and we cannot march until he is better.

On my way back from the sledges I saw some fresh guano on the sea ice, and looking about saw an Emperor penguin. I killed it and we carried it up to the hut; I hope it may do Browning good, as the seal meat certainly does not agree with him. We are all ready to start now as soon as he is fit to walk, but it is blowing a gale to-night.

September 27.—Still blowing, but clear. We found two seals up under the lee of some pressure, and killed one for extra meat; the other was the first we have been able to let go since the last autumn.

September 28.—Strong south-west wind and overcast in the morning, clearing and coming out finer in the late noon. Priestley saw six Emperors. We got five of them. I was very glad to get these, as they seem to agree with Browning much better than seal. He has been bad again and is getting pessimistic about himself.

September 29. — Overhauled the sledge runners, scraping and waxing them. We also carried down all the equipment that was ready. We are taking the 12-ft. sledge and the 10-ft., the latter being fitted with iron runners, which will be a great help on sea ice. The weather was overcast, with north-west wind.

September 30.—A calm morning. As Dickason and Browning were both better we abandoned the igloo after breakfast. Carrying down the rest of our gear occupied four of us most of the day, and I left the two sick men in the hut, cleaning the cookers, until the last load.

It came on very thick with snow in the afternoon and it was 6.30 P.M. before we pulled out. Snow drifts made the pulling heavy and by 8.30 we had only pulled a mile, and as we were all pretty tired after our long day's carrying we camped. Dickason was bad in the night, but we are all very cheerful at being on the march again, and the change from the dirt and dark of the igloo will do us all good. Our sledging rations also seemed sumptuous, the daily ration per man being :

2 pannikins of meat.	1 stick of chocolate.
$\frac{3}{4}$ pannikin of blubber.	8 lumps of sugar.
1 pannikin of cocoa.	A little pemmican.
3 biscuits.	

At the commencement of the winter we had some spare wind clothing, sweaters, mits, and underclothing, which we had landed from the ship. This I put on one side for the journey down and only issued it before leaving the igloo. There was not enough of everything to go round, but by making the clothes into lots and drawing for them we all got something. To keep them clean we only changed into them just before leaving the igloo, but the luxury of getting into dry clean clothing after the greasy rags we discarded was indescribable. We had been in the same clothes for nine months, carrying, cooking, and handling blubber, and all our garments were black and soaked through and through with grease. We were fairly well off for paraffin as we had only used the primus to cook our morning hoosh. Dickason's generosity in volunteering to work

ICE CAVE

[*See* p. 99

GROUP AFTER WINTER IN IGLOO

the primus always had also made a lot of difference, as he handles the stove with more economy than any other of us.

October 1.—We turned out at 5.30 A.M. The morning was still and overcast, but with the sun trying to break through. We got away by 7, but made slow progress, finding the drifts very heavy. My unit consisted of Priestley, Dickason, and myself, with the 12-ft. sledge, and as Levick had the iron runner sledge we had the heavier load. We had to relay most of the day, as Dickason could pull very little and Browning not at all. In fact the latter had to rest constantly, so our progress was slow, and by lunch time we had only made $2\frac{1}{2}$ miles. Our supply of oil would not run to hot lunch, so we had a cold lunch sitting under the lee of the sledge. Before leaving the igloo we had cooked some seal steaks over the blubber fire, but when examined in the light of day these looked so filthy and distasteful, that we discarded them in favour of shreds of raw penguin and seal.

The walking had made both Dickason and Browning much worse, so I had to camp at 6.30 P.M., having only done 5 miles. We are all very tired, but in good spirits at leaving the dirt and squalor of the hut behind. A lovely evening and every appearance of a fine day to-morrow.

October 2.—A fine morning when we turned out at 5.30. The surface was rather better and we did not have to relay, but it was all we could do to move the sledges. About 11 o'clock we got on to a blue ice surface and worked our way through a loose moraine. A bitter wind from the plateau got up about noon, bringing drift that in the squalls was so thick one could not see more than a few yards. The wind was fair, however, and we raced along over the blue ice until we suddenly came to a huge crevasse barring our passage. We proceeded cautiously along its edge to the eastward until we found a place where it was snow-bridged, and then leaving the sledges with Levick and Browning, the rest of us roped up and went across, testing it with our ice-axes as we advanced.

The snow bridge was 175 paces across, and except for one place on the weather side it seemed perfectly safe. I should like to have stayed and examined it, as from its width it had more the appearance of an inlet of the sea ending in a wide crevasse, but the gale was rising and the drifting snow so thick I thought it best to get the sledges across and push on; the surface was good the other side, and with the gale behind us, we raced along, trusting to the wind to steer by, as it was impossible to see where we were going.

The pace was too much for poor Browning, who was very bad again, and we had to camp at 5.30, having done about 8·5 miles. Dickason, I am thankful to say, is better and was able to pull to-day.

The wind dropped after supper, leaving us a lovely but a very cold evening.

October 3.—A very cold night, the wind getting up again at 3 A.M. and bringing drift. Levick had trouble with his primus and we did not get away till nine A.M. Soft snowdrifts made the going very slow and heavy, until just before noon, when we got on ice again among

SLEDGING.

rocks. These we examined, but found no sandstone. The drift was very thick, and, about 2, getting on undulating broken ice, I thought it advisable to pitch one tent, lunch, and wait for the weather to clear. About 3.30 the wind became rather worse, so we pitched the other tent and camped, the distance covered in the day being 3 miles. Browning looked very bad, but Dickason's condition is still improving.

October 4.—Blowing hard, with blinding drift. We delayed breakfast until 9 A.M., hoping it would clear, but as there was no improvement in the weather we turned in again, and as we were not marching we went on half rations of biscuit. Very cold.

October 5.—Turned out at six to find a slight improvement, so had breakfast ; but before we finished the wind and drift came down on us again as bad as ever, so that there was nothing for it but to coil down in our bags and wait. About noon the weather improved and we were off. The surface soon changed for the better and we made good way through some more scattered moraines which came from the Reeves Glacier. We noticed a marked open water sky to our left and front and pulled on till 6 P.M., hoping to make the inlet, as we wanted salt ice for the hoosh, but without attaining our object. It is impossible to pull longer, as the days are still short and we have no candles. We have made about six miles.

October 6.—We turned out at 5.45 to find the weather thick, but blue sky to the northward. We were back on a snow surface again, so we took the precaution of **waxing the runners, with good results.**

It was warm work pulling through the soft snow and we were glad to stop for lunch. We could make out the edge of the piedmont quite plainly, but could see nothing of the inlet until about 2 P.M., when we saw the mouth of it. A broad open-water lead several miles wide seemed to extend right along the barrier edge, but in the inlet itself the sea was frozen over. The snow was soft and the pulling very heavy, so it was 6 o'clock before we reached camp, on the north side of the inlet, about fifty yards from the cliff. Several seals and penguins were up on the sea ice, while snowdrifts gave us an easy road down from the barrier. The surface of the piedmont was broken by small crevasses here, one running right under the tent. We all enjoyed our salt-water hoosh and turned in very tired. Browning rather better. Dickason quite recovered. A lovely evening. Distance 8·5 miles.

October 7.—A beautiful morning after a comparatively warm night. We were away soon after 8, down the snowdrift slope and over a tide crack 4 ft. wide. The sea ice proved very heavy going, as it was covered with deep crusted snow through which we had a job to move the sledges. We saw rather an amusing incident here. A number of seals were lying along the tide crack, and just after we had crossed we saw one more struggle up on the ice and go to sleep with her tail within a few inches of the tide crack. She had hardly gone to sleep when a head came cautiously up, saw her, dipped down again, then coming cautiously up again, bit her hard. The poor beast squealed, hit at her assailant several times

PENGUINS DIVING

PENGUINS DIVING

with her tail and wriggled off as fast as she could across the ice, but the practical joker did not follow up the attack.

Beyond a stiff pull in deep snow we had no difficulty in getting our sledges up the snow drift and on the south cliff. Once on top we were troubled with a rather deep crusted snow surface, with long undulations which were fairly hard and good going on the summits, but with deep soft snow in the valleys. Curious conical mounds of blue ice showed up here and there. These are survivals, I imagine, of the séracs and icefalls visible on our right hand where the David Glacier flows down from the mountains, making a big disturbance. To avoid these we had to steer in a south-easterly direction. The day was fine but cold and we were all in good spirits, as even if we could not get down to Cape Evans by the sea ice, we could make certain of getting plenty of food here. Distance about 6 miles.

October 8.—Bright sun but cold westerly wind with low drift when we turned out at 5.30. We were away by 8 and the going was much the same as yesterday, only the ice hummocks were more numerous and the undulations steeper. In the afternoon the sun went behind nimbus haze and the light got very bad indeed, and was the cause of us nearly coming to grief. The snow was very wind-blown and slippery on the top of the undulations, but soft in the hollows, and we had been racing down the slopes to help us through the soft snow. Soon after 4 the light got so bad we could not see where we were stepping, and when well on our way down one of these slopes, I thought I saw a crevasse in front, so swung the sledge, and was going ahead to reconnoitre, when I found we were on the edge of a steep slope about 20 ft. high, which went sheer down into a barranca. We had to get the sledges up the slippery slope again—no easy job—and try round. After about a mile we found a place we could cross, but the delays of roping up to prospect made our day's march small. Dickason is bad again. I suppose it must be the heavy pulling. Distance 6 miles. The weather thick, with slight snow.

October 9.—I turned out to look at the weather at 4 A.M. and found it snowing and so thick I could only just see the other tent.

By 7 it was better though still thick, so after breakfast we started and steered a more easterly course to try and get out of this broken country. The light and surface were vile, while a cold westerly wind did not improve matters. We found ourselves in country just as bad, so steered due south and went straight ahead, but even going as cautiously as we could we nearly repeated yesterday's experience, stopping the sledge just in time on the edge of the cliff and having to work back up the slope and round. The wind had increased to a gale with drift to add to our discomfort. About 4 o'clock, however, the sun came out, the wind eased, and we got into better country. Just before camping, from the top of one of the ridges I got a view of the coast line south of the Drygalski, and the sea ice in Geikie Inlet, so I hope the worst of the Drygalski is past. Dickason is much better, but Browning is very bad again. We camped soon after 6, all very tired. Distance 6 miles.

October 10.—Turned out at 5 A.M. to find a lovely day with bright sun but a cold wind. At 7.30 just after starting a low drift got up and the wind was freshening but bitterly cold—so cold in fact that at lunch-time we only stopped long enough to eat some frozen meat and blubber, and then were off again over these endless undulations that give one the impression of always going up hill. At last on one of the undulations we saw sea ice to the southward, and a few minutes afterwards Dickason pointed to a white mass, looking like a cloud, which I made out to be Mount Erebus. While crossing another long undulation about three-quarters of a mile across, we came to a cliff barring our passage, but by bearing to the east, we found a place where we could cross the big crevasse that lay in front of it by a snow drift. The crevasse was about 10 yards wide, but well bridged. Once on top we saw the sea ice below us and about a mile and a half ahead. The drift, which had been blinding in the squalls, now cleared and we had a good view.

The sea ice seemed fast as far as we could see in all directions, and this was a great relief to us. The Drygalski had not been so formidable as I expected, in spite of the broken ice ; we only broke through into a few crevasses, although I have no doubt there are plenty there.

They are well bridged after the winter. We had no trouble in getting down to the sea ice, as hard snow drifts completely hid the south cliff. At 6 P.M. we camped, all tired but very pleased at having the Drygalski behind us and good sea ice in front. We had an extra biscuit and a stick of chocolate to celebrate the occasion. The night was very cold but fine. We have crossed to the westward of David's route.

I think distance about 7 miles.

October 11.—Westerly wind with heavy drift, and very cold. As there was no improvement after breakfast we turned in again. About 2 P.M. a solitary Emperor penguin came and called outside the tent. We went outside and killed and butchered him ; his heart and liver are in the hoosh pot as 1 write this. The remainder of his flesh, which is not bad raw when it is frozen, we cut up into thin strips to eat on the march. It was very cold work cutting him up in the wind.

The sun came out and the wind and drift eased in the evening, so Abbott and I re-packed the sledges, securing the wooden one on top of the iron-runner sledge. We find this the best arrangement for sea ice, although the resultant load is rather top-heavy. It was very cold and we got our hands very badly frostbitten.

October 12.—A cold wind but clear when we turned out at 4.30 A.M.

We were off before 7 over a fair surface. Soon after lunch we had some trouble with pressure ice, resulting in one upset. A lovely evening when we camped that night, Erebus and Melbourne both being in sight. Browning was better but still had bad cramping pains in his stomach. Distance 11 miles.

October 13.—A disappointing day, overcast, light northerly airs, and not much pressure, but a very heavy drag through deep crusted snow. We were all very tired when we camped. Distance 7 miles. We passed a track which at first we thought had been left by a sledge but afterwards proved to be that of a seal.

October 14.—The weather was much the same to-day as yesterday, but the surface was better. We pulled in shore to avoid heavy pressure which ran across our bows. A haze of snow crystals obscured the land, and this made the journey tedious and we were glad to camp, having done about 10 miles, but not I fear half that on our course. The prevailing ridges run about N.N.E.

October 15.—A fine morning, but cold wind from south. We turned out at 4.45 and for the first two hours made good progress. The sun came out quite hot and the wind dropped in the middle of the day, so that we were able to spend an hour over lunch. The mirage was wonderful, the pressure to the southward being seen inverted in the sky.

We came across more tracks, which I think must be seal. It is curious that we have seen no animals ; I can only account for it by presuming that this is old ice with no cracks. Soon after 4 we had to cross pressure ridges, for though we had been dodging them since lunch, they now became so high we had to camp and re-pack sledges. We shall have to relay the sledges to-morrow, taking them over one at a time.

Distance about 10 miles, but not half that on our course. A clear but cold evening.

October 16.—I suppose every now and then we swallow a bit of bad meat, and whether from that reason or some other, I was very bad last night with cramp and pains in the stomach, and this morning I am feeling cold

and sick. Levick gave me some medicine that put new
life into me. We have had a wearisome day of relaying,
with frequent upsets, and have been cutting a path through
high and heavy pressure ice, half hidden under a soft snow
into which we fell and floundered about.

At 5.30 the light was so bad that I camped. Distance
perhaps 3 miles, but it is impossible to gauge accurately
with this sort of travelling.

October 17.—Turned out at 5.15 to find snow falling,
and by the time we had finished breakfast a southerly gale
was blowing, with heavy drift, and it was impossible to
march, so we turned in and spent the day in our bags.

October 18.—The wind dropped in the night and the
sky cleared about 6, leaving a fine day. We have had
another heavy day's work relaying over bad pressure, but
yesterday's rest has done us all a lot of good and we went
at it quite fresh. We saw the Nordenskiöld ice tongue
ahead miraged up and looking quite close. About 5 P.M.
we came to the end of this infernal pressure, and saw
smooth surface between us and the tongue end, and by
6.30 camped on the smooth ice. I had noticed a seal up
about a mile west of us as we were relaying over the last of
the pressure, so after we had camped I went away on ski to
look for him.

After going about 2 miles I struck his tracks and
followed them till they disappeared down a hole. Through
the seal hole I tried to feel the lower edge of the ice but was
unable to do so. I take it therefore that the ice must be
at least 3 feet thick. This smooth surface we are on must
be due, I think, to the current coming up under the

A WEDDELL SEAL ABOUT TO DIVE

A WEDDELL SEAL ON THE BEACH

Nordenskiöld, causing this part of the sea to freeze over late in the season.

A cold evening with slight snow. Approximate distance 6 miles.

October 19.—A fine morning but colder. We turned out at 3.30, and after breakfast Levick, Abbott, and Browning went to the seal hole while we packed and started the sledges. They were successful this time and caught the seal asleep by the hole, and soon had him cut up and packed on one of the sledges. At 10 we stopped for lunch. The day was lovely for marching, being clear and cold, but the surface was vile ; no pressure, but soft sandy snow. We halted for a second lunch of raw seal at 3.30 P.M. Levick, Abbott, and Browning like it, the rest of us do not. We camped at 6.15, all very tired. Distance 9 miles. A lovely evening.

October 20.—A lovely morning, clear, calm, and cold. A stiff pull over a heavy surface brought us to the foot of the cliff of the Nordenskiöld ice tongue. The cliff here is about 50 feet high and very much indented. A few miles to the east a deep bay or inlet ran in to the southward.

A steep snowdrift enabled us to get on the ice tongue, but we had to unpack the sledges and carry most of the gear up, after hauling the sledges up to the top with the Alpine rope, as it was so steep.

We camped on the top at about 5 P.M. Priestley, Levick, and I then roped up and went on to see what the going was like for the next day.

We found long shallow undulations, and as far as we could see no crevasses. We shall cross it a long way inside David's route.   Curiously enough, there was hardly any tide crack between the sea ice and the tongue.

Several seals were in sight, but we did not kill any, as I am sure we shall get any amount south of this tongue. The tongue seems to be ice to within 2 feet of the top and the surface is rather a soft snow.   Distance 6 miles.

October 21.—Turning out at 5.30 A.M. we depôted all unnecessary gear and started considerably lighter. Should we have to turn back we can always pick this depôt up easily.   The day was lovely, but rather warm for pulling, and the surface soft but not bad going. We came across no crevasses and by 3.30 ran down an easy slope to the sea ice. The snow on the latter was rather deep. We lashed the wooden runner sledge on the one with the iron runners and pulled on till about 6, when we camped.

October 22.—A nice morning, but soon after starting a cold southerly wind got up, resulting in several frost-bitten noses. We were travelling over pressure well hidden by soft snow. In the afternoon we had some excitement seeing a dark conical object ahead, much the same shape as a tent. As Browning was rather bad, we left him with Dickason and Abbott to rest with the sledges, while Levick, Priestley, and I went on to look at it, but after going about a mile we made it out to be some black grit blown on to a conical piece of ice. On returning to the sledges we pulled in shore to try and get a better surface, but had to camp at 5 P.M. as Browning was so bad.   Distance about 6 miles.   We are about 1 mile from land, which appears to be low ice-covered foothills.

October 23.—I was bad in the night and did not wake till 6.30. The day was warmer, but I feel very cold and rather weak and slack. The light was bad, but we made fair progress. Passed inside a number of stranded bergs evidently broken off from the piedmont. About 4 P.M. we saw a seal near a stranded berg and we camped early, in order to kill and cut him up. There were tracks of several more near the berg, so I think we are coming to the land of plenty. A brain and liver hoosh did us all good. We are all feeling slack and stale. Distance 6 miles. We had to reduce to two biscuits per day owing to slow progress.

October 24.—A lovely morning, clear and calm with a few clouds over the mountains. While we were packing the sledges Browning went to the seal hole, but there were none up. The surface was heavy crusted snow with belts of pressure. During the day we passed a large number of stranded bergs and any amount of seals up round them, many of them with young.

Our route lay along a piedmont, evidently aground, judging by the steep slopes and crevasses in places. Soon after 4 P.M. we opened out a wide bay which I made out to be Tripp Bay. After this the surface improved. After camping, Levick and Abbott killed and cut up a seal.

There was a curious line of stranded bergs and pressure running parallel to the coast and about two miles off, which looks as if there might be a shoal there. Our distance to-day about 7 miles.

October 25.—Both Dickason and I had a bad night,

and I felt very cold when I turned out at about 5 A.M.
We soon got warm, however, for the snowdrifts between
the pressure were awful. We made out Tripp Island at
the head of the bay in the afternoon. It has been a very
tiring day, and as Browning was rather bad we camped
at 4.30. Distance 7 miles.

October 26.—A fine morning. We started away
after breakfast with both sledges, while Priestley went
into the bay on ski to look at Tripp Island and see if
Professor David had left his depôt of rocks there. We
knew he had depôted the specimens on some island on
the coast, but did not know which.

The surface had improved, so the rest of us were able
to get the sledges along at a fair pace and it was noon
before Priestley caught us up. He had seen nothing of
the depôt, but collected some rock specimens himself.
By 5 P.M. we were off another little island on the top of
which I made out a bamboo with my glasses. We
pulled in and camped under the north end. We had a
hard struggle over the pack, but within a few hundred
yards of land we found a smooth lead up and down the
coast. After this we made a point of keeping close to
the coast line on our journey, and it certainly paid us,
in spite of the extra mileage. After hoosh Priestley and
I climbed to the top of the island and collected Professor
David's specimens, also some letters his party had left
in a tin, addressed to Mrs. David, Dr. Mawson, Lieutenant
Shackleton, and to Commanding Officer, S.Y. *Nimrod.*
We brought all these down and packed them on the
sledge. When I got back to camp Levick came to me

about Browning's condition.   He was getting very anxious about him, suspecting organic trouble.   I suggested his and Browning's remaining at Granite Harbour with all the gear, while the rest of us pushed on with a light sledge to get provisions from Butter Point, where we knew there would be a small depôt, but Levick thought it best to bring him on, as, if the trouble was organic, the sooner he could be laid up in a hut the better.   We shall therefore push on, putting him on the sledge when he gets tired, and to keep his strength up give him one extra biscuit per day.   Seal meat seems to be poison to him. Our distance this day was about 8 miles.

October 27.—A fine morning.   Temperature warmer. We got away after breakfast, keeping inside Depôt Island and getting beautiful smooth ice nearly clear of snow, which lasted to Cape Ross, where we had to cross bad pressure ridges off the cape.   The ridges were so bad we had to cut passages for the sledges with ice axes.   We had smooth ice again to Cape Gregory, which is now an island, and we were able to make our way through the strait between Gregory Island and the piedmont ; after this we again struck a heavy surface.   We were now in Granite Harbour.   After pulling 2 miles through the deep snow we camped.   Distance about 12 miles.   The changes in the face of the piedmont are rather interesting. In 1902 Depôt Island was charted a point by the *Discovery.*   By 1909 it had turned into an island and was named accordingly by Professor David.   David reported Gregory Point a cape in 1909 and it is now (1912) an island.

We saw rock outcropping from the piedmont at various places, and no doubt these exposures will be points or islands at some near period in the future. Priestley collected specimens everywhere he could. We saw an enormous quantity of seals and young up, so this is evidently a great breeding-place.

October 28.—A fine morning ; we made fair progress over a snow surface. We had to make a détour into the bay to avoid pressure. A cold wind sprang up in the afternoon, and my nose, which had got very sunburnt all the morning, promptly froze, and when thawed out was very painful. We camped about 6 P.M. two miles north of Cape Roberts. No seals were up on the south side of the bay. Distance 10 miles. No sign of the ship or of Debenham's party.

October 29.—Turned out at 4.30 A.M. A fine day, but a bank of cloud to the south and a cold westerly wind. A two hours' march brought us to Cape Roberts, where I saw through my glasses a bamboo stuck on the top of the cape. Leaving the sledges, Priestley and I climbed the cape, when we found a record left by the Western Party last year before they were picked up, and giving their movements, while near by was a depôt of provisions they had left behind. We gave such a yell the others ran up the slope at once. It seemed almost too good to be true.

We found two tins of biscuits, one slightly broached, and a small bag each of raisins, tea, cocoa, butter, and lard. There were also clothes, diaries, and specimens from Granite Harbour. I decided to camp here and have a day off. Dividing the provisions between the two tents, we soon had hoosh going and such a feed of biscuit, butter, and lard as we had not had for 9 months, and we followed this up with sweet, thick cocoa. After this we killed and cut up a seal as we are getting short of meat and there is every prospect of a blizzard coming on.

Levick and Abbott saw a desperate fight between two bull seals to-day. They gashed each other right through skin and blubber till they were bleeding badly.

We had another hoosh and more biscuit and lard in the evening; then we turned into our bags and, quite torpid with food, discussed our plans on arriving at Cape Evans. We had quite decided we should find no one there, for we believed the whole party had been blown north in the ship, while trying to reach us. Still discussing plans we fell asleep. What with news from the main party and food (although both were a year old) it was the happiest day since we last saw the ship. I awoke in the night, finished my share of the butter and most of my lard, then dozed off again.

October 30.—The blizzard never came off. We turned out to find a beautiful warm morning. After another big feed of biscuits and a brain-and-liver hoosh we started in the highest spirits. The change of diet has done Browning good already. I took all the books, food, specimens, and records of Taylor's party, leaving only the old clothes.

I also left a note saying we were all well. The surface was fairly good with occasional belts of rough pressure ice that delayed us considerably. Taylor's journal speaks of Glacier Tongue having broken away from MacMurdo Sound and grounded on the coast south of Dunlop Island. It will be interesting to see if it is still there. At midday we camped for lunch, and the hot tea and biscuit made a great difference to our marching. This was the first hot lunch we had had and we all appreciated it. Between 5 and 6 the pressure was very bad; not high, but jagged and continuous, bruising our feet. Luckily we had the iron-runner sledge. Wooden runners would have been torn to shreds. Camped at 6.15. Distance 8 miles. Dunlop Island in sight about 3 miles ahead.

October 31.—A lovely morning. The south-west breeze of the night had dropped and the day felt warm. We suffered the same painful surface until within a mile of Dunlop Island, when we reached a smooth surface. We lunched on the north side of Dunlop Island. After lunch we searched it for records, but found nothing. Priestley collected some specimens. Resuming our march we got on to smooth ice between Dunlop Island and the mainland and kept a good surface until we camped at 6.15, half-way across the ' Bay of Sails.' Distance 11 miles: Mt. Erebus rising to the height of several thousand feet.

November 1.—5 A.M. A fine morning with heavy clouds to the south. We had a good surface and made good progress. Priestley collected from Cape Gneiss and Marble Point. We lunched at the latter cape, and at 3.45 we reached Cape Bernacchi, where we collected the remainder of Taylor's depôt, three-quarters of a tin of biscuits, one bag of pemmican, and ditto of sugar, raisins, tea, and cocoa. The pemmican and raisins were most acceptable, as we had finished ours. Priestley collected some specimens and we started away again at 4.30, across pressure towards Butter Point. At 6 P.M. we camped about 1 mile south of Cape Bernacchi with smooth ice ahead.

We are certainly having the most lovely weather, clear, calm, and cold enough to make marching a pleasure. A large number of seals and young up.

November 2.—5 A.M. A fine morning. Got away early over good snow surface, reaching Butter Point at 2.30. There was a good deal of pressure off the point, so leaving the sledges on the good ice we walked the half mile to the depôt. We had been seeing a large number of seals and young since Granite Harbour, but just off Butter Point the number was extraordinary.

Getting up to the depôt we found an enormous quantity of stores, also a note from Atkinson saying he had tried to relieve us last April but had found no ice beyond this spot. As there was no further message we were anxious for the safety of this party, as we know how unreliable the autumn ice is. As to what had happened it was hopeless trying to speculate. This had upset all our theories and I had a vague feeling something was wrong.

I therefore decided to leave one tin of biscuits here and get right across the sound as soon as possible. Taking a few luxuries such as chocolate and jam, we went back to the sledges and pulled in a south-east direction until about 7 P.M., when we camped. Distance 14 miles. Weather fine. The latter part of our march we were delayed by pressure ridges running north and south.

November 3.—5.15 A.M. Weather overcast, surface good, with belts of heavy pressure, the ridges running north and south. Some of the smooth ice had struck me as being rather new ice. At 11.30 our iron-runner sledge broke down hopelessly, one side coming off. We had a hasty lunch, packed the sleeping-bags, records, and a little fresh food on the other sledge, depôted all the remainder, and then started on again. The smooth-ice leads between the pressure were suspiciously dark and greasy-looking, so after going about half a mile we sounded with an ice axe and found we were on thin soft ice, which cannot have been much more than a day or two old. Turning the sledge we went back at a run, not stopping until we got on to better ice by the old sledge. Taking the rest of the food we then started W.S.W. towards the Eskers. Several leads were so new we had to cross them at a run, and it was 7.30 before we found sound ice, with no weak leads between us and the shore, and then I decided to camp.

November 4.—Weather overcast and warm. We turned out at 4.30, and after breakfast Priestley, Abbott, and Dickason went back with the empty sledge to get the remainder of the depôt, and if possible fit on the iron runners, while Levick, Browning, and I went back with packs to get more food. We had a long tramp to Butter Point and back over rough ice, and we had done 18 miles before we got back to camp, Levick and I with a 50-lb.

pack and Browning with a smaller one, as he had not quite recovered.

The change in Browning's condition owing to the biscuit is marvellous.

A week ago he could just walk by the sledge on a march of 8 or 10 miles; to-night, although tired, he is none the worse for his 18-mile walk. We found Priestley and his party had already arrived with the rest of the depôt when we got back, and to my great joy he had been able to fit the iron runners on to the 12-ft. sledge.

November 5.—We turned out at 3.30. A lovely morning, with bright sun. After breakfast we started away, steering for the Dailey Islands, but we were forced to make a détour to the west to avoid rotten ice-leads.

The mirage was extraordinary. At one place we thought we saw three men pulling a sledge; Priestley and I walked towards them; they apparently stopped; Priestley started semaphoring while I looked through my glasses. No result. Suddenly they turned and I saw they were Emperor penguins, miraged up in a way that made them look like figures. These leads of bad ice seemed to run into Blue Glacier, but I thought I could see good ice beyond them, so we raced the sledge straight across, getting over without a mishap. Once over we found old ice behind a pressure ridge, and after crossing that struck the Barrier edge, here about 4 feet high, with snowdrifts leading on to it. A large number of seals and Emperor penguins were on the old ice. Here we lunched. The Barrier edge runs out in a tongue, and we had struck it on the north-west corner We were thus able to steer direct for Hut Point over the tongue. At 5 P.M. we came up to the pinnacled ice lying on the east side of the tongue.

This pinnacled ice is very rough and gritty and is evidently the remains of an old moraine of the Koettlitz Glacier. By skirting to the north of this we found a lane of old sea ice on which we could travel until we had passed it. Enormous crowds of Emperors were here. In one bunch I estimated there were about 300. After travelling about 6 miles on this old ice the pinnacled ice gave out and we were able to head for Hut Point again over the Barrier. I had hoped to get into Hut Point the same night, so camped for hoosh at 6.30. Resuming our march we went on till 1 A.M., when I found we were still 7 miles off. I therefore camped, had some cocoa, and turned in. We had done a good march, twenty-one hours since we turned out, and had we been able to hold a straight course we should have easily got in.

November 6.—Another fine morning. We marched till 1 P.M., when our sledge broke down, the whole runner coming off. As we were only 1 mile from Hut Point, I camped. Priestley, Dickason, and I walked in to look for news and get another sledge, as I was sure some would be there.

As we neared the Point we noticed fresh tracks of mule and dogs.

I pointed them out to Priestley, and said, ' I hope there is nothing wrong with the Pole party, as I do not like the look of these.' He said, ' No more do I.' We ran up to the hut and found a letter from Atkinson to the ' Commanding Officer, *Terra Nova*.' I opened this and learnt the sad

Dickason   Abbott   Browning   Campbell   Priestley   Levick

LIEUT. CAMPBELL S PARTY ON THEIR RETURN TO CAPE EVANS

news of the loss of the Polar Party. The names of the party were not given, and finding Atkinson in charge of the search party which had started, I was afraid two units, or eight men, were lost. Finding a sledge only slightly damaged I took that back to the camp, getting back there about 5 P.M.

We were all rather tired, so instead of starting straight on to Cape Evans, we had supper and went to sleep. Before turning in we made a depôt of the broken sledge, all rock specimens, clothes, and food, so as to travel light to Cape Evans. I was very anxious to get there as soon as possible, as I thought there was a chance that there might be one or two mules or enough dogs to enable me to follow the search party. It had been a great disappointment for us to have missed them by a week, as we were all anxious to join in the search.

November 7.—4 A.M. A lovely morning. After a hasty breakfast we were off, arriving at Cape Evans at 5 P.M. We found no one at home, but a letter on the door of the hut gave us all the news and the names of the lost party. Very soon Debenham and Archer returned, giving us a most hearty welcome, and no one can realise what it meant to us to see new faces and to be home after our long winter. Our clothes, letters, &c., had been landed from the ship, and we were able to read our home letters, which we had only time to glance at in the ship in February. Archer provided a sumptuous dinner that night, and we sailed into it in a way that made Debenham hold his breath. A bath and change of clothes completed the **transformation.**

November 8.—Weather overcast, with a cold south-easterly wind of medium •force. I went round with Debenham and was much surprised at the amount of stores. If we were down for another winter there should be no lack. Our clothes had been landed by the ship. There was nothing we wanted except boots, of which I served out one pair to each.

It was hopeless to think of following the search party, the only transport being a few dogs that had been left behind as they were slow or weak. Atkinson's plans were to push on and search to the top of the Beardmore Glacier unless he found traces of the party before, so there was no hope of catching him. I find our party are not so fit as I thought. Most of us have developed swollen ankles and legs (œdema), and when the flesh is pressed in the holes remain there.

From November 8 till the return of the sledge party we were all very busy transcribing our last winter's diaries, developing photographs, and renewing what of our outfit we were unable to replace.

On the 11th Levick, Abbott, and Dickason left for Hut Point, and the next day but one they returned, bringing with them our records and specimens. They had taken all the provisions left on our broken sledge to Hut Point.

November 25.—A mild blizzard. Priestley and Debenham had arranged to start for Cape Royds to-day, taking Dickason, but decided to wait for better weather.

At 8 P.M. two dog teams with Atkinson, Cherry-Garrard, and Demetri arrived. They had found the remains of the Polar Party 11 miles south of 'One Ton Depôt.' Atkinson brought back all their records and personal gear, which I asked him to take charge of personally.

November 26.—I went with Atkinson to Hut Point with a dog team.

It was a fine, clear day, and leaving Cape Evans at noon we got there about 2 P.M. The surface was good and I walked up to the Gap and saw the rest of the party in camp at 'Safety Camp.'

November 27.—The remainder of the party pulled in about 2 A.M., and it was very pleasant meeting them all again. Atkinson and I left them there and returned to Cape Evans, getting in at 5 A.M. next morning.

November 28.—A fine day. The party with the mules arrived at 1 P.M. Although five mules out of seven were brought back we had to shoot two of them, as they refused all food and were in a very bad condition.

We now settled down to routine work and short sledge journeys on Ross Island, and for geological survey work, Priestley and Debenham taking a party up Mt. Erebus.

The ship arrived January 18, just as we were starting to prepare for a third winter.

THE WESTERN JOURNEYS

By Griffith Taylor, B.A., B.Sc., B.E., F.G.S.

[*See* Folding Map, p. 290; and The Birdseye Views, pp. 420, 422, 425.]

CHAPTER I

KOETTLITZ, FERRAR, AND TAYLOR GLACIERS

The following chapters describe the doings of six members of the Expedition during a detailed exploration of the 'Western Mountains' in South Victoria Land. A few words as to the scene of our operations and the *personnel* of the parties will serve as an introduction to the narrative of the sledge journeys.

As you stand on Cape Evans with your back to the steam cloud of Erebus you see across McMurdo Sound a glorious range of mountains running due north and south and rising to 13,000 feet in the south-west. These are the Western Mountains. Their southern limit is the extinct volcanic cone of Discovery, and far to the north one can follow the same range of snow-clad peaks until it merges with the grey line of the horizon. Beyond this grey line was Granite Harbour (76° 50′), and that marked the northern limit of our survey; while the Koettlitz Glacier (in 78° 20′), which hid the lower slopes of Discovery,

SHOWING THE CWM VALLE S

was the 'farthest south' reached in our two sledging trips.

On clear days we could see every little cup-shaped valley which roughened the mighty scarp of Lister, so sharply that it seemed impossible that they were seventy miles away. Due west was the valley of the Lower Ferrar Glacier, while the long gleaming snow slope at its mouth was the Butter Point Piedmont—the starting place for all Western exploration, where depôts have been made even since the butter was left there by the 1902 expedition.

Hidden behind the ranges was the Great Ice Plateau. From this height of 7000 feet descended the great rivers of ice—the Koettlitz, Ferrar, Taylor, and Mackay Glaciers— with which the following pages are concerned.

Now as to my mates. What is the 'Call to the Wild' which seems to draw men back to the Antarctic? In my opinion it is the association with picked companions, especially chosen for their suitability for the environment, which constitutes the charm of life in the Antarctic. The deserts of Australia or the wilds of Spitzbergen would appeal equally to me with the same companions.

There is a famous old school near Sydney where for many years there were representatives from two families, the Debenhams and Taylors. So that Frank Debenham and myself were old friends and graduates in geology of the same 'Varsity. In later years at Cambridge there was an informal club of research students in which Wright of Caius and Taylor of Emmanuel were fellow-members. Debenham's experience as Commissary-General at many a camp in Australia made him invaluable sledging—

while Wright was an expert in traversing snow-clad country, for he often spent·his vacations from Toronto Unive sity surveying in the Canadian backwoods.

Next may I introduce Tryggve Gran, the youngest and yet the most travelled officer in the Expedition except our leader himself. Interested in sport, travel, music, literature, and languages, 'Trigger' never let a day pass without enlivening our march by some of his many adventures.

Of the two petty officers, Edgar Evans coached the first party, all of whom were new chums, in Antarctic sledging. He was one of the *Discovery* men and was an ideal sledge mate ; while Forde, another giant of the navy, was sledge master on our Granite Harbour journey.

It is interesting to note that the six men represented six nationalities. Debenham and Wright come from Australia and Canada ; Gran is a hardy Norseman ; Forde is Irish ; Evans came from Cardiff ; while I was the only member born in England. If I have dwelt on this question of *personnel,* it is because it is so important a factor in exploration, and these few words help to explain the unbroken harmony which existed during our six months' sledging.

On January 26, 1911, Captain Scott handed to me the Sledging Orders governing our movements on the first Western Journey. They give a comprehensive account of what we actually carried out, and I therefore insert them here, omitting only a paragraph concerning Hut Point.

' DEAR TAYLOR,

'I purpose to disembark a sledge-party of which you will have charge, on the sea ice of McMurdo Sound as near the Ferrar Glacier as possible.

[*See* p. 210

THE FIRST WESTERN PARTY IN A NATURAL ICE-TUNNEL AMID THE
PINNACLES OF THE KOETTLITZ GLACIER
(Edgar Evans standing)

' Your companions will be Messrs. Debenham, Wright, and Petty Officer Evans.

' You will have two sledges with food and equipment for eight weeks.

' The object of your journey will be the geological exploration of the region between the Dry Valley and the Koettlitz Glacier.

' Your movements must depend to some extent on the breaking of the sea ice. Your best and safest plan appears to be to carry all your provision up the Ferrar Glacier to a point in the medial moraine abreast of Descent Pass, and to make a depôt at that point. With a fortnight's food you could then continue the ascent to the junction of the Dry Valley glacier and descend the Valley of that glacier. On returning to your depôt you will be in a position to observe the extent of open water, and you can either descend the glacier and pass to the east around Butter Point, or climb Descent Pass, descending by the Blue Glacier or by one of the more southerly foothill glaciers, and thus continue the examination of the Koettlitz Glacier area.

' On completion of your work you should cross to Hut Point, being careful not to camp too near open water. . . .

        ' Wishing you the best of luck,
                    ' Yours sincerely,
                        (sgd.) ' R. Scott.'

With regard to our equipment only one feature deserves comment. We carried an exceptionally large photographic battery, which was necessitated by the character of the problems which engaged our attention. For instance, Wright was chiefly interested in the forms of ice-structure which we encountered. The most delicate ice-crystals, which withered at a breath, must needs be photographed *in situ*. There was no possibility of his bringing back specimens for study in the hut during the dark winter months. For similar reasons a somewhat bulky polariscope—in which sheets of ice were examined in polarised light—formed part of his load, and was vulgarly referred to as 'the Barrel Organ.' He also had charge of the theodolite.

Debenham was engaged on the more usual work of collecting rock specimens and mapping their occurrence in the field. For this purpose another camera was essential, since in general his investigations were carried out on the cliffs at some distance from the rest of us.

The subject which primarily interested myself was the physiographic aspect of the region, or, as it may popularly be described, 'The last chapter in the geological history of Antarctica.' In other words, How has the land surface been affected by the flow of glaciers, by the action of wind, frost, water, and ice ? And a second and more interesting question I set myself was, How do the resulting features differ from those observed in more temperate regions, where water plays such an important part and ice erosion is absent ?

On January 27 Pennell took us across the Sound in the *Terra Nova* from Glacier Tongue to Butter Point, where we arrived about 4 P.M. We spent some time packing our gear on our two sledges. The total load was arrived at as follows :

	Lbs.
Two sledges and steel runners . . .	
Food for eight weeks	
Tools, tents, &c.	
Instruments, cameras, &c. . . .	
Four personal bags . . .	
	1046

We had heavy equipment for four men—averaging about 270 lbs. each—but as we were only proposing to take one sledge for a considerable portion of the journey this was of little importance.

From the coast we had a magnificent view of the lower portion of the Ferrar Glacier. [*See* Illustration, p. 420.] The valley was about four miles wide and extended south west for thirty miles. Up this we were to journey, ascending 3000 feet in the next few days.

Everyone noticed the grand sweep of the cliffs at the side. The northern face for twenty miles is a marvellous wall-like cliff about 3000 feet high—as straight and smooth as if planed by a giant carpenter. And indeed it is a typical glacial valley, where the lateral spurs, such as break up the continuity of an ordinary *river-cut* valley, are entirely wanting.

We started about 6 P.M. and pulled the sledges about four miles before camping for the night.

I asked Evans to cook for the first week, as he was experienced with the cooker and primus lamp. Debenham's reputation was such that I was sure he would master polar cooking sooner than any of us. So he became cook's-mate and assistant—to rise to chef next week. Wright agreed to take the third week, and I thought by that time I might have learnt enough to improve on my own very modest culinary attainments.

We started on a Friday, and our calendar was reckoned from cook's day to cook's day. There was never any doubt as to which day of the week it was, because each cook was so keen to relinquish his post at the close of his term of office !

While Evans was initiating Debenham in the mysteries of pemmican, Wright and I walked across the sea ice a mile or so to the south and reached a 'lateral tongue' or prolongation of the main glacier. There was a sudden rise of some three feet, and the surface in place of being level and comparatively smooth was carved out into deep irregular bowls with overhanging margins. These were in all probability giant 'sunholes,' and their floors were covered with a most beautiful carpet of snow crystals.

Examined closely each crystal was like the segment of a fan strengthened by cross-ribs, and these 'fan-plates' were often half an inch across. The surface as a whole reminded me strongly of the appearance of a coral reef— and it was about as pleasant a sight to us as the latter is to the navigator. Wright was the only one who appreciated their beauty, we others being more concerned with the numerous capsizes caused by this 'coral reef' structure, which characterised the whole of the lower Ferrar Glacier.

We returned to the tent, and as usual at starting found it impossible to eat all our pemmican. It seemed much too rich and abundant;—alas, how fleeting was this opinion !

Next day, January 28, we sledged several miles up the glacier, but spent all the afternoon examining a beautiful hanging glacier which lay like a great white mantle flung on the northern wall of the Ferrar Valley. To reach this side glacier we had to cross a much weathered portion of the Ferrar's surface. Large dome-covered ponds into which we fell at frequent intervals made one of us remark, ' Just like a promenade on the roof of the Crystal Palace.'

As usual the rock slopes were fringed by a colonnade of gigantic pinnacles thirty feet high separated by narrow crevasses. The sun glistening on the icy minarets and beautiful icicles made a most impressive sight. Beyond this we soon reached the talus or débris slopes below the ' Double Curtain ' glacier. A stiff climb up this brought us to the snout of the tributary, and we found that this ' mantle of ice ' ended in a vertical face forty feet thick. While Wright and Debenham investigated this region, I climbed up 2500 feet and stood on the shoulder of the Kukri Hills.

A wonderful panorama was spread out before me which was especially striking to the south-west. Here jutted out the three grand gables—like the roof of a Gothic cathedral—which were so appropriately named the Cathedral Rocks. Below this we were to leave our first depôt.

As we returned to the tent some two miles off we came across several parties of Emperor penguins stolidly awaiting the end of their moulting season. They probably totalled one hundred. Only one individual was garbed in new and shining raiment, and him I slew in preparation for a change of diet if our appetite failed on a pemmican régime.

All next day we pulled steadily up the glacier to the west, encouraged by Evans's opinion that we should meet better sledging surfaces higher up the glacier.

On the 30th we had very heavy going up the broad ice undulations and about noon got among the crevasses. We all slipped in at various intervals, but they were quite narrow and gave us no trouble. The snow was a foot thick in many places and alternated with 'glass-roof' ice into which we fell frequently. However, we kept on till 9 P.M., when we reached the big moraine below Cathedral Rocks, and there made our depôt as Captain Scott had advised.

Above our depôt the slope was steeper, but we had only half the load to pull, and towards 6 P.M. on the next evening we reached the top of the lower Ferrar and found ourselves on a small ice plateau about 3200 feet above sea level. We now marched along the grandest geological section it has ever been my good fortune to see. The cliff to the north, 3300 feet high, was capped by yellowish sandstone. Beneath this were two wonderful horizontal sheets of dark lava which had intruded through the granite base so that the rocks looked like a gigantic sandwich composed of alternating yellow, black and red layers. The lower slopes of the red granite were covered by the old lateral moraine, a layer of dark débris left by the Ferrar Glacier when it almost filled the valley we were following.

We pushed on till 9 P.M., descending slightly as we proceeded to the north, and camped on the glacier filling the upper end of the Dry Valley. The exploration of this glacier—which Scott had rapidly traversed in 1903—was the work before us during the next fortnight. Captain Scott has honoured me by giving it the name of Taylor Glacier.

I kept too near to the Kukri Hills on descending into the Taylor Glacier and we struck an extremely steep slippery surface consisting of clear ice cut into rounded hollows a foot across. This characteristic surface—like giant thumb-marks in a piece of putty—was full of small crevasses, and here the sledge repeatedly 'took charge.' We rolled about all over the place, and someone remarked that we had all the appearance of being drunk and none of the pleasure of it !

To our surprise, after five days' pulling over heavy snow in the Ferrar Glacier, we found no snow in the parallel Taylor Valley, only about 10 miles farther north. After lunching among the scattered blocks of the medial moraine we descended about a thousand feet, the sledge doing its own pulling. Debenham and I went on ahead with slack traces, while Evans and Wright enlivened the valley with what they were pleased to call 'cheerful song' ! A strong keen wind was blowing up the valley, but the most remarkable feature of this region prevented it from becoming obnoxious. There was no drift-snow !

Imagine a valley 4 miles wide, 3000 feet deep, and 25 miles long without a patch of snow—and this in the Antarctic in latitude $77\frac{1}{2}°$ S. By this time we could see the

' snout ' of the glacier just below us.   The slope became too steep for the sledge and at six o'clock we halted to try and find a site for our camp.

Beyond the snout was a wide, bare stony trough, extending many miles to the east.   The lower slopes were strewn with reddish granite boulders.   Here and there on the upper slopes piles of intensely black fragments— for all the world like coal dumps—marked recent lava flows.

Between the serrated crests of the giant cliffs towering five or six thousand feet above us were cascading rivers of ice.   These hanging glaciers spread out in great white lobes over the lower slopes of dark rock, and in some cases the cliffs were so steep that the lower portion of the tributary glacier was fed purely by avalanches falling from the ice fields up above.   And, most amazing of all, not a snow-drift in sight.   It was warm weather most of the time we spent in Dry Valley—rising sometimes above freezing-point—and everywhere streams were tinkling among the black boulders, so much so that this valley, in spite of its name, was certainly the wettest area I saw in Antarctica !

About a mile back from the end of the glacier we made a permanent camp.   We could drag the sledge no further, and I recognised that ' packing ' on our backs was the only way to map this snowless region.

Bare ice surrounded us, forty-foot ice cliffs and a wide ' glacier moat ' separated us from the steep rock slopes. Nowhere could we find a place to stand easily—while it was impossible to pitch the tent.   However, the centre of the glacier was cut up by surface streams into deep gullies whose sunny southern sides were cut into a series of

ALCOVE CAMP IN A SURFACE GULLY OF THE TAYLOR GLACIER

'PACKING' FROM ALCOVE CAMP TO THE SEA

(The Taylor Glacier is in the background ; Wright, Edgar Evans and Debenham are crossing
Lake Bonney)

picturesque alcoves. They were most beautiful specimens of Nature's architecture, the steep walls of clear ice being fretted by the sun into a thousand pilasters and niches. We lowered the sledge down 20 feet into one of these Gothic apses, and found ideal conditions for a sheltered camp. We had a strongly running stream—an inch deep —alongside; and though the wind howled along the surface of the glacier nothing was even disturbed in Alcove Camp.

We spent two days mapping the vicinity, and then started our trek to the sea. We packed up the tent, our sleeping-bags, and five days' food. Our method of march was rather amusing. Wright carried his pack in the Canadian method by a ' tump-line ' round his forehead. He took the theodolite. P.O. Evans wrapped his goods and the tent round the tent poles and proudly carried them like a standard over his shoulder. Debenham copied the Australian swagsman with a bundle in front nearly balancing the main bulk behind. I found, as usual, that a strap over the right shoulder (as used by the Italian harpist) suited my convenience best. Very reluctantly we left our trusty cooker behind, but Debenham carried his camera and half the food, while I bore the remainder and a veritable goldminer's dish, to try for gold in the gravels of Dry Valley.

We marched down a narrow gap, cut through a great bar of granite, and saw ahead of us quite a large lake, some three miles long. It was of course frozen, but through the thick ice covering we could see water plants, and below the steep cliffs the water seemed very deep. We lunched at the east end of the lake—the first of many cold meals, and like all of them consisting chiefly of biscuit and butter, varied by biscuit without butter. However, we had a cake of chocolate each afternoon and a little cheese.

Hereabouts the wide valley was filled with morainic débris, and we passed close to several of the cliff glaciers. I was much surprised to find that the bed of the valley now commenced to rise, for we knew we were approaching the sea. We continued to ascend and could see no way out of the trough. Immediately ahead was a great rock barrier across the valley and evidently several thousand feet high. [*See* Illustration, p. 420.] However, in the next few miles I counted no less than thirteen dead seals which had somehow come up from the coast, and I felt sure we could easily manage anything they could traverse.

Soon we began to open up a narrow defile down the north side of the valley, but this outlet—a sort of notch one thousand feet deep scored in the bottom of the trough—was apparently barred by a tributary cliff glacier.

It was now nearly six o'clock and my shoulder was aching with my pack. Judging from the readiness of the others to drop their loads, I concluded that they felt the same. But we all had an idea that a few minutes later would give us a view of the sea.

We wondered if we could pass around the snout of this wonderful tributary immediately in front. It opposed a face of ice 40 feet high, but just where it butted into the steep (south) slope of the defile there was a gap. So narrow was this that one could almost touch the ice face on one

side and the side of the defile on the other. Through this
we carried our packs ; through this in the other direction
the seals must have laboriously crawled to die far inland.

We could not see the sea, but found the defile occupied
by a frozen lake a mile long. There were dry gravelly
banks around this lake and here we pitched the tent. We
had brought no floor-cloth, but after the wet and icy floor
of the ' Alcove ' camp—where Wright had slept in a pool
of water three inches deep—we found the warm gravel
most comfortable. We had our frugal meal, washed down
by cold water from the lake adjacent. The latter was
distinctly medicinal and had no outlet, so ignoring climatic
differences we unanimously christened it Lake Chad.

I was quite worried to know what had become of the
broad stony valley which Shackleton's men had seen from
the coast in 1908, and wondered if we were side-tracked in
some tributary valley. So after dinner P.O. Evans—who
was always eager for extra work—accompanied me to the
top of the ridge immediately south of the tent. It was a
stiff ascent of 1600 feet to a flat bare expanse obviously
planed by bygone glaciers. To my surprise I saw that a
much larger rounded valley lay immediately north of this
ridge, but this ' Round ' Valley, unlike the defile, did not
connect with the Taylor glacier. To the east some ten
miles beyond a broad débris-strewn plain lay the sea, and
in the far distance we could see the glaciers on the slopes
of Erebus and the pyramid of Beaufort Island.

Early on the 5th Evans and I started for the coast, while
Debenham and Wright investigated the rocks and glaciers
near the defile. We proceeded S.E., passing severa

tributary glaciers, and had to cross many streams running across the plain from the southern wall. We reached a suitable station on the eastern slopes of the Kukri Hills and I took a round of angles with the theodolite which linked Dry Valley to Ross Island. We got back at nine o'clock and found that Debenham had collected many interesting minerals from the marble outcrops of the defile.

Next morning Wright and I ascended the Riegel which so nearly barred the valley. We climbed 2400 feet and then walked to the top of the scarp facing up the valley to the west. So tempestuous was the wind that we could not stand against it, much less use the theodolite. At last there came a lull, and almost before we had the theodolite ready the gale had veered to the east—diametrically opposite—and continued to blow almost as fiercely from that quarter. Our apparent fine weather in the west was, I think, largely due to the fact that there was so little snowfall there; in fact, this region would have been an arid desert even in more favoured climes.

After supper I took the prospecting dish and washed for gold in the gravels alongside the lake. There were numerous quartz ' leads ' in the slates with which metamorphic and eruptive rocks were associated, while water was abundant in Lake Chad. In spite of these favouring conditions neither Debenham nor myself could get a ' colour.' Only a ' tail ' of magnetite in the dish rewarded our perseverance. So we depôted the dish on a boulder in the defile, for we knew that there would be no water available for gold-seeking in the remainder of our journey.

On the 7th we trekked back to Alcove Camp. We lunched below the 'Matterhorn,' one of the most striking peaks in the Western Mountains. It appears to be composed of a cluster of dolerite pinnacles surmounting a pyramid of granite. We took careful angles to ascertain its height, which we estimated at 9000 feet. Great was my astonishment when we plotted our results in the hut to find that our peak was a bare 5000 feet. In the absence of trees or houses or any standards for comparison it was absolutely impossible to estimate any height or distance in these icy regions, and we soon learnt to profoundly mistrust our own guesses and to openly disbelieve anyone else's !

The warmth of the last few days had ruined the Alcove as a camp site. We had much difficulty in finding another. But about 100 yards north in the next deep gully was a patch of moraine exactly like a heap of road-metal. We levelled this as well as we could, and slept none the worse for what P.O. Evans called ' a few feathers in the bed.' I draw a veil over our performance at supper, the first hot meal for nearly a week !

Before we left this region Debenham climbed 2500 feet up the south slope and mapped a great wall of basic lava which clung like a black wart on the glaciated shoulder of the valley. On the opposite side, still higher, we could see a beautiful little crater of the same dark rock, which proved conclusively that the volcanic fires had illumined the glacier since ice had filled the trough to the brim.

We made good speed up the glacier and camped again

at the west end of the Kukri Hills. After supper Wright
and I went over to the great 'glacier moat' which separates
the ice from the granite cliffs. I was very anxious to
see whether there was any evidence of erosion by the
glacier on the cliffs at the foot of the moat.

We carried ice axes and 120 feet of Alpine rope. At
the edge of the glacier there was a sharp curve formed
by a snow cornice. Carefully peering over the edge,
we could see there was a frozen stream about 200 feet
below.

Wright lowered me over the edge—which I found was
formed of soft snow and projected, like the eaves of a
house, about ten feet. Some thirty feet down was a sort
of platform and then the steep edge of the great glacier.

Wright paid out the rope and I let myself down to its
end, about 80 feet above the moat. I started cutting steps
down the remainder, but my ski boots were so worn out
I got no grip, and I reached the moat purely by the force of
gravity. My instruments were luckily not damaged and
I found the depth to be 207 feet, while the moat was
100 feet wide at the bottom. Débris screened the cliff foot
and I could see no planation by the ice.

I managed to cut steps up to the rope and reached the
platform under the cornice. Wright hauled away man-
fully, with the natural but unexpected result that the rope
cut through the snow cornice and his efforts resulted in
my head being enveloped in snow, and there I stopped.
I cried 'Lower away,' reached the platform again, and
crawled along under the cornice, but could see no way out
of the *cul-de-sac*. Gloomily I returned to the rope and

descended to the moat, arriving in exactly the same manner, save that the skin vanished from the knuckles of my left hand this time! However, after tramping some distance north we found a place where the cornice had broken off, and here I was hauled up, my ice axe finding a tender spot in my leg as I reached 'glacier' *firma.*

Our rest was disturbed all night by a sound like continuous volley-firing. This was due to the cooling temperatures causing the glacier to contract and split.

In the forenoon Wright and P.O. Evans explored the ice falls and moraines near Solitary Rocks while Debenham and I walked towards Knob Head. The direction of the moraines revealed the interesting fact that all the ice from the Plateau was moving into Dry Valley and not into the Lower Ferrar as was previously supposed. The Ferrar and Taylor glaciers are 'apposed' glaciers linked like Siamese twins by the col at Knob Head. Originally they were quite distinct, and they will again be separated when the ice has dwindled a little farther.

That evening we discussed literature. P.O. Evans disliked Dickens and Kipling, whom Debenham and I enjoy thoroughly. He preferred a well-known foreign writer whose name he very sensibly pronounced Dum-ass. Our sledging library was quite extensive, for each of us had devoted a pound of our personal allowance to books. I will give the catalogue, if only as a caution to later explorers. Debenham took my Browning and the 'Autocrat'; Evans had a William le Queux and the *Red Magazine*; Wright had two mathematical books, both in German; I took Debenham's Tennyson and three small German books. The *Red Magazine*, the ' Autocrat,' and Browning were most often read ; Evans' contribution being an easy winner. Somehow we didn't hanker after German.

On the 10th we descended 1200 feet down a series of undulations and reached our depôt at Cathedral Rocks. The skua gulls had found the carcase of the Emperor and our chance of a variation in the menu had departed with the gulls.

On the 11th Wright and Debenham carried out a very important operation to determine the movement of the Ferrar Glacier. They fixed stakes right across the glacier which were aligned on two prominent peaks. Some six months later Captain Scott re-measured this line and found that very considerable movement, amounting to 30 feet, had taken place during the winter.

Meanwhile P.O. Evans and I prospected for a route up the steep snow slope of Descent Pass. Evans had been with Armitage when he used this route in 1903. We found the conditions very different. Soon we were sinking nearly two feet at every step in soft snow, through which I knew it would be almost impossible to drag the sledges. The slope soon increased to 11°, so that we found some difficulty in progressing even unencumbered. There I first made the acquaintance of the ' Barrier Shudder.' Every now and then a shiver would shake the surface and we could hear the eerie wave of sound expanding like a ripple all around. Sometimes one could see the whole snow surface sinking slightly, and at first the effect was very unpleasant.

We had been roped for two miles and were still

ascending. We now began to get among crevasses, though few were visible through the thick sheet of snow. Quite suddenly I slipped in to the thigh, and sounding with the ice axe just in front found two inches of snow over the crevasse and very little more behind me. I was evidently standing in a narrow bridge. At the same time Evans called out that he was over another about 15 feet behind, so that for a few moments things were rather involved. He got back on to firmer ground and hauled me back, and when we saw the surface begin to cave in bodily we decided, in Evans' graphic language, to 'give it a miss.'

We seemed to be in the least impossible part of the pass, and I could see plenty worse ahead. So I decided to abandon this route and continue down the Ferrar to Butter Point and so reach the Koettlitz Glacier *via* the Piedmont Glacier.

During our absence Wright had also slipped into a crevasse while fixing the stake nearest Cathedral Rocks. We inspanned after lunch and moved down the glacier to our old camp at the mouth of the Ferrar.

The morning of February 13 was bright and clear. We could see no change in the sea ice filling New Harbour where we had crossed it a fortnight before. I therefore headed south-east towards Butter Point. Here we had an experience that might have ended our journey prematurely.

We got along at a good rate for two miles, when Evans drew my attention to something black sticking up in the ice just ahead.

We had noticed an unusual creaking sound, which

I put down to ice crystals falling, but this strange object demanded investigation. I ran forward a little, and the black spike was obviously the back fin of a killer whale. The creaking was really a warning that the bay ice was on the move. Meanwhile the ice I was on moved off with a jolt, a mark of attention from the killer which we did not appreciate. However, I jumped the three-foot crack which resulted and we hastened to the fixed ice nearly two miles south. It was a case of ' *festina lente.*' We could not drag the heavy sledges more than 2 miles an hour and were continually crossing cracks where the oozy snow and creaking showed how insecure was our passage. Soon after we reached the Butter Point piedmont the whole bay ice moved off in great floes to the northward, so that seven miles of it had broken away since the ship landed us. It is quite impossible to tell whether sea ice is solid or not, for the first cracks are so small and the elevation of the eye so little that the only safe way to traverse sea ice in late summer is to keep off it !

We expected to find the Butter Point piedmont an easy level surface, but of its kind it was the worst I met with down South. All the afternoon we were plugging up an interminable snow slope. Just as one got one's foot braced to draw the sledges through the clinging snow, it would break through a crust and sink nearly to the knee. Then we would meet a few yards of firmer surface and bet whether we could make a dozen steps before the soft ' mullock' started again. Even worse was the jar when you expected deep snow and found a firm crust one inch below the surface. I carried a pedometer, and when

we had done 27,500 of these paces I felt we had earned
our supper.

Blue Glacier now confronted us. **P.O.** Evans and I
prospected across the snout and were glad to find that
though it showed crevasses in places, yet it was so free from
snow that we should have no great difficulty in crossing
them. They curved round parallel to the coast, and of
course lay along the line of our march, so that we came
on to them end-on and fell in several times. But by the
evening of the 15th we were safely camped in the rugged ice
south of the crevassed portion. Evans as usual enlivened
us with navy yarns. He illustrated the kindness of the
sailorman by a story of a mate of his who started a poultry-
farm. To Jack's disgust the ducks in his yard had no
belief in altruism and with their broad bills gave the
hens no chance. ' So,' said Taff Evans, ' evenchooly he
gets a file and trims their bills like the hens, and then
everything went all sprowsy ! '

If anyone had asked us what we should like sent
post haste from civilisation there would have been a
unanimous vell of ' Boots ! ' The rough scrambling over
the rocks and jagged ice of the past fortnight and the
alternate soaking and freezing they had experienced had
ruined mine completely. Deep constrictions formed in
the leather across the toe and behind the ankle and raised
great blisters, and even boils in Debenham's case. I had
no sole on the right foot, but within the next day or so
the temperature fell considerably and the thin leather
lining froze as hard as steel and so protected my foot.
For days a loose boot-nail which had accidentally been

pressed sideways into the sole when it was wet clung like a leech !

Each morning we had a painful ceremony when it was necessary to don our frozen boots. Remarks more fervid than polite flew about the tent, and some of us found that quotations from the poet philosopher lubricated the process.

> '. . . Gritstone,—gritstone a-crumble :
> Clammy squares that sweat, as if the corpse they keep
> Were oozing through '

was supposed to be a very potent incantation. We carried no blacking, but this ceremony was called ' Browning the Boots.'

Open water washed the face of the Blue Glacier. Black snaky heads—reminding me of prehistoric plesiosaurs—could be seen darting about amid the brash ice. They were Emperor penguins, which swim with their bodies submerged.

To the south of us stretched the sea ice, which was evidently rotten and ready to move north. Beyond the Blue Glacier on the right stretched a broad fringe of moraine which extended fairly continuously along the north side of the Koettlitz Glacier. Immediately ahead of us was a fifty-foot ice cliff, but some distance to the south we found a lower place and managed with the Alpine rope to lower the sledges down to the sea ice. We crossed the ' pressure ice '—where great cakes had been up-ended to form a frozen rampart—and reached a good sledging surface at last. Near by was a great pool of water

THE LOWER

Most picturesque in appearance, but as a sledging proposition it can only be described as infernal.' Mount Discovery is visible to the South

containing many seals, where jostling ice pancakes were surging about, so there was obviously no time to lose. We pushed gaily south and camped that night in a little gravelly dell among the moraines.

All night long we could hear the groaning of the sea ice as it ground on the coast : a most melancholy sound, composed of varying notes of which I wrote an analysis in the by no means stilly watches of the night as follows : ' A tiger's growling purr, *plus* the sough and whistle of the wind through a draughty house, with an undercurrent of the creak due to hard breeches rubbing on a new leather saddle.'

On February 17 we arrived at the lower reaches of the Koettlitz Glacier. For the lower twenty-five miles this great ice-river rises but little above sea level. But what a river ! South of the Dailey Isles, where it merges with the Great Ice Barrier, it is ten miles wide. A region of icy pinnacles and bastions, of lakes and winding gullies, as if a storm-lashed sea had suddenly been clutched in the grip of King Frost. Most picturesque in appearance, but as a sledging proposition it can only be described as infernal !

Soon after leaving the sea ice we plunged into a maze of ' glass-house ' and ' bottle-glass ' ice, whose names almost explain themselves. The former were great curved platforms often thirty feet wide, which threw us all together in the middle and then dropped us several feet through the ' glass ' into a pool of water beneath. The ' bottle-glass ' was due to the sun melting the ice ripples into a thousand spikes and edges which received us when we fell—which happened every few minutes.

Finally we sledged along the ' lower storey ' below the glass-house surface—on the floor of the drained lakes ; twisting round ice pillars, pulling the sledges under sheets of projecting ice, lifting them over barriers. But it got worse instead of better, and at last I decided to return to the land and make our depôt here instead of higher up the Koettlitz, as I had hoped to do. To reach the moraine we had to cross a sort of ' rip ' where a strong deep current of water flowed northward. Along this seals used to appear and would stop to study our movements with some interest.

This camp on the moraine marked the end of the third week. We celebrated it by killing a seal, and next day fried his liver. This was also a memorable day because, as someone remarked, I started cooking and we all lived through it !

I cut off a piece of the seal's belly-skin and sewed pieces over my worn-out boots. It wasn't a very neat job, for it was done with a marlin spike and waxed yarn— but as soon as I started walking the soft seal-skin changed to armour-plate, and when ultimately I wanted to remove these ' brogans ' I had to break them off with my geological hammer.

We spent two days exploring the very interesting region behind the moraines. Long parallel valleys, each containing a dwindling valley glacier, led towards the scarp below the Royal Society Range. Thirteen thousand feet above us towered Mount Lister, but we rarely saw the crest, for it was buried in clouds for the greater part of our journey.

On the 20th we left one sledge at the depôt and made another attempt to penetrate the fastnesses of the Koettlitz Glacier.

We had to cut tracks along the bottom ot the glass-house channels, and Debenham and I pulled while Wright and Evans devoted all their energies to lifting the sledge over the obstructions. The sledge dropped two feet and rolled upside down on one occasion, and later Wright went through the roof and was completely lost to sight in one of the glass-houses. By 6 P.M. we must have progressed almost two miles—and this with a light load! A thick snowstorm came up and we camped amid weird surroundings. All round us were ice sculptures of every conceivable shape. There were great wedge-shaped blocks, so fretted by the sun that they looked as if formed of wicker work. We called these 'fascines.' Others resembled giant pedestal-tables with fringes of icicles. Near the tent, displayed on one of these tables, was a great white monster with an armour-plated back, head, legs, and tail complete. We called this halt 'Armadillo Camp' in recognition of the genius of King Frost.

During the next four days we struggled up the middle of the Koettlitz Glacier. It was a strenuous time, but I recall a pleasant noon halt when P.O. Evans earned an honest penny. We saw him playing with the rope which lashed his sleeping-bag. Says Evans, 'I'll show you how to make a clove-hitch with one hand, and I bet you a 1s. 3d. dinner (our usual currency) you can't do it after you've seen me do it six times!' Debenham took the bet, and we all watched Evans closely. Then 'Deb' tried, and to

our joy succeeded, for the ‚handy-man was rarely ' done.'
But he never turned a hair, and booked the bets that now
filled the air. Again Debenham proceeded to try, and
failed—and Wright and I were equally unsuccessful.
Evans made quite a haul, but after saying he had never
seen anyone do it by sheer luck before, he proceeded to
teach us the dodge ; and later Debenham became quite
a knot-master under his willing tuition.

' A fine sunny morning, the first for many days.
Even this scene of desolation looks cheerful.' Thus
my sledge diary for the 21st. But the route did not improve. I wrote : ' We got going on awful stuff—rounded
pools of ice, between tables. It got worse and worse,
and after many bumps and leaps and falls I decided to
prospect. We had done half a mile in the hour. . . . We
started again about 3 P.M. Awful heavy work over
" glass-house " and leaping three-foot chasms, between
high fascines and across decomposing rivers of ice.'

About 4.30 we saw a ragged piece of skin projecting
from under an ice-table and found that it was part of a
large fish. We spent half an hour chipping it out and
recovered the dorsal spines, skin, tail, and the vertebræ.
These were preserved in a yellow fatty substance smelling
like vaseline and quite soft. I made rather a ludicrous
mistake here. I carefully preserved a very hard irregular
mass coated with this flesh, thinking it was a bone, but
later, after we had carried it for days on the sledge, we
found that this ' pelvic bone ' as we called it—melted
in warm water ! No head was found, and in this respect
the fish—which was possibly about four feet long—agrees

with the four large headless fish found by the *Discovery* Expedition. We had a hot discussion in the hut as to this problem of decapitation, but came to no definite conclusion, for it seemed too far for seals to carry it.

That night we slept at Park Lane Camp. We had been traversing a frozen park, set out in circular beds with winding paths in every direction. The 'flower beds' were represented by elevated masses of ice thirty feet across, exactly like an apple-pie with a raised crust—even to the four cuts made by the housewife across the top! The last two days we had only progressed seven miles, and for five of them we had carried the sledge rather than dragged it. [*See* Illustration, p. 422.]

Next day, however, we found that to the south the glacier was nearly continuous. It had not been dissected by thaw-waters to nearly the same extent, and by 4 P.M. we managed to advance ten miles to the south-west. We camped on a platform of weathered ice, so rotten that it resembled a layer of honeycomb. We found that this honeycomb ice was very common in this part of the Koettlitz.

We tried to find an easier way out of the numerous undulations which now characterised the surface, but unsuccessfully, and so plugged on south-west. We used to 'pully-haul' up one side (i.e. hand over hand) and then toboggan down the other. P.O. Evans was an expert steersman, while we others used to keep the ropes clear. But we had some nasty falls, especially Evans, who got a cut deep in his palm from a piece of 'bottle-glass' ice, in spite of his thick mitts.

VOL. II.

At noon we came across a picturesque tunnel in the
ice, about three feet wide, seven feet high, and one hundred
feet long. It had been cut out by thaw waters which had
now drained away.

In and out wound the lanes, forming a regular network
through all sorts of picturesque pinnacles. Here was one
like a yacht on stocks, there a perfect wedding-cake
twelve feet high, again a lady's bonnet, and so on in infinite
variety. At close of day we pitched Camp Labyrinth.

On the 24th we emerged from the pinnacles and
reached the coast moraines again near Heald Island.
Here I decided to make our terminal camp. In a gravelly
hollow we pitched the tent and next morning was devoted
to a 'make and mend.' All our sleeping-bags and finnesko were wet with the sloppy ice-floors of the last week—
for we had not been able to find any snow-drifts on which
to camp. They are much warmer and drier than ice.

Behind the tent to the north were slopes about 1000
feet high leading to empty 'hanging' valleys. These
radiated from the base of the Lister scarp, which rose
in one steep face 10,000 feet to the summit. This face
was pitted by gigantic cup valleys or, as they are technically
called, cwms, and presented a spectacle which probably
could be paralleled nowhere in the world.

Looking southward across the Koettlitz from the
mouth of one of these hanging valleys one could see
some sort of plan in the icy maze which had so bewildered
us. Above Heald Island the valley was filled with the
glacial stream in a normal uniform mass, interrupted only
by crevasses and falls. But to the east of Heald Island

[See p. 211

THE KOETTLITZ GLACIER, JUST NORTH OF HEALD ISLAND, SHOWING ICE
PINNACLES, ETC., NEARLY ONE HUNDRED FEET HIGH

it took the form of a glacier ' delta.'   Below the falls the
ice descended to the east in a series of broad undulations,
a portion of which we had traversed on the 23rd.   Long
promontories of ice fifty feet high extended from the
unbroken glacier mass and probably represented the
crests of the undulations.   These degenerated at the ends
into icebergs and monoliths of ice, and these again had
weathered into the bastions and pinnacles.   Lower down
the thaw waters had etched these into still smaller units,
and along the coast just below me the streams had formed
a well-defined if narrow avenue of smooth ice, which
promised us an easier return.

On these slopes I found an ice-scratched block—the
only specimen I had seen in a hundred miles of moraine
débris !

I returned to the tent along the margin of the glacier
and was amazed to see seal tracks in the fresh snow.   We
were over twenty miles from the sea and had not seen any
possible route for seals on our outward journey.   Yet here
were two seals—asleep as usual—on the old glacier ice.   I
disturbed one of them to see what it would do.   He
sneezed and grunted at me.   When I teased him further
he began to warble !   I heaved a lump of ice at him, where-
upon he lolloped twenty yards to a wet patch, lay over on
his side, and produced a whole octave of musical notes from
his chest, ranging up to a canary-like chirrup.   Finally
he crawled under a deep ledge, and vigorously butting with
his shoulders, opened out a hole and flopped under the
avenue ice.

I soon reached camp and found that Wright and

Debenham had both met parties of seals. We all thought of the constant stream along the tide crack by our last depôt and came to the conclusion that this was largely fresh water and formed the main drainage of the Upper Koettlitz. By this sub-glacial stream the seals penetrated nearly thirty miles inland up the Koettlitz Glacier.

On the 26th we crossed the glacier to Heald Island— which projected a thousand feet above the glacier and separated it into two streams of ice. While Debenham collected garnets and other interesting minerals, I climbed the island and sketched the topography up the glacier.

In the silts amid the ice we found large sponges and a fungus-like alga. The sponge must have been brought up by the ice from marine waters at some period far back in history. The alga had probably grown in a glacier pond, since drained away.

Next day we marched twelve miles west to explore a large tributary glacier which we could see across the low-level lateral moraine. After crossing two miles of moraine we suddenly came on a steep gully about 100 feet deep, at the bottom of which was a strongly flowing stream. This originated in a lake three-quarters of a mile long, but for a considerable distance flowed under the moraine, and ultimately entered the seals' sub-glacial stream and so reached the sea. Coleridge's lines entered one's mind :

> 'Where Alph the sacred river ran
> Through caverns measureless to man
> Down to a sunless sea.'

So we christened this stream the Alph River.

ICE CRYSTALS ON THE ROOF OF A CAVE AT THE HEAD OF
THE ALPH RIVER

A STEEP GULLY CUT BY THE ALPH RIVER THROUGH THE ANCIENT
LATERAL MORAINE OF THE KOETTLITZ GLACIER

We marched along the lake and up the gully beyond. Here a tributary entered from a large cave in the moraine wall to the north. The roof of this cave was coated with most beautiful ice crystals, which resembled pine twigs in shape and were about two inches long. Many brownish ice stalactites and stalagmites fringed the walls of the cave, and Wright was lucky in obtaining some beautiful photos of these structures.

At 4 P.M. we reached our goal—the steep face of the Walcott glacier, but as the weather looked stormy we had to retreat immediately. Wright and I compared compass readings here. The needles swung extremely sluggishly, but we found they were reliable to four degrees—which is about eight times the ordinary error. The fact that magnetic south was nearly due north also complicated matters here! We marched back by a different route and discovered a strong outcrop of basic lava about fifty feet thick which was rich in olivine and had caught up fragments of garnet rock in its passage through the earth's crust.

The month of March opened with a bright sunny morning, just suited for our proposed climb up one of the hinterland ranges. We climbed up the slope about eight hundred feet and so reached the level floor of the 'hanging valley' just behind the camp. We marched along this to the north end of the valley towards a prominent peak on the eastern ridge. A stiff climb over snow slopes and rugged granite led to the summit, which we reached at 1 P.M. The aneroid made this 3000 feet above sea level. It was a beautiful day and we could see Erebus,

Discovery, Morning, and the Pyramid up the Koettlitz.
Lister itself, as usual, was in the clouds, but nearly all
below was visible. We could see numerous hinterland
ridges reaching from the Lower Koettlitz to the Lister
scarp, and satisfied ourselves that no lateral ' Snow
Valley' existed below the scarp such as has been indicated
in earlier maps.

It was very cold on this hill (which we called Terminus
Mountain) ; and after swinging the theodolite and taking
several photographs we hurried back to the tent down
Ward Valley.

On March 2 we started our homeward trek ; nothing
could be worse than our outward track up the middle of
the glacier—though we were able to study the changes
of the glacier ice and so did not regret it. I therefore
decided to hug the coast on our return, though near the
depôt the ice was so full of silt from the moraines that we
had not seen any feasible route along the coast thereabouts.

For the next few days we followed the course of the
sub-glacial Alph river. Some four miles down stream
from Terminus Camp a rampart of ice pinnacles commenced, which recalled the monoliths of Stonehenge.
These walled off the rough sea of the Koettlitz Glacier from
the frozen surface of the ' river.' This broad lane was here
a quarter of a mile wide and consisted of a level surface
broken up by deep sunken ' paths.' The more elevated
areas were preferable for sledging, for the paths occasionally
let us through into water. The whole structure was due
to the drainage of water away from rivers and lakelets
whose surface had frozen.

Mt. Dromedary Mt. Huggins

THE SOUTH-WEST END OF ALPH AVENUE, SHOWING OUR RETURN ROUTE BETWEEN THE ICE
PINNACLES AND THE MORAINE

This splendid track—which we called ' Alph Avenue '
—enabled us to proceed with unexpected ease, and each
day we halted and explored one of the numerous tributary
valleys which characterised the hinterland.

Each valley was of the same type. A great bar of
débris—a terminal moraine in fact—some three hundred
feet high blocked the mouth of the tributary. Within this
was a bare rounded valley extending to the foot of Lister.
Some five miles from the coast was the snout of a tributary
glacier which had originally deposited the moraine, but now
was shrunk back to a mere shadow of its former self.

All along our route were groups of seals, and numerous
skua gulls enlivened the surroundings. Coming back from
one of our détours I was much amused to see Wright
crawling about among the seals in his investigation of
the ice—while thirty skuas were anxiously awaiting the
demise of this obviously crazy seal !

The summer was over now and we were getting fifty
degrees of frost in the nights. The weather was gloomy,
the sun rarely appearing till it had sunk below the level of
the pall of stratus.

We had an eventful lunch just before reaching our
depôt. We pitched the tent and fastened the door to keep
out the wind. I was sitting next the door with my precious
lumps of sugar on the floorcloth when I noticed that water
was creeping into the tent. In a few seconds it was
several inches deep. We bolted our raisins, pocketed the
lumps of butter and sugar and rushed out with the sleeping-
bags. There was a small lake all round us, rapidly rising
round sledge and tent. The water was rushing out of a

crack one hundred yards below us, probably driven back by a high tide. We had quite a pilgrimage to get our sledge packed again, having to walk round the newly formed bay.

The avenue petered out here, after furnishing us with a magnificent highway for twenty miles. We had some pretty rough work for the next mile or so, but reached our depôt safely on the evening of the 5th. We had a fine feed of seal liver fried in blubber. Debenham was cook and P.O. Evans was frankly sceptical as to the result. He took his whack gingerly, but handsomely acknowledged it tasted much better than in *Discovery* days. We turned over the fry with my bowie knife and found that safety-pins made excellent forks.

On the 6th we started across the head of McMurdo Sound to reach Ross Island. We had now two sledges to pull, but the surface was good and we soon approached the Dailey Isles. We made an interesting discovery here. All around were heaps of large sponges—a foot in diameter—buried in snow and ice. Among the long spicules we found Bryozoa, Brachiopoda, Serpulæ, mollusca, and a fine ' solitary ' coral.

That evening we climbed West Dailey Isle—a mass of volcanic lava 600 feet high—to try to see the extent of open water. The head of McMurdo Sound is occupied by a broad wedge of pinnacle ice about twelve miles wide at its base. It was necessary either to cross this or go right round it. We had had such heavy work with one light sledge that the latter route seemed the best, even though it was more than twice the distance.

For the next two days we marched north—almost the opposite direction from our destination at Hut Point. At noon halt we found that Debenham had two toes frostbitten—owing to a tight boot—but with rubbing they came back all right. We camped at the edge of the Pinnacles, which here were over thirty feet high and separated by deep gullies filled with snags, glass-house, and all manner of obstructions.

Next day we moved along the edge of the Pinnacles, which led us towards Butter Point, much to our disgust. During the forenoon we had heard weird ' blowings ' on our right, but it was rather a shock to come on a great bay in the Pinnacle ice, where the latter had recently broken off, and to see our friends the killer whales cruising around only 100 yards ahead ! We had to turn at once and march willy-nilly into the Pinnacles, so as to put a little distance between ourselves and the recent break of ' Orca Bay.'

Before going many yards into the Pinnacles we came on a ' river ' of salt water, fifty feet or so below the general level. Luckily the pancake ice from Orca Bay had jammed in this ' river ' and it was strong enough to carry the sledges. We hauled them hand over hand up the further bank.

After lunch we came to a fifteen-foot drop and we had of course to adopt relaying. Either Debenham or myself went ahead as quickly as possible and found a route by climbing pinnacles or bastions. The other three pulled the smaller sledge as indicated by the guide. After a mile or so we all went back and pulled the heavy sledge up to the other.

Next day passed in the same way, but we were cheered

by the sight of a patch of smooth surface ahead of us. Though only four miles off it took us nearly two days to reach it. Bad sandy patches delayed us and ruined the runners. On returning with the second sledge we could often see what looked like wisps of yellow tobacco in the lee of the jagged points of ice. These were long filaments of ash torn from our unfortunate runners.

So passed Edgar Evans' birthday, in honour of which we had some superfine chocolates which seemed in some way to bring us in touch with civilisation again.

At noon on the 10th we reached sea ice again beyond the Pinnacles and had good hopes of reaching Hut Point by night, for it was only a little over ten miles away. I wrote in my diary : ' The surface got so much better that we decided to get to Hut Point or bust! About 5 P.M. we decided to bust, for there was five miles of water between us and the hut. So we deviated with what speed we might to the south, gradually veering in the teeth of a young blizzard.'

In the morning we could see frost smoke rising from the water apparently for miles right across our track. In place of reaching the hut in one day we evidently had a long détour to make to get around the open water. We called this place ' Camp Had Again ' for obvious reasons, and started off, after digging out the sledges and tent, once more directly away from our objective.

We pulled six miles south before lunch, leaving Hut Point behind us on the left. The end of the great bay seemed in sight now and I felt justified in bearing east a little. We were only half a mile from the water when we came on sledge tracks, and these puzzled us greatly. We thought they must have been made by a depôt party but could see no depôt. I wrote ' It is not possible it has gone out, as undoubtedly some of the Barrier has ? '

As a matter of fact these were the tracks of the rescue party who had tried to save the ponies when Bowers, Cherry-Garrard, and Crean went adrift only ten days before. In view of our experiences the next few days I was glad we did not know of this disaster.

A strong drift was blowing when we broke camp, but we could see the sun and had bearings, so we moved round the open water to the north. After two miles we saw something black which turned out to be a fodder depôt. We built it up, for it was nearly invisible, and left a note for the Depôt Party, which was waste labour, for they had all returned a week before.

The wind increased in force, but we kept on till noon, when we came to open water and a great crack in the Barrier. Here the surface rose several feet quite sharply and Wright nearly slipped in as we were crossing. The drift was getting very much worse and we could see nothing a few yards ahead. I felt this was a bad position and turned inland ; we pulled about three-quarters of an hour and could not get any farther through the blinding snow. We managed to pitch the tent and then sat down to wait till the blizzard would let us move somewhere less exciting and farther from the breaking edge of the Barrier. Here, however, we stopped all through the next day and until ten on the third day.

It was the worst blizzard I experienced while sledging

in the South, and in consequence my sledge diary is rather
scrappy. I wrote : ' Finally decided to have an early
supper and turn into our wet bags. We lit the primus
and let the flame singe our feet to warm them. Talked of
Cambridge cakes and teas and other delights. Evans
told a cheerful tale of the snow round the tent at Cape
Crozier which pinned them in for five days in September
1903 ! We can't see 100 feet anywhere. The rime is
dripping down my neck and covering our bags. Drifts
are slipping off the tent. Wind veering somewhat
southerly from south-east. Now and again we peep
out of the door, but no improvement. Couldn't get on
to the shore probably to camp, as the water is evidently
exceptionally far to the east. . . . Guess we 'll shiver it
out. The booming of the lid of the biscuit tin outside
is like the Inchcape Bell !

The next day was much the same, but though the
blizzard blew as strong as ever, driving the drift in great
sheets into the open sound, yet I felt that as we had got
through one day and night all right, so we should the
next ; which is very common if unscientific logic !

On the 14th it lulled a bit by 10 A.M., and as we knew
the direction I decided to make for Castle Rock. The
blizzard had piled a long snow slope in the lee of our tent,
100 feet to the north-west of the sledges. We dug out
the sledges and packed the gear, and then marched out,
the wind helping us materially.

I anticipated some trouble from the tide crack next the
land which P.O. Evans had crossed in 1903. However, all
was lost to view in the mist of drift, though we seemed

to be ascending. Nevertheless, we could see Castle Rock at intervals, and steered by that. I thought we must have crossed the tide crack unknowingly, when the sun appeared and showed us we were one-third of the way up the promontory! With its customary irrationality Antarctica had decided to dispense with a tide crack in 1911, though the next expedition will probably find a chasm fifty feet deep where the Barrier presses on Ross Island.

We joyfully had lunch, transferred all necessaries to the big sledge, and pulled up the 1000 feet to Castle Rock, which we reached in two hours. We had a short rest and then proceeded to tackle the last two miles which lay along the crest of the promontory. Here I saw Evans over-cautious for the first time, but I can well understand his feelings. This was March 14, and on the same day in 1903, after a heavy blizzard, he and his mates were in the same spot trying to reach the hut. They went astray in the drift, and poor Vince lost his footing and slipped down Danger Slope into the sea.

However, there was no drift at this height, and we proceeded easily enough past Castle Rock and got on to the broad ridge beyond. After a mile or so we saw four men over toward Crater Heights. A great sight; though it was comic to see them marching in a row in their swollen wind-clothes. Except for their swinging arms, they looked to us just like a row of the Emperor penguins we had seen in New Harbour. They were Wilson, Bowers, Atkinson, and Cherry-Garrard. These told us the news and took charge of our sledge, while I went off and made my report to Captain Scott.

CHAPTER II

THE GEOLOGICAL EXPEDITION TO GRANITE HARBOUR

DURING January, February, and March 1911 the Western Geological Party had investigated the coast and hinterland south of Cape Bernacchi to Mt. Discovery. Captain Scott decided that this survey should be continued northward to Granite Harbour and that special attention should be given to the hinterland at this locality, if we could find a track up the ice falls of the Mackay Glacier.

His sledging instructions to me commence as follows : 'The objects of your journey have been discussed and need not here be particularised. In general they comprise the geological exploration of the coast of Victoria Land.

'Your party will consist of Debenham, Gran, and Forde ; and you will cross the Sound on or about October   . [Date not filled in.—G. T.]

'You will depart from Butter Point with provision as under :—

'11 weeks' pemmican,

'10 gallons oil,

'18 weeks' remainder food articles,

'25 lbs. cooking fat,

and make along the coast to Granite Harbour. You

THE SECOND WESTERN PARTY THE DAY THEY WERE PICKED UP BY THE SHIP

Taylor, Debenham, Gran, and Forde

will leave at Butter Point 2 weeks' provision for your party for use in case you are forced to retreat along the coast late in the season, and for the same eventuality you will depôt a week's provision at Cape Bernacchi.

' On arrival in Granite Harbour you will choose a suitable place to depôt the main bulk of your provision.

' As the commanding officer of the *Terra Nova* has been referred to the Bluff Headland shown in the photograph on page 154 " Voyage of the *Discovery* " as the place near which you are likely to be found, it is obviously desirable that your depôt should be in this vicinity.

' I approve your plan to employ your time thereafter approximately as follows :

' During what remains of the first fortnight of November in exploring north of Granite Harbour.

' During the last fortnight of November in exploring south of Granite Harbour.'

It was originally intended that we were to have the honour of starting the ' long trails ' during the second summer.   But owing to an unfortunate accident Debenham injured his knee, and when the time came for our start he was quite unable to leave his bunk.   The motor party left and then the Pole party.   We had probably a month's sledging on the sea ice ahead of us—and we knew that the ice might break up and float north early in December, so that it became a serious question how long I could delay the start.   On the 5th Gran, Forde, and I pulled our heavy sledge beyond the great shear crack (2½ miles) and left it there.

On November 7 Dr. Simpson, Debenham, Nelson and

myself held a council. We decided that Debenham could not do anything safely for a week. If he tried to hobble along his leg would never improve and it would probably lame him for life. Nelson very kindly volunteered to take Debenham's place and help us across to Butter Point with our sledges. Then we would return by Friday night, when we trusted to find Debenham able to start.

We pushed off at 9.45 with the small sledge, and in about an hour picked up the other, and then our troubles began. We found that we could only just drag the two along at the rate of about one mile an hour. We were all pretty soft after the winter and as usual found the first day or two extra special hard work. Crossing the thicker snow drifts the sledge runners stuck so much that the waistbelt on which one pulled seemed to dislocate one's pelvis !

At one o'clock we were only 4½ miles from the hut. As we were pitching the lunch camp the drift was rising rapidly and before we could get the tent properly fixed a blizzard was upon us. Everything was soon obliterated. At first I thought I could see the Western Mountains 30 miles away, but later found out that I was gazing at a snow ' pressure ridge ' about ten yards off !

Let us look round the tent and see how we have profited by the previous season's sledging. In the roof is a larger ventilator. This, strangely enough, keeps us drier—for the steam from the cooker escapes instead of condensing on the bags and tent. By special request our floorcloth is eighteen inches wider, and now our cameras and instruments do not get buried in snow as heretofore. But greatest blessing of all is an ordinary scrubbing-brush. This lies just inside the door where a man may reach in and find it—brush himself free from loose snow outside the tent, then brush his boots when inside the tent, and finally sweep the floorcloth. It was wonderful what a difference this made to our comfort—for previously any little mass of snow first melted on one's body or bag and then froze into a cake of ice which had to be re-melted before one was warm enough to sleep.

Our chance of a rapid journey to Butter Point soon became very slender. The snow drifted nearly to the peak of the tent and drove in the windward side as a great swelling bulge. The sledges were soon covered a foot deep. There we lay ' all that day ' and read and talked and snoozed till 7.30 next morning.

On the 8th we had done over 3 miles by lunch time and could see the cracks in the glacier of Butter Point so clearly that it seemed only five miles off. But it was a long twenty l

In the afternoon we did three more stages until we had been on the go for eleven hours. Eight miles seemed a poor result for such an expenditure of energy.

At 4 o'clock on Thursday we were twenty-three miles from the Hut. It was gloomy weather, but the surface had not been so soft and we still hoped to reach Butter Point. However, we saw the sky darkening to south'ard. Gradually Minna Bluff vanished, then Erebus clouded over, Castle Rock disappeared, and we knew that another blizzard was upon us.

This time it lasted 36 hours. Early on Saturday morning I could just see the Western Mountains. The drift covered the door and of course the sledges were buried. We put up a depôt flag and started back at 4.30 A.M. for headquarters. We had now only the sleeping-bags, cooker, tent, and one day's food. But owing to the surface, that 23 miles was stiff going. I thought we should be in by noon, but it took us just twelve hours to reach the dead penguins and refuse which unavoidably characterise the vicinity of Cape Evans.

I note that we immediately rushed the cook, and that the menu consisted of soup, rissoles and fruit tart, of which I had three extra helps and still felt hungry!

Debenham's leg had not improved much, but we decided to start with him on Tuesday (14th) and Nelson (and Anton) again volunteered to help us along, and if necessary they could fetch Debenham back.

It blizzed till 3 P.M. on Tuesday. We could then just see the Western Mountains and it seemed useless to wait longer. There was a great barrier of stranded bergs off the Cape, and in the lee of these several miles of clear ice—swept by the blizzards—appeared. The wind blew so strongly behind us that Debenham was able to ease his leg by sitting on the sledge. We managed six miles before night. Next day we were half-way across the Sound. On Thursday (16th) it was very thick. Large 'fluff-balls' of snow were falling, but there was little wind. I felt justified in pushing off and trying to steer by the compass, for we could only see about 200

MOULTING PENGUIN

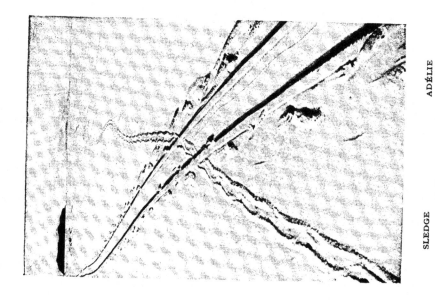

SLEDGE   P N   ADÉLIE

yards ahead. Debenham walked behind the sledge with the compass as near S. 65° W. (mag.) as he could keep it. Forde and Nelson glanced back to see his signals, and I tried to sight bits of ice pinnacle in our line ahead. It was eerie work. No sound, no sight, just gray-white mist enveloping us. Behind, Debenham's black figure— in front, a sheet of white with a few dark patches, any of which might be a small lump of ice ten yards off or a huge pressure ridge 200 yards away !

After several miles of this blindfold work, we were wondering how we were getting on—for the compass is by no means reliable so near the magnetic pole. Suddenly we realised Crusoe's sensations more closely than ever before. We were over twenty miles from the hut and there for the first time saw our footprints of the previous week ! Nelson offered a reward of his raisins for the man who saw the depôt first, and Anton soon won them. We reached our sledge at 2 P.M. and all six lunched merrily in our tent. Anton enlivened the meal by giving us a Russian groom's opinions on marriage in very broken English.

The passing of this blizzard was a beautiful sight. Gradually the solid billows of gloomy cloud drifted to the north, leaving a brilliant blue sky. The straight edge of the storm nimbus was fringed with mackerel cloud as if a great grey curtain were being drawn away from the glorious snow-clad mountains of the west.

We reached Butter Point on the evening of the 17th. About 300 yards up the snow slope is the depôt which has been used by all the Western Parties since 1903. Here we found the boxes left for us by Captain Scott in September. We dragged up the small sledge and loaded it with meal, cocoa, sugar, and pemmican. Then on the second trip we dragged down 330 lbs. of biscuit.

Then we had a busy time in the two tents opening pemmican and cocoa tins and sorting food. When Forde and Gran repacked the two sledges we had over 1200 lbs. to drag along.

Load of the Western Geological Party

' Tent ' sledge		
' Biscuit ' sledge		
Boots, stove, crampons		
Sleeping-bags (4)		
Personal gear (4)		
Tent, cooker, &c.	35	
	——	285
Theodolite	12	
Cameras and plates	30	
Repair bag, &c.	5	
Geological tools, &c..	15	
Shovel and ice axes (3)	16	
	——	78
Food, &c. (14 weeks), at 56 lbs. a week, less 4 weeks' pemmican	744	
Oil	100	
	——	844
Total		1207

and a less load I knew we should have a hard task when
Nelson and Anton left us.

We left Butter Point on the 18th, and after seeing us
well started the ' Convoy Commando ' exchanged farewells.
We gave them three cheers and Nelson and sturdy little
Anton marched steadily across to Cape Royds, thirty miles
away. Henceforth for over three months we were left
to our own devices. We were now really starting, although
the relaying to date had almost totalled a hundred miles,
in all of which Nelson's assistance had been invaluable.

So we moved off, Debenham linking in ; for to our
great joy his leg was certainly not worse for its drastic
treatment. The sun was bright and we wore amber or
green glasses. Through them the snow looked like the
rippled sand at the mouth of a shallow river. Forde
turned out in an Antarctic Panama with a brim slightly
less than a yard wide. Gran and Debenham had felt
hats with ear flaps. I just tied my felt hat down à la
coal scuttle until it was too cold, and then we had to wear
our ' balaclava ' helmets.

Now we started a fortnight's relaying. Weary work
at best, but when the course lies on sea-ice—which may
go out any day—and your retreat is barred by a vertical
ice-barrier thirty feet high, an anxious time as well.

We now started a regular routine of five stages a day.
After breakfast we packed the sledges and left the ' biscuit '
sledge flagged at our camp. Then pushed on about a mile
with the ' tent ' sledge. Flagged that and tramped back
to the other. Pulled it to the ' tent ' sledge and then
rested five minutes and criticised the Antarctic generally

and the snow surface more particularly ! So that in about two hours we had shifted our half ton a whole mile, and walked three in doing it. Then on again for another mile with the tent sledge. Here we pitched the lunch camp. Debenham boiled the tea and got the tent fixed while we three brought up the lighter biscuit sledge. In the afternoon we managed three of these stages, Debenham as before having the tent ready when we brought in the last sledge.

On November 20 we reached Cape Bernacchi. It was an awful surface. We crossed a layer of loose ice crystals in which one sometimes sank to the knee. Debenham's knee got a very painful wrench so that he could do no relaying. However, he started the plane table survey which he carried on throughout the whole journey—thus producing by far the most detailed sledge map of any part of Victoria Land.

We left a depôt of one week's stores here, as ordered by Captain Scott. We stuck a bright tin on the pole (as well as the flag) which shows up well when the sun is bright.

The outlook was not promising. Ahead of us was a wide bay filled with screw-pack. This is sea ice which has been jammed haphazard on to the coast. Many of the upturned blocks were eight feet high. Snow had fallen on this surface and filled in some of the hollows, and a more inviting man-trap or leg-breaker it would be difficult to imagine. However, by next day's noon we were through the worst of it. It was such hurried, tiring work that we had no leisure for photography. There was a quaint

THE WILSON PIEDMONT GLACIER, SHOWING THE CONTINUOUS ICE CLIFFS. THEY ARE A MILE
DISTANT FROM THE SLEDGE, WHICH IS ON SEA-ICE

[See p. 238

SHOWING THE CAMP OFF THE PIEDMONT TONGUE

COULOIR CLIFFS

spoor standing up in relief two inches above the snow
and made by an Emperor penguin, of which I should have
much liked a stereo-photo.

On the 21st we came up to an old friend. Nearly filling
a small bay was a giant berg about two miles long with
a black spot near the north-east corner. This was the
end of Glacier Tongue which had broken away on March 1
in the big gale and settled down fifty miles or so away on
the other side of the Sound.

The fodder depôt had been left on the tongue by Oates
in January and served as a useful survey mark. Our
best route lay within this mass of transported ice. It
was a good omen that there were some twenty seals
basking off the cape, for we knew we should have to live
largely on seal meat during our stay at Granite Harbour.

As we pulled under the thirty-foot ice cliffs of the broken
Tongue we could see remarkable snow folds apparent in
some fresh sections—which tend to show that much of it
had grown *in situ* (in its former position) from snow
cornices and drift rather than from mainland ice. .

The mainland shore was now almost wholly covered
by the southern portion of the huge piedmont glacier
which extends in an unbroken ' Chinese Wall ' of ice to
Granite Harbour. It was an imposing sight and an ugly
one to a sledging party travelling over the sea ice—for as
one moves north there are fewer and fewer places where it
can be ascended, and its thirty-foot barrier affords a poor
lee in time of trouble. This piedmont was moulded
over hill and dale in an alternation of icy dimples and
pimples, but several rounded domes and ridges projected

as Nunatakker—or *Nunakoller* as I prefer to term these *smoothed* rock outcrops, for *tak* means a peak.

The next morning (22nd) we had to cross a bay about six miles wide. As we lugged our heavy sledge close to the numerous seals they would raise their heads and gaze superciliously at us, then roll over on the other side and go off to sleep again ; no doubt much preferring their own lot in life.

Returning from the first trip we felt a strong southerly wind. I decided to try our sail as the wind was dead behind us and as there was no drift.

Forde superintended the rigging of our ice-yacht. The mast consisted of four of the tent poles, the other two going across and forming yards. The leather ' bucket ' uniting the poles formed a sort of pulley over which the main halyard was passed. Two sheets to the poop (as I suppose the rear of the sledge yacht should be called) kept the sail steady. These terms are probably not used in their strict nautical sense !

We had a great job to start the two sledges—for as usual after waiting a short time the runners froze to the surface. However, Debenham ' broke her out,' the sail filled, and when we once got going we found the half-ton quite manageable.

We felt we were progressing at racing speed when we accomplished a mile in forty-five minutes with both sledges, which before had taken two hours. But needless to say we had to pull with all our strength at the same time, though the wind must have almost accounted for one of the sledges. The miles piled up and we did 6½ geographical miles by 7 P.M., instead of 4½ by 9 P.M. as heretofore.

Between two bergs we had to cross a 'working' crack several feet wide. We were much amused at the efforts of a young seal which was baa-ing loudly and trying to climb a huge mountain eight inches high !

We reached Dunlop Island at noon the next day, helped by the wind and sail. There was a strait about a quarter of a mile wide separating it from the mainland cape. This strait consisted of blue glassy ice covered in narrow belts by thin wettish salty snow. This next mile led to the worst language I think I heard on any sledge journey ! My journal states : ' The wind drove the whole 1200 lbs. across the ice, while our combined efforts, almost bursting blood vessels, were needed to cross five yards of the thin snow. When we were on the snow—where you could grip—the sledge was on ice and needed no pulling. When we were on ice the sledge was on detestable sticky stuff and wouldn't budge. We had a merry time and cursed the glassy ice and its mate.'

From Dunlop Island as far north as we could see stretched an icy barrier, the furthest visible promontory of the piedmont being almost due north, though the maps of this coast showed a well-marked bend to the west

Unfortunately the wind changed in direction, and after it had nearly blown the sledge over I decided to ' down sail ' and steer nearer the coast.

We reached a spot where it was possible to climb up the ice. Here by the tide crack we pitched our tent. Gran and I climbed up 200 feet, crossing a few rather large crevasses. We could see no open water within ten miles.

On the 24th we got off at 9.30. I decided to try one sledge first and tack on the other if all went well. There was no wind and it was very hot. We could only just drag *one* sledge along and had only managed to get a mile northward by 1 P.M. Debenham had wrenched his knee, I sprained a leg muscle, and our progress was practically nil. So I decided to pitch the tent and go in for night marching, when the temperature would be below freezing-point and the surface harden a little. A queer state of affairs! I wrote: ' It was too hot to keep inside the sleeping-bags so I lay outside without a coat, in one pair of socks and finneskoes till about 6—when Praise Be it got cooler! '

Night marching commenced about 9 P.M. The surface was much better and as usual was best when a sort of ' pancake patchwork ' of ice projected above the soft snow. We were never able to use the sail again and had to relay practically all the remainder of our journey.

To the east appeared a brown island about 100 feet high and a quarter of a mile long. We hoped this had been missed by previous explorers, and while Debenham and I took angles with the plane table and theodolite the other two made a détour to examine our ' find.' Unfortunately it turned out to be a ' silt-berg '—a mass of ice filled with mud and moraine material. Many of the ' doubtful islands ' marked on Polar charts no doubt originated in the same way.

We had so far had neither time nor opportunity to

examine the geology of the coast we were skirting. It
was apparent also that as we proceeded northwards the
glaciers had retreated less, and except on the capes no
rock was exposed. From our low position we could only
see the summits of the 'facetted' walls marking the three
great valley glaciers which opened into the Piedmont
Glacier. Far away to the east, Erebus was throwing a
huge steam banner to the south. Later in the evening,
after some premonitory puffs, the banner shifted to the
north. We now had an imposing view of the great black
'fang' of the old crater wall, and just behind this the
lower dark dome of Terror contrasted strongly with its
snow-covered rival Erebus.

It was very warm in the tent (though the air
temperature outside was only + 18°) and owing to the
sun effect on the dark tent water lay in little pools on the
cloth valance. Luckily this altered before we started, or
the surface would have rivalled seccotine ! I finished my
day's notes with the remark : 'I don't take very full
geological notes for obvious reasons—we only see a piece of
rock about every three days ! '

I will copy some notes I made on our sledge routine at
this time. 'Our first movement, when we try to take
1200 lbs. at one fell swoop, is to " break out " the sledges,
so as to free the runners from ice. Then I give a Hipp !
cautioning Debenham not to strain hard, and the runners
come away grudgingly and you feel as if they were pulling
you asunder. Once under way they improve and we
can do as much as three-quarters of a mile in an hour,
while the sweat rolls off us, groans rend the air, and Forde

curses audibly! Gran slips about on the ice and nearly
kicks out Forde's patella. I get up steam too much on
easy ground till I hear Forde out of time. We come to an
ice ridge and there's bound to be soft snow just beyond.
You step into this just as the sledges start up the little
slope, slip down nearly to the knee, flounder about, and the
whole caravan stops! So twisted I my right leg and it
twinges all the time, while Gran diagnoses burst veins
with great gusto. . . .' How Debenham got through
with his disabled knee I don't know. We used to yell out
'Crack' as Gran and I stepped into them first, and so he
managed to keep out of some, but he suffered some awful
wrenches with gallant fortitude.

On Sunday the 26th we camped amid a cluster of
icebergs not far from a low rocky cape.

It was very heavy pulling through the snow which had
collected around the bergs. As we reached the screw pack
at the cape I wished to photograph the great cubes of sea-
ice thrown 20 feet up on to the rocks by previous gales.
Gran went ahead, and almost immediately cried out that
Granite Harbour was in sight. I hastily climbed up
through the granite blocks and there it was; we were
right at it! This was Cape Roberts, and it formed the
south extremity of the outer part of the harbour. We had
arrived three days sooner than the coast charts had led
us to expect, and who so joyful as we!

Looking north-west we could see a large and deep bay,
some ten miles across, very like New Harbour in appearance. It contained two inner fiord valleys—of which the
southern is occupied by the Mackay Glacier and is much

'OVERLAND OVER CAPE ROBERTS' TO AVOID THE SCREW-PACK

The sledge has just crossed the tide crack, here twenty feet wide, between the sea-ice and the land-ice

[See p. 250

HEAVY SLEDGING IN NEW SNOW OFF POINT DISAPPOINTMENT

the larger. I took several panorama photos with Forde in
the foreground collecting skua eggs—or rather trying to,
for they had not laid any yet, though many pairs were
evidently considering the subject. Their nests—mere
hollows two inches deep in the gravel—were ready, but
they merely sat about on cold feet, and stretched their
wings and squawked at us.

There was a low snow-covered col across the cape and
Forde found a feasible track over it which thus avoided the
rough screw-pack off the cape. So I agreed to try an
'overland' route with the sledges.

Now arose an interesting question. Where was the
Rendezvous Bluff photographed on page 154 in the
'Voyage of the *Discovery*'? After lunch—a midnight
feast as we were now marching—we inspanned and
made straight for a hanging glacieret we named the 'Spillover.' We did a long march to 'see round the corner.'
We crossed several working cracks and reached a small
knob of granite beneath frowning ice cliffs. About here
a huge bluff rose into view which we decided must be the
Discovery Bluff. It looked rather higher than 500 feet
and we saw it from another angle, but no other headland
seemed at all similar. I wondered if we were in some
other bay altogether, for it differed considerably from
the *Discovery* position. We returned from First View
Point for our other sledge. On our second trip it seemed
as if we would never reach the Point, for in our eagerness
we had done a two-mile stage. The weather looked
thick to south'ard and there was a threatening table-
cloth on Erebus. We hauled the sledges over some wide

tide cracks and bumpy ice and put up the tent in a little alcove.   Here there was not room to spread the poles properly, so the tent flapped under the blizzard.   We were safe however on *fixed* ice for the first time for days, even if it was only a yard or so wide!

On leaving View Point we proceeded due west up the south side of Granite Harbour.   We saw ahead of us an ice tongue projecting into the bay ice.   We had to cross a nasty tide crack quite twenty feet wide, but luckily only a foot or two in the middle was of pulpy ice.   Very heavy clouds rolled up from the south and it started to snow, so I decided to camp in the lee of the tongue. We made a good pitch on the ice with splendid snow blocks for the carving from a big drift alongside.

Dates and meals were rather hard to adjust at this time.   Midnight would be in the middle of a march, and supper would be celebrated at 8 A.M.   However, as night marching was no good for surveying, I decided to go back to day work now we were inside the Harbour. An opportune blizzard kept us to the tent long enough to enable us to straighten out the calendar!

It continued to snow.   We cut out breakfast and kept comfortably to our bags all morning.   We had lunch normally at 1.30.   Our last meal had been a lunch (at midnight) and Gran caused some amusement by demanding the chocolate for the missed meal.   During this blizzard I was cook, and trying to increase my culinary skill I wrote down full notes of our menu.

Breakfast.—Pemmican (looking like lumps of block chocolate) is put into the aluminium cup to full measure.

Meanwhile enough snow or ice has been melted in the cooker to cover the bowl of a spoon. The pemmican is added to this. Some water is taken out in another cup and the 'thickers' stirred up in it. The latter consists of three spoonsful of wheat meal or peaflour, with salt and pepper to taste. Debenham had a happy knack with the 'thickers' which made the hoosh slip down in a most comforting and glutinous way. I tried boiling hard and mixing soft and *vice versa*, but finally discovered that the art consisted in dropping the 'thickers' in just as the hoosh boiled and pouring it out 'good and quick.' About twenty minutes over the primus cooked the pemmican hoosh. Then cocoa (or tea) is made by pouring water from the outer cooker into the inner cooker, where a flavour of pemmican is superadded to it. I liked cocoa best for marching, the others preferred tea, so we had alternate days, though the sledging law says 'cocoa.'

With regard to biscuits we were in two camps. At Shackleton's depôt we found a cache of ordinary biscuits and Debenham preferred these, so I agreed to take a small tin along in lieu of an equal weight of sledging biscuits. So that Gran and I had two sledge biscuits each while the 'soft-teeth' ate Shackleton's brand. Forde dropped a cake of chocolate in his cocoa. *Nous autres* preferred to eat it at lunch.

Lunch.—We always had tea; Gran and I liked it weaker and the other two had the last pannikins full. Six lumps of sugar per man were served out, and as many raisins as you could carry out of the bag in your spoon. (N.B.—It had to be a *dry* spoon.) Butter was

whacked out if you hadn't had it already. I made mine
last lunch and supper by putting a bit by, though sometimes the bit vanished under the hot hoosh if I forgot
to take it out of the pannikin. Three biscuits each
and a cake of chocolate.

Supper.—Cocoa follows hoosh. We have two biscuits
and a cake of chocolate. One spoon was used in our
camp for measuring, stirring, tasting, eating soup and
tea, &c.—all alternating gaily as different operations
employ the cook. I believe other camps followed
the rule, 'One man—one spoon—one cup,' but we
were strictly socialistic. If your tea or hoosh was too
hot you stood it on the floor. If you didn't watch it,
it might melt its way out of sight—but that was a most
infrequent incident. 'Shut-eye' was played to ensure
fair division; the cook pointing to the fragments of
chocolate or butter and the blind person giving one
of our names. The cook has to share out food, stir the
hoosh, watch the primus, and generally hop around; so
that he has a busy time. This doesn't matter except
at supper, when he doesn't get his feet warm in dry socks
as soon as the others.

When the snow stopped, Gran and I walked to the
root of the ice tongue and climbed up the granite cliffs
to the west of it. On the top we found a bare plateau
300 yards wide on which were some large lichens and
a small patch of true moss, quite perky at + 15° and
evidently prepared to grow vigorously if permitted.
The tongue was a mile long and exhibited the usual
regular waves in its profile.

On the next day we continued west. The clear sheet
of ice we had seen ahead of us was now covered with
snow and our hopes of easy sledging were not fulfilled.
At lunch time the sun was so hot that the surface was
not traversable. We halted therefore and Gran and I
walked south to a small bay.

There was a wonderful granite cliff with overhanging
glacier streams connecting the upper ice with the lower.
Probably not long ago a continuous ice sheet covered
this 150-feet cliff, but now only comparatively narrow
ribbons of ice are left, though these are quite continuous
in spite of the steep fall. They were, however, in an
unstable position and we heard several avalanches—
hence our name for it of Avalanche Bay. Just to the
east of these 'ice-ribbons' was a rock outcrop which
seemed to me the first spot in the harbour whence the
top of the piedmont ice could be reached if the bay ice
went out.

After supper we pulled on towards the Discovery Bluff.
The surface improved somewhat and we started out for
more relay work. We could see Discovery Bluff quite
close, and after half a mile I judged we were half-way
and went back for the second sledge. Then on again
and it never seemed to get any nearer. Instead of half
a mile it was two miles. Bringing up the second sledge
was a weary grind. As Debenham said when we arrived,
'We were too tired to think!' We got in about midnight
and pitched camp on the tide crack. There was a young
seal—still in its woolly coat—lamenting its mother's
absence with great persistence. 'Baa-aa!' it said, like

a cross between a lamb and a very vigorous young bull.
This resounded from the granite cliff above us—and
occasionally the mother re-echoed it from the tide crack,
where she wisely kept. I was glad to see eight seals
here—most of which I intended to kill. Gran caught
the young one by the tail, which increased the bellows of
anguish. It then bolted to the water, in which it swam
readily, and we turned in amid a chorus from the seals.

On the 30th we journeyed on round the steep face
of the Discovery Bluff and opened up a fine little bay
with a regular beach of granite boulders. Here was
much lichen and lots of 'knobs' of dried-up moss. I
climbed up a few hundred feet and got a good view to the
south-west, where a beautiful glacier came into the
harbour at such a low angle it seemed to offer a feasible
route to the hinterland. Debenham had discovered
a nice patch of gravel and a suitable site for our stone
kitchen, so we decided to make our headquarters on this
point, which we christened Cape Geology. The beach,
in honour of our country and of the mossy verdure, and
in memory of our isolation, we named Botany Bay !

We had lunch about 3 P.M. and then we marched off
to get the wherewithal for our first seal-hoosh. A seal
lay only a quarter of a mile west of the camp. I poleaxed
her with an ice axe and we cut her up under Forde's
direction. Forde's right hand was still in bandages
from the serious frostbite of September and, indeed,
his third finger had not recovered by the end of our
expedition.

It was rather a sanguinary business, especially for

tyros. Gran fairly paddled in blood, and I fear I was little better. We took all the meat we could carry and Debenham had about 40 lbs. of blubber.

By this time about a dozen skuas had assembled. We did not frighten them, for we wished to attract as many as possible and later abstract their eggs. I wrote : ' About six pairs are breeding along the beach here, so we ought to get a dozen " new laid," and save them a world of trouble by killing them also.' (I'm afraid we were not very altruistic !)

Now we set to work at our stone kitchen. All the way from Cape Evans we had dragged a blubber stove strongly made in sheet iron by Bernard Day. The granite hereabouts weathered in long joints and we found a natural hollow about a yard wide and three yards long. The lower walls of the hut were therefore of solid granite about fifteen feet thick—which should ensure freedom from draughts. We broke out blocks from the floor and Gran smashed off a troublesome projection by repeatedly dropping a boulder weighing a hundredweight upon it until it decided to cave in.

At 10 P.M. I made a great discovery. I saw something black floating in a little pool, and closer inspection revealed a cluster of minute insects. The others had almost dropped to sleep and I was much chagrined at the luke-warm reception of my news. ' They'll keep till to-morrow, won't they ? ' was the tenor of their remarks.

Hitherto only a few odd legs and tails in some moss had been recorded for the Insecta from 77° South. Later Debenham found there were lots under many of the

R 2

pebbles. Here they clustered in a film of ice. As one turned a pebble to the sun they would thaw out and crawl around for exercise. I got a brush out of the medical chest and spread a sheet of paper with seccotine. Then brushed them off carefully on to the paper and so embalmed several thousand. We also got a few lively little beggars about one quarter the size of the big blue ones. The latter were nearly one millimetre long.

The first of December was my birthday, and I received congratulations. We ran up the sledge flags and our black and red depôt flags in honour of our arrival at our rendezvous. Debenham said he couldn't let me cook on my birthday and kindly offered to prepare the festive board. Meanwhile Gran, Forde, and I brought in our other sledge from two miles back.

Gran presented me with a bottle of prunes and one of Savoy sauce, which he had lugged along from the hut in his personal gear :—a present only to be fully appreciated by those whose menu was as limited as ours.

About 5.30 a long streamer of smoke announced that the famous stove was going, and Debenham produced a splendid liver fry, followed by cocoa in very quick time. ' I could have eaten two whacks of the fry easily.' After we were snugly in our bags in the tent, I divided off half a box of fancy chocolates. These were provided by Fry's for just such a contingency, and we passed a resolution that the leader should write and thank Fry's for their gift ; for crunching those elaborate chocolates brought one nearer to civilisation than anything we experienced sledging.

GRANITE HUT, CAPE GEOLOGY
Forde and Gran are cooking at the blubber stove, whose chimney projects behind
the 'sledge' roof-tree

[See p. 277

FORDE COOKING SEAL-FRY ON THE BLUBBER STOVE AT CAPE ROBERTS

Next day was spent in getting meat from another seal and in finishing the hut walls. From our rate of consumption I reckoned that one seal would give us 2½ meals of liver and ten meals of meat, while his blubber would cook about 30 meals.

Debenham and I flensed the seal-skin on a block of ice. This consisted in removing the white tallowy two-inch layer of blubber from the outer leather with sharp knives. It was rather a troublesome task in which we were *not* assisted by the numerous skua gulls which surrounded us. This skin was one of three we required for the roof of the stone hut.

Gran and Forde worked very energetically on the latter. Gran was so keen at lifting huge blocks of granite that I had to caution him against straining his back. We used a sledge for the roof tree, and sewed the skins together and then pulled them taut by heavy stones hung round the edges. Finally the hut looked quite snug with the smoke pouring out of the chimney (and also it must be confessed out of the front), and the *tout ensemble* was very like an Irish shebeen in Forde's opinion. Gran was reading Jules Verne's 'Mysterious Island' this trip, so we named our sample of Polar architecture 'Granite House' from that exciting melodrama.

On the 3rd Gran and I set about placing a letter on the Rendezvous Bluff as Captain Scott instructed me. We climbed up one of the big couloirs about 500 feet and then got on to a projecting spur, where we fixed a stout bamboo pole in a crack 3 feet deep in the granite—which just admitted the staff. I left a letter for Pennell as to our depôt. We then hurried down the cliff and went out to slay another seal. We had a difficult time trying to pack the hide, blubber, and liver on the sledge. The rounded portions ran about all over the sledge. Gran swears they worked their way up hill and came out of the folds of skin in which we tied them.

I threw some bits of meat into the ' shear crack ' while washing the liver, and the water was soon full of amphipods. These are humble relations of the shrimps, and Gran declared his intention of trying for bigger ' fish ' here if he could make a hook. However, we never had time to test this food supply.

On the 4th I decided to climb the Bluff. First we skirted low cliffs, below which were large ' joint-channels ' in the granite with carpets of thick fungus-like moss. These were green underneath, but the tufts were still black, contracted and dryish. Then over crags to a slope of talus débris in which I found a large frondose lichen about 8 inches across with well-developed branches and pseudo-roots. We got to the top in an hour, and our doubts as to the height were justified. The Rendezvous Bluff was sixteen hundred feet high instead of 500 as we expected !

We got a magnificent view of Granite Harbour and its hinterland.

Far to the east Erebus was wholly visible, while to the west we could see the great ice plateau. Right out to sea was Beaufort Island, and there was no open water near the harbour. Closer was the cluster of fifteen bergs near

Cape Roberts and the small tongue of ice where we had camped during the blizzard. But a most amazing discovery was that the whole inner part of the harbour was occupied by a great glacier tongue some five miles long and a mile wide. This projected out to sea from the Mackay icefalls and ended in three splay 'fingers.' It was a hundred feet above the sea ice and crevassed beyond description for the greater part of its length.

Across the harbour was a low plateau about 1000 feet above the sea, formed of black dolerite. Small glaciers hung over the steep cliffs, one being the 'Spillover' mentioned previously. Then looking west came the crevasses of the Mackay icefalls, as impassable and impossible as Dr. Wilson had described them. But in the south-west corner was the smaller New Glacier, and I felt sure we could get up that way somehow.

About twelve miles up the glacier was a huge nunatak with a cap of black dolerite rising into three peaks. This cap reminded me of a Chinese junk, but Debenham objected to Junk Mountain and suggested Gondola Mt. It was sad to find out later that Professor David on his journey to the Magnetic Pole had seen and fixed this peak and called it Mount Suess!

As will be seen, we investigated this most interesting rock island in the upper Mackay Glacier fairly thoroughly.

On the 5th, about 4 P.M., we started off with a week's provisions to map the northern coast of the harbour. We had only one sledge and got along in fine style—the first easy sledging we had met—and as it turned out practically the last! We camped at 6.30 at the end of

the Mackay Tongue, for we should lose sight of all our
survey stations if we went farther.

The sky looked very ugly—the sun dimly glaring
through gloomy clouds, while a low thick bank of dark
stratus covered the eastern horizon. The barometer
fell nearly half an inch in twelve hours, and we were quite
expectant of a blizzard, for similar conditions on a smaller
scale preceded the blizzard at the piedmont tongue. Our
meteorology was quite sound. The first furious blizzard
we had experienced now commenced, for the wind force
was about 7, while the drift was thick and wetting. I
will copy my diary here.

' 10 *a.m.*—We have a pretty snug camp on snow one
foot thick which you can accommodate to your hip bone,
but which it is difficult to stand the primus upon (especially
as the cooker base is full of fat, and is now our frying pan
at the hut !). It started snowing about midnight and
clothed the tent by 3 A.M. I woke to hear the tent flapping
and shaking down young avalanches, and it's been going
strong ever since.

' 2 *p.m.*—Still blizzing strongly ; there have been one or
two lulls of a few minutes, but they don't seem to mean
much. It is snowing like fury too, pattering on the tent
like rain on wooden shingles. If you budge from the tent
(Debenham did so to get a note-book) you get very cold
because the drift melts and wets you at this high temperature of + 23°. We had a meal about 11 A.M., Gran
cooking a good pemmican with a large supply of broken
biscuit therein. This strong S.E. wind blows practically
direct from Cape Roberts on to the tongue on our lee, so

I don't much fear it will shift out this ice. Anyhow we can't move and I'm learning to take these blizzes philosophically. Besides, the bags are dry and warm, and when I tire of writing this diary I snooze a bit, and then read Harker's "Petrology" (Debenham's), and then snooze more. Or Poe's "Tales" (too fantastic and Oriental to please me, most of them), or "Martin Chuzzlewit," or German Grammar. Forde is reading the "Mysterious Island" which Gran has nearly finished at last. Debenham started to work out a latitude but is now "wropped in Morfus." Last night's "hoosh" was an enormous success, 2½ pots of Forde's concentrated seal-hoosh mixed with water and meal made a top-hole hoosh —very tasty and all indigenous !

'6 *p.m.*—The tent is beastly sloppy. We have just finished our lunch, and if we can't get away, that is our last meal to-day. To-day is a queer camp—the first down here where we have actually been dripped on when no primus is going. We have put the cooker under the tied-up door and it is filling I see. Forde is dressing his hand and Debenham keeping warm very sensibly in his bag.

'*Noon.*—It is now noon and we are still snowed up off the end of the Mackay Tongue. Forty-three hours now and we have not got away. It dripped most of the night, for the temperature was + 27° outside and warmer inside. There was a puddle by the door, but Gran's and my bags have absorbed most of that, and Debenham's is wetter. I put on my boots, wind coat, and puttees and dug out the thermometer. The sledge is buried two feet under snow.

Debenham's big camera tripod shows above the snow and a bamboo pole—also the top of the shovel—but the rest is clean buried. . . . Then I came in and had breakfast.'

We had lunch about 2 and now saw blue sky occasionally to the east. Gradually the whole snow cloud blew over *en masse* to the west, leaving blue sky and a bright sun. We dug out the sledge, nothing of which showed, and tried to start off. We harnessed up alternately so as to beat out a track in the soft snow. The going was awful and the sledge pulled us flat on our faces in the snow—of course wetting us through. However, we managed to do about a mile in 3 hours and pitched camp in the middle of North Bay.

This blizzard is evidently the same which delayed Captain Scott at the foot of the Beardmore, more than 800 miles south of where it trapped us.

On the 8th we had an eventful day. We were about two miles from the coast, the nearest land being the flat glacier-cut shelf which we named the Kar Plateau. 'We loaded up the sledge and found we couldn't move it. It just stuck with the prow covered with soft snow. So we stuck up the flag-pole and " packed " all we could carry on our backs. Gran went first with his very heavy bag (half water) and the tent-poles. He plugged away in great style, but made rather a devious track as different parts of the coast appealed to him. By the time we arrived near the land Gran was manœuvring with the tent-poles to try and cross the tide-crack. This was a rotten affair. An ice foot 2 feet or more high, separated from us by a couple of feet of open water, ·was bad enough

—but nearly forty feet of the floe was soft and mushy, so that through the thick snow you could not tell which was hard ice and which open water. There were seals all over this mushy stuff and we came unexpectedly on their holes nearly buried in snow. Debenham and Forde were looking down one to see the thickness of the mushy ice, when a seal leaped out three feet, and as Forde pathetically put it " nearly frightened a loife out of me, Sorr!"' Meanwhile Gran had laid the poles up against the floe and left his bag just behind, when the mush gave way and in he went. He rescued his bag, and clinging to the poles he somehow managed to crawl up the ice foot, but he was pretty wet and soon very cold.

We traversed some distance to the north, Gran on the ice foot and myself on the mush. At every footstep water oozed up, and this doubtful belt was forty feet wide. I managed to get to land, but we could not have got the sledge over. We returned to find Debenham had gone through also. So I determined to make our survey from where we left the sledge and to return immediately thereto.

First, however, we had to get Gran off the ice foot. He threw his bag out towards us and as I went to get it I went in nearly to my waist. Luckily I managed to lean back on to less rotten mush. Then we lashed the bag ropes together and threw them to him. He threw the tent-poles on to the mush and then launched himself spread-eagle on the poles. The whole floe rocked up and down like a jelly, but the poles kept him up and he reached us without further mishap.

This slush—half ice, half snow—was much riskier than broken floe, for there was nothing to grip, and I think Forde voiced our opinions when he said : ' You done a wise thing to give that place a miss ! ' Gran and I were pretty chilled when we reached our tent, but soon got warm in our bags and slept off any ill effects.

We had an even more difficult time returning. My diary records it as ' hellish.' We managed the two miles with the light sledge in four hours, during which we experienced an interesting anatomical phenomenon—as if our insides were getting driven out of our backs by the drag of the harness !

Next day by evening we reached Camp Geology again. Everything was buried in snow. A tin of biscuits weighing 40 lbs. had been blown six feet off a rock. Granite Hut was half filled with snow and we later found that our flag-pole on the bluff, although of male bamboo two inches thick, was broken into a dozen strands.

December 10 was a Sunday, and we registered our highest temperature of + 40°. We expected the warmest day early in January, but it rarely rose above freezing point any more that summer. In the evening Gran and I planted his sea-kale seeds on a patch of mossy soil inside a granite hollow. It seemed a bit wet, but Gran assured us it would be up in a week and eatable in a month ! Our mouths watered at the thought of cabbages, though I don't think we others were optimistic.

The ship was due to pick us up in about a month to take us 200 miles north to Terra Nova Bay, and so of course we thought of a sweepstake as to its date of arrival. Unfortunately we couldn't decide on a stake. Money was no use. We should get any food we liked when we got on board. ' Gran suggested the *first bath* for the winner. But this though very sensible didn't catch on, for as we have no clean clothes probably we won't waste time on it ! '

The next few days, sledging on the sea ice was impossible, so I decided to survey and collect near our headquarters. I took angles for the latitude and longitude of Cape Geology (obtaining 162° 49') and was able to corroborate our sledgemeter record as to the correct position of Granite Harbour. Debenham and Gran climbed to the highest point of the Rendezvous Bluff and found its height to be 1624 feet. They saw open water off the harbour.

The skuas now commenced to lay. Gran said that he got his first egg from a nest half full of water, and declared that the bird looked much relieved when her uncomfortable charge was removed. Two of the nests which I saw seemed to show faint signs of intelligence on the part of the owners. In place of a mere hole in the wet gravel one had about twenty long feathers arranged round the edge—while the other was improved by the addition of some dried moss which the bird had picked from a foot away. I am afraid this intellectual activity on their part did not preserve their eggs !

We boiled four and I tasted my first Antarctic egg. They are the size of a small hen's egg, brown in colour with black, tawny and buff flecks on them. They have not so much taste as those of the common fowl and the albumen is translucent and bluish. They were very good and I could have managed six, though the Polar record of sixteen was I felt sure beyond my attainment.

The movement of the Mackay Tongue was an interesting problem. The sea ice was puckered into great pressure ridges off Cape Geology by the irresistible outward movement of the glacier. Great diagonal cracks traversed the floe from the same reason. So I decided to try to fix a stake on the Tongue, and with the theodolite we could accurately fix its progress to the east.

The chief difficulty was to get a mark. We had no wood to spare. Stones would sink into the ice. Finally I used the broken end of the signal pole. I tied some sealskin on the top for a flag, and painted it well with blubber soot, of which unlimited quantities coated Granite Hut. Gran and I walked over to the Tongue and marched 200 yards up it quite easily. Then we suddenly came on many deep crevasses masked by snow round which we had to steer carefully.

I sighted south with the theodolite to the tent on Cape Geology and north to a large crack in the granite of the Kar Plateau. These directions were not collinear of course at first, but I moved the theodolite until they were. This took a long time and we had to go back to get round a crevasse before we got it fixed. Returning we had hard work to find a track and got lost amid the parallel crevasses, which had an awkward tendency to join after you had followed them for a few hundred yards. On our return I found it was an excellent station, the stake lying directly in line with the crack in the cliff 5 miles off across the bay.

As a result of the seal-flensing to provide a roof for Granite Hut, I cut myself rather frequently. This was usual and a matter of no moment generally. Seven of these cuts healed up in a few days, but one on my right hand gave rise to much trouble. We carried a medical chest full of pills, and Debenham was sledge doctor and knew as much of medicine as Dr. Wilson could get on a sheet of notepaper. He felt an expert at snow-blindness, frost-bites and dyspepsia, but my hand baffled him. However, Gran had served on many vessels in his naval training and at first I had great faith in him. He gravely felt my pulse, and then the arm-pit. 'Do you feel any pain here ? ' I truthfully said ' No ! ' ' No blood poisoning in that finger,' says Gran. Next day it was worse, and Gran proceeded to lance it with great gusto, with the result that the thumb and two fingers swelled double normal size. For a week I could not sleep, and I tried all sorts of bandages and most of the pills—as expert opinion favoured frost-bite, rheumatism, or blood-poisoning. Gran remembered aspirin as good for rheumatism—so the patient swallowed two. Then he said he meant salicylate, so I took two of them ; and then he cheered us by telling us how a former invalid with whom he had had medical dealings died on his hands !

However, on the 16th we sledged to the head of the harbour to examine the numerous capes and bays and to try and find a path up to the great inland plateau. First of all we made for a low dark cape from which the Mackay Glacier had receded slightly. From our hut it looked just like a black hand stretched out from a snowy cuff—so we named it Cuff Cape. We found it a very interesting spot with moraines, rock-striae, perched blocks, and other evidences of past ice action in great profusion.

The next few days we explored and mapped a head-land which we called the *Flat Iron* from its resemblance to the sky-scraper of that name. On its southern face was a deep bowl-shaped bay with a little hanging glacier at the back, and possessing a dry gravelly beach. Here in the Devil's Punch Bowl beneath the Devil's Thumb we stayed till December 23.

It was a grand collecting ground. Almost every variety of granite, diorite and gabbro occurred on the Flat Iron. Debenham found a great 'dyke' of marble included in the granites, and containing large specimens of natrolite, pyroxene, and amphibolite. The New Glacier had only just ceased to cascade over the Devil's Ridge into the Punch Bowl, and the condition of this narrow granite ridge exposed after its submergence by a huge glacier was of extreme interest to the physio-grapher.

There were several pretty little tarns on the slopes, and Gran celebrated Midsummer Day by a dip, in which I would willingly have accompanied him but for my disabled hand.

Towards the end of this trip I began to be able to read my own left-hand writing. Unfortunately no one else has succeeded in doing so, and I find that the meaning of many (no doubt) most valuable notes is now lost to me also!

By Christmas Day we were back at Cape Geology

PRESSURE ICE BLOCKS NEAR DISCOVERY BLUFF, DUE TO THE THRUST OF
THE MACKAY GLACIER TONGUE ON THE SEA-ICE

THE DEVIL'S PUNCH BOWL, AN EMPTY CWM IN THE SOUTH-WEST
CORNER OF GRANITE HARBOUR

ready to tackle the hinterland. We celebrated the day in a manner worthy of the occasion. Forde rigged up all our sledge-flags : Gran's, which was given to him by Queen Maud of Norway, Debenham's and mine with Australian and Cambridge emblems, while Forde, not to be outdone, cut out a white harp from a linen specimen-bag and sewed it on some green burberry ! We had a fine lunch. Twenty-seven skua eggs had been collected, and Forde took the precaution of cracking them first. The first shewed considerable development—but he went into the fry, much to Gran's disgust. Then about four fair ones and then eight bad ones ; and finally we had two each—a thirty per cent. success ! We opened the Christmas bag ; a slice of pudding each, with ginger and caramels. An epicurean feast I warrant you.

A dense sea fog rolled in that night and enveloped everything, and next morning all of us (except Gran, whom nothing harmed) had rheumatic pains. Luckily this wore off later. It was Debenham's birthday, so we finished the box of chocolates, and Gran gave him a long-treasured box of cigarettes.

At noon of the 27th we once more reached the Flat Iron. I was at first of the opinion that the New Glacier would be the easier route, but the others favoured the Flat Iron, and their arguments decided me to try that route. We found it much easier than the glacier would have been. However, it was no joke reaching the snow plateau behind the Flat Iron. We had to climb one thousand feet of rough granite-strewn slopes carrying the sledge and fourteen days' provisions on our backs.

Gran and Forde managed the thirteen-foot sledge, while Debenham and I transported gear, but it took a long time and many traverses to get everything up to our camp on the snow. Luckily my disabled hand did not prevent sledge-hauling or packing, but it was now a long time since I had been able to sketch, photograph, or use the theodolite.

From the camp we could see open water, but it was a long way off; so that I wrote: ' It must go out a mile a day, or Pennell will have trouble to meet us.' I remember we spent that evening discussing a proposed sledge trip in Norway over the little ice-cap of Justedals Brae.

We left our snug gravelly camp after breakfast and pushed off up the great glacier. We were well knotted to the sledge and I went on a longer line so as to prospect for crevasses. It was comforting to think that though I couldn't help to pull anyone else out, the other three would have no difficulty in dragging me up. We zigzagged down from the Flat Iron on to the snow plateau. This was about ten miles wide and seven miles long. It was bounded by the long red ridge of granite ahead of us which we called the Redcliff Nunakol. On the south were the crevasses of the new glacier, while on the north were the icefalls of the Mackay, like a suddenly frozen storm-tossed sea. Gran said this would be called Skauk in Scandinavia, so we adopted that name.

The surface was covered with deep snow and there were many east-west depressions in this, into which we fell occasionally. I am not sure if they were crevasses;

they may have been subglacial streams. We heard here the eerie 'Barrier Shudder,' as the surface fell in around us, but familiarity made us disregard this.

There was a wonderful series of peaks to the south, rising about 5000 feet high and separated by the snow-filled bowls which are technically called cwms. Mount England was a very prominent object to the south-east, confronting us with a giant wall of granite 4000 feet high. This was seamed by couloirs and gullies, down which small snow avalanches formed white tongues leading to the crevassed slopes of the New glacier below.

About four o'clock we deviated to the south so as to camp on the Redcliff Nunakol. We descended a little the last mile and finally crossed a large frozen lake and reached a gravelly point on the nunakol. Here we pitched a comfortable camp about 30 feet above the glacier. Alongside was a little waterfall flowing from a marshy flat on which some moss was growing.

We spent December 29 surveying this island in the glacier. It was about 1000 feet above the glacier, but its rounded contours showed that it had been over-whelmed by the ice flood, fairly recently in geological time. About 5 miles farther west was Gondola Mountain (Mount Suess). This was a true nunatak or 'lonely peak'; for it towered 3000 feet above the glacier and its jagged summit had not been planed by the Mackay Glacier at its period of maximum flood.

Forde carried the theodolite up for me, and I managed to sketch the panorama. It extended over sixteen pages of my notebook, and under the circumstances was a work of art ; for there was a cold wind blowing, and I hadn't been able to draw for weeks. Many of the boulders had pot holes eroded in them, I think by wind and frost action. I boldly attempted to draw these also, sitting with my boots among them and drawing the latter also to show the scale !

We were confined to the tent by snow all the next day. Debenham and I made a chess-board on the back of his plane-table and cut out card discs for the pieces. After several weeks we began to realise the appearance of the men, and later we played many games while we were waiting on Cape Roberts.

On the last day of 1911 we left this camp and moved west to Gondola Mountain. The glacier was deeply snow-covered, and though we sank in it the sledge pulled pretty well. There must have been plenty of crevasses where the ice stream curved round the end of the nunakol, but though we sank in a foot or two at times, yet the snow was so deep we didn't break through anywhere. The sun came out to cheer us, and later in the day we reached a scattered moraine of granite blocks. The ice had been melted here in the previous summer, and we heard the old familiar creaking and splintering of 'glass-house' and 'bottle-glass' which reminded Debenham and myself of our trip up the Koettlitz Glacier.

Finally we came to a sudden ice cliff about 100 feet high, but just not too steep for tobogganing. So we 'let her go' and slid down into the stream-cut gully which fringed the Gondola Ridge.

This was the most interesting locality I saw in Antarctica.   On nearer approach the likeness to a gondola
disappeared, as the great granite buttress supporting the
dolerite capping came into view.   I must apologise for
comparing this fine mountain to a decayed molar tooth,
with three black cusps and a rounded hollow between,
but there was a great similarity in shape.   To the north
of the nunatak was a low ridge about two miles long,
composed of granite and separated from the mount by a
col or pass which rose but little above the glacier level.
All along the eastern slopes were piles of moraine
material.   Great cones of débris, built up of granite,
dolerite and a yellow rock (which we were glad to recognise
as Beacon Sandstone), stood out like watch-towers on
the morainic rampart.

Towards one of these, like a railway embankment of
yellow sand, we directed our way.   We carried our gear
to the top, smoothed off the site somewhat, and then
pitched our camp on mesozoic sandstones—probably the
first time this has been done in Victoria Land!   Just
below was a little lake dammed by the embankment, and
when I cut through three inches of ice near a big black
boulder, a bountiful supply of water welled up in the
hole.   On the bank was some dark shale, by far the most
promising rock for fossils that we had yet seen.   Before
the day was over Debenham had found some, and we
examined all the shale carefully and obtained many
specimens.   They were vesicular horny plates shaped
like the tiles capping a roof ridge.   Some were about
two inches long and had a well-marked keel.   Others

had a beautiful bluish lustre, and there were bits of wood in the shale also. (They are very like the armour-plates of certain mesozoic fish, but they have not yet been submitted to a specialist.)

A heavy cloud-fog descended over us next morning, but in the afternoon cleared off a little. The dark pall shrouded Gondola Mountain, but hung about 3000 feet up for the most part. Gran and I explored the Gondola Ridge behind the tent. Some of the fine-grained boulders were beautifully polished by the friction of the glacier ice. I thought I saw a skua egg here, but it was a piece of mottled sandstone exactly the same size and shape. All the crags were *roche moutonnée*, i.e. rounded by the ancient glacier, the lower eastern face being almost mirror-like in places from the scour of the ice. Here and there we came on large perched blocks, sometimes precariously poised on three or four small pebbles.

During the night we found it rather cold. Consequently I slept with my head right in the bag and awoke rather late from an exciting railway accident! However, nothing was lost thereby, for the heavens still encompassed us. Forde put in some good work with wax ends on my boot, and I searched the shales near the tent and found more 'sarpent critters,' as Seaman Evans christened all our fossils.

Debenham made another discovery; this time of some lumps of coal, and we got many specimens later of the same material. All these were in the moraine just north-east of Gondola Nunatak and I was anxious to find their original home. The 3rd was a more pro-

mising day, and Gran and I determined to circumnavigate
the nunatak if possible.   We walked along to the south
over the great moraine which fringed the granite ridge.
There were some large blocks of granite in this, some
twenty feet across.   There was of course much of the
basic rock (dolerite) also, for we could see that the cap
of the nunatak was formed of jointed columns recalling
those of Staffa.

On the south-west face of the nunatak we saw a long
lenticular mass of yellow sedimentary rock lying above
the red granite, but below the black dolerite cap.   It was
quite inaccessible, being about 1000 feet up, but I have
little doubt that the shales and coal were associated with
this formation, for the moraine trended exactly in that
direction.

Meanwhile Debenham and Forde had reached the central hollow of the nunatak, but had not time to ascend
one of the ' cusps.'

On the 4th—leaving Debenham busy with the plane
table—we others attacked the nunatak.   Gran had his
camera, I took the theodolite in a ruck-sack, and Forde
carried the legs.   The eastern face of the nunatak consisted of a giant granite bulwark 1800 feet above the ice.
Dark dykes had weathered out somewhat, so that it appeared to be pierced for guns.   We scrambled up the gap
between the bulwarks and the deck of the Gondola and
found the latter occupied by two little lakes.   From here
we separated, Gran making for the north-west cusp while
Forde and I chose the south-west peak.   The slope was
very steep and consisted of granite and sandstone up to

2000 feet. Then everything was covered by the broken columns of dolerite. I think, however, that hereabouts the sandstone layer was *in situ*, and in view of the paucity of fossiliferous beds in Victoria Land, all such occurrences have an especial interest.

I reached the top about 2 A.M. and found it 3000 feet above the tent. Gran soon appeared on the other peak, which the theodolite made 100 feet lower—much to his disgust!

The view was magnificent. A few feet away was a thousand-feet precipice above the lower talus slopes. Out to sea we could see miles of open water, with floes drifting about therein, but it looked no nearer than a month ago. I guessed it 10 miles east of Cape Roberts (Pennell said the pack ice was nearer 30 miles wide). Some four miles to the south was a gap in the mountain wall where a low-level distributary glacier seemed to flow into the next great valley. The gigantic cliffs at each side were topped by natural forts composed of Beacon sandstones and shales. I have named this interesting glacier the Miller Glacier—while Debenham christened one to the north the Cleveland. He naïvely explained that his friends must have a large glacier because there were such a lot of them!

To the west, about ten miles away, was the ice plateau descending in ice falls and marked by two (rock) nunakols. There was apparently a fairly easy route to the ice plateau to the south of this nunakol—certainly shorter and probably not so crevassed as the route *via* the Ferrar and

Flat Iron

PANORAMA FROM DISCOVERY BLUFF, LOOKING

East

Forde and Taylor

Cuff Cape

MACKAY GLACIER TO THE GREAT ICE PLATEAU

Miller Glacier   West

south-west—10,000 feet I should think, but all our survey angles were so acute that it is difficult to fix their distance exactly. To the north-west was a fine black-capped peak where the glacier left the Plateau. This I called Mount Tryggve Gran.

We were due back at Cape Geology about the 8th, so I felt that this was our western limit. We spent another day surveying the nunatak and collecting more coal and fossils, and left about noon on the 6th for our return to the rendezvous. We reached our Flat Iron Camp without incident and devoted a day to collecting and photography.

One photograph was an epitome of the physiography of the region. I note that it shows 'The ice face, the crevasses, the skauk, young " calved " bergs, low moraines, retreating glacier, high moraines, granite pavements, shear cracks in the bay ice, the ice tongue, the facetted cliffs, cwm valleys, overflow glacierets, hogback ridges, non-glaciated peaks, the old glacier flood floor, and the junction of the granite and the dolerite.' All this on a single $\frac{1}{4}$-plate negative !

Each day I entered up the meteorological log. The clouds were described also, very often by the word *overcast*. But this afternoon we noticed the sea fog rolling in below us, gradually blotting out the bay, then the ice tongue and the headlands below. I was some distance away from the tent and before I could return the camp was completely hidden. The others also managed to get back safely, but the cold and the high cliffs round the Flat Iron made it a nasty place to be lost in the fog. We could do

nothing much that afternoon and I described the weather
in one word as *undercast* !

We had a chapter of small accidents while we were
transporting our gear down to the sea ice 1000 feet below
us. I found on arrival that the cap of the theodolite
stand had joggled off. I returned and met Forde. He
looked at *his* load and found the handle of the primus
pump had disappeared. We spent some time searching,
but it was quite useless among the rough granite blocks.
Just as we started pulling on the sea ice Debenham
missed the sight-ruler, an indispensable part of the
plane table. Luckily he found this about a mile back
and Forde managed to make some ingenious leather caps
that served instead of the other lost articles.

According to orders we now spent the last week
surveying the neighbourhood of the rendezvous. The
blubber stove was going strong most of the day to melt
water or cook supper. We used to light it with paper
rubbed in the blubber. The black sooty blubber oil
would leak out and melt the ice on the floor of the hut.
The soot caked all the cooking utensils, and spread itself
liberally over us. Gran could always be relied on to
make any special delicacy such as porridge, for which we
saved our 'thickers' and a little oatmeal we had. This
used to take him about three hours in the cold hut—
while we worked out sights or wrote notes snugly in the
comparatively clean tent.

Moreover on these occasions Gran enlivened the cape
by carolling grand opera. When he felt the cold and soot
and smoke rather too much for him ' Pagliacci ' or ' Bertran

du Born ' would sink to pianissimo. Then we would shout
our ' Bravos ' and ' Encores ' and the northern Caruso
would start off again and away flew the skuas. So by
degrees a steaming pot of ' good stoof, that will stick to
your ribs ' was brought to the tent by our hardy Norse
mate.

We found Gran's seakale sprouting in their rock garden.
No less than twelve dicotyledons! I'm sure they were
the first grown under natural (or rather unnatural)
conditions in 77° South. Unfortunately they only flour-
ished a week, and even the native mosses did not get
green that summer—which made me sure it was a very
cold January.

On the 10th there was an addition to our circle. Gran
found two skua chicks in one nest and took one as a pet.
He tried to feed it, with the result that it nearly died ;
so he returned it. However, one of the pair of chicks is
always killed in the first week or so.

Gran and I went over to the Mackay Ice Tongue to
determine accurately the movement of the latter in the
past thirty days. We reached the stake without much
trouble by prodding for the crevasses and then set about
finding its progress to the east. Gran had my Goerz
glasses, and lying full length on the snow he observed
Debenham. The latter was stationed at the theodolite
some two miles off at Cape Geology, and signalled to Gran
with a flag as to which way I was to move. Finally I
got just in a line with my transit of December 14. I
measured the distance to the stake and it was 82 feet !
The glacier moves nearly a yard a day. Debenham's

conjecture that the *Discovery* made no mention of this imposing tongue because it was *not* imposing in 1902 ! is very likely correct.   It may easily have been several miles shorter when Captain Scott first saw the Rendezvous Bluff.

The date of our relief now approached.   Captain Scott wrote : ' It will certainly be wise for you to confine your movements to the region of Granite Harbour during the second week in January. . . . You will of course make every effort to be at the rendezvous at the proper time, January 15.'

There was nothing further to do near Cape Geology. One of the most difficult portions of our retreat was the nine miles between Cape Geology and the mouth of Granite Harbour.   I decided—after consulting the others —to leave for Cape Roberts on the 14th, for there we should also be in a better position to see the ship, while if the bay ice ' went out ' there was no feasible way out of the *cul-de-sac* at Cape Geology.

We packed up all we should require at Terra Nova Bay—where we were to spend the last four weeks of summer—and left the 600 lbs. of specimens, spare boots, &c., at Cape Geology, where they could be picked up by the ship.

We moved off at 7.30 on the 14th.   We had a very heavy load for one sledge—900 lbs. I believe—but I hoped we could pull it without relaying.   The surface was bad, being several inches deep in new-fallen snow.   We took an hour to do the first mile and then had to cross one

wide and were literally torn in the six-foot bay ice by the irresistible pressure of the Mackay Tongue. The edges were ragged—and composed of interlocking promontories. By means of these and an island jammed between we got our load across safely. The east was very gloomy and it started to snow. In previous years this bay had been clear of ice in January—so that I did not want to be caught in a blizzard on it in the middle of that month. The surface improved slightly, but we next struck a 30-foot shear crack filled with mushy snow. A little searching showed us a possible track. Debenham and I tied together and crossed first and then the others, and then we judged the sledge might do it. I expect it would have sunk like a stone if the ice had given way, but we had to get over here or nowhere.

The snow came down thickly now and we plugged ahead, steering by compass for the small piedmont tongue where we had been held up two days on our arrival. Suddenly we seemed to run into a snow slope—and by a mighty expenditure of energy we got the sledge up on to the tongue and were safely on fixed ice for the time.

We soon got the tent pitched, for there was not much wind, and had some tea. I will quote my diary.

'We were all in a cold sweat—for the work is very hard, and yet you don't keep warm. However, we got into our bags and were soon warm, if damp. This blizzard was but temporary, and about 4 P.M. it blew over to the west. I crossed the tongue to see the descent on the other side. It was about five feet down a steep snow slope. Beyond was a narrow shear crack with two seals, but the big crack at the end of the tongue went farther east. We pulled over the glacier and down the slope past the seals without difficulty. Then on a little farther and saw a crack to our right. It seemed only about a foot wide, and I was testing this weak spot with the ski-stick, when the soft snow on which I was standing collapsed and I went into the water. Luckily I grabbed Deb's hand, and Forde and Gran got my harness. I was jerked out like a cork from a bottle and was never so near flying ! None saw the others pull, and they all thought I felt very light ! We plugged on to the east and came to the main wavy crack—an ugly blighter 30 feet across of mushy water. Luckily this also narrowed at the bend, and after some searching we pulled over him also.

'I was getting jolly tired here. However, we could see our destination at last and so pushed on. A keen wind came up from the south-west and swept over the 100-foot glacier wall to the south, driving snow across our course. We crossed a little crack which Debenham thought was new since the snowfall ! To our left were many birds about a mile away and black patches of ominous appearance were showing. Debenham climbed on the sledge and was sure it was open water, and I agreed, but we couldn't do anything and pushed on. I got some relief for my blessed tired legs by marching a longer stride, and we plugged on hoping it would hold firm another hour. However, at long length we began to see details in the never-ending glacier wall on our left—icicles, crevasses and snowdrifts—and at last could make out a feasible slope up on to the cape and felt safe. I had cramp from the pulling and couldn't move for a time.' It was, however, a distinct anticlimax when we got to the top of the cape to see that we had been misled by some queer shadows, that there was firm ice for at least seven miles and no sign of water anywhere! However, our experience at New Harbour made both Debenham and myself realise the risk we were running if the break-up of the ice—now long overdue —had eventuated.

'*Monday, January* 15, 1912; the day on which we were to be relieved. Nary a relief—nor any sign of it, and skuas squawking round us!

'We surveyed our cape expecting to find lots of pools of water, but there is none anywhere. Everything is covered with snow except the big boulders and three patches of gravel—of which we have annexed the largest.' When we arrived each was inhabited by a pair of skua gulls— which we may call White, Black, and Gray. The Whites had one egg, the Blacks a young chick, and the Grays two eggs. The history of these families was pathetic in the extreme.

We dispossessed the Blacks, and I put young Blackie in a new nest—just as well made as his own—which I scraped out a little distance away. The parents fled squawking and left the chicken cruising about on strong stumpy legs with the head low like an apteryx. All night long it yelled for food, so next day I transferred it to the Whites' nest near the warm egg. Meanwhile Debenham set up the blubber stove on a rock ledge near by, to get to which he crossed the Grays' nest rather frequently. They resented this, but sensibly made the best of a bad job and ate up *their* eggs.

The further history of young Blackie was chronicled by the Sledge Poet :

' Lo ! A miracie hath happened,' said returning Skua-White,
' Here's our nest just full of chicken, full of howling appetite.'
Said Skua-White unto his mate, ' For fear this should become a habit
We'd better eat *our* egg—Besides, you may be very sure *he'd* grab it.'
    So little Blackie reigned supreme
    Until one day when he was fed
    By the kind and humane leader,
    Foster father, foster feeder,
    On rich and tasty lumps of blubber
    His little tummy stretched like rubber,
      Stretched too much . . . and now *he's* dead.

The skuas are the most quarrelsome birds I know. They would fight for hours over the carcase of a freshly killed seal before they realised there was enough food for ten times as many skuas—and by this time the flesh would be frozen so hard they could make no impression on it. The penguins have their own peculiar propensities, while the seals used to amaze us by their callousness.   The day after we reached Cape Roberts we killed a large seal and cut it up while another twenty yards away watched us quite casually and did not budge for hours.

There was nothing much to do on the cape.   It was triangular in shape, and about half a mile long.   It rose about 50 feet above the sea ice.   The broad base of the triangle was covered with snow which gradually merged into the Piedmont Glacier.   There was no ice wall here, so that the glacier was presumably stagnant at this corner. The great granite tors of the cape were all flattened, showing that they had been planed off by a former extension of the ice sheet.   Debenham spent some time making a detailed plane table survey.   I fixed several theodolite

A PANORAMA OF CAPE ROBERTS, WHERE THE WESTERN P

Gran   The Hays

AVALANCHE CLIFFS ON THE SOUTH SIDE OF GRANITE HARBOUR. HERE THE PIEDMONT ICE

OLATED FOR THREE WEEKS. LOOKING NORTH

Mt. England

[See p. 241

CWM ON THE LEFT, BUT IS DISCONTINUOUS OVER THE CLIFFS ON THE RIGHT

stations, but as the days went by our life settled into a monotonous round.

I cut the meals down to two a day. We had plenty of seal meat and biscuit, but all the other stores were approaching their last week.

We used to have supper about 7 P.M. Every other day it consisted of a half ration of pemmican—for though seal meat is not so black as it's painted (and it's very black indeed), yet we had eaten little else for a month, and were all heartily sick of it. Then we turned in and used to yarn or read till about 3 A.M., when we managed to get to sleep. We turned out at noon and had a biscuit and seal lunch. During the afternoon we used to walk over the cape and inspect the cracks in the sea ice. One man was kept fairly busy cutting up seal meat, while the cook coaxed the stove to cook the fry.

Debenham was our only smoker, and certainly found tobacco a great solace. I had brought socks instead of tobacco, and had looked forward to jeering at him when his tobacco and socks gave out. Unfortunately our socks lasted much better this trip as our boots were stronger, and I never used my spare socks!

Gran started a drama—a great 'nature play,' full of storms and wrecks with a strong substratum of melo-drama. It was called 'Tangholman Lighthouse' and we used to urge him to fill it full of incident and cut out the 'nature' part of it. I read 'Martin Chuzzlewit' for the nth time and found it, as always, very interesting; while Forde tackled 'Incomparable Bellairs'—a book which charmed Gran—but luckily Forde made it last a very long time.

VOL. II.

We played chess with our cardboard pieces. I think
we were fairly even, though Debenham often tried risky
openings, to my advantage.   The place of Seaman Evans
as Society Entertainer was taken by Gran. His varied
adventures in Arctic seas, among the Andes, in Turkey,
Venezuela, and other of the less known regions of the
earth interested us much. He was, I remember, very
anxious to experience the delights of 'station life' as
portrayed by Debenham.

January 20 was Gran's birthday. I was sorry I
couldn't return his kindly present (of Savoy sauce, &c.),
but I told him I would give him a ship during the day.
The Sledge Poet contributed the following Birthday Ode
dealing with Gran's avowed Nietzschian principles ; which
is here published—if the Editor thinks fit—with Gran's
gracious permission.

ODE TO TRYGGVE

ON HIS 23RD BIRTHDAY, CAPE ROBERTS

(Chanted at ye Full Pemmican Feast)

O Tryggve Gran, O Tryggve Gran,
I would thou wert a moral man.
    And yet since we
    (The other three)
Are just as moral as can be,
A 'soupçon de diablerie'
Improves our little company.

O Tryggve Gran, a holy calm
Is most essential in a psalm ;
But prose should be a thought less calmer
When elevated into drama.
    And yet though we
    (The other three)
Are critical to a degree,
We wish success some future day
To the first Polar ' Nature Play.'

O Tryggve Gran, thou art a man
Who hath compressed within a span
Of three and twenty years, such deeds
That hearing which, each man's heart bleeds
    Among us three;
    And yet though *we*
Are kind to every girl we see,
I have no doubt each lovely creature
Would rather help *you* follow Nietzsche!

O Tryggve Gran, you should be dead
A-many years ago—instead
Of which, he saves you oft,
That ' Little Cherub up Aloft.'
    And therefore we
    (The other three)
In this new principle agree
(As with your luck no man can quarrel)
'Twill serve us best to be *unmoral*!!!

I was just writing the last line of the poem (?) when Gran
yelled out ' Ship Ho ! ' We had seen ships many times
already, but he was certain of this, so we turned out, and
there under the fang of Erebus we could see some top-
masts. Later we could make out three masts and black
smoke—so we knew it was the good old *Terra Nova*, and
not the *Fram*, which burned smokeless oil fuel.

We set about elevating our flag farther up the glacier.
We took it up a long way, nearly to the top as we thought.
On our return we saw it was only one quarter of the way
up, a good example of the trickiness of snow slopes in
this respect. I arranged night-watches to observe any
signals or sledge parties, and we turned in hoping to be
aboard in twenty-four hours.

[Nay, gentle reader, you are not at the end of my
narrative ; it was just twenty-four *days* before we were
relieved !]

T 2

Next day she was in much the same position, about twenty miles away across the screw pack and broken floes. About two miles away a great crack stretched north and south. It was fully eight miles long, and seemed to presage the breaking up of the sea ice.

On the 22nd we could not see the ship. A strong south wind sprang up and the gradually clouding sky seemed to portend a blizzard. 'The stronger the better,' I wrote, 'if it will only drive out this blessed floe.' We took a few photographs. There were two Emperor penguins moulting on each side of our cape, but Debenham reported that they were too frightful to photo ! Forde and I had a day with my stereo-camera taking various interesting details around the cape—planed granite blocks, pressure ice in the bay; and then the Emperors, awful as they were, several seal and berg pictures, &c.; but sad to relate all these negatives were smashed when the sledge fell over the glacier cliff.

I did not entertain the idea of trying to reach Pennell across the screw pack. We should get into a more precarious region each mile, and we could not communicate with the ship to ensure her awaiting us. Pennell could send a party, with safety at either end, if he desired. I was, however, very glad later to find that Pennell also considered the pack absolutely impossible for sledging from the ship.

We saw her during the next few days, and then she never showed up again.

On the 27th a blizzard started, which we hoped would move out the ice. It tore our sledge flags badly, so that

GRANITE BLOCKS PLANED BY ANCIENT GLACIERS AT CAPE ROBERTS. FIFTEEN BERGS APPEAR TO THE SOUTH

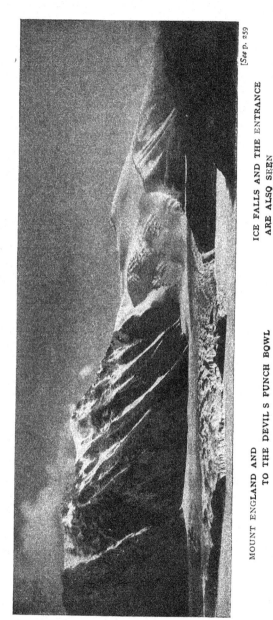

MOUNT ENGLAND AND ICE FALLS AND THE ENTRANCE
TO THE DEVIL S PUNCH BOWL ARE ALSO SEEN

[See p. 259

we brought them down from our distress signal 350 feet
up the glacier, leaving only the big depôt flag there.

It was very trying work with the blubber stove, for
there was no shelter on the cape. When there was any
wind the flames would blow out of the door and give
no heat at all. The water did not get tepid in half an
hour; whereas on a calm day it would boil in twenty
minutes. I spent an hour trying to cook the fry and
barely succeeded in melting the fat. We decided that
the stove could not be used in high winds, even though
it was in a sort of ice cave, and the cook sat in the door
to keep the wind out !

Our rations had been cut down by half for a fortnight.
Three or four biscuits a day, butter every other day,
chocolate one stick; pemmican one-eighth; sugar and
tea two-thirds. However, we had plenty of seal meat,
and as we were not working we required much less food.

So passed several days. Gran spent all one afternoon
making chupatties. The lid of the camera box was his
pudding-board. He used the wheat meal ' thickers ' for
dough, and collared our allowance of raisins. The cakes
were cut out with the rim of a cup, and then fried in a
mixture of butter, fat, blubber, and soot. Anyhow the
result was highly successful, though the inside was somewhat wet and the whole cake I should now consider
distinctly heavy !

Each day we started the last bag of something precious.
First the pemmican, then the chocolate, then the butter.
Only one seal had been visible for some days, and I decreed
her doom. She lay on a large piece of ice which was

rising and falling with the swell. We reached this across an ice island, surging about in a large pool. In spite of all this movement, no more of the ice moved north as far as we could judge.

On the evening of February 1st I held a council. Captain Scott's instructions read : ' I am of the opinion that the retreat should not be commenced until the bays have refrozen, probably towards the end of March. An attempt to retreat overland might involve you in difficulties—whereas you could build a stone hut, provision it with seal meat and remain in safety in any convenient station on the coast.'

However, he gave me permission to begin the retreat in February if we were not relieved in January, and I began to prepare for this event, for I felt sure we could traverse the piedmont glacier.

Cracks seemed to be spreading on the sea ice even while one was watching it. The surging ice-blocks in the tide-crack, now twenty feet wide, rose several feet. Now and again a huge shock, as of a big rock bumping on another, announced a new crack, while a constant roar, like that of a distant lion, announced the periods of maximum of the swell rolling in from twenty miles away.

On February 3 Debenham, Gran, and I climbed the glacier slope behind our camp to prospect for a path. We roped up and proceeded about three miles southward, keeping well behind the crevasses. These are numerous on the steep seaward slope, but we met with none on the fairly level ground, though we could see them just below us. The surface was not very good, usually two inches deep in snow and occasionally a foot deep. This did not promise easy sledging; but the snow was dry now, and I was going to cut down the weights to a minimum.

We could see open water about twenty miles off, but a huge mass of ice pack was apparent as far north as we could see. There seemed to be a broad belt of pack, at least sixty miles long, which was quite absent in January 1902.

Obviously our exploration of Terra Nova Bay was impossible now, and it looked as if the ship would never reach us at Cape Roberts. With good luck we might cross the piedmont glacier to Cape Bernacchi in a few days, and Pennell might find it easier to reach us there, while we should at any rate be nearer to headquarters. There was also a week's food there, and we had now only a fortnight's sledging stores left.

On February 4, Gran and I explored the sea ice below the piedmont for about four miles to the southward. We passed through the fifteen bergs in the little bay, and then got among the screw pack. This was covered with snow and afforded us extremely heavy going, as may be imagined. Near the shore was a perfect network of new cracks with the ice 'working' all the time. Below the glacier wall was a deep tide crack four feet wide, but where some ice blocks had fallen in we managed to get across to fixed ice. As a result of this journey I decided to march first along the sea ice, and then climb up the piedmont at this point.

Next morning I wrote a long letter to Pennell which we all signed. We made a depôt on the highest point of the cape, and fixed a flag alongside with the letter in a little tin match-box. The journal for Captain Scott I left in the food cairn in my ditty-bag. I remorselessly weeded out every one's gear. We took nothing but what we stood up in, and our notes and the instruments. Luckily most of Debenham's and all Gran's negatives were films, but I had to leave nearly all my plates and my cherished Browning. I knew we had some bad crevassed country to traverse—thirty miles of this—and then I expected thirty miles of coast work, largely over moraine and rock, where we should have to portage the sledge and all our gear on our backs. This would bring us to Butter Point, whence our route was the same as in the previous summer. With a light sledge it was just possible we might be able to raise it if it slipped down a crevasse; and this was quite a probable event, for in traversing along a piedmont glacier the party moves *parallel* to the crevasses. One thus reaches them imperceptibly, and the whole party with its outfit may be marching over a crevasse, whereas in crossing them at right angles this is rarely the case.

We turned our backs finally on Cape Roberts at 11 A.M. on February 5. Our flag waved bravely, and below it was the cairn of stones covering the food left there by Scott's orders. If we had to return it would give us a breathing space; but I never saw the cape again. For many months the flag was left in solitude. The screw pack never broke adrift that winter. In the

next spring six desperate men sledging southward, to
more endurable—though, as they thought, no less solitary—
quarters, here found the first news of the main party.
Our depôt possibly saved Petty Officer Browning's life. It
certainly gave the Northern Party their first bearable day
for many months. Brave old flag—it hangs in Tewkesbury
in Priestley's home, and there my old Browning was
restored to me after many months!

So we marched on. We were all stiff and out of
training, and the sledge did not pull easily, but we reached
the tide crack and crossed it much more readily than
I expected. After lunch we pulled up the steep slope
of the glacier and to our delight found the surface grow
harder almost every hour. But other troubles were
upon us. So much so that for three days I felt it doubtful if anyone would ever read my diary! However,
on the evening of the 8th I wrote up the 5th (and succeeding days) as follows:

'Then quite suddenly we came on huge crevasses
all round the shop. Some open—which I took care not
to keep too close to, and others bridged. They seemed
too wide to do anything with, but after cautioning the
others to tread quietly, I prodded across safely, though
the ice axe pushed in all its length easily. Then the
others followed and the sledge after. Gran fell in at
the near edge and saw the straight wall. Several of
these were over 20 feet wide, but we had to chance them,
and tested them all before the sledge started. Then we
marched along between two fairly visible ones and luckily
they didn't join. The surface got flatter and they died

out gradually, so that we made fair progress. We came
to another enclosed snow basin, and I felt sure the seaward slope would be safer. So it was, though Forde
went down a small one. We pulled along this up to
a sort of col about 8 miles from Cape Roberts, and
here, as we were well beyond the mouth of the Big Valley,
we camped.

'My only fear now was that bad weather might
cover the glacier with soft snow, for I felt that all the
big crevasses would be lidded and the little ones could
hardly swallow the lot of us.'

Next morning we made the harness traces longer,
so that only one man at a time need cross even a wide
crevasse. We had to traverse the mouth of another
large valley glacier. Three of these debouched on the
piedmont glacier from the Western Mountains, and
the pressure from the northernmost (the Debenham
Glacier) was responsible for the crevasses of March 5.
The second valley glacier was not so large, but we anticipated trouble. We had a stiff pull uphill for three
quarters of a mile, but some of the snow was so hard
that the sledge runners made no mark! This was an
ideal surface, for one's feet did not slip on it, though
occasionally the sledge skidded. We were about 700 feet
above the sea here and entered a col just below a huge
snow hill.

'Afterwards we were cutting around the hill afore-
said when suddenly appeared many crevasses. So we
deviated abruptly and ascended the hill sharply. We
encountered three, into one of which I fell, but they were

not very wide. The moral of this is, Don't go for the break of a hill facing and near the sea, but stick to hum-drum grades if possible; if not, still don't go for the break of a hill!'

The somewhat frivolous tone of the above note is evidence that it was written when we had traversed the worst of the piedmont. It was always the case 'down South.' One never got photographs or 'instantaneous pen-pictures' of anything really exciting. It was always a case of 'Get a move on, and get out of this good and quick,' so that one's diary lost most where it would have been most interesting.

We were now behind Dunlop Island and about 1250 feet up the piedmont. We were astonished to find that the floe had all broken up to south'ard. Long curved cracks parallel to the coast marked where pieces were continually floating off. We congratulated ourselves on our safe position on the piedmont, for we should have sledged into this without knowing it, had we continued much farther on the sea ice. Small bergs looking just like white yachts dotted the open water, which seemed to extend south to Castle Rock. There was no sign of the *Terra Nova*. We began to think she had come to grief, for Pennell knew we were free to move off on February 1.

After supper Debenham got out his plane table and continued his survey. He was at first much puzzled by the position of his station on the stranded Glacier Tongue to the south-east. He realised soon, however, that it had twisted round, and was even now preparing to continue its journey to the Nirvana of warm northern waters.

We had been blessed with sunshine the last few days. I do not believe we should have managed to dodge the crevasses otherwise, for in dull weather you cannot tell any difference between a ten-foot hollow or a ten-foot hummock when it is only a yard or two away. However, as a result of the sunshine Forde had a bad touch of snow-blindness. Debenham got out the medical chest. He ground up some $ZnSO_4$, picked it up on a paint-brush, and dropped it in the corner of Forde's eye. Later in the night I gave Forde another dose, for the pain is pretty considerable.

The next day my right eye was sore and watering in spite of the amber glasses, and I feared I was to become a patient also. We plugged along over an absolutely level snow plain, where Debenham, without warning, dropped into a crevasse over which I had crossed without puncturing the lid.

In the afternoon my eyes gave out, and I put bandages on the right eye, and gave up the lead to Debenham. It was an astonishing relief to cease from staring at the glaring surface, and either pull along with shut eyes or keep one eye on the gratefully dirty back of Debenham's white woollen jacket!

Debenham led us safely past three huge crevasses, and we halted for a spell among a cluster of smaller ones. That evening we climbed up the snow hill behind Gneiss Point about 1350 feet above the sea, and as we had now passed the third valley glacier, I felt we had finished with the crevasses for the time being. We camped on hard

The zinc sulphate may truthfully be described as an ' eye-
opener,' but later the cocaine in the mixture calms things
down ! You are advised ' to keep your face cool,' but
unfortunately I had to keep my head in the bag to get
warm. However, Forde was pretty right next day and
my eyes soon stopped aching, though everything appeared
double for many hours !

On the 8th we reached the land near Cape Bernacchi.
There was a steep ice slope 200 feet high at an angle of
30°. Luckily it was much honeycombed and sun-eaten.
We put grummets (rope brakes) on the sledge and
managed to get it down by 1.30 P.M. We had a very
cheerful lunch, for we knew the depôt was only a few
miles south. Then we found an ice-foot all the way
along the edge of the rocks and moraine which led us
right to the Bernacchi cairn. This was a regular ice
pathway about 20 yards wide. It was due to sea-ice
which had become cemented to the shore, the tide crack
being farther away from the rocks and defining that
part of the floe which had lately drifted away to sea.

No one had visited our depôt. New Harbour was
full of new broken floe, but a fine ice-foot seemed to
promise well for our next march.

We stayed a day at Cape Bernacchi, for I wished
to get a good station for the triangulation of this coast.
Gran and I took the theodolite to the top of a hill 2900
feet high at the north-east end of Dry Valley. We named
this Hjort's Hill in honour of the maker of our trusty
primus lamp. As we were climbing this hill Gran swore
he could see the ship off Cape Evans through the

binoculars. It seemed clear to me also—smoke, cross-trees, hull, and 3 masts, but after an hour or so we decided it was only a miraged crack in the Barne glacier. Our disappointment was very keen, though I am now not so sure that we did not really see the ship, some forty miles away. We could see the twenty-foot débris cones behind the hut quite easily on a clear day.

I wrote the usual letter to Pennell. I had left two in Granite Harbour and two on the piedmont now, though it did not look as if any would ever be read. All through the 10th we skirted New Harbour, finding a fairly feasible ice-foot between the granite-strewn slopes and the open water. We came across a Spratt's biscuit box here—which was evidently left by the 1902 expedition. We saved a considerable détour by crossing the head of the harbour on the sea ice and camped below the Kukri Hills, where I halted rather early to get a round of angles. We were held up here all next day by a snowstorm, which we spent reading and sewing.

On the 12th we rounded the Kukri Hills, and when the ice-foot petered out we were luckily able to continue on the sea ice. We had lunch amid a colony of over forty seals, and then reached the southern side of the Ferrar Glacier, where we camped on a rather wet and muddy heap of 'road metal' moraine.

We were now safely round New Harbour, and curiously enough crossed the sea ice at the mouth of the Ferrar on the same day of the year as when we nearly went out to sea on our first sledge journey. Henceforward we knew our route. We had plenty of food at the Butter

THE MOUTH OF DRY VALLEY SHOWING THE COMMONWEALTH GLACIER DEBOUCHING INTO IT FROM THE SOUTH.
NEW HARBOUR APPEARS ON THE RIGHT

Point depôt, which we reached that evening, and knew
we could reach the old *Discovery* hut before the end of
the month.

This depôt had been blown over and wrecked generally.
We took some pemmican, butter, and chocolate, and
next day proceeded south along the Butter Point piedmont, leaving another note for Pennell. The surface
was much better than the preceding year, but curiously
enough we found quite a number of small crevasses.
Debenham and Forde fell in together in one of these, and
the burly Irishman jammed so tightly, it was quite a
business pulling him out of it ! In the evening we reached
the Strand Moraines. These are great piles of ancient
silt, gravel, and erratic blocks which were dropped here
by the ancestor of the present Koettlitz Glacier. At
the southern end of these moraines—which were several
miles long—was quite a large lake. We tobogganed
down to this and across to a nice little gravelly delta just
made for the tent. We found that the open water reached
just to this point, the sound still being frozen to south'ard,
though obviously breaking away in great sheets. I
wrote that night : ' No *Terra Nova*. We should have
been picked up at Evans Coves (Terra Nova Bay) to-
morrow.' We had the choice of two routes now. Either
to cross the snout of the Blue Glacier, or to take to the
sea ice and coast round the latter. We had done the
former and knew it would only take a day. The latter
might be quicker, though a great calved berg blocked
the route about two miles ahead. Debenham preferred
the glacier, the other two the sea ice. I made a bet with

Gran that we couldn't get the sledge between the calved berg and the glacier without unloading it. This had a rather interesting outcome. I finally decided to keep to land ice on the principle of ' the Devil you know being preferable to the Devil you don't.'

It was annoying to find that the Blue Glacier had so completely changed its complexion in the twelve months. In place of clear blue ice where one could see every crevasse, it was one uniform sheet of smooth snow, and we soon began to fall into the crevasses. In a very short time we had all been in a couple of times, and it was evidently an unhealthy region for sledging. I deviated to the edge of the glacier to try and lower the sledge on to the sea ice ; and we soon got abreast of the calved berg, where we halted a few minutes.

Away to the south-east we could see a blizzard coming up, and I wanted to get a snug camp in the gullies south of the Blue Glacier. We had an argument as to who had won the bet, for there was a high jumble of ice where the calf jammed the parent glacier. The other two decided in my favour, and so we pushed off on the top of the glacier edge to the wished-for camp. Gran was dissatisfied with the court's decision and kept glancing back to the scene under discussion. Just as we were dipping down the slope which cut off all view to north-ward he yelled out : ' Ship Ho ! '—and there she was over the top of the black moraines.

' We turned back good and quick to retraverse the crevasses, for she was four miles off and we were afraid might miss us, as a snowstorm was brewing in the east.

THE RELIEF OF THE WESTERN PARTY BY THE 'TERRA NOVA' OFF THE MOUTH OF THE KOETTLITZ GLACIER

She steamed along past the berg and out along the floe.
We pulled back hard, crossing crevasses carelessly, but not
falling in much, and finally could make out that she
had a flag on the gaff, apparently recognising us. We
kept along the edge of the glacier till we could find a
place to get down. Here was a drop of 30 feet, almost
vertical, with a big tide crack and a tide pool at the
bottom. Gran went down first, and then I got down
half-way. Unluckily, as we were lowering the sledge
Forde was pulled over by his harness and fell right on to
Gran, who was squashed into the snow while the sledge
came down on top of us. It nearly broke in the middle ;
however, we lugged it over to the ice and set off hot-foot
over the two miles of ice. The ship now anchored near
the floe and four men came to meet us. They harnessed
up and told us the news. We heard that the Southern
Party were going very well, that there was no sign of
Amundsen, and that there had been no accidents of
importance.' Also that they had not been able to communicate with Cape Evans until a week before, and
had been unloading stores every available moment before
they came over to search for us. And then the world's
news at first hearing made us feel safer in the Antarctic.
The disruption of China, the Franco-German-English
trouble in Morocco, the Italians and Turks in Tripoli, and
the great strikes in England. We had missed an eventful
year during our sojourn in the peaceful regions of the
South.

It was no easy business reaching the ship. The sea
ice was rapidly breaking up, and moving off to the

northward in great rectangular fragments. Finally the ship butted a cake of floe towards the fixed ice and held it there long enough to get the sledge over.

Once on board we made a dive for our mail. A pillow-case full for each of us, and all home news satisfactory.

We had been picked up just a month later than the date fixed by Captain Scott. We were now only a few hours' sail from Cape Evans, and looked forward to a change and the comforts of the hut. But the blizzard we had been watching caught us and was succeeded by many others, and not for ten days did we get near the hut. In fact, during the ensuing three weeks there were only three hours in which we could get into touch with headquarters, before we turned our faces to the north.

So ends my narrative. During the six months that we had spent sledging we had mapped a hundred miles of coast and hinterland, our detailed surveys extending. in places over thirty miles from the sea. Our general scientific results are briefly described in the final chapters of the book. All our collections were safely brought back to England in the *Terra Nova* in 1913.

What is the best personal result of our sledge journeys ? A group of friends who are closer than brothers. Here's luck to my mates—to Debenham, Wright, and Gran !

SPRING DEPÔT JOURNEY

By Commander Edward R. G. R. Evans, R.N.

On September 9, 1911, the depôt party, consisting of Lieutenant Evans, Gran, and Forde, left Cape Evans to dig out the depôts at Safety Camp and Corner Camp. As later on the dog teams were to take out quantities of stores to Corner Camp it was deemed advisable to visit this spot, and if necessary put new flags to mark it, and build up the cairn.

The party started at 8 A.M. on ski, in beautifully fine, clear weather. We saw remarkable earth shadows on the clouds over Erebus.

Nelson came with us to Glacier Tongue, and while we had four men we travelled at 3 miles per hour; directly he left our speed decreased materially.

There is no doubt a four-man team has enormous advantages over one of three. The increase in permanent weights is very slight, consisting only of a sleeping-bag and a small personal bag; the only disadvantage is the difference in the time taken to cook meals. When marching against time the three-man unit saves nearly half an hour a day.

We passed Meares driving home from Hut Point, but

he was half a mile inshore and didn't come out on account of the dogs, who are very hard to control if they get near another sledge team.

There was no object in camping for lunch on the sea ice, and we pushed on to Hut Point for lunch. The distance by sledgemeter was 13 miles 300 yards (statute 15 miles 264 yards). We found Meares had left everything at Hut Point in splendid order, and we soon had the blubber stove going and a meal cooked. At 5.15, it being quite fine, we repacked sledge and marched 4 miles out towards Safety Camp. We stopped about 9 P.M., had supper, and turned into our bags.

Our camp was on the sea ice, and we noticed an extraordinary change in the temperature after rounding Cape Armitage; the thermometer at Hut Point showed – 21° and on camping it was – 42°, with a sharp biting breeze coming away from the Barrier. Minimum temp. – 45°.

On the following day we started off in a light easterly wind, temperature – 36·5°, and hauled our sledge to Safety Camp, which is distant from Cape Evans 22 miles 452 yards (statute). We dug out the depôt, tallied stores, and then put up a wind recorder of Simpson's.

It was interesting to see how Safety Camp had drifted up during the winter. It took many hours to dig it out, and although this depôt contained, amongst other things, 73 bales of fodder, each of 107 lbs. weight, the snow had completely covered it.

After lunch we took 6 tins of paraffin from here and marched 8 miles 641 yards between 5.30 and 8.30 P.M. At 9 P.M. the thermometer showed 45·2° below zero.

THE SHADOW OF MOUNT EREBUS ON THE CLOUDS

The temperature fell a good deal during the night and we could scarcely sleep. Gran, using an eiderdown bag inside his sleeping-bag, was warmer than the other two of us, but later on our journey the eiderdown bag was like a board and he had very little if any advantage from it.

On September 11, at 7 A.M., the temperature was − 58·2°, the minimum for the night being − 62·3°.

At 9 A.M. we started off, and marched 5½ miles by sledgemeter (statute 6 miles 530 yards).

We built cairns at every night and lunch camp, and small 'top-hats' whenever we had a halt. Corner Camp is very difficult to find, as landmarks are so often obscured by cloud and drift in this vicinity. One of our objects was to mark the track clearly.

We stopped for lunch at 2 ; the land was entirely obscured by mist, although the sky was clear overhead. Thermometer at − 43°.

The surface in the forenoon though variable was fairly good ; we marched another 5¾ miles by our sledge-meter during the afternoon and camped at 8.30, the weather gradually becoming worse, wind from W.S.W., with low drift. By the time our tent was pitched a fair blizzard was on us. Temperature − 34·5°.

By 10 P.M. the tent was well drifted up, weather squally, but all snug inside. We had with us the new pattern double tent, which is a horrible thing—it shortens the space down so, and is the most trying thing to spread in a breeze. To quote my diary : 'There is a sharp difference of opinion as to the value

of this invention. Naturally the maker, Petty Officer
Evans, is very proud of it, but the other seamen hate
it. However, we shall give it a good test now, likewise
the ski-shoes, which I like immensely if they are the
right size; if too big they are trodden down and spoilt
very soon, but if too small one's toes get frost-bitten
where the shoes pinch.'

Tuesday, September 12, 1911.—Blizzard continued till
8 A.M., when wind decreased to force 5; it however still
continued to drift until 10 A.M., when wind dropped to
force 3, weather overcast and snowing. Temperature – 19°;
the minimum for the night being – 40°. The wind in
creased to force 6 with drift at 11 A.M., but by 2 P.M. it
was fine enough to make a start, which we did in a biting
cold wind. We built a good cairn here, but it was cold
work.

We marched this day till 8.30 P.M., when it was very
nearly dark and very misty. Surface bad after the
blizzard; we covered 7 miles 783 yards (statute). Temperature on camping – 46°.

September 13, 1911.—The diary continues : Having
shivered in my bag all night, at 5 o'clock I told the others
to get up, both of them being awake. We cooked a meal
and prepared to scout for Corner Camp. On going out
to take the meteorological observations found min. temp.
– 73·3°. Present temp. – 58°. I don't think anyone was
surprised, as it was very cold during the night. I got a
glimpse of Observation Hill and the sun, and I found the
bearing of the former was N. 70 W. instead of N. 68 W.,
so we struck S.S.W. for a short distance and then saw the

flagstaff of Corner Camp. On arriving at the depôt found the whole cairn buried thus :

so dug out all the forenoon and eventually got all stores out and tallied. We left one tin of biscuits here, two bags of treacle, six bags of butter, and six tins of paraffin. We put all biscuit tins and sacks of oats on end on the top of the cairn we built. The complete tally of stores is ·

Sledging biscuits	.	9 cases	Cocoa		6 bags
Butter	.	14 bags	Oil		11 cans
Cheese	.	. 6 ,,	Oats		3 sacks
Tea	.	. 2 tins	Sugar		6 bags
Fodder	.	. ½ bale	Chocolate .	.	6 ,,
Pemmican	.	6 bags	Raisins	.	6 ,,
Cereals	.	. 6 ,,	Treacle .		2

The cairn is now like this :

We left at 5 P.M. and started to march to Hut Point — non-stop run — as I wished to get my gear

nicely dried at C. Evans before going out with Meares
on the 20th. We had no wish to remain at Corner
Camp, as all the time we were digging it was drifting a
little and blowing about 5, temperature – 32°—about all
we could 'stick.' After striking camp we marched till
10.30 P.M., doing 9·5 miles by sledgemeter. When 4 miles
from Corner Camp the wind dropped to a calm. At
10.30 had pemmican and tea, then at midnight started
off, and steering by stars kept on a W.N.W. course till
about 5 A.M. (September 14), when we had a light breakfast of tea and biscuit. Off again before 6, and continued
marching until we came to the edge of the Barrier about
12.45. We did not stop at Safety Camp, but marched
straight to Hut Point, arriving at 3 P.M. At the hut we
had a meal of tea and chapatties which Forde made. We
ate steadily till about 5.30, and then discussed marching
to C. Evans. Had we started we might have got in by
3 A.M., but not before; but we had marched all through
one night, and besides digging out Corner Camp we had
marched 30 miles 40 yds. by sledgemeter, equal to 34·6 stat.
miles, which on top of a day's work was good enough
for me. We therefore prepared the hut for the night.
Turned in about 7 and soon fell asleep. Gran woke Forde
and myself about 10 P.M. with cocoa and porridge, both
of which were splendid. We then slept till 9 A.M. on
the 15th.

September 15, 1912.—Turned out at 9 A.M., cooked a
fine breakfast, and then washed all the cooking gear,
cleared out the hut, got on our marching gear, and at
2 P.M. started off for C. Evans. We had an easy march

LIEUT. E. R. G. R. EVANS SURVEYING WITH THE FOUR-INCH THEODOLITE
WHICH WAS USED TO LOCATE THE SOUTH POLE

on the sea ice and arrived back at 9.25 P.M. Found that the sledge party Capt. Scott is taking W. had left that morning, and that I was not going on my second trip to Corner Camp as the dogs will not start for another month. I found by comparison that my watch had lost two seconds since I left nearly a week ago. Turned in about 11.30 P.M., and was soon snoring.

Marching average ·

				m.	yds.
Sat. Sept. 9, whole day				19	1186
Sun. „ 10, half „			.	8	
Mon. „ 11, whole „	.	.	.	12	
Tues. „ 12, half „	.	.	.		
Wed. „ 13, whole „	.		.		
Thu. „ 14, „ „	.	.			
Fri. „ 15, half „	.		.		
				102 .	

Time out of hut, 6½ days. Allow off for two diggings and blizzard 3½ days, equals 5 days' marching.

THE LAST YEAR AT CAPE EVANS

WITH THE FINDING OF THE POLAR PARTY

By Surgeon E. L. Atkinson, R.N.

CHAPTER I

THE ATTEMPT TO MEET THE POLAR PARTY

In writing the record of the second year I must give all credit to A. Cherry-Garrard. It is entirely from his diaries and from the official diary kept by him that these records are compiled. To make matters clear it would be as well to go over the events after the return of the first Southern Party. It consisted of A. Cherry-Garrard, C. S. Wright, Petty Officer Keohane, and myself. We returned to Cape Evans on January 28, 1912. The orders then given to me by Captain Scott were for myself and Demetri, with two dog teams (if Meares were returning in the ship), to proceed as far south as possible, taking into consideration the times of return of the various parties, and in order to hasten the return of the final party. The dog teams were in no manner a relief expedition and were simply meant to bring the last party home more speedily.

On our return to Cape Evans the ship had not as yet been communicated with. Indeed communication was not established until February 4, owing to bad sea ice intervening.

On February 9 we started landing stores from the ship, and in this all hands were employed.

On February 13, the sea ice having started to break up in the south bay, I judged it advisable to make a start with the two dog teams for Hut Point, 15 miles to the south of Cape Evans, a journey across sea ice. It was from this point that the Barrier could be reached and the return of the Southern Party hastened by the dog teams. The two dog teams, Demetri the Russian boy, and myself were kept at Hut Point by bad weather until February 19. On the night of the 19th the weather began to abate. At 3.30 A.M., while we were in our sleeping-bags, Petty Officer Crean reached the hut and brought in the news of Lieutenant Evans' breakdown beyond Corner Camp. Crean had done a remarkable walk of over 35 statute miles to get what relief he could, leaving Lashly to look after Evans, who was in a very serious state and with only a small supply of food left. Within half an hour of his arrival a very thick blizzard came on and it was impossible to make a start. The blizzard kept on the whole day, and it was not until 4.30 on the afternoon of the 20th that a start was possible. Demetri and I then made a start with both dog teams. The weather was exceedingly thick and we could only see a very short distance. We travelled, with one rest for the dogs, until 4.30 P.M. the next day. Then the weather being too thick to travel we camped, judging that we were somewhere near the camp with Lieutenant Evans and Lashly. During a temporary clearness we saw the flag which Lashly had put up on the sledge about 2 miles away. We found Lashly and Evans within the tent. During the whole of that night and the next day the blizzard continued and it was impossible to travel. The

story of Lashly's and Crean's devotion will no doubt be
told in another place. Lashly looked after Evans, and
his nursing arrangements were splendid.

At 3 A.M. on the morning of the 22nd we made a
start, Evans being in his sleeping-bag on the sledge. The
teams travelled well, and with only one break 15 miles
from Hut Point we reached home and safety for him
at midday, after 5 hours' actual travelling. Considering
his condition, I judged that if I were able to obtain help
from Cape Evans it would be better for me to stay with
Lieutenant Evans and for Wright or Cherry-Garrard to
take my place with the dog teams and to go south with
Demetri.

On February 23 Demetri went to Cape Evans, and that
same night Wright, Cherry-Garrard and Davies the carpenter came up to Hut Point. Having regard to his work,
it was better that Wright should not take command of
the dog teams, and so it was settled that Cherry-Garrard
should do this. After due consideration of weights and
the probabilities of the date by which the final party could
return to certain depôts, it was decided that the dogs
should take 24 days' food for themselves and 21 days' food
for the two men, carrying in addition two weeks' surplus
supplies for the Southern Party complete and certain
delicacies which they had asked for. The totals brought
the weight carried by each team up to the most economical
travelling limit for the time of year. As there was no
dog food in any of the depôts except at Corner Camp
or along any of the route, it meant that, counting in
this supply, 24 days was the limit of their usefulness.

Again, it cannot be too firmly emphasized that the dog teams were meant merely to hasten the return of the Southern Party and by no means as a relief expedition.

The next two days, February 24 and 25, were devoted to giving the dogs a much-needed rest and to making up provisions and dog food. Indeed, owing to bad weather, it would have been impossible to have made a start on these days. The following record of the journey of the two dog teams is taken entirely from Cherry-Garrard's diary ·

February 26.—Since it looked fair last night, at 2 A.M. they decided to start. There was a strong wind and a fair amount of drift at the time. The dogs proceeded well to Safety Camp and then on to the biscuit depôt, 15 miles from Hut Point. There they were rested for a short while and finally started at 6 P.M., and reached Corner Camp at 10 P.M. The dogs were working splendidly and together, and completed the distance of 30 geographical miles for the day in thick weather and with a head wind.

On February 27 they again had a head wind and low drift; they made good 10 miles and then camped for tea; proceeding afterwards over a very good surface but with bad light, they completed 18½ miles for the day, seeing but one cairn, which they only made out when it was 20 yards away. They camped in the nick of time, as a blizzard broke upon them and they had great difficulty in getting the tent pitched. The dogs pulled well and were very fit and not done up. It may be noted in passing that the difficulties of camping and breaking camp are enormously increased in bad weather when there is a unit of only two men instead of four.

Next day, February 28, they started at 7.45 P.M. on a
beautifully clear day and ran 10 miles up to the time they
camped for tea. The surface was good, with very large
sastrugi. On one of these, while Demetri was ahead,
Cherry-Garrard's sledge upset; he had to unload the
sledge partially in order to right it. As it was righted the
team took charge. Cherry-Garrard clung to the sledge
but lost his driving stick, and it was not until the team
had taken him over a mile to the south that they were
stopped. The weather was coming on thick, and it was
an anxious time as their weekly bag, cooker and tent poles
had been left behind. Eventually both teams returned
and the sledge was re-packed. A blizzard came on and
they were unable to travel until the next afternoon. There
was a strong wind and the temperature began falling on
this day. They completed 16¾ miles for the day.

February 29 proved a good clear day and they reached
the Bluff Depôt in latitude 79° south. The sledge-
meters had been giving a great deal of trouble and did
not tally; this, with the bad light, increased the difficulty
of navigation enormously.

On March 1 they started about mid-day after giving
the dogs a good rest, which they needed after their long
runs of the previous days. They proceeded for 10 miles
without seeing anything. The weather came on thick and
they had to camp at 6.30 P.M. It cleared a little later and
they made good two more miles. The party on this day
saw a snowy petrel. The position of this bird so far south
and away from food is remarkable.

On March 2 they had a cold and sleepless night with a

low temperature and a blizzard blowing from the north-west. The rate of travel was so quick that the dogs' run was finished early and the two men had to spend an unusually long time in their sleeping-bags, which in this cold weather was bad for them and bad for their gear. About mid-day the weather cleared enough to let them start.

On March 4 they reached One Ton Depôt in the morning, travelling during a clear night and morning. A blizzard came on after their arrival and the temperature had fallen considerably. Cherry-Garrard, owing to the low temperature, found his glasses of no use and had to trust to Demetri to pick out the cairns. Owing to the cold weather and the thin coats of the dogs he rightly decided to give them more food.

On March 5, 6, 7, and 8 they had exceedingly cold weather and blizzard. On none of these days would it have been possible for them to proceed south had they wished to do so. This party had no minimum thermometer, but on most of the nights before the sun had set the temperature had fallen to nearly minus 40°, which probably meant a minimum temperature of between 40° and 50° for the night. The dogs were in bad condition and feeling the cold. Demetri also declared that he felt far from well. These days of bad weather left Cherry-Garrard with the alternative of holding on at the camp or of travelling south for one day and allowing one day to return to the One Ton Depôt. Owing to the difficulties of keeping the right line with dog teams, he very wisely decided to remain at One Ton Depôt, leaving himself with only 8 days' dog food to return on.

Strict injunctions had been given by Captain Scott that the dogs should not be risked in any way.

On March 10 they depôted their two weeks' supply of provisions for the Southern Party, including several smaller delicacies. One Ton was then supplied with sufficient man provisions for a party of five for over a month. On this same day they started their return journey at 8 A.M. after a very cold night. Their gear and sleeping-bags were all iced up and neither of the men in good condition. The dogs at the start went practically wild, Demetri's sledge crossing Cherry-Garrard's and smashing the sledgemeter adrift. They fought as they went in their harness and had no idea of direction. This continued for six or seven miles and then they got better. After this the weather became gradually overcast and navigation became difficult. After camping, they again proceeded slowly by compass, completing 23 miles for the day, but had no idea of their whereabouts at the end.

The next morning, March 11, the weather was so overcast that they could not start. Quoting from his diary : 'Started at 2 P.M. with just a litle patch of blue sky, but we did not know where we were going and stopped at 8 miles in a blizzard. I think we were turning circles most of the time.' During the night and morning of March 12 they had a very heavy blizzard and very low temperature. Demetri declared that he could see the Bluff and that they were right into the land. This meant that they would be amongst the ice pressure and crevasses. They steered east away from this, and the weather clearing slightly, they saw White Island and headed back toward this. The temperature now remained below minus 30 for the whole of the day and the dogs and men began to feel the effects of the low temperature and high winds.

On March 13 they got a point of land to steer upon, realising that they were well to the east of what their position ought to have been. They did 18 miles for the day and camped in a fog. The year was closing in and the time of the travelling day was much decreased. Demetri thought that he saw the flag of Corner Camp to the west and steered for it. Luckily the foot hills cleared and they were able to avoid the ice pressure and crevasses of White Island, for which they had been steering. The total run for the day was about 11 miles.

On March 14 they had a clear day and realised that they were a good deal out of their reckoning. Getting under way they thought they saw what was a cairn; making for it, they found it was a great open crevasse or chasm with pressure on the farther side miraged. They then made out south-east and crossed several big crevasses. Soon after this they saw the motor one mile to the east, and Corner Camp 2 miles beyond that. They ran on past Corner Camp and eventually reached the Biscuit Depôt 15 miles from Hut Point. On this day Demetri nearly fainted and declared that he was completely done. Their main anxiety now was whether the sea ice between the edge of the Barrier and Hut Point still remained in.

On March 15 they were held up all day at the Biscuit

Depôt by a blizzard, Demetri's condition causing Cherry-Garrard great alarm.

On March 16, after a night of blizzard, they started at 8 A.M. They reached Hut Point late in the afternoon, meeting there Petty Officer Keohane and myself. Both men were in exceedingly poor condition, Cherry-Garrard's state causing me serious alarm. The dogs were frostbitten, and miserably thin, while in many cases their harnesses were iced up and frozen to them. They were quite unfit for any further work that season.

Cherry-Garrard under the circumstances and according to his instructions was in my judgment quite right in everything that he did. I am absolutely certain no other officer of the Expedition could have done better.

CHAPTER II

LAST EFFORTS BEFORE THE WINTER

On February 23, when Demetri went to Cape Evans to try and obtain help, he had a letter from me to Lieutenant Pennell, commanding the *Terra Nova*, conveying my request. After Cherry-Garrard and Demetri had left on the 26th, Lashly, Lieutenant Evans, Wright, and myself were left at Hut Point.

On February 29, the sea ice having gone out to within a quarter of a mile of Hut Point, the ship arrived. Lieutenant Evans in his sleeping-bag was placed on a sledge and removed on board the ship. She returned to Cape Evans, landing Wright and Lashly there, together with some stores. She then proceeded north to Evans Coves to try and pick up Lieutenant Campbell and his party. Lieutenant Evans' condition being still serious I had to accompany him. After several unsuccessful attempts to relieve Campbell, the ship returned to Cape Evans on March 4. Here, Keohane was picked up, and he and I were landed by the ship at Hut Point. Until the arrival of the dog teams on March 16 we occupied ourselves killing seals and laying in a store of meat and blubber before the return of the Southern Party. The ship, meanwhile, had proceeded north on a third attempt to

x2

relieve Campbell and his party. Owing to her small coal supply, she could not stay in the Sound later than March 8, and thus she was unable to notify us at the base of her success or failure in this undertaking.

On March 16, Cherry-Garrard and Demetri came in and reported that they had seen no sign of the Polar Party; they also reported the early break of the season, exceedingly low temperatures and the bad weather on the Barrier. The condition of both men was such that it was impossible for them to do any further sledging that season. I told Cherry-Garrard that we should have to make another journey to try and get to the Polar Party; he readily agreed and said that he would be quite ready himself after a few days' rest. The taking of Demetri, owing to his health was out of the question. On the third day after his return Cherry-Garrard collapsed in the morning, suffering from an over-strained heart; it was a very sad blow to him to realise that he was unable to help during this anxious time, and it was a hard measure to have to tell him that further sledging that year was impossible for him.

Realising that something had to be done, I proposed to Keohane that he should come out alone with me. He was cheerful and willing and proved of the very greatest service during a very trying time.

We discussed fully the probable dates of the return of the party to certain points and the possibility of two men being able to render them material assistance. Owing to the bad light and the time of the year, the probabilities were that they could only be met at depôts.

MOUNT EREBUS

On March 26 Keohane and I, having eighteen days'
food for ourselves and the major portion of a week's
ration for the Polar Party, started south. On the first
day we made good about nine miles after a very hard pull.
The temperature was exceedingly low but the weather
fair. Our minimum thermometer failed on this journey,
so that there was no accurate record of the temperatures.
After a sleepless night we started at 8.30 and made good
another nine miles. The day was overcast and there
was no point to steer by. The weather continued cold
and there was practically no sleep at night in the tent
occupied by only two men.

On March 29 it was again overcast, with strong
breeze ; we made good eleven miles and then, the weather
clearing, we realised that we were too far in to White
Island amongst the pressure.

On the 30th we made out from White Island, then a
few miles south of Corner Camp. We returned to the
motor, taking up the sledge left there by Lieutenant
Evans, and then on to Corner Camp. Taking into consideration the weather and temperatures and the time
of the year, and the hopelessness of finding the party
except at any definite point like a depôt, I decided to
return from here. We depôted the major portion of a
week's provisions to enable them to communicate with
Hut Point in case they should reach this point. At this
date in my own mind I was morally certain that the
party had perished, and in fact on March 29 Captain Scott,
11 miles south of One Ton Depôt, made the last entry in
his diary.

A partial blizzard sprang up and we set sail; with this help we made good 8 miles during the two hours of light remaining to us.

On March 31, snow was falling heavily and we got under way in a very bad light. Our condition was bad, as owing to the low temperatures we had got no sleep. We made good to the Biscuit Depôt, 15 miles from home, and then proceeded in the dusk for one more mile.

The next day, April 1, with a strong following breeze and a sail to help us, we reached Hut Point after dark. We were both glad to be in and to get some sleep. By this time all hope of the return of the Southern Party had been given up. Cape Evans was separated from us by open water and it was then impossible to get help from that quarter while, for all we knew, Campbell and his party had still not been relieved and were somewhere on the coast. I regarded their relief at this time as being of prime importance. To effect this it was essential to get help from Cape Evans, as at Hut Point we had two sick men and two men who were capable of sledging at that time of the year. We watched the Sound anxiously for any chance of being able to get across the sea ice to Cape Evans. Almost every day it froze over in a thin sheet, only to be swept away by high winds. The temperatures recorded at this time of the year were 10° to 15° lower at Hut Point than they had been in the previous season.

On April 10 the two Bays, one between Glacier Tongue and the Hutton Cliffs on the peninsula and the other between the Glacier Tongue and Cape Evans, having frozen over, I decided to make along the peninsula with

Keohane and Demetri, lower ourselves over the cliffs and make for Cape Evans. Leaving Cherry-Garrard necessarily at Hut Point to look after the dogs, we made our way along the peninsula and had only slight difficulty in lowering ourselves and the sledge over the cliffs with the Alpine rope. On this occasion our luck was most distinctly in. We had reached this place about 10 miles from Cape Evans at 2.30 in the afternoon; we then expected, owing to the bad surface of new sea ice, to have a pull lasting well on to 12 midnight, instead of which the ice had a firm and even surface and was devoid of any slush and ice-flowers such as are usual. We set sail before a strong falling breeze, and all sitting on the sledge had reached the Glacier Tongue in twenty minutes. We clambered over the Tongue, and our luck and the breeze still holding, we reached Cape Evans, completing the last seven miles all sitting on the sledge in an hour. There I called together all the members and explained the situation, telling them what had been done and what I then proposed to do, also asking them for their advice in this trying time. The opinion was almost unanimous that all that was possible had been already done. Owing to the lateness of the year and the likelihood of our being unable to make our way up the coast to Campbell one or two members suggested that another journey might be made to Corner Camp. Knowing the conditions which had lately prevailed on the Barrier, I took it upon myself to decide the uselessness of this.

April 11 and 12 were spent in preparing gear and securing provisions.

On April 13, about 10.30 in the morning, with Wright, Gran, Keohane, Williamson, and Demetri I started back to Hut Point. The surface of the sea ice had then completely changed and was covered with slush and ice-flowers ; a trying blizzard started, and after a very hard pull we had to run for shelter to the little Razorback Island. We camped there and had tea. Soon after, the blizzard abated somewhat and we got under way. We made very slow progress, and after a very hard day's pull could only reach the Glacier Tongue, seven miles from home. The next morning we awoke, made our way over the Tongue, and reaching the cliffs had some difficulty in getting up. The sledge was held at arm's length by four men while one clambered up and by the help of his knife eventually gained a sure footing and was able to help the others. Except for the steepness of the climb, the remainder of the journey to Hut Point was easy. There we found Cherry-Garrard greatly relieved at our return, as the ice had been blowing out of the Sound, but had luckily remained in in the two bays. We reached Hut Point on the 14th.

The 15th and 16th were occupied in drying gear and making up provisions for four weeks. I decided to take C. S. Wright, who was a skilled navigator, Petty Officer Williamson, and Keohane. The season was well advanced and a great part of the travelling and camping had to be done in the dusk.

On April 17 we started across the sea ice, and after 5 miles we reached some old sea ice which had probably been there for two years or more. We then proceeded over a very good surface through a cold day towards the pinnacled ice, and completed 13 miles for that day. The minimum for the night was minus 43°. We did not sleep very well and started breakfast at 7 A.M. in the dark. The temperature for the whole day was about minus 40°. We made good progress over this same old sea ice and luckily we were able to skirt the edge of the pinnacled ice. We camped finally about four miles from the Eskers on the western shore, four miles of new sea ice intervening between us and them. On this night there were five penguins on the old sea ice by our camp. This was disturbing, as it meant the near presence of open water. The minimum for the night was minus 45°. When the morning broke, we saw that a blizzard was impending and we knew it was a matter of speed if we were to cross the new sea ice in safety. Luckily the wind favoured us. We set sail and practically ran with the sledge for two miles before it. The wind then falling light our progress became very slow over a bad surface. To add to our anxiety we could see several Emperor penguins making towards the old sea ice and big leads opening and frost smoke rising from the breaking up of the new sea ice. Eventually we reached the Eskers in safety. We proceeded over a very bad surface from Butter Point for four miles and then, a strong blizzard setting in, we had to camp. This blizzard proved far from being a friend. With it the temperature rose to zero, and our clothing and our bags, which were already full of ice, became saturated, making us in a very uncomfortable state.

On the 20th in the morning, after 3 miles, we reached the depôt on the northern end of Butter Point. This depôt had been left there earlier in the season by the ship. We camped and had some tea. Having struck camp, while we were harnessing up Williamson exclaimed, ' Lord, look at that ! ' The sea ice at the foot of the Point was gradually breaking up and sailing out to sea. This meant that it was impossible for a party to travel up the coast to the relief of Campbell, and we necessarily had to turn back from this point.   It also meant that it was impossible for Campbell and his party to make their way down the coast and that in all probability he and his party would have to winter at Evans Coves. The question of their travelling on such sea ice was infinitely more disturbing than the question of their wintering there.

As one instance of the loyal way in which I was supported during the whole of this season, I can quote the following : ' Wright, from the very first, had been entirely against this journey. He had some knowledge of a previous sledge trip on the western coast. Not until after I had told him that we should have to turn back, did he tell me how thankful he was at the decision. He had come on this trip fully believing that there was every probability of the party being lost, but had never demurred and never offered a contrary opinion, and one cannot be thankful enough to such men.'

We depôted two weeks' provisions at Butter Point and started to make our way back to Hut Point, our only anxiety being lest the new sea ice had blown out in the blizzard which had delayed us at Butter Point. That night we camped near the northern end of the Eskers and awaited the morning with some anxiety. To our joy we found that the 4 miles of new sea ice was still in in part. Again with a favouring wind we set sail and ran before it for 2 miles. The wind again fell light, and to our consternation we saw the Emperor penguins walking solemnly toward the edge of the old sea ice, which probably meant that there was open water between us and it. But eventually we reached safety and camped for a meal, then in a bad light completed 6 more miles.

Next morning, the 22nd, a blizzard caused a late start. We made for the end of the pinnacled ice, hoping to find our ice still in. As we approached, dense volumes of frost smoke were seen arising from where it had been. This was serious, as it probably meant we should have to make our way through the pinnacled ice, an undertaking which meant several more days in the bad light and bad going. Luckily for the party, there was a narrow ledge or ice-foot projecting from the edge of the pinnacled ice. Alternately along this and along the edge of the pinnacled ice we made our way, stumbling and falling in the holes and capsizing the sledge. After 7 miles we made our way through, and although we could not then see our whereabouts, we knew the remainder of the journey would be pretty plain sailing.

On April 23 there was a blizzard in the morning, a very strong wind and low temperature. There were no land marks to steer by, and using the sastrugi for this purpose we only completed $3\frac{1}{2}$ miles by 1 o'clock and then camped for a meal. Soon after, the weather cleared slightly and we started to make our way to Hut Point. We found that the sea ice had again gone out close to Hut Point, but by keeping well to the south and completing 15 miles, a very good march for the day, we arrived at Hut Point in the dark. I have never known a journey have such an effect upon a party in such a short time.

On the 23rd, the day we returned, we saw the sun for the last time until his return in August. The greater part of this journey was done in the dusk. Wright, owing to the low temperature, was unable to wear his glasses. The light being bad and he short-sighted, he marched under a very great disadvantage. I have spoken before of his loyalty and good-comradeship. Petty Officer Keohane behaved splendidly on the Barrier in the latter end of March and beginning of April and again on this journey. Williamson's conduct was also splendid in every way. The next few days we spent at Hut Point drying out our gear, which was badly iced, and getting some sleep, which we all needed. We began to realise that it was a question now of making the best of circumstances and waiting till the spring of the year before anything further could be done. At Hut Point Cherry-Garrard, Gran, and Demetri had remained, and their task of waiting had been by no means the easier one.

As winter drew on, we had now to return to the base. On April 28 Wright, Gran, and Keohane started to make their way back to Cape Evans over the sea ice. Soon after they had rounded the point it began to blow very stiffly and they ran for safety to the Glacier Tongue; they crossed very thin and bad sea ice, Wright having to go

DEMETRI GEROFF

GRAN WITH MULE 'LAL KHAN'

ahead at the full length of the Alpine rope. When they arrived eventually at Cape Evans it was dark and blowing a blizzard. They were lost on the Cape for some time, but eventually found the hut and were in safety.

On May 1 Cherry-Garrard, Demetri, Williamson, and I returned to Cape Evans with the two dog teams. There we started to settle in for the winter and gradually took up the winter routine.

Everything was well at the hut at Cape Evans and work, scientific and otherwise, had been proceeding as usual. We early realised that for the sake of everyone concerned the routine followed in the previous year must be continued in this as far as possible. It was a necessity for us to keep up our work and interests and exercise, so as to avoid slackness and depression and to keep fit and useful through the dark months. The North Bay had only frozen to within half a mile of the hut and had been continually freezing and blowing out.

The seven mules, which had been given by the Indian Government to Captain Scott to enable him to carry on further exploration in the second year, were in excellent condition. Lashly had received certain instructions from Captain Oates when Evans' party left them on the Plateau at 87° 37'. He had been in entire charge of the mules and continued so throughout the winter. Their condition throughout was splendid and spoke volumes for the care with which he looked after them. These mules were suggested to Captain Scott by Captain Oates, and they justified his hopes in every way. The mules had been exercised regularly whenever the weather permitted, and already the seven leaders had adopted their four-footed charges. The ship had also brought down fourteen new dogs. Three of these died soon after landing, and eventually only four of them proved to be of any use for sledging. A litter of pups had been added, but these died owing to their mother leaving them.

Debenham had been doing the meteorological work and Nelson, who was in charge, had carried out the magnetic observations. Crean was in charge of the sledges and sledging gear and Williamson had charge of the sewing-machine, with Keohane to help Crean and Williamson. We early appreciated the efforts of a really good cook in Mr. Archer, who had been landed for this second year. Besides being a good cook he proved a good companion and was always lively and cheerful. Lieutenant Gran took charge of the stores and also of the four hourly meteorological observations. He proved a most efficient stores officer and in his observations was continually trying to break previous records, which he was very often able to do in this exceptional season. Cherry-Garrard was again our editor for the *South Polar Times* and took over the care and preparation of all the ornithological and zoological specimens obtained. Hooper, the steward, took over the management of the acetylene plant, thereby relieving someone else of a very thankless task.

The mules were apportioned as follows ·

To Nelson	.	,	.	.	.	Khan Sahib
To Gran	.	.	.	.	.	Lal Khan
To Crean	.	.	.	.	.	Rani
To Keohane	.	.	.	.	.	Begum

To Williamson . . . .

To Hooper . . . . .

To Archer . . . . .

A regular night watch to take hourly observations of aurora, to look after the mules and to keep in the fires was also kept. Since our numbers were so much reduced the men were asked to take their nights, and to this they cheerfully agreed. We numbered altogether thirteen souls in the hut. Weekly lectures were arranged to be given by the various officers, and instead of confining these to merely scientific subjects, other items of interest were lectured upon.

CHAPTER III

THE SECOND WINTER

ON May 3rd to the 5th we had an exceptionally strong blizzard wind. In the evening the gusts recorded by the anemometer were between 70 and 88 miles an hour, a strength considerably over that of any previous observation. The ice was again blown from the North Bay. During the whole of the night the force of the gale increased, and toward morning it began to take off. When Gran checked the instrument at 8.30 A.M. it registered for 3 minutes the rate of 104 miles an hour, and by this time its force had abated considerably. It was exceedingly difficult at this time of the year to obtain any seals owing to the lack of ice in the South and North Bays.

Simpson had some hyacinth bulbs sent down to him, and under Hooper's care these, embedded in a basin full of white sawdust, burst into bloom and lasted for some considerable time.

It was strange at this time of the year to see the open water right up to the hut. The sky effects were beautiful towards the north at midday, and on a calm day their reflection from the open water was splendid.

Demetri and Keohane busied themselves in building

a dog hospital. This was essential, as several of the dogs had not as yet recovered from their trip to the Barrier in March. It was large and comparatively warm and much appreciated by the invalids.

The exceptional weather with repeated blizzards of great force during the whole of May kept both man and beast very much confined to the hut. This one felt more than the previous year, as besides being confined to the hut, when it was possible to get exercise we could only do so for a short distance on the Cape, whereas in the previous year the sea ice had extended for some 30 miles to the north of us. There was now open water to the south.

Crean and Keohane had already started mending most of the sleeping-bags, which were in sad need of repair. Luckily the ship had left us with a good supply of reindeer skin and there was plenty to go round and fill up the bare patches in the sleeping-bags.

The mule gear which had been supplied by the Indian Government showed the very greatest forethought in every detail. There were only very slight alterations to be made, more especially in the texture of the gear. The mules had been supplied with a form of canvas snow-goggles, for the ponies in the previous year had suffered badly from snow blindness. These goggles saved the mules from this amount of discomfort when they were on the Barrier. We also realised that owing to their small hoofs they would probably have to use snow-shoes. These had been supplied, and on trying the mules with them most of the animals after a very short time took to them quite naturally.

Debenham had been given charge of all photographic

gear; and was out continually taking photographs of
general and scientific interest.

On May 10 Nelson lectured on the tides, the main interest
of his contention being that with the greatest declination
of the moon the movement of ice was more probable.

A never-failing source of amusement after dinner
every night has been a form of bagatelle which is played
on a mess table. The table was covered with a strip
of green Willesden canvas stretched between two long
boards which formed the cushions. Between these boards
at the top of the table a bridge fits, having in it a number
of holes. The object is to get the balls into these holes,
the score being according to the number above the hole.
A competition was arranged and the lowest scorer of the
competition received the Jonah Medal. Having obtained
this, he had to announce at luncheon each day 'Gentlemen,
I am the Jonah.' This he continued to do until someone
else had relieved him of the medal.

The ice in the North Bay now froze again to a thickness
of 4 to 5 inches. Nelson started again to build his igloo
on the ice in the South Bay to carry on his biological
work. When he had pricked the ice the water came
through and flowed over the floor of his igloo. The ice,
being thin, was pressed down at the spot where the weight
bore on it.

On May 13 we had a wonderful aurora display about
6 P.M. and this was believed to be the brightest that had
been seen at Cape Evans. The greater part of the sky was
covered, but the most vivid shafts ran north-east and
south-west. Debenham tried with various exposures

to photograph the phenomena, but unluckily failed to get any results. We started again our fish trap, which was let down by digging a hole through the ice; this was at first successful and we had a fair number of fish. The flesh of these fish was so sweet that they were, in the ordinary way, quite unpleasant eating. Archer, by soaking them first in vinegar and water, made them much more palatable. Keohane and Williamson, after a great deal of trouble, caught some of these same fish by hook and line.

On May 25 we had some slight excitement. Wright needed a lamp to heat his magnetic hut, and Nelson and he, while experimenting with one and increasing the pressure in the lamp to give a better flare, unluckily managed to burst it. Immediately the whole end of the table and part of the floor was a mass of flames. With blankets and a fire extinguisher these were soon put out and no harm done. Nelson, whose face was down by the lamp when the explosion occurred, had a very lucky escape. Our fish trap, which had been failing in the number of fish caught each day, was blown out to sea with the ice from the North Bay. This was a serious loss, but we managed with some wire, iron bars, and two hoops to make another but smaller one. About this time some of the geological specimens which had been brought back by the first and second return parties were handed over to Debenham. These had mainly been collected in the scattered moraine under the Cloudmaker. To his surprise and joy several fossils of plants and small marine animals were found in some of these.

Y 2

One of the dogs, Vaida, who had been ill since his return, was allowed a ceitain amount of latitude; he frequently came into the hut and would take up his position there, appreciating the warmth and comfort and strenuously resisting ejection at any time. Altogether he regarded himself as having taken on the duty of a house dog.

On June 1, the ice appearing sound, Demetri and Hooper with a dog team went to Hut Point, doing the journey there and back in the same day. One of the dogs had been lost on our return to Cape Evans; but no trace of this animal was found on arriving there and he was never seen again.

The first week of June proved practically calm and we had our coldest temperatures of the winter.

However, as a little ice remained in the North Bay we were able to get more exercise for men and animals. From the 8th to the 13th we had a most exceptional blizzard, both for the warmth of temperature and the amount of drift. It was quite possible in this blizzard to move a few yards away from the hut and be lost for some considerable time. The ice again blew out and we had a wonderful show of phosphorescence in the sea. Once beneath the ice foot we saw a seal chasing a school of fish, the fish outlined with phosphorescence and the seal with a glowing snout and all his body bright, in hot pursuit.

In the previous season Wright had had great trouble in maintaining an even temperature for his pendulum observations. To overcome this a large hole was cut in the floor of the dark room and a kenyte boulder embedded in it, upon which the pendulum was set. With this arrangement he was able to take his observations more accurately and in greater comfort.

Bv this time the weather seemed to have broken and we had an almost continuous series of blizzards. Meanwhile we had noticed one peculiarity about the mules. The ponies in the previous year had refused to go out when there was any wind and drift blowing. The mules, on the other hand, objected strongly by kicking their stable and squealing if they were not taken out for exercise under these conditions.

On the 19th preparations were begun for our celebra tions of Midwinter Day on June 22. Debenham was busv making the slides for a lantern lecture. Gran and Williamson were busy behind a blanket making a Christmas tree. This consisted of a central bamboo with lateral stems and the whole imbedded in a pot of gravel. There was a present for evervone with an appropriate oration on its presentation. The whole was lighted with electric light, by arrangement with the physicist.

On June 22, Midwinter Day, Cherry-Garrard, our editor, presented us with anɔther number of the *South Polar Times*, and the remainder of the afternoon was spent as a holiday in reading this, playing bagatelle, or making preparations for a happy evening. The whole hut was decorated with the Christmas tree, sledging flags, and some red bunting. A large white ensign was hung over all as a canopy. Nelson presented each member with a

very pretty menu card.   These were cut out of cardboard
and painted to represent Adélie penguins.

The menu was :

Cape Evans,
June 22nd, Midwinter's Day.

Croûte Erebus.   Amandes Sellés.

Crême de Volaille Ferrar.

Noisettes d'Agneau Darwinian.

Centre Filet de Bœuf rôti.

Asperges en Branches.

Pommes de Terre Naturel.

Poudin Noël.   Pâté d'Eunice.

Compôte de Fruits.

Charlotte Russe glacée à la Beardmore.

Buszard's Cake.   Dessert.

After dinner, when various healths had been drunk,
Gran jumped out of the dark room dressed as a clown,
with his face powdered and painted.   His acting was
splendid, with a joke for everybody and sometimes a
piece of poetry which he declaimed to the men as they
came forward to receive their presents.   Gran made an
excellent clown, and the whole entertainment went with a
roar from beginning to end.   Then Debenham put up his
lantern and gave us a lot of pictures of all kinds: leaving
Dunedin, in the pack, Cape Crozier, the Western Mountains,
ponies, and many more.   He had taken a lot of time and
trouble over these slides and they were excellent and
added to the enjoyment of everybody.   The evening was
closed by a sing-song.   Each day now we knew meant one

MIDWINTER DAY, 1912—THE OFFICERS
Left to right, Cherry-Garrard, Wright, Atkinson, Nelson, Gran

MIDWINTER DAY, 1912—THE MEN
Left to right, Archer, Williamson, Crean, Hooper, Keohane, Demetri

more towards the return of light and usefulness, and
preparations were started for the future sledging season.
After dinner I called together the members and told them
what I proposed to do in the coming season, stating the
reasons and asking for their criticism. Two alternatives
lay before us. One was to go south and try to discover
the fate of Captain Scott's party. I thought it most
likely that they had been lost in a crevasse on the Beardmore Glacier. Whether their bodies could be found or not,
it was highly desirable to go even as far as the Upper
Glacier Depôt, nearly 600 miles from the base, in the hope
of finding a note left in some depôt which could tell
whether they had fulfilled their task or turned back before
reaching the Pole. On general grounds it was of great
importance not to leave the record of the Expedition
incomplete, with one of its most striking chapters a blank.

The other alternative was to go west and north to
relieve Campbell and his party, always supposing they
had survived the winter. If they had come through the
winter, every day of advancing summer would improve
their chances of living on in Terra Nova Bay. At the
same time there was good prospect of their being ultimately relieved by the ship, if indeed she had not taken
them off in the autumn. As for ourselves, it seemed most
improbable that we could journey up the coast owing to
the abnormal state of the ice. Instead of being frozen
for the winter, the whole Sound to the north and west of
Inaccessible Island was open water during July; the ice
was driven out by the exceptionally strong and frequent
winds, and there was little chance of a firm road forming

for the spring. Under these conditions officers and men unanimously supported the decision to go south.

Nelson at the end of June had started some lectures upon heredity. These proved to be of great interest and led to several discussions amongst the men and officers. They were so popular that they had to be continued for three weeks. The weather in June as a whole was immeasurably worse than it had been in any previous season. Comparison of the records will show this in figures, both as regards wind and snow. though not in actual lowness of temperature. Our hut was becoming gradually snowed in. After these blizzards in the dark it was almost an impossibility to walk far in the camp because of the huge drifts. Pyaree started giving some trouble with her capped knee on her near fore-leg. This continued for some time and she was unable to get exercise and lost condition. The ice, which had been fairly permanent again, blew out in a large bight to the south of the Cape. In the afternoon now we occasionally saw some colour in the northern sky, a presage of the light that we were to have. One never appreciates fully the blessing of an amount of light until one has been through a good deal of darkness. This time also we started bagging off the rations for the future sledging season. Owing to the probable length of our search these were of considerable bulk.

On July the 16th we had probably the most beautiful day of the year. The whole northern sky was filled with opalescent clouds, and owing to some white ice instead of the black water in the North Bay, the increase of light seemed very appreciable. The mules were now exercised regularly on the ice in the South Bay, and by this means their leaders were able to take them over greater distances. Their condition began gradually to improve, and the way they had come through the winter so far reflected great credit on the care taken by Lashly

On the 19th the plans for the Southern journey were laid before the other members. Debenham, who had been suffering from an old knee injury at football, and Archer were the two members who would have to remain by the hut.

It was a sad blow to both of them to realise their position, but they accepted it cheerfully. The plan was to provide enough provisions to enable two parties, each a unit of four, to ascend the Beardmore Glacier, and two dog teams with a unit of three men to return from some point not as yet settled. Of the men ascending the glacier, four were to remain at the Cloudmaker and collect geological specimens, photograph, and do survey work. They would then proceed to the foot of the glacier and continue doing this same work until the return of the others, for all this time they were needed as a support by the advance party. This advance party, the other unit of four, would ascend to the top of the glacier if it were necessary to go so far. On their return to the foot of the glacier both units would march home. At this time it was believed by most of us that an accident had occurred to the Southern Party, probably at the lower reaches of the Beardmore, in bad weather, and that sickness had nothing to do with the disaster.

As there was no food either for dogs, mules, or men in any of the depôts, the initial starting weights would have to be very large. To help as far as possible some small depôt journeys would be made in the spring. During the whole winter so far the cheerfulness of the party had been splendid under the most trying conditions, but there now seemed to be an added sprightliness with the return of light.

Nelson had been occupying his time by a very ingenious method of predicting occultations. He predicted altogether nearly fifty, but unfortunately was only able to get one or two observations. These observations were for obtaining the exact longitude. The whole Sound at this time to the north and west of Inaccessible Island was open water. We had two enormous drifts of nine to ten feet high leading from the door of the annexe down to the sea. The latter end of July the weather broke up entirely and we had a repetition of our usual blizzards for the season.

LOOKING WEST FROM CAPE EVANS.

CHAPTER IV

THE SECOND WINTER: Continued

In August, with the gradual return of light, we were able to get about more and consequently took more exercise. A small ski slope was made running down from the rear of the Hut and also a small jump was fixed by Gran. On fine days there was a continual stream of men labouring slowly up the slope and making their way down again with varying success. The sea ice conditions still continued bad and there was some doubt now as to whether we should be able to make our way over the sea ice to Hut Point.

On August 12 for the first time we saw the sun's rays on the summit of Erebus and the smoke rising from the crater was painted a beautiful pink. One of the difficulties that we had to encounter for the next sledging season was the lack of sledge meters. We had only one left, but Lashly, our handy man, was trying his hand at the manufacture of another under the direction of Nelson. By means of a bicycle wheel and the front fork of a bicycle he made out head and wheel, while the register was made from the meter attached to the dynamo. This looked

CHAPTER IV

THE SECOND WINTER: CONTINUED

IN August, with the gradual return of light, we were able to get about more and consequently took more exercise. A small ski slope was made running down from the rear of the Hut and also a small jump was fixed by Gran. On fine days there was a continual stream of men labouring slowly up the slope and making their way down again with varying success. The sea ice conditions still continued bad and there was some doubt now as to whether we should be able to make our way over the sea ice to Hut Point.

On August 12 for the first time we saw the sun's rays on the summit of Erebus and the smoke rising from the crater was painted a beautiful pink. One of the difficulties that we had to encounter for the next sledging season was the lack of sledge meters. We had only one left, but Lashly, our handy man, was trying his hand at the manufacture of another under the direction of Nelson. By means of a bicycle wheel and the front fork of a bicycle we got our lead and wheel, while the register was made from the meter attached to the dynamo. This looked exceedingly promising, and after it had been used over short distances gave very good results eventually. On the Barrier it proved of assistance up to One Ton Depôt and then had to be abandoned.

The new sledges, called Finnesskis, were the cause of much discussion. Six had been ordered from Hägen of Christiania, and these arrived with tapered runners, the breadth of the runner in front being 4 inches, diminishing to 2½ on the after part of the sledge. We tried these sledges with the old 12-foot, man-hauling over various surfaces and with equal loads. In every case the new sledges ran more easily, but it was impossible to judge if there was sufficient bearing surface for them with heavy loads on the soft Barrier surface. They eventually proved to be of the greatest service, and animals or men could move loads on these sledges which it was impossible for them to move with the ordinary 12-foot and broad runner. The idea of the sledge was that the broad front portion should run over and smooth and prepare the track for the after tapered portion.

There was very little alteration needed in any of the other gear. Each individual had his personal likes and dislikes and adapted his gear accordingly. In the rations there was only a very slight alteration, our old summit ration being adhered to with the addition of extra sugar, a stick of chocolate, and one onion per man per day.

On August 22 we celebrated the return of the sun with a special dinner, and ended up proceedings with a sing-song. It was not until the 23rd, however, that the sun was seen, and then only by Nelson, who saw its upper

rim from the top of the ramp. Almost every day now
we saw the earth shadows cast by Erebus and Mount
Discovery. These looked like dark cones of shadow
running across the sky from east to west.

During these bad conditions of ice in the winter we
necessarily had to be careful of the dogs. Some of these
were confirmed hunters, and it was through the ice going
out during a blizzard that we lost the best leader that
we had. Noogis was a dog who had been Demetri's
leader on the southern journey in the early part of the
year; he had never lost heart on that journey and had
been a great factor in cheering the other dogs and getting
them along as well as they did. In the earlier part of the
year he had once before been taken out to sea by the ice
blowing away, but on that occasion he made his way
back by the ice-foot around the Barne Glacier. On
this occasion he was blown out during the blizzard and
we never saw him again.

Our feeding during this winter, with the idea of
preventing scurvy, had a very welcome addition in the
shape of fresh vegetables. These consisted of potatoes
and onions which had been brought down by the ship.
As the party was so reduced in numbers, this store lasted
practically throughout the winter and proved very acceptable. In September we also had another addition in
the shape of the Emperor penguins; they came up on the
ice in the South Bay in very large numbers, and nearly
every day for some time we were able to secure fresh food.
The flesh of the Emperor penguin is better and much less un-
palatable than seal; it was appreciated by the men where
seal would only have been eaten as a preventive measure.

The number of dogs who were fit for work on the Barrier made exactly two teams. This left at the hut seven dogs who could work but were unable to stand the trials of a long journey. Debenham started to exercise these dogs for geological purposes around the hut. Small as the team was, it made up in obstinacy and trouble for its size.

The chief trouble was getting away from the Cape down a pretty steep ice-foot, and the old leader, Stareek, generally refusing to do his duty when he was within reach of the hut, their direction at first was uncertain.

On September 3, Wright, Debenham, Cherry-Garrard, and I made a small trip over the Barne Glacier to Cape Royds, Shackleton's winter quarters. Our main object was to secure a few luxuries and to leave some spirit and apparatus there for work to be done amongst the penguins in the summer. We found on arriving that the bays and the whole of the Sound as far as we could see were practically free from ice.

On September 5, during a stiff blow, our chimney caught fire. The chimney consisted of an upright piece which went through the hut about the middle. A galley and a stove were at either end of the hut; from each of these a funnel ran and connected with the central upright piece. The fire started at first in the centre and gradually spread down towards the galley or cooking range. We got the flames under control by covering the chimney on the outside with large slabs of snow, the inside of the hut meanwhile being full of smoke and smuts. After some trouble the funnel was disjointed, taken out and swept through.

THE HUT AFTER THE WINTER

During the worst time the funnel for nearly half its length was red-hot and glowing, and the heat inside the hut was very uncomfortable.

On the 6th, with the idea of giving the members exercise, Nelson, Gran, Crean, and Archer started for Cape Royds over the Barne Glacier. Gran made a complete list of all the stores at Shackleton's quarters and the party returned on the following day.

The exercise of the mules was now carried on over a longer period, sledges were made up and they were harnessed in and drew their loads on alternate days. The only mule that gave us any serious trouble was Gulab; but Williamson throughout was most tactful and painstaking with this mule, who proved eventually to be the best beast that we had. Pyaree's capped knee started now to give us a great deal of anxiety, and up to the last week in October before she started we thought that she would be unable to go. As it was, she went on to the Barrier with a stiff foreleg, but she worked splendidly as the strain wore off and proved to be the second best mule of the lot.

Owing to the uncertain condition of the ice it was essential to remove as many stores as possible to Hut Point. On September 18 to 22, a party went there with dog teams, taking down a load of stores and with the idea of putting the hut in order. The hut had nearly been buried by the inclement season, but after a great deal of digging had been done it was made more habitable. The hut at Cape Evans had been very much snowed up by this bad season and our roof in one part began to sag from the weight of snow upon it. This was continually removed and as continually was replaced by the next blizzard. During the remainder of this month several trips were made by the dog teams to Hut Point, taking down stores. The ponies also were given extra food so as to get them in better condition for their trip on the Barrier.

It was proposed after the previous year to make their allowance 11 lbs. per mule per day, a ration consisting of oil cake and oats in the proportion of two of oil cake to one of oats.

On September 26 we had a partial eclipse of the moon which we saw very clearly. The maximum shadow fell just before midnight, and we thought we should be unable to see it, for the moon rose behind clouds to the north of Erebus, but it cleared in time and Nelson was able to get his telescope fixed up. Our winter now was practically ended. With the return of light the health and cheerfulness of the party, which had been excellent throughout, improved still more, and we knew now that only a month intervened before we should be away on the Barrier. Scientific work had been carried on throughout the winter, although in certain branches this had been necessarily prohibited by the absence of sea ice.

On October 12 Debenham, Demetri, Cherry-Garrard, and I went down to Hut Point, and on October 14 took the two dog teams out to lay a depôt 12 miles south of Corner Camp. This consisted mainly of pony and dog food and was essential in order to relieve the ponies over the first four days of the journey, on which they would have to encounter heavy surfaces. On the return, as one

THE RAMP AND THE SLOPES OF [illegible]

THE RAMP AND THE SLOPES OF EREBUS.

of the dog teams was crossing a large crevasse, four of the dogs broke through the crust and the sledge was practically anchored by their weight. With the help of the other dogs these were gradually hauled out, popping out of the holes like corks from a bottle. As the sledge and team were on the crevasse at the same time it was fairly anxious work. The dogs bolted and a driving-stick was left by the edge of the crevasse. This was a good but unintentional mark by which to avoid it in future. The depôt was called Demetri Depôt in honour of the Russian dog-boy.

On October 19 four of the mules came down from Cape Evans to Hut Point, bringing loads ; they did the journey splendidly and gave great promise of their future usefulness. Debenham meanwhile had been making a geological survey of the peninsula and Cherry-Garrard had been helping him.

On October 25 Cherry-Garrard and Demetri with two dog teams went out to Corner Camp, taking with them a further supply of dog biscuits and fodder. This was the last journey before we started south on October 29.

CHAPTER V

THE FINDING OF THE POLAR PARTY

ON October 29 the mules all came down with their leaders to Hut Point and everything was ready for a start on the journey south. It was decided to march at night as we had done in the previous season, so that the mules would be moving during this cold time and camp during the warm portion of the day.

At 7.30. P.M. on October 30 the seven mules and eight men making up the Pony Party started south. C. S. Wright was in command, as he was a skilled navigator. The mules and their leaders were as follows :

E. W. Nelson, leading Khan Sahib ; T. Gran, leading Lal Khan ; W. Lashly, leading Pyaree ; T. Crean, leading Rani ; T. Williamson, leading Gulab ; P. Keohane, leading Begum ; F. J. Hooper, leading Abdullah.

Wright was in command and went ahead, setting the course and standing by to give any help he could. The mules' weights up to Corner Camp would not exceed 500 lbs. This was because of the deep and bad surface usually occurring over this area. The tents were under Wright and Nelson. It was proposed to march twelve geographical miles every night, but, as their progress was uncertain, the question of this distance was left entirely to Wright's judgment.

Gran. Williamson. Keohane. Wright. Demetri.

SOUTHERN PARTY 1912

Photo. by F. Debenham.

Pyaree started lame, but within a few days had lost any slight trouble which she had. Gulab had proved that he would chafe easily with the breast harness, and in his case a collar was taken as well. Their first day they did twelve miles, camping about six miles to the S.E. of Safety Camp. Where the sea ice joined the Barrier there was a wide tide-crack, and Khan Sahib unluckily fell partially into this; he was a very quiet animal, and with the aid of an Alpine rope and hauling on his fore-legs they got him up and over on to the surface.

The next day they made good another twelve miles over a slightly worse surface, camping within six miles of Corner Camp. Owing to the dogs' experience in the earlier part of the year, we realised that this area was more crevassed than it had been previously. I had left it to Wright's judgment as to whether the leaders of the mules were to be linked up by the Alpine rope in going over these last six miles. He thought it fit to do this and they proceeded in that order. The surface they encountered was exceedingly deep and heavy, and only two of the mules struck crevasses and these, luckily, without any mishap. The mules were so tired when they had finished the six miles to Corner Camp that Wright decided to remain there for half a day.

On November 1 the two dog-teams, with Cherry-Garrard, Demetri, and myself, started to follow the mules. The dogs' loads, which had been made out to allow about 75 lbs. per dog, proved to be heavy from the start; the progress was exceedingly slow and we completed fifteen miles for the first day. The next day, again over a very bad surface, we completed another fifteen miles and reached Corner Camp. There we had a very reassuring note from Wright. He said that the mules were going well together and, instead of having to be split up into fast and slow mules, they broke camp and pitched camp, with one exception, all together, for Khan Sahib, Nelson's mule, was peculiarly slow, and in the temperature we were encountering on the march Nelson found it of the greatest difficulty to keep himself at all warm. This mule would usually lose three-fourths of a mile on the others while they were completing two miles. Nelson invented a method of walking two steps forward and jumping one back, in order to keep his circulation up to the mark.

They proceeded, building cairns of snow at intervals of from two to four miles in order that we might follow their tracks.

I saw from the way that the dogs were going that we should have great difficulty, with their present weights, in catching the mules before they reached One Ton Depôt. On Wright's satisfactory report I decided to entrust everything to the mules and to use the dogs as a means of lightening their heavy loads. The mules' weights had increased from Corner Camp up to nearly 700 lbs. per mule. This was far in excess of any weights hauled by the ponies in the previous season, and here we saw the advantage of having tapered runners to our sledges. The beasts, with comparative ease, were able to move these heavy loads on the sledges, where they would have been unable to do so with the broad runners of the previous 12-foot sledge.

Wright proceeded the next day to Demetri Depôt,

twelve miles south from Corner Camp. The mules here took on their full loads and proceeded south before we could get up to them. Here the remainder of the surplus weights of the dogs was left.

Kasoi, one of the dogs, had refused for that day to work; no amount of beating would induce him to do so. We therefore took him off the trace and tied him with the harness to the rear of the sledge. Demetri's team, who were following, realised that something was wrong with this dog: they pulled their very hardest with the idea of getting up to him and finishing him. Kasoi realised what this meant, and it decided him in favour of work as nothing else could have done. He resumed his pulling, and never slackened his trace afterwards.

On the night of the 4th and the morning of the 5th of November we had got on to a very good surface; we started early and light, in order to reach the mules before they had started, and this we eventually did after we had made our twelve miles. In view of their condition and the tired dogs I decided to give animals and men a day's rest at this place. The weather, which had been windy and drifting up to now, had begun to clear and would give the animals some chance of drying off, as well as having a good night's rest.

Gulab, Williamson's mule, had been badly chafed by the breast harness on his shoulder. Williamson had changed him to his collar and almost immediately after the first day of this he chafed again. Throughout the whole of his journey Williamson took the very greatest care of his animal and invented various new and clever designs for taking the weight of his draught off his chafed shoulder. Eventually Gulab's tail was brought as an aid to this. By means of a back strap connecting his collar and his tail most of the drag was taken off his shoulder and, under these conditions, the chafe began to heal.

About this time, as the lights were very strong, the mules began to show signs of snow-blindness. It was then that their snow-goggles were tried for the first time. We found that they were of the greatest use and generally stayed on while the mules were on their lines ; they were of the greatest comfort to the animals.

The mules would not eat their ration of oil cake and oats at all. They showed a liking for everything except their ration. They would eat man or dog biscuits, tea-leaves and tobacco, ash and various portions of garments, with the greatest of relish, but they needed the utmost care and coaxing to be induced to touch their ration at all. They were picketed by their fore-legs, as the ponies had been in the previous year, and they showed the greatest ingenuity in getting themselves free and strolling about the camp, testing various articles of the store goods.

The same routine was kept by this party. The morning march was seven miles in length ; they then camped and had tea, which lasted for about one hour and a half. When camp was struck, they marched on for five miles more, completing the twelve geographical miles for the day. Their speed on march was favourable compared with that of the ponies of the previous year. Our surfaces were so hard and good that the mules did not with their small hooves sink appreciably into the snow.

The dogs' weights here having been much reduced, they were able to relieve the mules to a large extent. The routine of the march was now changed : from one to two hours after the mules had started, the dogs followed them. The change in the dogs and in their rate of progress was now wonderful : when they had something to follow, and especially when the mules came into view, they proceeded during the whole of the day at a full gallop.

Abdullah, Hooper's mule, had constituted himself leader throughout, and continued so until his return from the Barrier towards the end of November. This was a difficult feat, as the first mule has always the added hardship of having to break the track.

The surface was extremely good, hard, and almost marbled, and the sledges followed the animals easily.

Each night, on camping, a wall was built for the mules, consisting of large slabs of hard snow dug in the Barrier ; they were a considerable amount of trouble, but afforded shelter to the beasts from the wind and drift. The mules had so eaten their covers that it required much ingenuity to make these useful for protecting the beasts.

The day's rest had done everyone good, and on a glorious day we proceeded and soon finished the twelve miles for the day.

On the night of the 6th and 7th we started at 10.30, and, on a slightly worse surface, did seven miles up to lunch. All along this way we had been building cairns of snow at intervals of from two to four miles apart. The day, which was cloudy, cleared towards morning, and was much colder. During this time we were marching in temperature which ranged from minus 20 to the lowest of minus 29. In the daytime, when the sun had reached its full height, the temperature would rise almost to zero.

On the night of the 7th and morning of the 8th of November we made the old Bluff Depôt in 79° South and re-built it, placing a new flag of black bunting on the pole. Here we left two boxes of dog biscuit for the dogs returning on their journey back from the south. The surface again continued good, and never in any previous experience had it been so hard and good as far south as this.

On the night of the 8th and 9th we continued over this same good surface, before a slight north-easterly wind and a cold day. The dogs had now again begun to fail. They seemed to lack enthusiasm and spirit; I believe that in their case they had had too much work upon the Barrier and were spiritless and easily depressed by the lack of anything to see. In the previous year we had had certain ' cuts ' of land for the Bluff Depôt and Corner Camp. It was quite easy to see from these that both camps had changed their positions owing to the gradual movement of the Barrier, year by year. Approximately, and judging very roughly, the movement in either case had been about half a mile for the year.

On the night of the 9th and 10th we came again to a curious phenomenon of the Barrier surface. As the mules proceeded ahead of us loud crackling roars could be heard from time to time. These were caused by a subsidence of the surface over a large area, as an animal or man trod upon it. The depth of the subsidence was only a fraction of an inch, but the resulting report was exceed-

ingly loud and startling, if unexpected. The mules soon
settled down to the roars and became accustomed to them,
but it was always a source of great interest to the dogs.
As soon as one of these subsidences with its roar came
to them they started off at full gallop, expecting at any
moment some animal to appear. They had been accustomed in Siberia to dig out animals lying up snowed in.
These subsidences were a great help and kept the dogs
interested, and they ran very well.

On the night of the 10th and morning of the 11th we
made One Ton Depôt, coming up five and three-quarters
miles to it. I decided to give men and animals a half-
day's rest here. It was a beautiful sunny and bright day
but with some wind. Here we found the stores which
had been left by Demetri and Cherry-Garrard. One of
the tins of paraffin on top of the cairns had leaked and
spoilt some of the stores placed at the foot of the camp.
There was no hole of any kind in this tin.

Our progress up to this point had been made in a day
and a half less time than it had taken us on the previous
year, and that was with the mules drawing full loads for
the whole of the time. There was no doubt that our
surface had been infinitely better than in the previous
season. Everything was favourable and the health of
men and animals was splendid.

On the night of the 11th and morning of the 12th,
after we had marched eleven miles due south of One
Ton, we found the tent. It was an object partially
snowed up and looking like a cairn. Before it were the
ski sticks and in front of them a bamboo which probably

was the mast of the sledge. The tent was practically on the line of cairns which we had built in the previous season. It was within a quarter of a mile of the remains of the cairn, which showed as a small hummock beneath the snow.

Inside the tent were the bodies of Captain Scott, Doctor Wilson, and Lieutenant Bowers. They had pitched their tent well, and it had withstood all the blizzards of an exceptionally hard winter. Each man of the Expedition recognised the bodies. From Captain Scott's diary I found his reasons for this disaster. When the men had been assembled I read to them these reasons, the place of death of Petty Officer Evans, and the story of Captain Oates' heroic end.

We recovered all their gear and dug out the sledge with their belongings on it. Amongst these were 35 lbs. of very important geological specimens which had been collected on the moraines of the Beardmore Glacier; at Doctor Wilson's request they had stuck to these up to the very end, even when disaster stared them in the face and they knew that the specimens were so much weight added to what they had to pull.

When everything had been gathered up, we covered them with the outer tent and read the Burial Service. From this time until well into the next day we started to build a mighty cairn above them. This cairn was finished the next morning, and upon it a rough cross was placed, made from the greater portion of two skis, and on either side were up-ended two sledges, and they were fixed firmly in the snow, to be an added mark. Between

THE LAST REST
(The Grave of Scott, Wilson and Bowers)

the eastern sledge and the cairn a bamboo was placed, containing a metal cylinder, and in this the following record was left :

'November 12, 1912, lat. 79 degrees, 50 mins. South. This cross and cairn are erected over the bodies of Captain Scott, C.V.O., R.N., Doctor E. A. Wilson, M.B., B.C., Cantab., and Lieutenant H. R. Bowers, Royal Indian Marine—a slight token to perpetuate their successful and gallant attempt to reach the Pole. This they did on January 17, 1912, after the Norwegian Expedition had already done so. Inclement weather with lack of fuel was the cause of their death. Also to commemorate their two gallant comrades, Captain L. E. G. Oates of the Inniskilling Dragoons, who walked to his death in a blizzard to save his comrades about eighteen miles south of this position ; also of Seaman Edgar Evans, who died at the foot of the Beardmore Glacier. " The Lord gave and the Lord taketh away ; blessed be the name of the Lord." '

This was signed by all the members of the party. I decided then to march twenty miles south with the whole of the Expedition and try to find the body of Captain Oates.

For half that day we proceeded south, as far as possible along the line of the previous season's march. On one of the old pony walls, which was simply marked by a ridge of the surface of the snow, we found Oates' sleeping-bag, which they had brought along with them after he had left.

The next day we proceeded thirteen more miles south, hoping and searching to find his body. When we arrived at the place where he had left them, we saw that there was no chance of doing so. The kindly snow had covered his body, giving him a fitting burial. Here, again, as near to the site of the death as we could judge, we built another cairn to his memory, and placed thereon a small cross and the following record : ' Hereabouts died a very gallant gentleman, Captain L. E. G. Oates of the Inniskill-ing Dragoons. In March 1912, returning from the Pole, he walked willingly to his death in a blizzard, to try and save his comrades, beset by hardships. This note is left by the Relief Expedition of 1912.'

It was signed by Cherry and myself.

From here I decided to turn back and to take, as far as possible, all the stores to Hut Point. I then thought that by any means that lay within our power we should try to reach Lieutenant Campbell and his party. As the sea ice would in all likelihood be impossible, we should probably have to take the route along the plateau, ascending the first Ferrar Glacier and making our way along the plateau as far as we were able.

On the second day we came again to the resting-place of the three and bade them there a final farewell. There alone in their greatness they will lie without change or bodily decay, with the most fitting tomb in the world above them.

Our journey back was uneventful. Two of the mules had to be killed because of their condition and to give food to the dogs. Five returned from the Barrier, and for the remainder of their days had as good a time as we could give them.

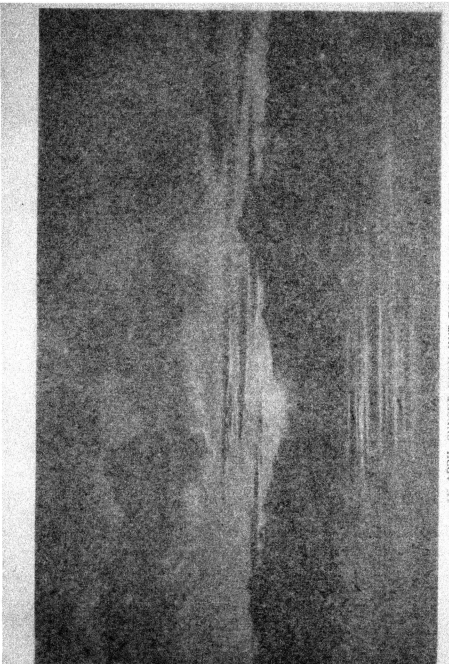

AN APRIL SUNSET FROM HUT POINT, LOOKING WEST.

at the place where he had left them, we saw that there was no chance of doing so. The kindly snow had covered his body, giving him a fitting burial. Here again, as near to the site of the death as we could judge, we built another cairn to his memory, and placed thereon a small cross and the following record : ' Hereabouts died a very gallant gentleman, Captain L. E. G. Oates of the Inniskilling Dragoons. In March 1912, returning from the Pole, he walked willingly to his death in a blizzard, to try and save his comrades, beset by hardships. This note is left by the Relief Expedition of 1913.'

It was signed by Cherry and myself.

From here I decided to turn back and to take, as far as possible, all the stores to Hut Point. I then thought that by any means that lay within our power we should try to reach Lieutenant Campbell and his party. As the sea ice would in all likelihood be impossible, we should probably have to take the route along the plateau, ascending the first Ferrar Glacier and making our way along the plateau as far as we were able.

On the second day we came again to the resting-place of the dead and built there a final

bodily cross, with the most touching in all the world

Our journey back was uneventful. Two of the mules had to be killed because of their condition and to give food to the dogs. We started from the Barrier, and for the remainder had as good a time we could give them.

AN APRI SUNSET FROM HUT POINT, LOOKING WEST.

On the morning of November 25 two dog teams, with Cherry-Garrard, Demetri, and myself, having pushed ahead of the mules, reached Hut Point. Cherry went into the hut and returned with a letter and his face transformed. I think we had then the best news that any men could wish for many, many a long weary day. Campbell and his party, having all survived the winter, had made their way down, arriving at Hut Point on November 6.

We proceeded in all haste to Cape Evans, there to have the goodly sight of their rounding countenances. They had filled out wonderfully on the good and unusual food, and each and every one was now heavier than he had ever been in his life. It was a sad home-coming for them after their hard time.

I can only here say that I can never be sufficiently grateful to all the members of the Expedition who were with me during this bad season, for their entire loyalty and good-fellowship; never one moment's trouble and always cheerful and willing.

THE ASCENT OF EREBUS, DECEMBER 1912

By Raymond Priestley

A party of six left Cape Evans on December 2, 1912, with the main object of surveying the old crater, and if time permitted making an ascent to the rim of the present active crater. It was originally intended that in the final climb Professor David's route should be followed, but our researches in the old crater led to the adoption of quite a different way, and one where a sledge could be pulled to a height of considerably over 9500 feet, at least 3000 feet higher than the Shackleton Expedition party were able to reach before being obliged to abandon theirs.

We left our Cape Royds camp (1000 feet above sea level) on December 4. It was not an ideal day for starting, and for the first 2000 feet of the ascent we groped from nunatak to nunatak through a thick cloud, and Debenham was unable to commence his plane table survey.

We lunched above this cloud belt, and although it swelled slowly upwards we were, with the exception of a very few minutes in the early afternoon, able to keep ahead of it until we camped beneath a prominent cone about 4,000 feet above sea level, which is well seen on the sky line from Cape Evans, and which would therefore be an important point of Debenham's survey, linking the portion

THE RAMPARTS OF MOUNT EREBUS

of Erebus visible from Cape Evans and Cape Royds with
the country beyond the shoulder, which was the last ridge
visible from winter quarters.

As we were caught by the fog in the act of camping and
the landmarks below had been blotted out all the afternoon
by the belt of cloud, we were obliged to wait here until the
weather cleared and we could fix the cone, and so persistent
was the bad weather that it was not until 10 A.M. of the
7th that we struck Reflection Camp, as we had named it,
and were able to proceed.

Our first objective, the Northern Nunatak, or Demetri's
Peak as we afterwards named it, was within easy reach by
lunch time, so I decided to camp at a large nunatak about
a mile and a half from the peak and take a rope party to
examine it. So far all the rocks we had passed had been
the typical kenyte so familiar to us at Cape Royds, but
we found ourselves now camped on basalt, an allied but
distinct rock which was not seen by the Professor's party,
who had kept close in to the main crater and had not
attempted any side issues such as our present divergence.
After lunch I took Gran, Abbott, and Dickason, leaving
Debenham with Hooper to help him to continue his
survey, and made straight for the peak, which we reached
without crossing any bad country, though crevasses were
numerous above our route.

We climbed the small triangular hill from bottom to
top, making its height 300 feet, and from the top we
obtained a good view and a photograph of the old crater
and of a strongly seracced glacier which loomed up as a
bad obstacle in our examination of the district.

The peak proved more interesting geologically than was expected, and we took back a good crop of specimens and photographs.

From here our route to the old crater itself proved steady, steep (for sledges), and uninteresting, and we camped on the gravel of a small nunatak on the lower side of the crater glacier at 5 P.M. on the 8th (8000 feet).

From this point Debenham was able to initiate the survey of the crater, and the next day all six of us carried one tent and equipment for three men a mile or two up the side of the glacier and established a camp in a gully nearly 9000 feet above sea level. After making this camp I took a rope party of four across and collected from the lower fang of the crater, while Debenham took Abbott and continued his plane table survey. What I saw from the crater side of the glacier decided me to make the final climb from a point about half a mile beyond the Gully Camp, and so I sent Gran with two of the men back for a supply of food from a depôt we had laid three or four miles back and almost on the Professor's route.

After lunch I returned with the other two, and we struck the single tent at our lower crater camp, collected all spare gear and depôted it and the extra food, and on the return of the other three we pulled the sledge with its skeleton equipment as far as the Gully Camp, where we spent the night.

On the morning of the 10th we again pulled out, and by 11.30 A.M. we were camped in the position from which I had decided to make the final ascent. After discussion with Debenham, I selected Gran, Abbott, and Hooper to

REMAINS OF AN EXPLOSION CRATER ON EREBUS
(9,000 feet)

EREBUS PARTY, DECEMBER 1912
(*Left to right—top*: Hooper, Abbott, Dickason; *bottom*: Priestley, Gran)

accompany me to the top, leaving Debenham, who had slight mountain sickness, to continue his survey, and Dickason, who was feeling the height more than the other two men, to help him.

From here we were taking a single camping equipment —tent and poles, bags, inside cooker, primus, oil, and four days' provisions on full ration, and after this had been apportioned each man was permitted to take a reasonable amount of personal gear. All hands dragged the packs on the sledge some distance up the first snow slope, but the gradient soon became so steep that we were obliged to anchor the sledge with ice axes and assume our packs, while Debenham and Dickason tobogganed back to camp on the sledge.

By climbing about a hundred feet at a time and taking long spells we were able to make steady if slow progress up the rock ridges, which were here nearly continuous as far as the rim of the second crater. The only difficult bits to negotiate were when we were obliged to cross the snow-slopes from ridge to ridge, and these were only dangerous because, owing to scarcity of ice axes, the four of us were able to have but three between us, and I was never sure where the fourth man would fetch up if he slipped. This necessitated step cutting and slowed us up considerably, and it was not until three hours and a half after we had left the sledge that we reached the rim and saw the second crater stretching out in front of us.

Our first care was to select a good site for our camp, and after that was pitched to cook our evening meal and turn in. The clouds prevented our getting a view of the

active crater and no photographs were possible. The only
effect the height had on us as yet was to cause sleepless-
ness and a slight shortness of breath, but we were already
beginning to experience some discomfort from the low
temperatures, and the whole time we remained at or above
this elevation the mercury remained obstinately below
−10° F., and at one time registered −30° F.

The 11th saw us still shrouded in cloud and, except
for a short walk in the immediate neighbourhood of the
camp, we got nothing done; but Gran woke me at 1 o'clock
in the morning of the 12th, to find the weather so magnificent that I roused all hands at once and we got breakfast,
deciding to take time by the forelock and not risk a change
of weather.

The only drawback to the morning was a low
temperature, −15° F. to −18° F., and a cold southerly wind
which gave us a good deal of trouble, as the high altitude
very much decreased our chances of resisting frostbite.
From the scenic point of view the volcano could not have
been better, for it was very active, and the steam cloud was
being carried steadily northward by the breeze. As we
approached the active crater we secured photograph after
photograph, and I also took several looking back at our
camp and the old crater in the background, and at Mount
Terror and Mount Bird. A good description of these two
upper craters has already been given by Professor David;
and repetition would be unnecessary and useless. The
principal impression they have left on our minds is that of
absolute bareness and desolation.

As our altitude increased we were more and more

SOUTH FANG, OLD CRATER

HIGHEST CAMP IN ANTARCTICA—ACTIVE CRATER

troubled with shortness of breath and fatigue, and were obliged to rest every hundred yards or so; but we reached the summit of the active cone within two or three hours of leaving the camp, and while Gran made a cairn for the record I had prepared, I endeavoured with the help of Abbott and Hooper to light the hypsometer; but the breeze was too stiff and enfiladed the crater rim so that no adequate shelter could be obtained, and after wasting half a box of matches and getting several frostbitten fingers we were obliged to desist.   Gran and I then took a series of photographs on the rim of the crater, but we were unable to see more than a few feet down because of the steam and sulphur vapour, which caused us considerable inconvenience even during the short time we spent on the rim, for every slight variation of direction of the wind resulted in our complete envelopment by the vapour, which was not too good to breathe in.

After a short while on top Hooper reported that his feet were frostbitten, and I at once ordered him back to camp, telling off Abbott to accompany him and to collect a rucksack full of pumice on his way down.

Gran and I continued slowly down the cone, collecting felspars as we went, and I had descended about 500 feet when I discovered to my annoyance that instead of the record we had left a tin of exposed films at the summit. Gran immediately volunteered to fetch this and place the real record, and as I wished to collect thoroughly I continued slowly on my way down.   I had reached the second group of fumaroles and was beginning to photograph them by the time he should have reached the top, when there was a loud explosion, and amongst the smoke I could see large blocks of pumice hurled aloft. This eruption made me extremely anxious for Gran's fate, especially as he did not appear on the farther side of the smoke cloud as soon as he was due, so in spite of breathing trouble I made good speed up the hill, and had reached within fifty feet of the top in record time, and without a halt, when he strolled out of the steam cloud all serene and looking none the worse for his adventure. He had had a unique opportunity of observing an eruption of Erebus, and that the opportunity was not wasted can be seen from his description, which is as follows ·

'Whilst making some notes of the things I had seen, I heard a gurgling sound come from the crater, and before I had realised what was happening I was enveloped in a choking vapour. The steam cloud had evidently been much increased by the eruption, and in it I could see blocks of pumiceous lava, in shape like the halves of volcanic bombs and with bunches of long drawn-out hair-like shreds of glass in their interior. The snow around me was covered with rock dust and the smoke was yellow with sulphur and disagreeable in the extreme.'

Gran was fortunate in not experiencing any worse effect of the eruption than a slight sickness during the next few days, which we both attributed to the sulphur vapour. I think of the two of us my own experience was the worse for, as he says later in his diary, 'It is no joke taking a mountain by storm, especially with the barometer standing at eleven inches.'

The hair-like lava I had already noticed on the slopes

THE SUMMIT OF EREBUS

of the crater, and it is doubtless of the type known as Pele's hair.

Gran made his escape from the steam cloud on the western side of the mountain, and so was able to get a good view of the Western Mountains, and believed he could see a range stretching back and cutting across the plateau at about the latitude of Granite Harbour.

We then returned slowly to camp, collecting as we went, and arrived in about 9.30 A.M., to find that Hooper s feet had recovered and that Abbott had collected a fine lot of specimens.

After our return to camp we rested in our bags for a few hours, and then struck camp and glissaded down the 2000 feet till we rejoined Debenham and Dickason, covering in a few minutes a distance that had taken us three or four hours on our upward way. During our absence the latter had made good use of their time, finishing the survey of the old crater and collecting from moraines left by an ancestor of the crater glacier.

We spent the night camped here, and the next morning proceeded on our way down the mountain, using ice axes in rope grummets at the after end of the sledge as brakes and making such good way that the same day we picked up all our depôts, and camped within striking distance of Hooper's Shoulder, as we afterwards named the Southern Nunatak, in time for a late lunch.

In the afternoon Debenham, Abbott, and Hooper and I walked over to the shoulder, photographed it and collected from it, and by 6 P.M. we were back in camp.

The final descent was delayed until the 16th by bad

weather, but on that date we pulled as near Cape Royds as we could take the sledges, and from there packed our own bags and such equipment as we required to Shackleton s Hut, where I reported to Lieutenant Campbell and gave him an outline of the trip.

VOYAGES OF THE *TERRA NOVA*

By Commanders E. R. G. R. Evans and H. L. L. Pennell

First Voyage

To connect the thread of the story it is as well to run briefly over what occurred before Campbell landed at Cape Adare.

On January 28, 1911, Captain Scott and the southern depôt laying party having left, the ship proceeded for King Edward's Land with Lieutenant Campbell and his party on board. Ice preventing her from getting beyond Cape Colbeck, Campbell ran into the Bay of Whales, intending to land there; but finding Captain Amundsen had selected this site and built his hut here, he proceeded to the opposite extreme of Ross Sea to try and land on the north coast of South Victoria Land as far to the west as the ship could get. No landing place, however, could be found on this coast at all except at Cape Adare, Robertson Bay, where there is a moraine on which Borchgrevink wintered in 1898. There being no alternative he decided to build his hut here.

During the 18th and 19th the work of landing the stores for Campbell's party was carried out as rapidly as *Feb. 18 and* possible, a dead flat calm lasting the whole *19, 1911.* time. Heavy pack ice, setting round the ship, *Cape Adare.* prevented all communication with the shore between 1 and 2 P.M. on the 18th; and at 4 P.M. on the

19th the ship was again being pressed by the ice, only more heavily than on the previous day, so that it was necessary for her to steam to her anchor.

At 8 P.M. the order was given to weigh and stand off, and the night was spent by the ship in doing magnetic work, as fortunately the middle of Robertson Bay was clear of ice.

At 3.30 A.M. the moraine was again approached, and the watch that had been landed to work on shore were *Feb. 20,* re-embarked. An adieu to Campbell's little *1911.* party was hooted on the syren and the *Terra Nova* steamed to the N.N.W., in a calm, but with a rapidly falling barometer, to try and get round the pack that always extends north of North Cape.

Her orders were to explore to the west of North Cape as far as the coal supply allowed.

Six A.M. found her clear of the pack off the entrance to the bay. All hands set to to clear up the decks, batten down and prepare for bad weather, and it was well on in the forenoon before they were able to get any rest. By noon a strong wind was blowing from E.S.E. and freshening, and the sea was beginning to get up, so fires were banked and she was snugged down to lower topsails.

Blink appearing on the port hand, course was altered to north to keep away from it, when snow obscured everything.

At noon on the 21st course was altered to W., and shortly after the ship ran very close to an iceberg which *Feb. 21,* showed us that the range of vision, estimated *1911, 68° 41′* at half a mile for ice, was considerably less than *S., 168° 29′* *E.* had been thought. During the afternoon she crossed Ross's track, the most westerly track in this sea up

to date. At midnight steam was again put on the engines,
the wind and sea having died rapidly and the weather
cleared. A sounding was taken in 1435 fathoms and course
altered to the S.W. to close S. Victoria Land again.

Bruce in the afternoon watch picked up some snow
capped mountains, and after this more peaks and lower
Feb. 22,   land were quickly raised above the horizon,
1911, 69° 10′ and a large number of icebergs appeared ahead.
S., 1 4° 30′
E.   The ship was brought up by pack at 9.P.M.
which stretched between her and the shore and parallel
to the coast, as far as could be seen.

Though several attempts had been made, no ship
previously had had the good fortune to get in sight of the
coast on this longitude, so the luck of the *Terra Nova*
was in this season.

This new coast-line discovered by Lieutenant Pennell
has been christened Oates Land, after Captain L. E. G.
Oates of the Inniskilling Dragoons.

The land was tantalisingly covered in cloud. Nothing
could be done till the morning, and so the night was
spent trawling and swinging for variation. A sounding
gave 178 fathoms. The trawl was particularly interesting and made ample amends for the delay. As soon as
it was light enough to see, we tried to close the land as
the pack did not look especially heavy. Clouds still
hid all except the lower land.

An hour and a half showed the futility of attempting
to get through, and at 5 A.M. the attempt was given
up, the ship being then 8000 yards from the end of a
glacier tongue and in 134 fathoms of water. This tongue

appeared to run down from snow-covered rounded hills,

Feb. 23, 1911, 69° 29′ S., 162° 49′ E. while behind it a rugged range of hills ran down to a point, apparently forming the eastern point of a large bay, as away to the west could be seen high cliffs with outcroppings of rock, but everything in that direction was much obscured by mist or haze. The ship's position, fixed by sun and moon, was 69° 43′ S., 163° 17′ E.

Forty-seven icebergs could be counted from this spot, all being in the pack and probably mostly aground. This trend of the land to the northward would well account for the hang of the pack and icebergs north of North Cape.

At 8 A.M. the ship started to skirt the pack to the westward, noting what details could be made out of the coast, which were not many. The routine now was for Rennick to sound every forenoon and middle watch, and if in comparatively shallow water, as often as time could be spared. The sounding-machine was worked by hand, and on many nights was a cold and patience-trying job.

As she worked westward the pack pressed the ship out

Feb. 24, 1911, 69° 4′ S., 161° 19′ E. from the land, and in the afternoon a light fog and snow came down again. In the middle watch it blew a strong wind from the S.E., with thick snow, and she was hove to.

The snow stopped about 8 A.M., but the day was dull and one could not see far. Course was shaped S.S.W. and

Feb. 25, 1911, 68° 50′ S., 5° 11′ E. by 2 the *Terra Nova* was stopped by pack with what appeared to be a miniature archi- pelago close to the southward. These turned out to be icebergs, probably aground, and some of large

size, but when this was discovered the weather brightened
and a cliffy coast-line was seen to the S.W.   Following
the pack along towards the land, it was soon seen that
there was clear water inside the pack.   This water extended, apparently, up to the land, and at one place the
line of pack was not more than a mile broad.   After
sounding in 154 fathoms the ship was worked into the
pack with high hopes of finding another place like
Robertson Bay, which is often clear of pack, though the
entrance is usually more or less guarded by it.

At 5 P.M., after an hour's struggle, the attempt was
seen to be hopeless, the ship was only a third way through,
and the pack grew heavier as she advanced.   A light
wind had sprung up and this had closed the pack, so that
the ship was caught and unable to move at all.   This was
very disappointing and the position was not free from
anxiety as, undoubtedly, there is a fair tidal stream in
these waters, and grounded icebergs do not make pleasant
neighbours in such circumstances.

As the sun got low the day improved, the clouds
broke, and in the sunshine we had a good view of the
land, though the upper parts of it were always shrouded
in cloud.   The ship appeared to be off a point (or angle)
in the coast, apparently forming the western end of a
large bay to the east of us.   The coast was steep and
rugged, half-bare rocky points separated by glaciers being
the chief features.   The hills behind did not appear to
be very high, but this is only guess-work, as the higher
land was obscured in clouds all the time and only occasionally a glimpse could be got when the clouds partially

lifted in one spot or another. There was no movement
in the ice in respect to the ship till 5 A.M., when Cheetham
reported a general easing up, and shortly after the ship
was able to turn and work out to the northward without
unusual difficulty.

After taking bearings and making sketches from the
edge of the pack we ran to the northward and north-
westward, with pack on the port hand and
the coast beyond the pack till 2 P.M., when the
coast made a sharp bend to the westward,

*Feb. 26,
1911, 68° 57'
S., 158° 53'
E.*

though the edge of the pack still continued to trend to
the northward. While one of the soundings was being
taken on this day a rorqual fouled the sounding wire
in a most extraordinary manner, and for a short time there
was quite an exciting and very novel sport of playing
whale, which naturally ended by the wire parting.

This was the last we saw of the land, the pack not being
finally cleared till in Lat. 64°23′ S. Many times false hopes
were raised by the ship running into clear water and being
able to turn west and even south of west towards where
C. Hudson is marked on the charts, but invariably it was
only a few hours before she would be turned and, as a
general rule, each noon position was east of the previous
one. On the whole, after leaving the coast, the floes were
of a less formidable character than those found off the north
shore of Victoria Land, but the interspaces were filled
with slush or else frozen over with new ice. This made
pack that earlier in the season would have been easily
negotiable now absolutely impassable. The nights also
were drawing out, and after dark the first appearance of

pack had to be the signal to heave to till daylight, which often meant till 6 A.M., as the morning twilight was found very bad for picking a way through the pack.

The sea was now frozen over in the sort of large lakes or pools of still, open water that were found in this sea, and though this ice was never more than a few inches thick, it made a considerable difference to our speed.

On March 2, while working through fairly loose pack, the wind that had been light westerly turned to E.N.E., *March 2,* with the immediate effect of closing the floes in, *1911, 67° 35′* and the ship was completely held up. During *S., 16° 16′* *E.* that night the wind shifted again to the southward and so topsails and foresail were set. It was merely waste of coal to try and steam through this ice, but the steady pressure of the ship under sail let her gradually, though very slowly, work through ; often held up by a floe for an hour or more, in the end she would manage to turn it and run ahead half a ship's length or so. This meant that in her wake was generally to be found a small pool of water clear of ice.

A number of whales (lesser rorquals) were in this pack, and they soon discovered this clear water and took advantage of it to come and blow ; as there was not room for them to come up in the ordinary way, they had to thrust their heads up vertically and blow in a sort of standing-on-their-tails position. Several times one rested its head on a floe, not twenty feet from the ship, with its nostrils just on the water-line ; raising itself a few inches, it would blow and then subside again for a few minutes to its original position, with its snout resting on the floe. The men amused themselves by pelting it with little bits of coal and other missiles, of which it appeared to be entirely unconscious. The grooves on their throats were plainly seen, quite clearly enough to count accurately; and sometimes even their moustaches could be distinctly made out, as also the white band on the flipper.

Fortunately (or unfortunately) the whale gun was out of action, and so there was no necessity to try and *March 4,* procure a specimen for biological purposes. *1911, 67° 11′ S., 160° 47′ E.* Whales kept close to the ship till noon on the 4th, when, the pack having eased up, steam was again put on the engines and she was able to make appreciable way.

The ship passed only some ten miles west of Young Island (one of the Balleny Group), but although it was *March 5,* a sunny day all the Balleny Islands were *1911, 66° 37′ S., 161° 42′ E.* covered in clouds, and no useful bearings could be taken.

At last, on March 8, when in 64° 23′ S., 161° 39′ E., she cleared the last of the pack, and in half an hour sooty albatross were round the ship, a sure sign that no pack was north of her.

The next fortnight was a struggle for the ship to keep to windward, the wind obstinately holding to the north side of west and generally blowing hard. Although so light, she was much stiffer than expected.

To the seaman of the present day used to iron ships it is a never-failing source of surprise and delight to see a wooden ship in a heavy sea. How nicely she rides the waves, like a living being, instead of behaving like a half-submerged rock.

The albatross and other deep-sea birds were a great pleasure; while south of Lat. 60° the pretty Hour-glass dolphin (first noticed by Dr. Wilson in the *Discovery*) was often round the ship.

On the 22nd, when ninety miles south of the Macquarie Islands, the long-hoped-for fair wind *March 22,* came at last and held till we made *1911, 56° 9'* Stewart Island. On the 23rd steam was *S., 159° 15'* *E.* again raised.

The pumps had been a nuisance throughout, and during a gale on the 24th the trouble came to a head · the ship was heeling between 40 and 45 degrees and jumping about considerably, and only a little water could be got through the engine-room pumps. The hand pump had been kept going all night, but during the morning also choked, and as soon as there was a little water in the well, it lifted a plate in the engine-room during one of the ship's bad heels and let all the ashes and coal down into the well. Both bunker doors had to be shut and could not be opened with safety; engines were stopped and steam kept for the bilge pump, whose suction was with great difficulty kept partially free by Mr. Williams. He kept a perforated enamel jug on the end of the suction, and stopping the pump every two or three minutes as the suction choked, removed and cleared the jug, replaced it and then restarted the pump; this process having to be kept up the whole time the hand pumps were being seen to. To accomplish his object Williams had to lie flat on the boiler-room plates, and when the ship listed to starboard, stretch right down with his head below the plates and clear as much coal away from round the suction as possible. This often meant that the water surged back before he could get his head out, and there can be few nastier liquids to be ducked in than that very dirty bilge-water.

Meanwhile for the hand pumps Davies had to take off the bottom lengths of the suction pipes, lift them, and clear them from below. To do this the flange rivets had to be bored out, and it took eight hours' incessant work to finish the job.

During the re-fitting at Lyttelton pumps and everything connected with them were thoroughly overhauled in all respects and never gave serious trouble again.

Paterson Inlet was made on March 28 and Lyttelton on April 1.

Throughout all her cruise the scientific side of the ship's work was undertaken as follows : Lillie had all the biological work and Rennick was solely in charge of the soundings, and it can be safely said that neither of them missed a single opportunity that offered ;

Meteorological Log : Drake ;

Zoological Log : Bruce ;

Magnetic Log and Current Log : Pennell ;
while the officer of the watch, at the time, kept a general lookout for anything of interest that might occur.

Lyttelton,
April 1–
July 10.
The ship lay at Lyttelton for three months, undergoing a general and thorough refit. Rennick was employed the whole time in plotting as much of the surveying work carried out in the

LIEUT. BRUCE

PRISMATIC COMPASS

LIEUT.

south as could be done in the time, and in preparing the charts for the forthcoming winter's cruise ; while Bruce looked after the refit.

Here we should like to take the opportunity of thanking Mr. J. J. Kinsey for the great trouble he always took to help the Expedition in every way that lay in his power.

Winter Cruise

The ship again left Lyttelton on July 10 for a three *July 10–Oct.* months' cruise, to carry out surveying work 10, 1911. round the Three Kings' Islands and between this *Winter* *Cruise.* group and the extreme north of New Zealand.

Hereabouts rather troubled waters prevail, as the swell from the Tasman Sea to the west meeting that from the Pacific to the east often causes a confused swell even in calm weather. The routine was to sound all day and have Lillie's plankton nets over all night, while opportunities for trawling were always taken as they occurred, Lillie being ready any hour of the day or night. On the whole a very good biological collection was obtained.

Occasionally a visit was paid to Mangonui on the east coast to take in fresh provisions, but, as a rule, the ship was hove-to for the night.

Lillie gave a series of popular lectures on evolution, which aroused the greatest interest fore and aft and did a great deal to break the monotony of the time.

Rennick and Mr. Williams very ingeniously adapted a motor (most generously lent by Mr. Kinsey from a motor-boat) to work the Lucas sounding machine, which quite trebled the ship's sounding efficiency.

Sounding work does not, as a rule, provide exciting incidents, the day when it is undertaken coming under one of two headings—suitable for work or unsuitable. On unsuitable days, if the wind was easterly, nothing could be done except to heave to and drift; if westerly, there was good anchorage inside North Cape (the extreme north-east point of New Zealand), and the whole company were on these occasions very thankful for the quiet days in the ship, in comparison with the tossing about experienced in easterly gales. Mr. Williams was also able to take advantage of these days to clean boiler tubes.

The time away was strictly limited to the period covered by the insurance of the ship, and so, on *Bay of Islands, Sept. 24-28, 1911.* September 22, she had to leave for Lyttelton. On the way down she called in at Russell, Bay of Islands, to take in fresh provisions and pick up her mail. Three days were spent here waiting for the mail and were much appreciated by everyone, as it is an exceedingly pretty and, historically, very interesting spot. Rennick without delay set about cleaning and painting the ship so that she might be presentable for Lyttelton, though frequent showers of rain did not help him.

Lillie and a companion walked over the peninsula to the tiny little Bay of Wangamumu, where there is a small whaling station belonging to Messrs. Jaggers and Cook. After a delightful walk through the bush, which took some seven or eight hours instead of three or four as expected, they were lucky enough to find Mr. Cook there himself, for he had arrived from the Southern Ocean only a few hours previously, and was preparing to commence whaling round this station.

Lillie was able to make arrangements to stay with them for a month.

On Thursday, the 28th, the *Terra Nova* weighed and proceeded south, calling at Wangamumu on the way, where Lillie was landed with all his paraphernalia for collecting and preserving specimens.

The ship arrived off Kaikoura at daybreak on the 8th and, being now close to home and with three days' grace, *Kaikoura,* was able to put in two days' sounding on the *Oct. 8, 1911.* hundred-fathom line and so to fill up a rather serious blank on the charts. The coast scenery here, on a fine day, is magnificent, as the seaward Kaikoura mountains run close to the coast and there are very many striking snow-capped peaks in the range.

On October 10 the *Terra Nova* was once more berthed alongside the wharf at Lyttelton. It is only fitting here to acknowledge the real hospitality shown the Expedition by New Zealand. From the Prime Minister downwards all were anxious to help, and the extent of this help received both from individuals and Government departments can only be fully realised by the ship's party, who found all difficulties smoothed away for them as soon as they arose. Dr. John Guthrie, M.D., of Lyttelton, took on the duty of honorary doctor, and Mr. P. Strain, of Christchurch, volunteered as honorary dentist. The services of both gentlemen were frequently and gratefully invoked.

The ship was rather over two months at Lyttelton,

and the time was just sufficient. Rennick was able to
finish the chart of the Three Kings and the
ship's soundings by working hard at it, although
the time was very short for such work.

Lyttelton,
Oct. 10–*Dec.*
15, 1911.

The mules, given by the Indian Government, had
arrived some weeks before the return of the ship and
were enjoying themselves in the fields on Quail Island,
while the fourteen Siberian dogs from Vladivostok
arrived during October. Everything that care and fore-
sight could do for the mules had been done before they
left India, and the Expedition owes a deep debt of
gratitude to Lieutenant George Pulleyn of the Indian
army, in whose care they were, for the trouble taken
over them. For some time before leaving India they
had been exercised in rocking-boxes to develop the
muscles especially brought into use by the motion of a
ship; and their equipment, which was sent with them,
had been thought out with the greatest care. As we had
only seven mules, the stables were built over the fore-
hatch on the foremost side of the ice-house, so that they
all were in the open air.

The dogs travelled unattended from Japan, and the
officers of the different ships in which the mules and the
dogs travelled took every possible pains to keep them
in good health, with the most happy results in both
cases.

Mr. James Dennistoun joined the Expedition here to
take charge of the mules on the way south.

Lillie had a very fairly successful month at
Wangamumu, as a good many whales were caught, all

VA,' 1912 VOYAGE

Left to right—Mr. Dennistoun   Engineer Williams, L   Pennell L   Bruce Biologist Lillie

however, of one species—the Humpback. On his return
from there he went off to Mount Potts in the South Island,
collecting fossil plants, being fortunate in obtaining some
specimens of the early Mesozoic flora.

The programme for the cruise as far as could be fore-
seen and according to the outline given in Captain Scott's
sailing orders to the ship was ·

1. Pick up Campbell and party about January 1 at
   Cape Adare.

2. Re-land them in the vicinity of Wood Bay.

3. Relieve the geological party about January 15
   at Granite Harbour.

4. Land mules, dogs, stores, &c., at Cape Evans.

5. Lay out various depôts according to the orders
   to be received at the Hut, in readiness for the
   next season's work.

6. Consistently with carrying out the above, to
   make biological collections, sound, and carry out
   other scientific work to as large an extent as
   possible.

Second Voyage

At daybreak on December 15 the ship slipped and
proceeded with mules, dogs, and all relief stores on board.

*Dec. 15,
1911. Leav-
ing Lyttelton.*
This year was the year of transport workers'
strikes at home, and it was only the extreme
energy and determination of our manager, Mr.
Wyatt, and the great consideration shown by the shipping
companies, that enabled the stores to be shipped out in
time. Until Christmas Day we had a high barometer and
fine weather, with fairly light but continuous southerly

winds. This made our progress slow, but the fine weather more than compensated for that.

Rennick sounded twice a day while on the New Zealand continental shelf and once a day afterwards, except for two and a half days round about Christmas, when the weather prevented this work being done.

The motor now worked without a hitch ; without it the necessity of crossing the Southern Sea quickly, so as to save the animals, would have allowed very few soundings to be taken. The smooth sea also allowed the mules to be moved in their stalls, so that the stables could be properly cleaned out and thoroughly disinfected.

The Sunday before Christmas, just as we were going to lunch, Nigger, the cat, fell overboard. He had been

Dec. 24, 1911, 60° 39′ S., 178° 39′ W.

baiting the dogs on the poop, got uncomfortably close to one and, jumping to avoid the dog, went overboard. Fortunately it was an exceptionally calm day ; the sea boat was lowered, and Nigger, who swam pluckily, was picked up and the ship on her course again twelve minutes after the accident. He was quite benumbed with the cold, but was taken down to the engine-room and well dried, given a little brandy to drink, and by the evening was all right again.

The first berg was passed on Christmas Day in 61° 31′ S., and the first belt of pack on the 26th in 63° 59′ S. It

Dec. 26, 1911, 63° 31′ S., 173° 23′ W.

was not, however, till the following evening that the real pack was met, and in the dog watches of the 28th ·it began to get heavy, eventually holding the ship up at 1 A.M. that night.

After once getting in the pack until they were landed, the mules were exercised at least twice, generally three *Dec. 29 and* times, a week. They were walked round and *30, 1911, 66°* round the main hatch and nearly all of them *46' S., 177°* *48' W.* used to take the opportunity to roll, which they greatly appreciated. With the numerous ring bolts, combing of the main hatch, and other obstructions, there was a certain amount of risk; fortunately there was no accident and the benefit they derived from being moved about justified the risk being taken.

The deck was always well covered with ashes, which were kept for the purpose instead of being thrown overboard when sent up from the boiler-room. Two or three of the mules were inclined to jump about a bit; Lal Khan, in particular, enjoying his outings a little too much, but Bruce always took charge of him and managed to keep him well under control.

Every day after leaving New Zealand the dogs were given a run round the upper deck, and whenever the ship was stopped in the ice they were exercised on a floe, which afforded plenty of excitement to the men as well as to the dogs.

Being held up in the pack always gives a good opportunity for work of different sorts to be done. Lillie has his plankton nets over, trying different depths; Rennick always sounds; and, if the sun comes out, observations for variation are taken with the landing compass on a floe outside the range of disturbance of the ship's iron; and, if a floe with ice that has not been splashed with salt water is near enough, the ship is watered, as there is no

knowing when the next opportunity may occur to obtain
fresh water.

During the 30th the floes were visibly breaking up,
and in the morning watch of the 31st steam was again
put on the engines and the ship able to make slow but
steady progress.

In the early hours of the New Year the pack was left,

Jan. 1, 1912,
68° 44′ S.,
178° 55′ E.
and no more pack was met till the ship got
to within five or six miles of Cape Adare at
9 A.M. on the 3rd.

Here very heavy pack was found and Robertson Bay
was full of it, but by waiting for the chance she managed

Jan. 3 and 4,
1912. Off
Robertson
Bay.
to get within a mile of the moraine on which
the hut is built by 11.30; all inside this was
heavy pack swiftly moving with the tidal
stream.   Nothing could be done, and with the satisfaction
of seeing people moving about near the hut, we had to
haul off to the centre of the entrance, where there was now
a space of clear water.   While waiting, Lillie got a satisfactory trawl in fifty fathoms—the first of the season.

At 4 P.M. the water on the north side of the moraine
cleared sufficiently to allow of an attempt at landing, and
after an hour's pushing through the pack she anchored
close in, in seven fathoms.

Rennick and Bruce immediately went on shore with
the cutter and whaler, and in spite of a nasty swell which
was breaking on the beach were able to embark some of
the stores.

In an hour and a half, however, the boats had to return,
as the pack was setting towards the ship, and she had to

weigh at once; it was not till 1 P.M. the next day that the pack gave signs of easing up again, and the ship took till 4.30 to work her way through and anchor again in the same position. The swell had now died down, and in two and a half hours Campbell and all his party, their collections, and all necessary stores were on board; just in time, for the pack was again setting on the ship.

Robertson Bay is not a nice place from the seaman's point of view. The tidal streams are strong, the pack ice heavy, there are very many grounded bergs about, and gales are frequent and fierce, while the uneven bottom suggests the likelihood of unknown pinnacled rocks. It was with great satisfaction, therefore, that we left the bay with Campbell's party on board in excellent health and spirits.

More pack was found lying off the coast of South Victoria Land and kept the ship well off shore till about *Jan. 7, 1912,* forty-five miles E.S.E. of the extremity of the *75° 15' S.,* Drygalski Barrier, when it became sufficiently *168° 37' E.* loose to let her turn in towards the Drygalski and work through it. With hopes alternately raised and lowered as the pack eased up or became heavier, the ship at last got on the north side of the Barrier and into clear water; and during the first watch of the 8th was secured alongside the sea ice at the entrance to what is now called Arrival Bay, about six miles north of Evans' Coves.

The gear and a month's depôt for Campbell's party were immediately disembarked, and with hands from the ship to haul a depôt sledge, he was left on a moraine about one and a quarter miles from the ship.

The ship slipped immediately her party returned, and meeting a good deal of fog and snow had some difficulty in working through the pack on the way out, being eventually held up during the forenoon of the 10th and kept there for thirty-six hours; but in the end she arrived off Beaufort Island during the afternoon of the 12th.

Jan. 10, 1912, 76° 53′., 1 5° E.

The prospect was not encouraging, as there was nothing but heavy pack in the direction of Granite Harbour and across the whole entrance to McMurdo Sound. It was, however, a glorious day, and the opportunity was taken to swing ship for magnetic constants, take observations for variation on the ice, sound, and try to collect plankton. In the Antarctic seas the water is often so full of diatoms that the fine meshes of the plankton nets choke as soon as they are put over. This, by stopping the passage of water through the net, prevents it catching anything and so renders useless many opportunities for collecting that would otherwise be favourable.

Jan. 12, 1912, 76° 42′ S., 167° 12′ E.

Till February 4 nothing could be done. On January 13 fast ice was found to extend as far north as the southern end of Bird Peninsula; and, when it was possible to work through the pack towards Granite Harbour, fast ice was found on the 23rd to extend thirty miles from the head of this inlet.

Jan. 13–Feb. 4, 1912. In or near McMurdo Sound.

These three weeks were one long succession of being caught in the pack and struggling to get out again. Whenever there appeared to be any change, the ship would steam over towards Granite Harbour or Cape Evans to look; for often it appeared as if the ice in the strait was really breaking up, but every time in reality it was found that only comparatively little had gone out.

The time, however, .was not wasted : whenever in a workable depth, with steam up, Lillie had his trawl out and so got six or seven trawls. Rennick got a number of soundings, though of necessity not in any particular line, and there were several opportunities for swinging ship and observing variation on fast ice, while an interesting series of Giant Petrels was obtained, ranging from white to the comparatively dark varieties.

Mather, who had taken great trouble in New Zealand to perfect his taxidermy, skinned all the ship's specimens.

At last, on February 4, the ship was secured alongside fast ice off Cape Barne. Atkinson came off with a dog team and reported all well, and was shortly followed by Meares and Simpson. They informed us that the ice was bad between the ship and shore, and consequently did not stay long, but took the mails with them he they left.

During the next two days two miles of ice went out *Feb. 6–14,* in a gale, and in the first watch of the 6th the *1912. Off* ship was at last secured alongside fast ice, with *Cape Evans.* safe ice between her and Cape Evans.

The dogs went ashore at once, the mules were hoisted out early the next morning and soon were safely ashore, after being on board fifty-four days. It says much for Dennistoun's care of them that they landed in such good condition.

Sledging the stores on shore was commenced at once ; but it was two and three-quarter miles to Cape Evans (i.e. five and a half miles on the round trip), so that the work was necessarily slow.

The unloading continued steadily till the 14th, with a break in the middle when a gale took another mile of ice out and so made work much quicker ; but on the 14th the ice started breaking up and yet did not go out ; nothing could be done, and as after a day no change took place the ship crossed over the Sound to Butter Point to see conditions in that direction. There were still nineteen tons of stores, including some coal, to be landed, but all the essentials were ashore.

At Butter Point a note from Taylor (in charge of the geological party) was found, saying that his party had

Feb. 15, 1912. camped there and gone on the previous day. *McMurdo* Following the coast south, this party was *Sound.* observed on the Blue Glacier, and they were soon on board, all well. It was fortunate that Taylor had realised early the impossibility of the ship reaching Granite Harbour and so had beaten a retreat south over the piedmont. His specimens he had been compelled to leave in a depôt at Granite Harbour.

Shortly after they were picked up it came on to snow and blow. Owing to the weather it was impossible *Feb. 19,* to land this party at Cape Evans, so the ship *1912, 75°* turned north to pick up Campbell's team. *27' S., 166°* *49' E.* Course was shaped direct for the extreme of the Drygalski Barrier, and the ship ran, with considerable pack to the east of her and loose pack in shore, until

heavy ice ahead forced her to turn back on her course
some twelve miles and then work through the eastern
belt of pack.

The following extract is from the ship's journal :

' Following the edge of the pack north, it was seen
to be very heavy and the blink gave no sign of open
water inside it until the ship was east by north thirty
five miles from the end of the Drygalski, when there
was a belt of pack some two miles broad and clear water
inside, at any rate for some distance : this belt was
entered at 2.30 P.M., and it shows the heaviness of the
ice that she was not clear till past 9 o'clock (a speed
of a third of a knot), although it was comparatively
loose-looking pack.

' The wind was rising as she worked through this
strip of pack, and soon after it came on to snow heavily.
Nothing could be done but to remain under easy steam,
to avoid the floes, if possible, and look out for bergs.
Before midnight it was blowing storm force and objects
were visible at only a few hundred yards.'

The storm continued for two days, the latter half
without snow, when Mount Melbourne showed up in great
beauty.

The open water the ship was in was about six miles
broad, and though across the pack another lead (or possibly
open water) could be seen, five miles or so distant, yet it
was absolutely out of her reach.

The wind was steady in direction from the south-west,
and the whole pack and ship drifted slowly but surely
north until it became imperative to regain the open

sea to avoid being caught in the cul-de-sac of Lady Newnes Bay.

Fortunately the retreat was open and the wind fair for taking it, and so on the 21st the ship had regained *Feb. 21,* her freedom of action, but was no nearer *1912, 75° 0′* relieving Campbell. That evening the storm *S., 169° 10′* *E.* eased down and course was again shaped for the Drygalski Barrier, with the hope that the ice which had previously barred her way might have drifted past the end of the Barrier. The pack (now on the starboard hand) was followed south as closely as possible, though snow often shut in everything to a ship's length and compelled her to stop till it was clear enough again to see where she was going. Gradually she was able to alter more to the west and north of west, until in the middle watch (23rd) she had rounded the southern end of the pack, some 20 miles south of the Drygalski Barrier, and was steering north through light pancake ice with, of course, the heavy pack again to the eastward of her. The pancake ice gradually became heavier, but she was able to make two or three knots at sixty revolutions.

Tempted on by what appeared to be water sky ahead, she rather unexpectedly came to a dead stop about *Feb. 23,* 4 A.M. and could not even go astern in her *1912, 75° 43′* wake, as the pack east of her was pressing *S., 164° 20′* *E.* in towards the coast and so consolidating the pancake ice she was in. At the same time the weather cleared and showed the extremity of the Drygalski Barrier to be fifteen miles due north. The water sky proved to be a myth.

HEAVY PACK IN WHICH THE SHIP WAS HELD UP WHILST ENDEAVOURING
TO RESCUE THE NORTHERN PARTY

After six hours the pressure eased and the *Terra Nova* was able to turn, taking, however, four hours' struggle to do so, and it took another twenty-six hours to escape from the ice which, on the day before, she had taken three hours to pass through. The alternative of leaving the ship in the ice and letting her drift with it past the Barrier was too dangerous to be more than thought of and cast aside, owing to the probable severe pressure that would be encountered while passing the Barrier itself.

The ship immediately proceeded to Cape Evans in order to report and to embark those going home, as it was probable that she would have to spend the remainder of her time trying to relieve Campbell.

As far as Cape Bird the ship passed through sea covered with pancake ice, and Ponting was able to get some very interesting photos of it in different stages of growth. Fortunately this ice only reduced her speed by about two knots.

After passing Cape Bird a strong southerly wind sprang up, so that great difficulty was experienced in making Cape Evans; but finally she anchored close in at 2 P.M. on the 25th, all the fast ice having gone out since she was last here. At 11 P.M. the gale lulled *Feb. 25,* for a few minutes and a boat was sent ashore. *1912. Cape* Simpson at once came off with the news *Evans.* that Lieutenant Evans was at Hut Point and seriously ill, and should be taken off as soon as possible.

The gale came on again at once, and it was not till

the first watch on the 28th that the ship could secure

Feb. 28. Off alongside the fast ice about ½ mile north of
Castle Rock. Hut Point and Atkinson and his party were
able to bring Evans on board. The opportunity was
taken to land two sledge loads of stores that would
be useful at *Discovery* hut.

The ship at once proceeded to Cape Evans, and by
everyone on shore and aboard lending a willing hand
the remainder of the stores (about nineteen tons) was
landed in the boats between 2 A.M. and 7.30 A.M., in a
perfect calm and beautiful weather.

As soon as the last boat came off, the ship left for
Terra Nova Bay again. It was essential that Lieutenant

Feb. 29, Evans should have a doctor with him for
1912, 77° 7′ a few days more and so Atkinson had to go
S., 166° 25′
E.   in her, though it was quite likely that she
might not be able to re-enter the Sound.

Conditions off Terra Nova Bay had not improved,
and the ship ran up and down outside the heavier pack

March 1 and trying it in places wherever a sign of weakness
2. Off Terra showed ; but with always the same result,
Nova Bay.   that after entering two or three miles through
pack which gradually grew heavier she would be brought
up. Once, indeed, she managed to work through to a
position north-east seven miles from the end of the
Drygalski Barrier, but even here she was 35 miles from
her destination, and this was the last flicker of reasonable
hope.

The following extract is from the ship's log :

' All day on outskirts of ice filling Terra Nova Bay

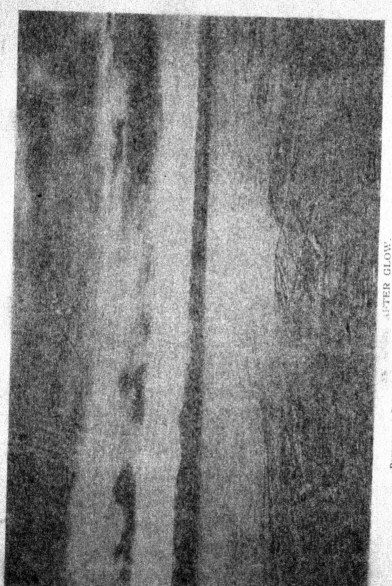

AFTER GLOW.

Photograph By Herbert G. Ponting.

Reproduced

the first watch on the 25th that the ship dropped anchor

Feb. 25,
Cape Evans. alongside the fast ice about ½ mile north of

Point and Atkinson and his party were

able to bring Evans on board. The opportunity was

taken to land two sledge loads of stores that would

be wanted at discovery hut.

The ship at once proceeded to Cape Evans, and by

everybody in the ship's company lending a willing hand

...

As soon as the last boat came off, the ship left

Terra Nova Bay again. It was essential that Lieutenant

Feb. 29,
1912, 77° 7′
S., 166° 25′
E. Evans should have a doctor with him for

a few days more and so Atkinson had to go

in her, though it was quite likely that she

might not be able to re-enter the Sound.

Conditions off Terra Nova Bay had not improved,
and the ship ran up and down outside the heavier pack

March 1 and
2. Off Terra
Nova Bay. trying it in places wherever a sign of weakness

showed; but with always the same result,

that after entering two or three miles through

pack which gradually grew heavier she would be brought

up. Once, indeed, she managed to work herself into a

position north-east seven miles from the

Drygalski Barrier, but even here she was of

her destination, and this was the last failure of

hope.

The following extract is from the ship's log

'All day on outskirts of ice along Terra

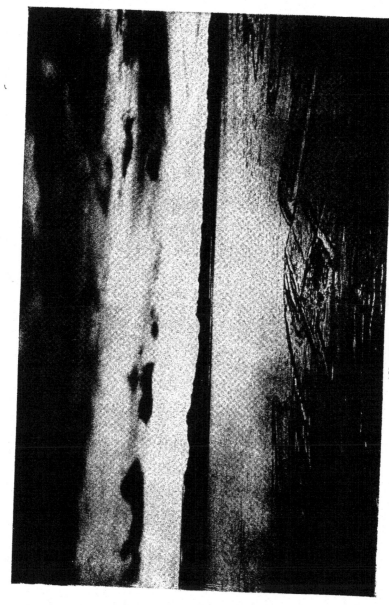

AN APRIL AFTER GLOW.

REPRODUCED FROM AN AUTOCHROME PHOTOGRAPH BY HERBERT G. PONTING.

and extending fifteen to twenty miles eastward from the extremity of the Drygalski Barrier. On the outskirts thin pancake and small, but very heavy, bay ice floes ; the heavy floes becoming more numerous and the new ice heavier the farther the pack is entered, till heavy pack with interspaces all filled with snow slush forms an impenetrable barrier ; in places this year's pancake, consolidated and up to one foot thick, in thick slush, forms equally impenetrable barrier owing to its viscous nature.'

In the forenoon of the 3rd the ship was again headed for Cape Evans. From several miles north of Beaufort *March 3, 1912, 76° 2′ S., 167° 26′ E.* Island to nearly Cape Royds the ship was passing through pancake ice, refrozen into large solid sheets of very varying heaviness but often sufficient to reduce her speed fifty per cent. The wait at Cape Evans was very short ; she was only delayed an hour embarking those members going home who had not been able to get on board before, together with Keohane, and then proceeded to Hut Point, where the ice had now broken away to within a quarter of a mile of the hut.

Atkinson and Keohane were landed and a few stores *March 4, 1912. Off Hut Point.* taken to the hut. The ship then ran for the Glacier Tongue to complete with water, and shortly after 10 P.M. (the 4th) proceeded again for Terra Nova Bay.

Although only twenty hours had elapsed between the time she passed Cape Royds going south, and repassed it going north, the ice had materially thickened, and between Cape Bird and Beaufort Island she forced through with considerable difficulty. The condition off Terra Nova Bay had, if anything, grown worse, and this time the ship was held up when 20 miles E.N.E. of the Barrier.

Finally, on March 7, taking into consideration the *March 7,* nature and extent of the pack and the time *1912, 75° 5' S., 168° 43' E.* of the year, the conclusion was reluctantly come to that the ship could not reach Arrival Bay that season, and so she turned north.

The next day a sooty albatross was around the ship— *March 8, 73°* a most welcome sight, proving the absence of *32' S., 174° 12' E.* pack to north of her ; and from now on large numbers of deep sea birds were always round the ship.

On the 15th and 16th the *Terra Nova* passed up the north-east side of the Balleny Islands, closer than any *March 16,* other ship had been able to get, except Balleny *1912, 66° 44' S., 164° 48' E.* himself ; but either it was foggy or else it snowed so persistently, that nothing was seen of them except on the 16th, when the fog suddenly rolled away for two hours and, through a rift in the clouds, a glimpse of Buckle Island was obtained—part of the side of a snow-capped mountain with the sun on it, a rarely beautiful sight, appearing to be quite detached from anything to do with the earth herself. Before this one of the beautiful little snowy petrels had appeared, telling of ice in the vicinity, so the course was altered more to the northward and, when the fog lifted, icebergs and smaller bits of ice were seen on the port hand. It

is seldom these little birds are found away from the close
vicinity of ice.

Fires were put out on the 18th, a good offing having
been made, the position being 64° S., 160° 12′ E.

Between the 21st and the 25th it blew hard, the
climax being reached on Sunday night (the 24th), when
March 24, a severe storm was raging, the most severe
1912, 55° encountered by the ship during her whole
51′ S., 165° commission. It is a wonderful sight to see a
49′ E.
comparatively small ship in a storm, particularly at
night; the marvellous way she rides over waves that
look as if they must break on board, together with the
dense darkness in the heavy squalls, relieved only by the
white crests of the waves as they break, is a sight that
makes up for a considerable amount of discomfort.

The gale was followed by two days' calm, when
Ponting was able to cinematograph the birds feeding
March 26 close under the ship's stern.
and 27, When off the coast of New Zealand a
20′ S., 167° school of sperm whales was seen and followed
33′ E.
for some time with the hopes of getting a photograph.
The animals, however, were too shy for the ship to approach
within reasonable photographic range.

At daybreak on April 1 the ship entered Akaroa
harbour to despatch the telegrams with the season's
April 1. news. Here we learned of Amundsen's
Akaroa. success in his undertaking.

On the 3rd she was berthed alongside the wharf in
Lyttelton again, and, needless to say, received with true
New Zealand hospitality.

The season had in many ways been a hard one for the engine-room department, but they never failed the ship in any of the difficulties in which she found herself, and, although conditions were often disheartening, the hands kept as willing and cheerful as if everything was going well.

Lieutenant Evans and Drake went home on Expedition business, the members of the shore party who had returned dispersed to their respective duties in civil life, and the men who had joined in New Zealand signed off temporarily for the winter.

Refitting and laying up the ship was hurried on as rapidly as possible and, by the help of the New Zealand Government, arrangements were made for the ship's party to survey Admiralty Bay in the Sounds.

The party were boarded at an accommodation house near French Pass and worked from motor launches, these latter being fitted with the ship's Lucas sounding machines.

The party consisted of thirteen, including officers, and three hands remained in the ship at Lyttelton as ship-keepers.

This work lasted from June 10 to October 15, when it was necessary to return to Lyttelton to prepare for the coming relief voyage.

On the whole for that part of New Zealand the weather this winter was unfavourable, but, in spite of this, a satisfactory amount of work was carried out.

On August 17 we had the great misfortune to lose

Brissenden by drowning. He was buried on the hillside overlooking the bay, and a marble cross erected to his memory. Robert Brissenden was a first-class man. careful and reliable, besides being a very good messmate, and his loss was very much felt by all.

THE THIRD VOYAGE

The ship left Lyttelton at 5 A.M. on December 14,
Dec. 14, 1912. A crowd of friends had collected to bid
1912. Lyttel- us farewell and send last messages to our
ton. companions in Victoria Land.

At 7 P.M. that evening we discovered a wretched man stowed away in the lifeboat. On being questioned the stowaway said he was a rabbiter and anxious to make a voyage in the *Terra Nova* : he appeared to be about thirty-five years of age and not very intelligent. As there was no object in taking this man south we shaped course for the nearest port, Akaroa, in order to land him. Fortunately, the Norwegian barque *Triton* was sighted at midnight, and her courteous captain relieved us of our stowaway, promising to land him in Dunedin.

The programme for the third southward voyage included the running of a line of soundings from Banks Peninsula to a point in Lat. 60° S., Long. 170° W. Thence the ship was to proceed due south until the pack was reached, sounding twice daily. After entering the pack she was to continue to force her way southward, keeping approximately on the meridian of 165° W., to sound over the less known portions of the Ross Sea, and to determine the nature and extent of the pack ice in this unexplored region.

The earlier southern voyages had mostly been made in more westerly longitudes.

In conjunction with the ambitious deep-sea-sounding programme Lillie was to make a number of quantitative plankton stations, and obtain trawls whenever the occasion was suitable. We also hoped to add materially to our magnetic observations for Variation, Dip, and Total Force.

The programme was fairly well adhered to, and thanks to Rennick's expert handling of the Lucas machine we obtained several soundings of about 3000 fathoms, when less ardent hydrographers would have surrendered to the bad weather.

On December 17 the Antipodes Islands were passed, the ship labouring in the heavy sea and occasionally rolling *Dec. 17,* her bulwarks under; it was not considered *1912, 49°* advisable to attempt a landing. These islands *12' S., 178°* *14' E.* are visited twice a year by a Government steamer, and have been examined pretty thoroughly, although rather sketchily surveyed.

On this voyage the ship was infested with rats, but Cheetham, our boatswain, who has crossed the Antarctic Circle fourteen times, showed himself an adept at rat-catching and soon freed the ship from the pest. He used to throw the rats over the side, and the albatrosses and mollymawks would swoop down and devour the vermin in an incredibly short time. We had all kinds of rat-traps in use, and even used mouse-traps to catch the young.

On December 26, in Lat. 63° S., we passed the first iceberg of the voyage, an old disrupted berg, and as we

Dec. 26, 63° 43′ S., 166° 36′ W. advanced southward all kinds of icebergs were to be seen. The ice-log shows a greater number and variety of bergs on this than on the two preceding voyages.

Dec. 29, 1912, 69° 28′ S., 166° 15′ W. The great belt of Antarctic pack ice was not reached until December 29, when we had attained the 69th parallel.

On comparison with the records of earlier voyages it will be seen that the northern limit of the pack this year lay two degrees farther south than found on voyages made in more western longitudes.

The only other Expedition that has explored this part of the Ross Sea was that under Sir James Ross, who found a line of compact hummocky ice in the same position in 1842 ; this confirmation throws some light on the trend of the pack in this quadrant.

We had expected to meet with pack ice on crossing the Antarctic Circle, and our expectations not being realised, the ship's company looked forward to an almost ice-free voyage to the Ross Sea.

Our hopes were frustrated. The day after entering the pack we encountered heavy bay ice, which retarded us to such an extent that we could scarcely make more than one mile an hour on our course. We had a tremendous struggle this season to get into the Ross Sea at all, and not until we had fought our way for over 400 miles did we really get through the pack.

The weather conditions this season were all that we could

wish for, and we had plenty of time at our disposal to carry out our scientific programme. When our way was barred by temporary congestion of the pack Pennell, Rennick, and Lillie would all get ahead with magnetic, deep-sea sounding, and biological work, mostly under favourable conditions.

Occasionally the sea was so discoloured by diatoms that we might have been steaming in the Thames estuary, and then again the discoloured area would be succeeded by belts of beautiful blue water wherein one could see crab-eater seals diving under the ship.

Quite the most fascinating sight in the pack ice was the exhibition of swimming by two crab-eaters in the open water leads on New Year's Day. They followed the ship and disported themselves like dolphins ; when we were forced to stop owing to the closeness of the pack the two seals rubbed themselves along the side of the ship.

We were disappointed at seeing no Ross seals this year, for we have secured no specimens of this animal at all.

Jan. 5, 1913,
71° 48′ S.,
166° 48′ W.
By January 5 we had worked through 168 miles of pack, averaging only 24 miles a day, and burning over seven tons of coal for each daily run.

Now we were confronted by small belts of ice composed of floes 15 to 20 feet thick and 100 feet in diameter. This ice was so hard that the ship could not break it. Whenever we collided with a floe the *Terra Nova* shook fore and aft, the officer in the crow's nest experiencing the most violent concussions.

On this day a penguin chased us for over an hour,

crying out ludicrously whenever one of us imitated its call.
The little creature became quite exhausted, as we were
steaming through lighter ice at the time and it had to swim
steadily after us. The poor bird was unable to reach the
ship, as the ' kick ' of the propeller swirled it away whenever it caught us up. As often as this happened the
penguin would struggle on to a floe and reel about like a
drunken man, until finally it lay still, thoroughly defeated.

We were completely beset with ice on January 6
Jan. 6 and and 7, and the officers spent their time working
7, 1913, 71° for Lillie, obtaining plankton and water-bottle
40' S., 166°
47' W. samples at many different depths.

Lillie put out his twenty-four mesh net at 1000 metres,
and obtained a lot of specimens, including a fine jelly-fish.

On January 8, the ice opening up, we proceeded slowly
on our way. We passed close alongside a low hummocky
Jan. 8, 1913, iceberg which had three Emperor penguins on
71° 41' S., it. They must have been there some weeks, as
167° 4' W. the surface of the berg was much soiled and the
snow trodden about over a great area. The iceberg was
too high for the birds to have regained had they once left
it. Two of the Emperors were very thin ; the third, an
enormous bird, was moulting and one could not make out
what sort of condition he was in.

Until January 14 progress was painfully slow, but on
this day the ship worked through into looser ice. The
pack was eventually cleared on January 16 in Lat. 74° 50' S.,
Long. 177° 15' E.

The night of January 17–18 was very still and a belt
of stratus cloud settled down, forming a thick fog ; the ship

nevertheless was worked through small ice belts and she rounded Cape Bird on the morning of the 18th. About breakfast time the sun dispersed the mist and shone brightly. The now familiar features of McMurdo Strait were clearly outlined to the southward, and our stout little ship steamed at full speed past Cape Royds towards our winter quarters.

We had spent the last twenty-four hours in ' squaring up ' and preparing our comfortable, if somewhat limited, accommodation for the reception of our comrades at Cape Evans. The mails were all sorted and each member's letters done up in pillow-slips with his name boldly printed thereon. We had only one piece of bad news, the death of poor Brissenden, for all the wives and relations were well, and eagerly looking forward to the return of the Expedition. Every telescope and binocular in the ship was levelled on the hut as Cape Evans opened out from behind the Cape Barne Glacier. The bay was free of ice and one or two figures were discernible outside the hut.

The ship rapidly closed the beach, and by the sudden lively movements of those ashore we knew that the *Terra Nova* had been perceived.

As we stopped engines a crowd collected before the hut and we could count nineteen men—it was an exciting moment.

The shore party gave three hearty cheers, to which the ship's company replied. The Commanding Officer, espying Campbell, shouted through a megaphone, ' Are you all well, Campbell ? ' At this our friends on shore became speechless, and after a very marked hush, which

quite damped our spirits, Campbell replied : 'The Southern
Party reached the Pole on January 18 last year, but were
all lost on the return journey—we have their records.'

The anchor was dropped; Campbell and Atkinson
immediately came off and told us in detail how misfortune after misfortune had befallen our gallant leader
and his four brave comrades. We listened sadly to
the story, and our feelings were too deep to be described.
We had actually prepared the cabins for the reception of
our lost companions, and it was with infinite sadness
that the beds were unmade, the flags hauled down from
our mastheads, and those undelivered letters sealed up for
return to the wives and mothers who had given up so
much in order that their men might achieve.

But however great our sorrow we had the consolation
of pride in the magnificent spirit shown by the Polar
Party. The manner in which these men died is in itself
an eloquent description of their characters as we knew
them. The absolute generosity of Captain Scott himself
runs through his dying appeal to the nation and those
letters of his with no word of blame or reflection on others
for the disaster, though he could not know that scurvy
had smitten the last supporting party, and that those
who would have come were fettered by illness and the
weather conditions that finally arrested the advance of
the dog teams.

It was characteristic also that he did not forget the
future of his Expedition, but left instructions and letters
to the end that the scientific results should be fitly
published.

The two devoted men who died side by side with
Captain Scott were fine British types. Wilson was a
wonderful fellow, whose magnificent judgment helped us
all to smooth over the little troubles which were bound
to arise from time to time, and who (it has been said
before and let it be said again) by his own example and
the influence of his personality was mainly responsible
for the fact that there never was a quarrel or an angry
word in the Expedition.

Bowers possessed an individuality that attracted his
companions enormously. He was, besides being a very
quick, clever worker, a humourist of the most pleasing
type. He bore hardship splendidly and stood the cold
probably better than anyone in the Expedition.

The conspicuous bravery of Oates was typical of the
man. 'The Soldier' was really loved by the men. He
had a dry wit that always left him uppermost in those
exciting arguments that did so much to cheer us during
the winter season. Patrick Keohane, a splendid Irish
seaman, remarked to us as the details of the story were
unfolded : ' Captain Oates did just what we all expected
of him, sir ; he was a fine man that, sir ; not much talk
about him, but chock full of grit.'

The fifth man of the Southern Party was a British
bluejacket of the finest type, who had made himself
invaluable. Edgar Evans was the sledge-master, and to
him we owed the splendid fitting of our travelling
equipment. He left a fine record of service, and his
example will do a great deal for the younger seamen
of the Royal Navy.

The *Terra Nova* remained at anchor off Cape Evans for thirty hours, and those on board did their best to help the Cape Evans party to settle down for the homeward voyage.

We heard that the shore party had that day (Jan. 18) commenced the work of preparation for a third winter; they were delighted to see us. A typical extract from the diary of a member may be quoted:

'*Jan.* 18.

Terra Nova in sight

Hurrah! Hurrah!

Great Joy———

Hurrah!

We are relieved, and God be thanked for that Teddy * is on board the *Terra Nova*. Everything all right there.'

Immediately greetings had been exchanged and the situation thoroughly grasped, all hands packed and transported the specimens, collections, and equipment to the ship. We worked all night, and in twenty-four hours had removed our effects to the *Terra Nova,* and closed the hut after clearing it up and making a list of provisions and equipment.

We have left at Cape Evans an outfit and stores that would see a dozen resourceful men through one summer and winter at least.

On Sunday, January 19, at 5.20 P.M., the Expedition

---

* 'Teddy' refers to Lieut. Evans, who was not expected to live after his bad attack of scurvy.

finally left Cape Evans and proceeded in the *Terra Nova* to Cape Royds, where a depôt of specimens left by Priestley's party on the Erebus journey was embarked.

We then steamed up the Sound towards Hut Point until brought up by the fast ice which still stretched out for nearly ten miles from the southern shores of McMurdo Sound.

Early on January 20 Atkinson set out with a party of seven to erect a cross in memory of our lost companions. It had been constructed by Davies of jarrah, an Australian wood.

This cross, 9 feet in height, now stands on the summit of Observation Hill, overlooking the Great Ice Barrier and in full view of the *Discovery* winter quarters.

IN

MEMORIAM

CAPT. R. F. SCOTT, R.N.

DR. E. A. WILSON, CAPT. L. E. G. OATES, INS. DRGS., LT. H. R. BOWERS, R.I.M. PETTY OFFICER E. EVANS, R.N.

WHO DIED ON THEIR

RETURN FROM THE

POLE.   MARCH

1912

TO STRIVE, TO SEEK,

TO FIND,

AND NOT TO

YIELD

The line chosen from Tennyson's 'Ulysses' was suggested by Cherry-Garrard. Atkinson's sledge team consisted of those who had taken part in the search for Captain Scott.

MEMORIAL CROSS ERECTED AT OBSERVATION HILL TO THE SOUTHERN PARTY

They took two days to convey the heavy wooden cross to the top of Observation Hill and erect it. It was well secured, and will remain in position for an indefinite time, as there is no dampness likely to cause rot in this high latitude.

During Atkinson's absence the ship's officers were employed surveying and carrying out magnetic work; the engineers took this opportunity of letting fires out and cleaning the boiler. Atkinson returned on the night of January 21, having put Hut Point in order and closed the old *Discovery* hut, which, like our own winter quarters, we have left well stocked with provisions and what equipment we could spare.

During the night of the 19th a large iceberg swept into McMurdo Sound and was carried by the current directly for us. Having no steam we had to set sail and stand away to the northward from the sea ice to which we were made fast. We had some excitement, as the wind was very light; the sails were just full enough to give us steerage way, and the great tabular iceberg drifted close across our stern.

The ship now proceeded towards Granite Harbour. Steam was ready by 5 A.M. on the morning of the 22nd, and encountering detached belts of ice we furled sail and worked close to the coast of Victoria Land.

At 2 P.M. the *Terra Nova* rounded Cape Roberts and secured to the fast ice off Granite Harbour.

Gran in charge of a party of six men went in to bring off a geological depôt left by Taylor and Debenham. It was a hard journey, 17 miles there and back. A big open

lead had to be crossed *en route*, and Gran's men negotiated
this by converting their sledge into a ' kayak,' using a
canvas cover which made quite a good boat out of the
sledge.   On their way home to the ship they had the
fortune to get on to a loose ice floe with their two sledges.
Ferrying in this fashion much time was saved, and the
party returned hungry and tired but successful at 3 A.M.
on January 23.

During the absence of this party some surveying work
was accomplished, and the astronomical observations taken
by the navigating officers in conjunction linked on the work
of Griffith Taylor and Debenham to the main survev.   Off
shore soundings were obtained by Rennick with a view to
throwing light on the neighbouring glacier movements.
Pennell carried out magnetic observations, Lillie trawled
with the Agassiz and obtained a fine haul, which included
enormous sponges.   In short, the usual beehive industry
in the scientific work was maintained.

At 3.30 A.M. the sledge gear was brought on board
by Gran's party ; they had secured all Taylor's and
Debenham's beautiful geological collections, consisting
largely of fossils and coral.   These specimens had been
left here a whole year ago.

This accomplished, we hauled in our ice anchors and
proceeded under steam as requisite for working through
the pack which barred our way to the Drygalski Barrier.

At 11.30 A.M. the ice became so heavy that we were
forced to turn round and return towards Granite Harbour.

All day we worked to clear out of the pack and made
only fair progress, the floes being so big that our weight

would not move them. The outlook was brighter at midnight, when we were doing 5 knots to the north-eastward, the ice-fields being less compressed. The punching and butting through continued with varying success till 9 P.M. on January 24, when the Commander concluded that it was a waste of coal and unfair to the ship to proceed. We stopped, therefore, and banked fires.

After a delay of seven or eight hours Bruce reported the ice to be opening tremendously, and we accordingly proceeded on January 25, as soon as steam was ready. Very gradually the old ship worked towards Terra Nova Bay. Shortly after noon we won through into a very big open lead and could make five knots on our course. We stopped to sound at 8 A.M. and noon, the soundings showing 437, 625, and 515 fathoms. These soundings show a 'deep' which I believe Professor David rather suspected. They were really taken for his benefit.

By 3 A.M. on January 25 we had worked the ship through the ice near Campbell's winter quarters and secured to the sea ice which extended a quarter of a mile out from the piedmont. This was particularly solid and slippery, being quite free from snow. Although so close to the shore we found the depth 198 fathoms.

We sent a party away under Priestley to pick up the depôt of geological specimens; the remainder of the Expedition visited the igloo where Campbell and his party spent the previous winter.

The visit to the igloo revealed in itself a story of

hardship that brought home to us what Campbell never would have told. There was only one place in this smoke-begrimed cavern where a short man could stand upright. In odd corners were discarded clothes saturated with blubber and absolutely black. The weight of these garments was extraordinary, and we experienced strange sensations as we examined the cheerless hole that had been the only home of six of our hardiest men. No cell prisoners ever lived through such discomfort. Most of the *Terra Nova's* crew secured mementoes of their visit to this unparalleled habitation.

We left a depôt of provisions at the head of the Bay, its position being marked by a bamboo and flag. This depôt contains enough food stuffs to enable a party of five or six men to make their way to Butter Point, where another large depôt exists.

Very early on January 26 we left these inhospitable shores, and steaming E.N.E. to get clear of the ice belts which stream up the coast, we virtually gained the open Ross Sea by the evening, on the return voyage to New Zealand.

An attempt was made to close the Balleny Islands, which do not all appear to be correctly charted, but thick weather and adverse ice conditions prevented our accomplishing this.

The *Terra Nova* stood well to the westward, as shown in the accompanying track chart, until she was in a good position for making New Zealand.

It is interesting to note that in latitude 64° 15' S.,

longitude 159° 15' E. the *Terra Nova* passed close to an iceberg twenty-one geographical miles in length.

On February 2, in latitude 62° 10' S., longitude 158° 15' E., during thick weather, the ship was beset with icebergs and at slow speed steamed for six miles along the face of one huge berg. She was in a narrow channel out of which she could not work owing to the close grouping of detached icebergs which lay on the other hand.

This last season the ice conditions appeared to be the worst on record as far as the exterior ice was concerned, but close to Victoria Land we were never seriously hampered.

The biological, magnetic, and hydrographical work was continued on our homeward voyage, and on February 10, at 3 A.M., the ship reached Oamaru, a small port on the east coast of South Island, New Zealand. Here Lieutenant Pennell and Dr. Atkinson were landed with the Commander's despatch, which was sent to the Central News for simultaneous distribution throughout the world.

The *Terra Nova* remained at sea until Wednesday, February 12, when she returned to Lyttelton.

Her entry into the harbour was very different from the happy return we had so looked forward to.

With flags at half-mast we steamed into the port and were berthed alongside the Harbour Board shed by Captain Thorpe, the harbour-master. Thousands came to meet us and quietly notified their sympathy, and for many days afterwards we received messages of condolence from all parts of the world.

THE VOYAGE HOME

The ship sailed from Lyttelton on her homeward voyage on March 13, 1913, under the command of Lieutenant Pennell. In the ward room, besides the Captain, were Rennick, Nelson, Lillie, Levick, Anderson, Mr. Williams, and Mr. Cheetham. When Bruce went home by mail steamer with Lady Scott, Nelson volunteered for the position of second mate, and proved himself a most efficient officer. Mr. Gibson Anderson of Christchurch volunteered for the voyage, and was taken on for coal trimming.

The ship had thirteen dogs on board, going home as pets of various members. Davies built platforms for the dogs ; these stood about ten inches off the deck and had a ledge three or four inches high, so that in wet weather the animals would be off the decks and in hot weather have air circulating under them, while, when the ship was rolling, they had the ledges to support themselves against. These platforms were a great comfort to them.

It was intended to run down the Great Circle track to 56° South and then east along that parallel. The ship made a good run down to 56° South, but then met easterly winds, fortunately, however, being able to *March 23, 1913, 56° 2′ S., 156° 25′ W.* pass about fifteen miles north of where the Nimrod group is charted (from information received nearly a hundred years ago), and got two soundings, both over 2000 fathoms. Captain Davis in the *Nimrod* on her way home in 1909 passed right over the charted position, but weather prevented them sounding. Either this group is charted a great deal out of position, or, what is more likely, does not exist at all.

North-east winds continuing, the ship was driven a good deal farther south than was intended and met with

March 27, 1913, 58° 51' S., 142° 29' W. a considerable amount of fog and thick weather. On the 27th she passed three bergs, and another one on the 29th, but the weather all these days was so thick that ice could only be seen at a very short distance. On the 29th, however, she was able to alter to the north-east and soon to leave these

March 29, 1913, 58° 39 S., 134° 54' W. rather uncomfortable latitudes. There was a marked dearth of birds all across the Southern Ocean, great grey shear-waters and the little black-bellied petrels being the most common, while the mollymawks and sooty albatross were only occasional visitors.

Cape Horn was passed on April 11, in a strong gale; but as the ship entered the Straits Le Maire at daybreak the next morning the wind dropped and the sun rose over Staten Island, ushering in a beautiful day; and from here, with very little exception, fine weather was experienced all the way to England.

While crossing the shelf on which the Falkland Islands stand, Lillie was able to trawl, and once again after leaving Rio de Janeiro, for the last time on the commission, the catch in this case being almost entirely composed of swimming crabs.

Trawling probably caused more excitement and interest in the ship than anything else she did, and the

instant a catch came in-board Lillie was surrounded by
an interested group of men, very anxious to see if any
startling novelty had at last been dragged up from the
bottom.

Across the Atlantic the plankton nets were put over,
when possible, for half an hour every night, and a good
series of catches was made ; the middle watch was chosen,
as experience had shown the practical impossibility of
entirely preventing garbage, ashes, &c., from being thrown
overboard during the day, and the nets faithfully collected everything that went over. At night, however,
after washing down the shoots and the ship's side where
ashes had been thrown over, the haul was made and the
net brought in absolutely clean.

Rio was reached on April 28, and the ship stopped
here four days, coaling, taking in fresh provisions, and
giving leave.

While crossing the Tropics the dog watches were
taken in the stoke-hold by the after-guard. This gave
each fireman a sixteen hours' spell free of watch two days
out of every three : a great boon when the conditions are
trying, as they undoubtedly are, in the engine-room and
stokehold in the Tropics.

The ship called at Fayal in the Azores, in order to
cable home, and anchored off Horta on June 2. She
was placed in quarantine, much to our chagrin, though
facilities were allowed for sending cables and getting
provisions.

At last, on June 11, the ship dropped anchor in Crow
Sound, Scilly Islands, where two days were spent painting

and cleaning up, and on June 14 she arrived at Cardiff, exactly three years after leaving.

Here it only remains to acknowledge the exemplary conduct of the ship's company, fore and aft. Every member worked to help the Expedition forward loyally and cheerfully, accepting each position as it came, all hands doing their best to help matters forward and to see the humorous side of everything.

UNIVERSITAS ANTARCTICA!

LECTURE ON THE ROSS ICE BARRIER BY CAPTAIN SCOTT
June 7, 1911, 8 P.M. (*From notes by Griffith Taylor*)

I. *Flotation.*—Let us first of all consider the question of the flotation of the Barrier. There can be, I think, no doubt that it is afloat. On pages 417–420 in the ' Narrative of the *Discovery* ' will be found an account of the Ross Barrier, in which we read that its face is 360 miles long, and that the sea exceeds 1800 feet in depth along the greater part of this distance.

The ice wall is 150 feet high here in places, and we must allow for a much greater depth which is submerged below the level of the sea.

The ratio of submerged to visible ice appears to vary, and should be investigated on bergs in our vicinity.

Even if it is 7 to 1, then the Barrier is afloat at its edge, and the same is of course the case if the ratio be taken as 4 to 1. Professor David quotes an example of 1 to 1, but that is certainly exceptional.

It seems certain that there is a layer of water under the great Ice Barrier, which has five times the extent of the North Sea.

II. *Limits.*—We have several observations of the ice front, notably Ross in 1840, and the *Discovery* in 1902. The latter showed a recession in general of from 15 to 20 miles, with a maximum of 45 miles. In 1911, however, Pennell reported that the conditions appeared to have changed little during the last ten years.

This means that 45 miles at any rate must have been afloat. The Ross Sea does not get shallower so far as we know.

We must remember that the wall near Balloon Bight varies greatly in height. If the ratio of the edge of the Barrier above and below water line be taken as 1 to 4, then the ice sheet seems to vary in thickness from 70 to 700 feet, with an average of about 400 feet.

But it is quite conceivable that this sheet is extremely thin in places.

III. *Crevasses.*—These natural breaks in the continuity of the ice have been studied in some detail. We observe that they are radial near the Bluff and White Island. They have parallel sides, both in plan and section. No crevasses seem to occur more than 15 miles from the land. Curiously enough, none of these seem to have any great depth, for I saw platforms about

50 feet down, and rarely got a lead down beyond 8 fathoms (50 feet).

Let us compare an ice sheet over land with a similar sheet extending over water. In the first type one could not expect uncrevassed areas of any size if the ice were *moving* over the land. (Though we must remember that the *stationary* ice over the Plateau is not crevassed.)

Again, over a sea surface the crevasses would only extend for a limited distance, in fact to sea-level, where they would freeze over. This may account for the limited depth observed.

Near the Barne and Shackleton Inlets the great lateral trench was filled with pools due to thaw waters, and this was 100 feet deep. If the sheet were 1000 feet thick, one would expect this 'rupture crack' to be much deeper.

IV. *Temperature and Pressure.*—The temperature in the crevasses seemed fairly constant near the land, but when farther away it seemed to rise with depth. This looks like the result of a subglacial sea.

The atmospheric pressures as taken on the journey to 82° S. varied very little from those at Hut Point :

$$
\begin{array}{lll}
\text{At } 79°, & + \cdot 045\,'' \text{ difference} \\
\quad ,, \;\; 80°, & + \cdot 04\,'' & ,; \\
\quad ,, \;\; 81°, & + \cdot 06\,'' & .. \\
\quad ,, \;\; 82°, & - \cdot 03\,''
\end{array}
$$

The barometric gradient probably rises as one goes south, so that one cannot use the barometer to obtain accurate levels.

One could get equal (and useless) readings all the way

if the change in *levels* corresponded to the change in barometric gradient.

In working up the meteorology notes, barometer figures based on Royds' journey—who went nearly *parallel* to the Barrier edge—were unfortunately used to obtain results for the Southern journey.

Finally, we may conclude that the tendency of all the facts is to support the ' Floating Barrier' theory.

V. *Movement of the Barrier.*—There is certainly not enough inclination in the Barrier ice sheet to account for its motion. The Bay of Whales (or Balloon Bight) has not moved much, and this may be taken as the eastern limit of the moving sheet. We don't of course know the extent of the ice sheet to the south-east.

Depôt A moved 608 yards in thirteen and a half months, which agrees closely with the 500 of movement observed by the *Nimrod.*

We must take note of the direction of movement observed, for this may not represent the total movement. It may give the minimum, and this result is very startling in view of the sluggish *land* glaciers.

Simpson suggests that the deposition of snow on the Barrier leads to an expansion due to the increase of weight. If it is 350 miles long and 400 feet thick, then the ratio of thickness to length is 1 to 5250. This can be adequately compared to a sheet of cardboard ⅛ inch thick and the length of this hut (50 feet).

The ice sheet can only move to the north. If we assume it moves 1000 yards, and that 175 square miles is the amount moved north, then the mass to be added to keep the breaking front about the same position is 11·7 cubic miles.

Let us consider the snow deposition. It is stated that about 4 inches of compressed snow falls per year. The blizzards evidently build up shallow flat hummocks here and there, and may cover the whole surface at the fourth effort.

The old *Discovery* Depôt was covered in 13 inches of old snow or 9 inches of ice.

If we assume the Barrier area is 350 × 350 miles, then we get a mass of 16·5 cubic miles.

The difference in these two interesting figures—16·5 cubic miles and 11·7 cubic miles—may be due to an ablation of the under surface of the sheet by warm water. However, we may assume that there is sufficient snowfall on the Barrier to account for the movement, which is a fact of the first importance.

At the edge of the Barrier there is a curved ascent, and ' doming ' is common in bergs. May not this curving be a result of the outward expansion ?

The movement of the northern glaciers seems to be much greater than that of the Beardmore and southern glaciers. Perhaps it is six times as great. But the slow movement in the south may still be sufficient to account for the ice sheet's advance.

The fact that the great lateral trench keeps open looks as if rival motions were at work.

As far as 170° W., Campbell says that the 1911 survey showed the western edge of the Barrier face to be stable, and with no change like that since Ross's time. Of course there may be catastrophic years. We know that icebergs are very plentiful in some years in the Southern Ocean. This last summer our Glacier Tongue broke away after remaining for many years.

VII. *Mainland Glaciers.*—There is very little evidence of large motion. David says the Nansen Glacier presses out the sea ice; but quite probably it is the other way, and due to the sea ice pressing against the Glacier Tongue. The movement of the glaciers is a measure of the pressure behind; they are, however, so cold in these regions that their movement is sluggish compared with those in temperate climes.

I do not think there is anything like 13 inches annual snowfall on the Ice Plateau. If there is recession along the coast, the same must obtain on the great Ice Plateau. The high level moraines decrease in height above the present surface of the ice, the débris being 2000 feet up near the coast and only 200 feet above near the plateau. However, the Beardmore from its great crevasses seems to show extra movement.

VIII. *The Inland Ice Sheet.*—All our data are hypothetical—we are erecting an edifice of theoretical bricks! We may give it the area of two-thirds of the circle drawn with a radius of 1200 miles.

There seems to be a descent from 9000 feet at the Pole to 2000 near the edge, and then a rapid fall at the sea line.

We may surmise 50 to 100 yards movement per annum across the edge of the Plateau, with a thickness of 700 or 800 feet; but all this is merely a fine effort of the imagination!

The ice cliffs all round the continent seem much the same. The depths over the shelf at the edge seem of about the same order also.

We must remember that the new set of facts of the Great Plateau bounded by the new range of mountains was never thought of before 1903, and is not fully digested yet.

I believe that the snowfall increases towards the fringe of the plateau sheet.

These facts suffice to account for the outflow of Antarctic bergs. In latitudes 66° S. and 73° S. we find the same thickness of the ice cliffs. It must, however, be admitted that much of this theorising is very weak.

Finally, with regard to the question of the high continental Plateau and the land under the ice sheet I will ask the Physiographer to descant.

DISCUSSION

As usual, Captain Scott called on the members in the order in which they sat at the table.

Oates commented on the difficulty of detecting differences in the Barrier level. He often saw herds of cattle on the ice surface which turned out to be débris of previous camps.

Wilson said that if the outward movement was due to a flattening of the Barrier mass, then he would expect the great Shackleton Inlet trench to fill up.

Wright suggested that it was aground before the great lateral trench was reached.

Taylor drew attention to the great amount of surface-sculpturing due, not to pressure, but to thaw waters and direct sun-melting.   Some of the shallow crevasses might be due to this and not to movement or pressure—as on Butter Point.

If the Ferrar Tongue had grown since Captain Scott's visit, then these Antarctic glaciers were by no means sluggish.   Might not the slope apparent at the edge of the Barrier be due to the greater weathering at the edge, due to the presence of warm waters and stronger winds?   He suggested that the word 'glacierised' should be used for lands covered by glaciers instead of 'glaciated,' which might be kept for land forms exposed on recession.

He discussed the probable structure of the continent, with 'block' coast near Ross Island and an 'Andean Range near America.   The level surface of the Plateau was largely due to the preservative action of the ice cap. But it would also seem to exhibit 'senile' features, due to a previous cycle of normal erosion.

Probably Antarctica was a primeval solid block of the earth's crust of the type known as a 'Shield.'

Nelson thought the increase in snow above would certainly be balanced by the solution below.   He thought the face of the Barrier would be curved to the north, unless something were affecting it besides purely mechanical agents.

Simpson said that simply lowering thermometers into the crevasses was useless.   They should be buried in ice in the crevasse sides.

Debenham said that the Admiralty Range was certainly not of a true Pacific type.

The meeting adjourned about 10 P.M., but a select group of debaters carried on the arguments until 12.15 A.M.

A RÉSUMÉ OF THE PHYSIOGRAPHY AND GLACIAL GEOLOGY OF VICTORIA LAND, ANTARCTICA

BY GRIFFITH TAYLOR, B.Sc., B.E., B.A., F.G.S.
(Senior Geologist to the Expedition)

IT is always a wise principle in research to proceed from the known to the unknown. So little has been written on the subject in question that we should have almost a blank sheet were it not for the geologists of Shackleton's Expedition, whose detailed work is not yet published.

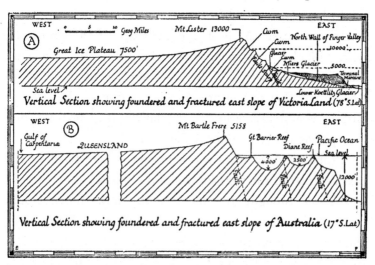

Let us glance at a map of the South Polar regions, how ever, and see if we can deduce any useful principles from neighbouring lands.*

* The section across Australia is from a figure by Professor David, F.R.S.

The physiography of the eastern coast of Australia has been subjected to a somewhat detailed investigation during the last ten years, with the result that it is found to exhibit splendid examples of subsidence, trough faulting, and rivers ' drowned ' by the sea. Great slices of the coast have sunk below the waves fairly lately in geological times, so that many of the great rivers of Eastern Australia now rise on the present coast (the old divide) and flow inland to the central lowlands. The features characteristic of this portion of the crust are therefore an elevated coastal region sloping gradually to the west and sharply truncated by ' faults ' on the east.

Let us now journey southward to Antarctica and take a birdseye view of the coast of the Ross Sea and of the great mountain range which leads from the Ross Sea and McMurdo Sound almost to the Pole. We notice at once that this range extends almost due north and south, as was the case in Australia, that it practically constitutes the shore line, that it has a steep eastern slope—often dropping ten thousand feet in a few miles—and that it descends gradually on the west to a uniform land mass of a plateau type.

It seems evident that these points of resemblance are not accidental. The great earth movements which affected Australia in middle and late Tertiary times also affected Antarctica. A readjustment of equilibrium raised the west and depressed the east in both continents. The central portion of Australia, consisting of ancient rocks which have been planed down to a uniform level by the normal agents of erosion—by rivers, wind, &c.—

is an example of a *peneplain.* It was formed in middle Tertiary times, and bears all the evidence of ' old age ' in a land surface. As we have seen, it has been elevated and now the rivers are cutting it down again, forming canyons all round its coastal edges, and the ' cycle of erosion ' has commenced anew. In Antarctica the land below the central ice plateau would appear to be a similar peneplain. The comparatively slight depth of the *outlet* glaciers seems to indicate that the ice cap is not very thick, probably one or two thousand feet only. The peneplain is, however, elevated to eight thousand feet instead of one to three thousand as in Australia.

It is, however, with the margin of the ice cap that these few pages are concerned. Just as in Australia beautiful canyons and falls have resulted from the attack of the weather on the margins of the plateau, so in Antarctica the ice rivers and agents of frost erosion have carved out their own characteristic topography.

We know from the fossils that warmer conditions existed in Mesozoic times in Antarctica, probably in early Tertiary times. Moreover, the elevation of the land so many thousand feet has undoubtedly given rise to a permanent refrigerating system of winds which has made Antarctic coasts much more inclement than they would have been with a less elevated interior.

There is practically no trace of *pre-glacial* topography such as might be shown by a moulding of the inland ice cap. We may picture the rock surface like that of upland Norway, as a gently rolling plateau. As the ice mantle covered Antarctica, occupying the more pro nounced swellings first, and then spreading in lobes of ice down the broad depressions, we may imagine that a very little difference in the contour might determine the position of the great outlet glaciers where the ice cap drained away to the sea. In other words, the glacier valleys do not appear to owe much to pre-glacial topography.

Let us now survey the marginal mountain range and the ice plateau more closely. The plateau seems to rise to 11,000 feet near the South geographic Pole, and decreases gradually to the north, being about 7000 feet at the South magnetic Pole. The mountain ranges have peaks, such as Markham and Lister, rising to 15,000 and 13,000 feet respectively, but the average height is perhaps about 9000 or 10,000 feet, while for considerable stretches near Granite Harbour they are only 6000 or 8000 feet high. Every 20 or 30 miles this fairly continuous range is broken by a huge 'outlet' glacier. Many of these are now well known, such as the Beardmore, which is over 100 miles long and 30 miles wide, the Ferrar, Mackay, David, &c. They form the only routes from the coast to the interior, and were it not for the *ice falls* where the glacier covers some irregularity in its rock floor, or the more dangerous *crevassed areas*, where it sweeps round a corner, or receives the thrust of a large tributary, they would not be difficult to traverse with sledges. The grade is not very steep, and they are to some extent sheltered from the blizzard drift which is the great obstacle to Barrier and plateau journeys. Their detailed topography is, however, very different from that of an area subjected to 'normal' erosion.

The regions more especially investigated in the two sledge journeys of the Western Geological Parties in 1911 and 1912 were the following :

(*a*) The Ferrar and Taylor outlet glaciers (77° 40′).

(*b*) The Koettlitz ice delta and its hinterland (78° 20′).

(*c*) Granite Harbour and the Mackay outlet glacier (77°).

(*d*) The Great Piedmont glacier between Granite Harbour and New Harbour (77° 20′).

Each of these regions presented its own peculiar

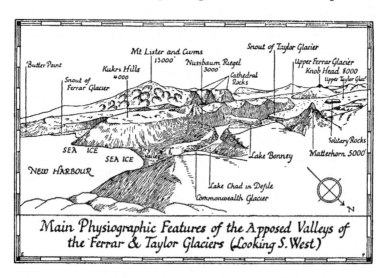

Main Physiographic Features of the Apposed Valleys of the Ferrar & Taylor Glaciers (Looking S. West)

topography, and the four were diverse enough to embody almost the whole cycle of glacial erosion within their domain.

(*a*) *The Ferrar and Taylor 'Outlet' Glaciers and the Dry Valley.*—These two glaciers are now connected by an ice col near Knob Head Mountain, but were originally

AN OUTLET GLACIER' VALLEY COMPLETELY FILLED WITH ICE. LOOKING UP THE FERRAR GLACIER TO THE SOUTH-WEST

Kukri Hills   Lake Bonney   Snout of Taylor Glacier

AN ICE-FREE OUTLET VALLEY, WHOSE GLACIER HAS RECEDED OVER TWENTY MILES FROM THE SEA. LOOKING
SOUTH-WEST UP DRY VALLEY TO THE SNOUT OF THE TAYLOR GLACIER

[See P. 209

THE   CIER,   OF THAW-WATERS ON AN ANCIENT

distinct parallel glaciers draining the ice plateau. As one marches up the Ferrar Glacier and notes its crevasses and ice falls, one wonders what the rock floor is really like—under the ice river. Just 5 miles to the north is another glacier which furnishes the answer to this question, for the Taylor Glacier now stops short 25 miles from the sea, and in Dry Valley we see how all the other valleys will appear when the ice age shall pass away from Antarctica.

Starting from New Harbour at the mouth of Dry Valley, the latter presents a typical catenary cross-section. A splendid pair of walls with the characteristic slope of 33° defines the glacier trough. There is no large terminal moraine near the sea, which seems to denote a fairly uniform and perhaps rapid retrocession of the glacier. About 6 miles from the coast a narrow defile appears on the north side, but the rounded valley floor rises gradually to 2000 feet over the greater part of the trough. West of this point there is a sudden drop from the Nussbaum Bar (or Riegel) into the next ' bowl ' of the valley. This is filled with moraine material to the depth of several hundred feet, for the drainage of the ' bowl ' is *away* from the sea to the salty waters of Lake Bonney. The defile previously mentioned is about 1500 feet deep, and would seem to be a water-cut gorge denoting an inter-glacial period.

Lake Bonney is about 3 miles long and is separated into two portions by a granite bar 500 feet high. This also is traversed by a narrow gorge on the northern side of the trough and is a smaller edition of the Nussbaum

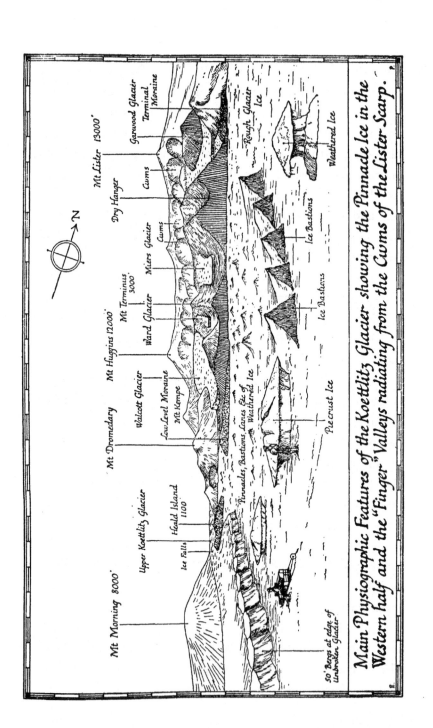

Main Physiographic Features of the Koettlitz Glacier showing the Pinnacle Ice in the Western half and the "Finger" Valleys radiating from the Cwms of the Lister Scarp.

N

Mt Morning 8000'

Upper Koettlitz Glacier

Ice Falls

Heald Island 1100

Mt Dromedary

Mt Huggins 12000'

Walcott Glacier

Low Level Moraine

Mt Kempe

Ward Glacier

Mt Terminus 3000'

Miers Glacier

Cwms

Dry Hanger

Cwms

Mt Terminus

Cwms

Mt Lister 13000'

Garwood Glacier

Terminal Moraine

Rough Glacier Ice

Weathered Ice

Ice Bastions

Ice Bastions

Pinnacles, Bastions, Lanes &c of Weathered Ice

Piecrust Ice

50' Bergs at edge of Unbroken Glacier

'Bar' or Riegel. Then about ½ mile farther west we reach the snout of the Taylor Glacier, which appears to be overriding moraine material at its extremity. The surface of the latter rises 600 feet in a very short distance, and is carved into alcoves and gullies by the sun—all of these erosion features presenting a steep face to the north and a gently sloping one to the south. The thaw streams on the glacier and in the moraine-filled Dry Valley all flow to the N.E.

Visitors to Switzerland will recognise how closely this alternation of 'gorge,' 'riegel,' and 'bowl' recalls the classic glacial valley south of the Saint Gothard Tunnel. Moreover, Lake Lucerne owes its cross-like plan to the action of two parallel glaciers—one of which overflowed (near the Rigi) into the adjoining valley. The same process is being carried on to-day where the 'apposed' glaciers of the Ferrar and Taylor valleys are joined in Siamese-twin fashion south-east of Knob Head.

(b) The *Koettlitz Glacier* cascades over ice falls near Heald Island and reaches sea level while still 20 miles from its snout. This 20 miles of low-level glacier is extremely interesting, for it would appear to be a stagnant area whose chief characteristics are due to the action of thaw waters on an old glacier surface. The pinnacles, bastions, and bergs have been described in the preceding narrative. Here again the drainage is directed diagonally across the glacier to the north-east. Some movement has taken place, for the edge of uniform glacier sheet on the south is fringed by great bergs which are differently oriented, though all sealed in the extremely ancient water-cut labyrinth of ice which constitutes the north-west portion of the delta.

Below the scarp of the Royal Society Range is a hinterland of parallel valleys. These are about 10 or 12 miles long, and are in many cases occupied by small glaciers in the western half of the valley. They are identical with the 'finger' valleys described in the reports on the glacial geology of the Rocky Mountains, U.S.A. Narrow ridges about 3000 feet high separate them. Some 'hang' a thousand feet above the Koettlitz. Characteristic hills, triangular in plan, occur where these valleys join, and all of them 'head' in beautiful cwms. Above these, cwms, and more cwms, fret the scarp of Mt. Lister over the whole extent of its 10,000 feet face. There is little doubt that we have here an example of the way the glacial cycle commences its operations, for this is a fault scarp of comparatively recent date.

(c) *Granite Harbour*, like New Harbour, is probably a relic of the period of glacial maximum when the ice flood exerted tremendous erosive power on its bed, and was able to erode far below sea level. We shall, however, never be able to witness these maximum forces in operation. Because a dwindling river has little effect on the topography it would be foolish to deny the action of a great river in flood; just as our observations in the Antarctic on a nearly stagnant or receding glaciation are not to be taken as descriptive of the most active periods in glacial history.

The first feature that strikes the geologist is that as one proceeds north there is less and less land exposed below

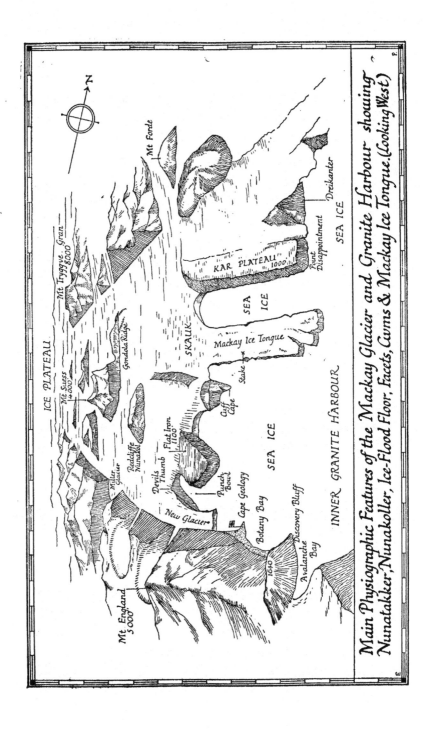

N

ICE PLATEAU

Mt Tryggve. Gran
8000

Mt Forde

Mt Suess
14000

Gondola Ridge

Miller
Glacier

Redcliffe
Nunatak

Mt England
5000

Devils
Thumb

Punch
Bowl

Flat Iron
1100

Cuff
Cape

New Glacier

Cape Geology

Botany Bay

1640

Avalanche
Bay

Discovery Bluff

SKAUK

Stake

SEA ICE

Mackay Ice Tongue

SEA
ICE

KAR PLATEAU
1000

Point
Disappointment

SEA ICE

Dreikanter

INNER GRANITE HARBOUR

Main Physiographic Features of the Mackay Glacier and Granite Harbour showing
Nunatakker, Nunakoller, Ice-Flood Floor, Facets, Cwms & Mackay Ice Tongue.(Looking West)

the snow and ice mantle. • This implies, I think, that the precipitation in the south-west corner of McMurdo Sound is extremely little, and increases both north-ward and southward. The most striking feature in the harbour—the Ice Tongue—has been described in the narrative. The Mackay Glacier moves 3 feet a day, as already recorded. Mention must be made of the ridge separating the new glacier from the Devil's Punch Bowl. This has certainly been covered quite lately by the new glacier. The harder dykes are striated, but the ridge is for the most part covered with granite débris. There is practically no englacial rock débris in the glacier, so that one is led to the important conclusion that the floor of the new glacier is covered with rock débris and that no erosion is taking place under this fairly large glacier. What was the floor of the Mackay Glacier at its period of greater area is exposed in many places 1000 feet above the sea ice in the form of rock-strewn plateaux.

One of the most interesting features is the evolution of the cwm which is indicated on all sides in the steep facetted slopes. On Discovery Bluff are the couloirs or chimneys; on Mt. England these become somewhat funnel-shaped; on the face of the Kar Plateau they deepen to a definite if shallow bowl. They obviously only originate on steep slopes where the icy covering is shallow. Avalanche Bay and the Devil's Punch Bowl are respectively filled and empty cwms, both at sea level. Along the southern crest of the valley are giant cwms each with its own glacier. Here the Miller Glacier has cut through the divide and links the Mackay presumably to the upper Debenham

Glacier. The walls are facetted, but not much facetting is visible—for the Mackay would seem to be filling its bed to a greater extent than the Ferrar or Taylor glaciers. Traces of a high level plateau at 3000 feet are evident all around Mt. Tryggve Gran, and the ice sheet drains thence into large tributary glaciers such as the Cleveland.

The upland topography is of three types. There are mountains, such as Tryggve Gran, whose shape is due to their stratigraphy. This peak is flat-topped owing to the presence of a dolerite capping. Others exhibit the typical cusps of the Matterhorn type, due to cwms encroaching on three sides. Others again, such as Mt. Forde, the Whale Back and Whitefinger, are now like giant *nunakoller,** for the cusps have yielded to the smoothing action of frost erosion.

Scattered over the glacier are the *nunatakker** (such as Mount Suess) and *nunakoller** (Gondola Ridge and Redcliffs) which have been described in the narrative.

(*d*) Space does not permit of any adequate account of the Great Piedmont Glacier. It has a seaward edge some 200 feet thick over the land, and for a considerable portion its front would appear to be floating, for here the edge is but 30 feet above the sea ice (and presumably 200 feet below water level). It rises to some 2000 feet above the sea about 3 or 4 miles from the coast, and is beautifully moulded over hidden *nunakoller*. One or two of these project above the ice about a thousand feet, and the mountains behind exhibit beautifully the relation of

---

* The two types of islands projecting through the ice sheet need to be distinguished. *Nuna-tak* is ' lonely *peak*,' and I suggest *nuna-kol* (*fide* Gran) for the *rounded* ridges which have been covered by the ice-flood.

lower glaciated slopes to· cuspate peaks. The plane
separating these topographic types is here about 3000
feet high. Behind many of the rocky capes the piedmont
appears to be nearly stagnant, or receding slowly, for the
ice either begins to thicken very gradually or is greatly
sun-weathered. In no case is there any evidence of pressure or 'overhang' on the capes, though the crevasses
opposite the valley glaciers show some movement, no
doubt due to the pressure of the latter.

In conclusion it will be of interest to trace the features
accompanying the growth of an ICE age as exhibited in
Victoria Land. Near Cape Evans the change of a snow
drift into a *glacieret,* and of the latter into a glacier, can
be studied in many places. The later stages depend
greatly on the topography. If the land is flat—i.e. part
of an old peneplain—the ice sheet merely spreads out
in great lobes, of which examples occur near the Solitary
Rocks on the flattened slopes north of the Taylor Glacier.
This grows larger and spreads out laterally, and, to my
mind, plays a protective part, as in the Great Piedmont.

If, however, we are dealing with steep contours, the
incipient glaciation—accompanied by water at this stage
—cuts out couloirs and shallow cwms. The next stage
is probably that represented by the scarp of Lister.
Ultimately some cwms encroach on others and dominating
'finger valleys' are initiated. These ultimately become
'outlet' glaciers.

The 'outlet' glaciers rise to a maximum, overriding
the slopes and carving out what later appear as shoulders
or benches. At this period there is true glacial erosion·

The *riegel* are overridden and planed down, the fiords
are cut out, the lakes are deepened. Later the snowfall
diminishes and the erosive power decreases, and the glaciers
dwindle through all the stages recorded by Hobbs. The
Beardmore Glacier with its tributaries largely entering
at grade, the Mackay with a few ' hanging' glaciers, the
Ferrar with a preponderating number of tributaries
hanging on the slopes of the main trough, are examples
of the earlier stages in this decline. The Koettlitz with
its tributaries 5 miles back from the main glacier and the
Taylor Glacier with its extraordinary ice-free outlet
trough 25 miles long are later stages in the retrocession
of the ice mantle.

THE GEOLOGICAL HISTORY OF SOUTH VICTORIA LAND

By F. Debenham, B.A., B.Sc. (Assistant Geologist to the Expedition)

It is now nearly fifteen years since the first landing was made on the mainland of South Victoria Land, since which time four scientific expeditions have visited it and returned with geological information. This has been, or is being, published in the form of reports of a more or less technical character. Therefore it seems advisable that an attempt should be made to condense this information into a popular narrative of what actual changes that area has undergone in past time, so far as they are known.

The tale must necessarily be incomplete, for the difficulties confronting geological investigation in those regions are naturally considerable, but enough has been done to warrant a preliminary interpretation of the known facts.

South Victoria Land at the present day is marked on the map as a strip of coast running in a southerly direction from Cape Adare (Lat. 71°) and merging into King Edward VII Plateau in the region of the Beardmore Glacier (Lat. 83°–85°). As appears in the physiographic account, it consists for the most part of a high level plateau terminated along the coast by steep escarpments, more or less indented by the action of huge overflow glaciers. It includes several groups of volcanic islands, the chief of which is the Ross Archipelago (Lat. 77°–79°). But in this narrative we shall include the Ross Sea and the Great Ice Barrier in the region, as inseparably bound up with Victoria Land in its history.

The oldest rocks met with in South Victoria Land, forming its foundation, or 'shield,' consist of gneisses, schists, quartzites, and crystalline limestones, much altered and folded by later earth-movements. On account of this alteration, much of their story is hidden from us, but we may compare them in age with the rocks of Western Australia or Eastern Canada—that is, they are of pre-Cambrian age. They were laid down for the most part by the agency of water, the schists and lime-stones being clays and chalks when they were formed. The sea-bottom on which these deposits collected was subject to continual up-and-down movements, changing the character of the deposit, for we find in rapid succession and in thin layers schists which were fine muds, next to quartzites which were sandbeds, and marbles which were either deep-water chalk deposits or shallow clear-water coral reefs.

On account of the complex folding of these beds, as well as the difficulty of obtaining a measurable section, we are unable to make any definite statement as to their thickness, but they cannot have been less than 15,000 to 20,000 feet. But figures are of little value, since there

is no method of ascertaining what thickness of strata
has since been denuded from the surface. The folding
and heating of the rocks has since quite destroyed all
evidence of the animal or vegetable life of that time,
though numbers of small graphite particles, found in
the crystalline limestones, may be the remnants of
carbonaceous growth in the ancient coral reef.

Our earliest view, therefore, of the region is that of
a sea bordered by land long since used up in forming
these deposits of mud, sand, and limestone. The gneisses
were in some cases huge intrusions of granite connected
with the up-and-down movements referred to, and in
other cases conglomerates, formed close to the coast-
line by waves or rivers. It is probable that there was
life of the lower forms in these seas, their skeletons being
now altered beyond all recognition.

Between the deposition of the crystalline schists
and the next succeeding strata there is a vast gap, yet
the mere existence of a gap in the geological record
means something, and we may interpret it as marking
a period of uplift in that area, so that it was dry land,
and instead of receiving further deposits, became the
source of deposits laid down in neighbouring seas. In
the vast period of time that this gap represents, most
of the alteration and folding of these rocks took place,
for the later strata are comparatively undisturbed. The
mechanics of these huge earth-movements are hidden
from us, but they partook of the character of a shrinkage,
and the strata were folded and plicated into only a
fraction of their former horizontal extent. Further, the

present directions of these folds tell us that the pressure came in a direction parallel to the Equator, the axes of the folds being nearly on a north and south line. However, with the opening of Cambrian times—a well-marked period in the earth's later history—the southern portion of our area was again below the sea, for in the Beardmore region we find beds of black limestone containing fossils of corals and of a primitive sponge-coral called Archæocyathus. The northern portion of Victoria Land was still probably dry land. The limestone is of unknown thickness, but its character tells us something. From its purity we can argue a clear though comparatively shallow sea, while from a number of limestone breccias found, we know that after consolidation it was broken up in places by earth movements, or even volcanic eruptions, and afterwards re-cemented again. But after this period of deposition the land again emerged from the sea, and no legible record is found until much later. A record of a somewhat illegible kind exists in a comprehensive series of granites which occur in profusion along the whole of the present coast-line. These are of infinite variety, and probably belong to many ages, but the majority seem to have been intruded after the Cambrian limestone and before the next succeeding strata. They were doubtless connected with the uplift of the whole region. In their intrusion through the pre-Cambrian schists they tore away and even assimilated huge blocks of schist and gneiss, which exist to-day as enclosures in the granite.

At the end of Palæozoic, or beginning of Mesozoic

times—that is, somewhat *later than when the great coal measures of England were being formed—the whole of the Victoria Land region became an area of deposition of a very interesting kind. For belonging to this period we find a very well marked series of rocks, named by Mr. Ferrar of the *Discovery* Expedition the Beacon Sandstone.

In the district visited by him, the Royal Society Range, the series is composed mainly of a dense sand-stone with thin beds of shale, and is at least 2000 feet thick. Farther to the north the series is represented by a similar sandstone, but associated with beds of coral, shale, and limestone. In the Beardmore district it appears as limestone, calcareous sandstone, beds of coal, and shale. There can be little doubt that these all represent deposits of approximately the same period under slightly varying conditions.

In the Royal Society Range (Lat. 78°–79°) the sandstone itself tells us a good deal. The grains of sand are very well rounded, as though wind-worn, there is much false bedding, the shale bands are thin, and there are remains of fresh-water plants in these bands. From those facts we can postulate a low-lying area with sand dunes or desert sand in the neighbourhood, which was collected and redeposited, probably by water. A semi-arid climate prevented any great amount of animal or vegetable life, for there are no fossils in the sandstone. There are, however, worm markings, ripple marks, and the casts of sun cracks, all of which mean conditions such as now obtain in parts of the Gobi Desert. As

far as is known, sea water had no part in this great series
of deposits. Yet the climate varied according to both
place and time, for in the Beardmore district there are
many coal beds and thick shale deposits, marking probably
a humid climate and a marshy topography. These conditions were repeated in a smaller degree in the Granite
Harbour district and to the north. Throughout the
whole area there must have been rapid, if not large,
rivers, for the sandstone in places contains small pockets
and bands of coarse conglomerate—a sign either of
coastal sea action or of rapid rivers.

For this period, therefore, we may not be far wrong
if we imagine a land somewhat approaching in conditions
the Southern Sahara or the outskirts of the Gobi Desert.
Too much emphasis must not be laid upon its desert
character, however, for our only evidence for that is the
wind-blown appearance of the sandgrains, and the absence
of fossils in the sandstone itself. The same conditions
probably held over what is now the Ross Sea and the
Great Ice Barrier, these being formed at a much later
period. The Beacon Sandstone series is the most
important yet found in that quadrant of the Antarctic,
for it is not only the latest sedimentary deposit of any
magnitude, but it undoubtedly has locked up in it great
stores of fossil evidence which have as yet hardly been
touched by geologists.

In the absence of later sedimentary deposits, the
more recent history of Victoria Land is somewhat
hypothetical, but one very definite period stands out,
marked by a geological phenomenon for which there are

few analogies to be found in the world. Perhaps the most characteristic feature of the whole of Victoria Land is the existence in practically all parts yet visited of a line of dark level-bedded rock, which stands out on cliff faces, produces pinnacled mountains, and generally dominates the topography. This is caused by intrusions of dolerite in the form of a sill, which from the district of its first description may be called the McMurdo Sill. From Lat. 71° down to Lat. 85°, and probably beyond, this dolerite is found, varying only slightly in character, and precisely similar in mode of occurrence. In places it occurs as one thick sill, nearly always columnar in form, up to 1500 feet in thickness; in others it splits into two or more sills of smaller size. In general it has intercalated itself between the strata of the Beacon Sandstone, but in some cases it has formed a sill through granite. In one particular district, that of the Ferrar Glacier, it forms a sill of 300 feet almost level bedded, dividing two very different types of granite. Its intrusion was for the most part quiet, and has left little effect, beyond a baking of the strata in its immediate vicinity. In places, however, it was evidently more violent, for huge blocks of granite or Beacon Sandstone are found in it, torn from their parent masses. The intrusion of these sills of molten rock probably raised the whole area to some extent, and prevented any further deposits. The true boundaries of the area intruded by the McMurdo Sill have not yet been located, but it can hardly be less than the size of the British Isles, and is probably much greater.

There is one more marked period in the history of

South Victoria Land. Probably about the middle of Tertiary times that part of the crust was subjected to further shrinkage stress of an even kind, which ultimately resulted in a series of great breaks or faults along the present coast-line. On the upthrow side of the fault the land was slowly raised into the present plateau, while on the downthrow side the land was depressed below sea level, and now forms the Ross Sea and the sea bottom below the Great Ice Barrier. Simultaneously with, and probably as an effect of this faulting, there occurred a great outburst of volcanic energy along the line of break. At many points volcanoes were formed, the chief centres being the Ross Archipelago, the Cape Adare Peninsula, and the Balleny Islands. This outburst is now just dying out, only two volcanoes being still active—Mt. Erebus on Ross Island, and Sturge Island in the Balleny Group. No recent deposits having been found, the later pages of the history of this area must come from its physiography, and cannot be treated of here.

For the work upon which this history is founded our thanks are due to the geologists of the various Antarctic Expeditions, chiefly Mr. H. T. Ferrar, of the National Antarctic Expedition, and Professor T. W. Edgeworth David and Mr. R. E. Priestley, of the British Antarctic Expedition, 1907-9. The 35 lbs. of specimens brought back by the Polar Party from Mt. Buckley contain impressions of fossil plants of late Palæozoic age, some of which a cursory inspection identifies as occurring in other parts of the world. When fully examined, they will assuredly prove to be of the highest geological importance.

SUMMARY OF GEOLOGICAL JOURNEYS

By F. Debenham, B.A., B.Sc., Assistant Geologist to
the Expedition

Owing to the early publication of this book before any of the material brought back has been examined, it is difficult to state the exact nature or importance of the geological results of the Expedition.

A summary of the work done will perhaps to some extent indicate its scope.

Of the three geologists accompanying the Expedition two were with the main party on Ross Island, Mr. T. Griffith Taylor and Mr. Frank Debenham. A third, Mr. Raymond E. Priestley, was with the Northern Party, stationed the first year at Cape Adare, the second in the Mt. Nansen region.

It had been among Captain Scott's original plans to maintain a geological party in the field during each sledging season, and this was carried out until the third season, when the Search Party took all available men.

The special geological journeys from the main base at Cape Evans were as follows :

In the autumn of 1911 a party of four, under Mr. Taylor, spent six weeks in the foothills of the Royal Society Range, examining and surveying about eighty

-miles of coast line, including Dry Valley and the Ferrar and Koettlitz Glaciers. Mr. C. S. Wright accompanied this party and studied ice phenomena under the most typical conditions.

The next summer another geological party under Mr. Taylor spent three months on the coast to the north of McMurdo Sound, making their base at Granite Harbour. During this, probably the most comprehensive geological journey yet made in the South, a complete detailed survey of the coast and the hinterland was made both by theodolite and plane table.

The Mackay Glacier was ascended almost to its outfall from the plateau, and fossils associated with coal beds were found. A complete physiographic study of the region was made by Mr. Taylor and some important measurements of glacier movement taken.

At the same time geological collections were being made on the Beardmore Glacier by various parties. The notes made by Dr. Wilson and the specimens collected by him and by Lieutenant Bowers are perhaps the most important of all the geological results.

The plant fossils collected by this party are the best preserved of any yet found in this quadrant of the Antarctic and are of the character best suited to settle a long-standing controversy between geologists as to the nature of the former union between Antarctica and Australasia.

In December of 1912 a party of six under Mr. Priestley ascended Mt. Erebus by a new route and spent a fortnight on the upper slopes collecting and surveying. The

positions of the former craters or calderas and of the
fumerole areas were carefully mapped and much of the
former history of the volcano ascertained.

In the Northern Party, stationed at Cape Adare for
the first season, a journey chiefly geographical and
geological was made along the coastline to the west.
Owing to unfavourable ice-conditions the party was not
able to go very far, but Mr. Priestley was able to make
a comprehensive collection of the slates and schists of
the region, supplemented in the summer by the recent
lavas of Cape Adare itself.

In the succeeding year, being landed by the ship at
Evans Coves, the same party made a journey into entirely
new country in the neighbourhood of Mt. Melbourne and
obtained further fossil evidence from the Great Beacon
Sandstone Series.

Throughout his journeys Mr. Priestley made a special
study of local ice conditions which together with Mr.
Wright's work with the main party will furnish a very
complete report on ice phenomena in the Antarctic.

From this summary it will be seen that the geological
work of the Expedition was particularly comprehensive
and was one of the chief items in the scientific syllabus
of the Expedition. The mass of material brought back
will be worked up and published in a special Geological
Report.

NOTES ON ICE PHYSICS

By Charles S. Wright, B.A.

These notes deal with a very few only of the subdivisions falling under the heading ' Ice Physics,' and are intended merely to give a popular survey of this interesting and by no means unimportant branch of scientific work.

As a practically new field of research, in the nature of things the work was largely observational in character, and until all the data are fully worked out all conclusions must be considered provisional and incomplete.

A consideration of the important place in the scheme of things occupied by the molecule known as H_2O would certainly lead one to give it the nickname of ' the mighty molecule.'

The climates of the earth are almost entirely controlled by water in one of its three forms. In the Northern Hemisphere we have long realised the effect of the Gulf Stream on our own lands; what then is the effect on the Southern Hemisphere of a stream of huge icebergs ever breaking off from the Antarctic continent and drifting northwards into low latitudes? Be it remembered that an iceberg at melting point is several times as efficient a reservoir of cold as an equal volume of water at the same temperature.

Consider only the simple case of an ocean current washing a natural ice barrier stretched across a strait and gradually eating its way through. How far-reaching will be the effect when the barrier is down! The whole history of the world might easily be changed by some such simple catastrophe.

SEA ICE

Possibly foremost among the different forms of ice to be studied was that of sea ice—being fast ice * formed in autumn on the surface of the sea by the action of the cold air above it. The process of freezing is a very interesting one to watch in cold, calm weather. As the temperature falls the sea becomes covered with small scale-like plate crystals up to one inch across of a delicate fern-like structure. They generally float flat upon the surface, but many are imprisoned in an approximately vertical position. After the surface becomes covered, the ice then grows in the ordinary way by accretion from below. In the initial stages, when the ice is only an inch in thickness, the felt-like mass on the surface has little rigidity, and even up to 3 inches thick moves freely up and down under the influence of a swell without losing its coherence in any way.

Sea ice is quite different in its properties from the ice formed on a pond or lake of fresh water, owing to the fact that some of the salt in solution in sea water is always imprisoned between the individual crystals in the sea ice. This imprisoned salt between the crystals does not

* Ice not in movement.

ICE FLOWERS ON NEWLY FORMED SEA ICE

freeze in contact with ice till a fairly low temperature is reached, and consequently sea ice when new and thin is never hard and rigid like fresh water ice. As a result ice even four or more inches thick is for sledging by no means safe, whereas the same thickness of fresh ice would be sufficient to support a regiment of soldiers.

In cold clear weather about thirty-six hours is required to form ice of this thickness, which is then of a dark slaty colour, but somewhat mottled owing to differences in transparency of the differently oriented crystals.

If the temperature of the air is below zero Fahrenheit, as the ice forms and while it is still only a couple of inches thick, the extruded salt on the surface commences to gather moisture from the air and grows upwards in beautifully shaped crystals, forming rosettes in almost infinite variety of structure, depending chiefly upon the conditions of temperature and humidity in the air above.

These 'ice flowers' have but a fleeting existence, however, for should the air temperature rise much above the temperature at which they were formed they melt again and collapse. Since the cryohydric temperature of common salt and water is zero Fahrenheit, it follows at once that no ice flowers can live above zero temperature (0° F.).

In the early part of the winter all additions to the thickness of the sea ice are due to conduction by the cold air above, but there is every reason to believe that later in the winter the sea ice grows to its great thickness of 8 and 9 feet largely by the deposition of frazil crystals from below.

There is very little •growth from above due to deposition of snow.

After the first winter, when the Sound was completely frozen over, the ice was seen on the return of the sun to be buckled in the form of low waves two or three inches high and about 150 feet apart from crest to crest. This phenomenon was due evidently to the dilatation of the ice on rising temperatures and was remarkable by reason that in each hollow a tiny crack was visible and remained open until the disappearance of the ice—Nature's provision for helping the break-up of the sea ice after a severe winter. In mild winters when the outer Sound is kept free of ice no such cracks or waves appear.

ICE FOOT

During the autumn, while the sea is as yet open and the temperature low, the whole shore line becomes covered with a coating of frozen spray, which on account of its saline constituents remains wet and sticky at even comparatively low temperatures, and provides pendent masses in an infinite variety of form, from a very stubby icicle to the so-called foot-stalactites, due to constant accretion of snow drifting from one direction only. About the same time there is growing on all shallow shores a low platform a few feet above the surface of mean sea level. This growth is due partly to drifted snow consolidated by spray, partly to tidal action, and partly to growth direct from the waves and sea.

This ice foot later on becomes frozen clear to the

GROWING ICE-FOOT, CAPE EVANS

bottom on shallow shores and remains fixed to the land during the winter, being separated by the working tide crack from the fast sea ice beyond.

PACK ICE

Pack ice, in distinction to fast ice, is not bound to the shore, but moves under the influence of local currents and wind. In the Antarctic, pack ice is evidently seldom formed at sea and largely consists of fast ice which has been broken away and carried off to sea by blizzards or some such transporting agent. The pack extends in normal years in December from about 66° to 71° S. Lat., a distance of 300 miles from north to south, and at times evidently fills the whole width of the Ross Sea.

Pack may be heavy or light, closed or open—the latter conditions being entirely dependent on local winds and currents. Thus heavy pack if open may offer no insuperable bar to navigation, whereas in closed pack, whether heavy or light, little progress can be made by ships. Heavy pack is usually associated with hummocks or pressure ridges rising to a height of four or five feet above the general level of the floe. These hummocks and pressure ridges are called upon to furnish ice for cooking and other purposes in the pack, being comparatively free from salt, owing, as mentioned previously, to the fact that the salt in the ice goes into solution and drains away, whenever the temperature rises above zero.

Towards the end of February the Ross Sea becomes comparatively free of pack and offers no bar to navigation.

Snow

Precipitation from the atmosphere occurred always in the form of snow in these regions bordering on the continent; sometimes, when the temperature was high, in the form of delicate six-rayed stars, or at lower temperatures in the form of hexagonal plates, little granular balls, or at still lower temperatures fine needle-shaped forms.

Not long, however, do they keep this form after falling. Immediately ' the mighty molecule ' starts its work, some crystals grow at the expense of others, the whole grows more compact, becomes hard, and while still containing much air is white and called névé. Later it completes its change by expelling the air and becomes the well-known blue ice.

During the summer one can see the whole transformation taking place before one's eyes in the course of a few days.

Crystal Forms

Not only in the form of snow, however, do these crystal forms occur. In crevasses, on the roof of the stables, on windows, and so on, countless varied forms are to be seen, each single form corresponding to a particular temperature, humidity, change of temperature, and change of humidity. Every slight lowering of temperature deposits its appropriate form and quantity of ice crystals on every object exposed to these conditions.

Thus on ice ponds or other masses of ice, at times the crystals are so deposited as to outline the form of the

ICE CRYSTALS IN CREVASSE

massive crystals in the ice — at times so as to show the orientation of the crystals on the surface.

Probably the most beautiful form of crystal, and certainly the most distinctive one, was to be found in huge masses in all crevasses. Single crystals measured up to 2 inches across, and were built in the form of hollow pyramids.

GLACIERS

It is, however, when in the form of glaciers that one appreciates to the full the power of 'the mighty molecule': huge valleys, 5, 10, 20, 30, even 50 miles wide, filled with moving ice, cut by this ice from the solid rock to a depth of thousands of feet—huge streams of ice moving by virtue of their own enormous weight at a rate of 30 feet a year even in the most dormant glaciers.

Hundreds of glaciers representing every type are to be found along the stretch of shore from Cape Adare to the Beardmore Glacier; some, like the Ferrar and Beardmore Glaciers, accommodating the outflow from the great ice plateau 9000 to 11,000 feet high, others flowing from local névé fields, and others little more than consolidated snow-drifts.

Owing to the fact that the 'snow-line' is at sea level, a very large proportion of the glaciers terminate in the sea and discharge bergs from their seaward faces as do many Greenland glaciers. More than this, however, the Antarctic glaciers, instead of coming to an end where they rest on the sea bottom, often preserve their entities as glaciers or streams of ice while projecting many miles

into the open sea. Examples of this type are furnished
by 'Glacier Tongue' between Winter Quarters and Hut
Point, and by the Nordenskiöld and Drygalski ice
tongues farther north. This latter pushes its way into
the sea a distance of about thirty miles and has a volume,
on a rough calculation, of fifty thousand million cubic
yards.

Probably the most interesting of the data collected
on glaciers were connected with their interior structure,
the size of the individual crystals, the amount of the
imprisoned air in the form of air bubbles, the occurrence
of silt bands and of bands of clear blue ice in horizontal
layers, and the occurrence and distribution of crevasses
and of pressure ridges in the glacier. This field, however,
is much too large to enter upon in this place.

THE BARRIER

By far the most unique feature of the Antarctic is
the occurrence of huge masses of floating ice, such as the
Great Ross Barrier, which fills up the whole of the narrow
end of the Ross Sea. This great sheet of floating ice has
an average depth of probably 600 feet and presents an
unbroken front to the sea 400 geographical miles in length
with a depth from back to front of over 300 miles. The
surface of the Barrier is comparatively level, and offers
little obstruction to sledging. The yearly snowfall from
observations by Captain Scott in the *Discovery* Expedition and from Sir Ernest Shackleton's work amounts
to about eighteen inches of consolidated snow of density

about $\frac{1}{2}$. From the same authorities we know that the yearly motion is in an east-north-easterly direction (close to Minna Bluff) at the rate of about 500 yards a year.

We have, moreover, data to show that no great change in the position of the seaward edge of the Barrier has taken place since the *Discovery* Expedition in 1901–04. Thus the Barrier may be considered for purposes of calculation as remaining *in statu quo* by virtue of the discharge of icebergs from its seaward face.

If this is so, we see that the volume of ice due to deposition, $\frac{18}{2} \times \frac{1}{12} \times \frac{1}{3} \times 400 \times 2000 \times 300 \times 2000 = 12 \times 10^{10}$ cubic yards (taking width as 400 miles, and length 300), should be converted into a strip of ice on the seaward side 400 miles long, 500 yards wide, and 600 feet deep $= 8 \times 10^{10}$ cubic yards.

This agreement of observation is a remarkably close one and proves that our fundamental statement is very close to the truth.

It should here be pointed out that in the above calculation no allowance has been made for the effect of glaciers pushing the Barrier before them and so adding to the apparent motion. That is, it is assumed the Barrier moves under its own weight alone. Luckily the Barrier may be subjected to further calculation, being in the happy position of a mass of ice resting on a frictionless plane at freezing point. Thus with certain assumptions regarding the rather uncertain coefficient of viscosity of ice and a slight excursion into integral calculus, we can arrive at the conclusion that the Barrier under its own weight would each year push out a distance of from

100 to 500 yards—a distance at least of the same order of magnitude as that found by observation.

From this we see we are probably justified in neglecting the volume of ice added to the Barrier and carried down by glaciers from the plateau, and may treat the Barrier as an entity by itself.

Consider now the effect of such a Barrier in equilibrium, enclosed on three sides and exposed to a continuous snowfall. Without any further mathematics it is at once clear that the velocity of motion at the seaward edge must be very many times faster than the velocity at the shore farthest from the sea. The tendency of a continuous snowfall would be therefore to accumulate a much greater thickness of Barrier on the side farthest from the sea. That this is not so is shown by the barometric observations of the sledging parties, which furnish convincing proof that the Barrier is still afloat quite close to the landward end, and further that a very good current circulation obtains under this part, since the single circumstance capable of preventing an accumulation of snow is a corresponding melting action, which again can only be due to water underneath the Barrier.

ICEBERGS

It has been noted that the Barrier and also land glaciers may discharge ice into the sea in the form of bergs. Since no bergs were ever seen in McMurdo Sound except in the late summer months, it may almost be taken that the prime cause of the calving of bergs from the parent glacier is due to the melting action of the warm sea water.

Bergs met with in the Antarctic can best be roughly divided into barrier or tabular bergs and glacier bergs. The tabular berg is recognised by its flat tabular form, whereas the glacier berg seldom has such a regular profile and often is formed of deep blue ice in contradistinction to the dazzling whiteness of the barrier berg. The tabular berg has a height up to 200 feet above sea and at times reaches the enormous length of 21 miles—truly a floating island. After partial melting it usually becomes slightly tilted to one side, or develops enormous caverns due to the action of the waves. In the final stages it may overturn or even disintegrate and after prolonged exposure to the elements is hardly distinguishable from the glacier berg.

The general tendency of the currents in the Ross Sea is to carry these bergs northwards into the warmer water, so that in late summer the greatest accumulation of bergs occurs at a fairly low latitude. As a result also of their great heat capacity they are not associated at this time of the year with pack ice as they are in the early summer.

That the number and distribution of these enormous reservoirs of cold has a real effect upon the climate of Australasia can hardly be doubted, and it is therefore evident that a close study and analysis of the data on this subject may well give results of the very greatest value.

GENERAL PHYSICS

[Simpson and Wright]

By Charles S. Wright, B.A.

The field covered in pure Physics by the Expedition was by no means a small one. It may conveniently be divided as follows :

(*a*) *Magnetic observations.*

These consisted in continuous photographic records by Eschenhagen magnetographs of the elements N.S. (astronomical) force, E.W. force, and vertical force. These instruments were placed in a cave dug into an ice-drift a couple of hundred feet to the south-west of the hut at Cape Evans. This furnished the highly desirable advantage of a constant temperature condition, important in that the sensitiveness of the instruments is dependent upon temperature. The light in the cave was furnished by a small electric lamp run from accumulators in the hut. Time signals were recorded on the trace every two minutes by means of a clock fitted with electric contacts, kept also in the hut and compared daily with the standard chronometer.

The programme of magnetic work included ' quick

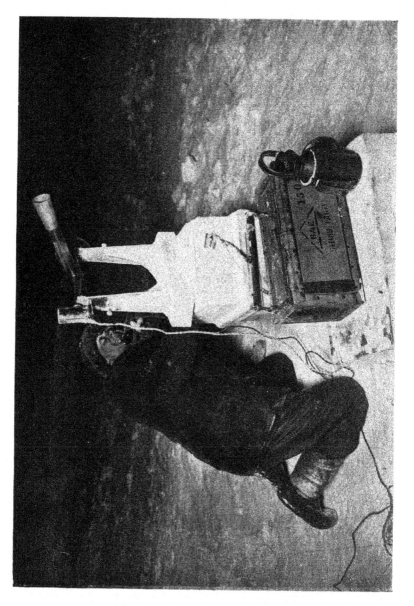

OBSERVATION WITH THE TRANSIT

runs' on international term days. 'Quick runs' are obtained when one moves the photographic paper at a much greater speed than usual, so as to have a more open time-scale. These were carried out at the same times by all magnetic observatories, in the hope that the comparison of traces would give definite information regarding the origin of magnetic storms.

Magnetic storms, though frequent, are not of hourly occurrence, and it is a matter for congratulation that one of our largest storms (also recorded by Webb's instruments with Mawson) occurs during the course of a quick run.

In addition to almost complete traces furnished by the magnetographs, absolute observations were undertaken once a week for standardisation of the traces, while observations for sensitiveness of the magnetographs were carried out once a month.

Observations of stars or sun, for time signals and for rating of chronometers, were made on an average once every fortnight. During the whole of the second year the rate of the standard chronometer varied only from 0·17 second losing to 0·25 second gaining, a very fine performance considering the adverse conditions it had to contend against.

The complete hourly records of auroras, which have been shown to be connected with sun-spot phenomena and with. magnetic storms, should when worked out give data of considerable value, especially when compared with the data collected by Priestley on the Northern Party.

(b) Atmospheric electricity.

(b) 1. Potential gradient.

During the whole of the first year and part of the second (until the almost continuous blizzards made observations useless) records of the potential gradient of the atmosphere were made in the usual way by use of the self-recording Benndorff electrometers. Owing to the mechanical difficulties of such work in cold regions, recourse was had to the lately discovered element ionium as a collector of the air potential, this substance being furnished by the great kindness of Prof. Giesel.

An interesting effect, noticed almost immediately on setting up the apparatus, was that in high winds, even when there was only the slightest amount of very low drift, the collector became charged to such an extent that sparks ½ inch long were continuously emitted by the charged system.

In order to obtain an estimate of the mean absolute value of the earth's electrostatic field in the Antarctic, comparison eye observations were undertaken over the level surface of the sea ice, similar to those undertaken at Melbourne for determination of the absolute value of the potential gradient over the sea.* These observations gave for the Antarctic a mean value of the same order as those obtained in other latitudes and over the sea.

(b) 2. *Radioactivity of the air.*

Numerous observations on the radium content of the Antarctic air were made during the first year, using the same apparatus as was used for observations on sea

---

* 'Atmospheric Electricity over the Ocean,' G. C. Simpson and C. S. Wright, *Proc. Roy. Soc.*, A., vol. 85, 1911.

air during the voyage of the *Terra Nova*. As might be expected (dry frozen surfaces can hardly disengage any great quantity of radium emanation), the variations in radium content were not large, but of the same order of magnitude as observed over the sea.

(*b*) 3. *Natural ionisation in closed vessels.*

The paper before mentioned contains the results obtained on the voyage of the *Terra Nova* from England to New Zealand, of which the section on Natural Ionisation may be summarised as follows :

(i) Variations in natural ionisation are due primarily to varying amounts of radioactive products in the air (disengaged, chiefly at least, from land surfaces).

(ii) These radioactive products are too diffusely distributed in the atmosphere to have any direct effect on the natural ionisation, and only become operative when deposited in the neighbourhood of the experimental station by precipitation, or by the earth's electric field (potential gradient).

(iii) There exists a minimum value to this natural ionisation (about 4 ions per c.c. per sec.) which has not by any method been reduced in value. This minimum would seem to be independent of the size or material of retaining vessel, and may therefore be best ascribed to a spontaneous breakdown of the enclosed gas, very similar to the spontaneous breakdown of radioactive substances.

From the above one can see that in places where the radium content of the air is very small (as over the sea), the variations in natural ionisation will also be small. Further work on the minimum value in the Antarctic (carried on in an ice cave at constant temperature) gave a value very slightly lower than that found over the sea, and showed, with a self-recording instrument, no variations greater than the probable errors of observation.

For further details of the above, and in respect to measurements of the ionisation of the air, the reader is referred to the paper before mentioned.

Samples of sea water were also collected from various depths for radium analysis, and will be worked out by Professor Joly, but the results are not yet available.

(c) *Pendulum observations.*

It will be known to the general reader that the weight of any substance as measured by the pull of the earth upon it is not an invariable constant. Thus a piece of lead or other substance weighed at sea level on a spring balance would be heavier at the Pole than at the Equator by about 5 parts in 1000. This difference may be considered as partly due to the weakening, as one goes towards the Pole, of the centrifugal force of the earth's rotation, and partly due to the increased force of attraction by virtue of the flattening of the earth at the poles, and consequent shorter distance from the centre of attraction.

Dealing with such small differences in value of the gravity constant ' g,' it becomes essential, if any theories are to be tested, that observations should be carried out with the most extreme accuracy.

The universal method of measuring ' g ' is by noting the time of swing of a pendulum, and as absolute measurements are of the utmost refinement and delicacy, comparative measurements are nearly always undertaken, and referred to similar observations at the standard station in Potsdam.

The pendulums used were of Col. von Sterneck's pattern and are gilt, three in number, swinging from agate planes in two directions at right angles to one another. The pendulums are swung at atmospheric temperature and pressure, and corrections are applied to reduce to normal.

The time of swing is measured by the method of coincidences, with reference to a special clock making an electric contact each second. This clock is used as the standard and rated (if possible) to $\frac{1}{10}$th second in the day, by observation of stars at meridian transit.

With care the value of 'g' should be accurate, after all corrections are applied, to one part in a million, but under the particularly unfavourable conditions in the Antarctic it is doubtful if a much higher accuracy than 1 in 250,000 is obtainable.

The difficulties experienced with the instrument in the Antarctic, though apparently trifling at this distance, were very real at the time. For instance, observation on stars for clock rate was usually complicated by a temperature of $-40°$ with a slight wind, quite sufficient to keep one nursing his nose, and to be very careful not to put one's eye to the telescope lest it freeze and remain there. Other little troubles, such as the stopping of the clock by a bodily shift of the wall of the hut upon which it was hung, also tended to reduce the accuracy of the observations.

During the first winter the pendulum observations

were made in a small cave.dug into an ice drift, but did not prove at all satisfactory, partly owing to the frost-fogging of the lenses and mirrors during the course of the observations and partly owing to the intense cold. There being more space in the hut during the second winter, a second series of observations was undertaken inside, a huge kenyte boulder being imported to serve as a solid base for the instrument. By cutting a hole through the floor of the hut and freezing the boulder to the frozen ground underneath, a very solid and rigid stand was formed. This second series was carried out in the dark room (by courtesy of Debenham), and the coincidences observed by telescope through a small window in the wall in order to reduce the temperature variation of the pendulums. The observations, though not equal to those obtainable in a fixed observatory, are quite concordant and should give sufficient data to substantiate definitely the theoretical formula at present in general use.

DR. SIMPSON IN HIS LABORATORY

METEOROLOGICAL REPORT

By G. C. Simpson, D.Sc.

Captain Scott's great desire was that good scientific work should be done on the Expedition. He therefore did everything in his power to help those to whom he entrusted the work by giving them all possible facilities and large financial aid, and he allowed me to use all the money subscribed in my native town and country for the scientific work under my charge. In consequence no Expedition has gone out so well equipped with stores and instruments for physical investigation. The following short statement of work done at Cape Evans will give some idea of the completeness of the outfit :

(*a*) An almost unbroken record by self-registering instruments of : temperature (two instruments), barometric pressure, wind force (two instruments), wind direction, sunshine, electrical state of the atmosphere, and the three elements of terrestrial magnetism.

(*b*) Regular observations of the usual meteorological instruments.

(*c*) An investigation of the upper air by means of balloons both with and without instruments, by which knowledge has been gained of the temperature and air currents up to a height of over five miles.

(*d*) Weekly absolute determinations of the magnetic elements.

(*e*) Hourly observations of the aurora during the whole period when it was dark enough to observe.

(*f*) A close study of the optics of the atmosphere.

(*g*) Accurate determination of the value of gravity by means of pendulums.

(*h*) A very thorough study of ice, as it occurs both in the air and on the ground.

In addition to the above a valuable set of meteorological observations was made at Cape Adare.

It is impossible to discuss here, even briefly, the results obtained, but it is quite clear that many of them are new and unexpected. Enough data have been collected to require many years for their adequate discussion by specialists. A few numerical results obtained during the first year are given in the table at the end of this article.

Throughout this book there have been constant references to temperature and wind—two meteorological factors which have been of vital importance to the members of the Expedition. It appears therefore that it would not be out of place to examine here these two factors from the scientific point of view to see what justification there was for the verdict passed on them from purely physiological experiences.

TEMPERATURE

The mean temperature at Cape Evans during the first year of our stay was – 0·4° F., which compares with – 1·3° F. found for the two years that the *Discovery* was in the same region. The corresponding temperature for a place in the same latitude in the Arctic is 2·5° F., thus the difference is not very great. The lowest temperature recorded at Cape Evans was − 50° F., which is not particularly low, for many well inhabited towns in Alaska and Siberia experience lower temperatures every winter. The real severity of the Antarctic climate is not shown in its low minimum temperatures, but in its low maximum temperatures. The July temperature at the North Pole has been calculated to be 30° F., the mean temperature at Cape Evans during December 1911 and January 1912 was 21° F. Thus the summer temperature at our base station over 900 miles from the South Pole was 9° F. below the summer temperature at the North Pole itself. It is interesting to compare the mean temperature throughout the months of the year at Cape Evans with that of a station in the corresponding latitude in the northern hemisphere. The comparison is made in Table I on the next page.

Thus during the three summer months our temperature was more than 15° F. below what would have been experienced at a similar latitude in the Arctic. The low temperature during the summer in the Antarctic is one of the outstanding features of its climate and has not yet received a really satisfactory explanation.

As stated above, the lowest temperature experienced at Cape Evans was − 50° F., but that was by no means the lowest met with by members of the Expedition. In July 1911 Wilson, Bowers, and Cherry-Garrard made a sledge journey on to the Barrier and they experienced

temperatures many degrees below those recorded at
the same time at Cape Evans. The lowest temperature
they encountered was – 77° F., which is the record low
temperature for the Antarctic and has only been sur-
passed in the Arctic at Werchojansk in Siberia—the coldest
spot on the earth. That the Barrier is much colder
than McMurdo Sound was made clear during the *Discovery*

TABLE I

Cape Evans. 77° 35′ S.		Northern stations. 77° 30′ N.	Difference.
February .	18·6		– 15·6
March	6·2		– 15·2
April . .	– 1·4		– 3·5
May . .	– 11·0		
June . .	– 11·8		
July . .	– 19·6		
August	20·0		
September	15·4	–	
October .	– 4·0	. – 5·4	
November	12·4	15·4	
December .	21·5	. 33·1	
January	20·7	36·9	

Expedition, but the temperature observations made by
the Norwegian Expedition at Framheim have shown
how great the difference really is. Framheim was only
sixty miles nearer the Pole than Cape Evans, yet the
mean temperature measured there was – 13·4° F., that is
13° F. lower than the temperature experienced simultaneously at Cape Evans. The cause of the great difference

of temperatures between the Barrier and McMurdo Sound is at present unknown, but it is hoped that the correct solution will be found when all the data have been discussed.

BLIZZARDS

It is a matter of experience, even in England, that great cold without wind is much easier to bear than a much higher temperature with wind. One does not wrap oneself in furs when going for a motor ride because of the cold, but because of the wind. It is the same in Polar exploration ; the wind is the chief enemy, not the cold.

Those who, previous to reading this book, have read Amundsen's ' South Pole ' cannot but have been struck by the fact that while this book is full of descriptions and references to blizzards the word hardly appears in the other. It is very natural to ask the reason for this strange difference. The reason is an important one, and if it had been known previously the history of the conquest of the South Pole would have been very different. *One can now say definitely that the blizzards which have been so fateful to British Antarctic exploration are local winds confined to the western half of the Ross Barrier.* The meteorological observations made simultaneously at Framheim, Cape Evans, and Cape Adare have thrown a flood of light on to the nature of these winds, and although at the time of writing the observations have not been sufficiently discussed to give us a complete solution of all the problems connected with their origin, many points of general interest have appeared, and an attempt will be made to summarise them here.

The velocity of the wind can be recorded automatically without much difficulty, and this has been done at many observatories, so that we know the chief characteristics of the wind in most countries. In the Antarctic a continuous automatic record of the wind was obtained at Cape Evans ; while at Cape Adare and Framheim frequent eye observations were made ; we have therefore the data for an interesting comparison.

The character of the wind in the British Isles is found to be very similar at different stations. Calms are very seldom recorded, and at the other end of the scale winds of a greater velocity than 50 miles an hour are rare. There must therefore be some intermediate velocity which occurs most frequently. The records of three years have been taken for Yarmouth on the Norfolk coast, and the number of times winds of different velocities occurred counted.

The result of the count is shown in the second column of Table II, from which it will be seen that at Yarmouth winds having a velocity of 4 miles an hour or less only occur on the average during 5·2 hours out of a hundred. The wind blows between 5 and 9 miles per hour for 23 hours out of the hundred, and velocities between 10 and 14 miles in the hour are met with during 28·4 per cent. of the time. Higher velocities than these occur less frequently, and during every hundred hours the wind blows at a greater velocity than 45 miles only during three-quarters of an hour.

TABLE II •

Frequency of Winds

Wind Velocity.	Yarmouth.	Framheim.	Cape Evans.
Miles per hour.	Per cent.	Per cent.	
0 to 4			
5 to 9			
10 to 14			
15 to 19			
20 to 24			
25 to 29			
30 to 34			
35 to 39			
40 to 44	1·5		
45 to 49	0·7		
50 to 54	0		
55 to 59	0		
Greater than 60	0		

The figures in the above table are plotted in Fig. 1, in which the thin line curve represents the data for Yarmouth. The curve shows clearly how the wind at Yarmouth blows most frequently with a velocity of about 10 miles an hour and that the frequency of higher and lower velocities falls off very rapidly on either side of the maximum. This curve is typical of all stations in the British Isles. In every case investigated, calms are of infrequent occurrence, while there is some velocity which occurs most frequently. The velocity which most frequently occurs varies from station to station, being least (about 5 miles an hour) at inland stations and greatest (about 10 to 15 miles an hour) at coast stations.

A similar analysis has been made of the winds at

FIG. 1

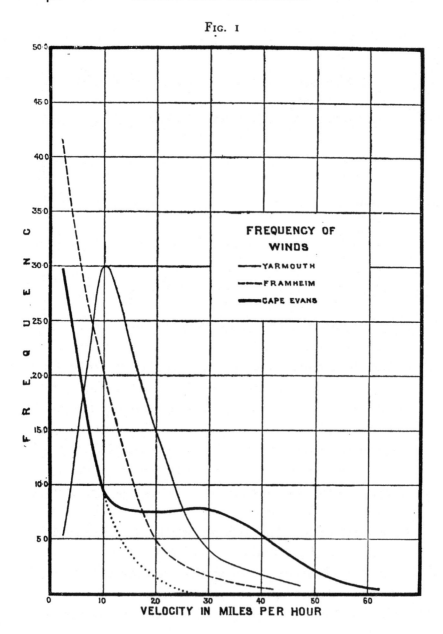

Framheim, the winter quarters of Captain Amundsen's Expedition. The results are shown in the third column of Table I, and are plotted by a broken curve in Fig. 1. It will at once be seen that the result is entirely different from that obtained for Yarmouth. At Framheim calms were of frequent occurrence and the wind blew at 4 miles an hour or less during 42 per cent. of the tota time. From this high percentage of calms winds of higher velocity fell off rapidly and regularly. It is important to notice that the shape of the curve for Fram heim is similar to that of the curve for Yarmouth from its highest point to its end. This shape is frequently met with in scientific work, and indicates that the change from maximum to minimum is regular without any outside factor influencing the natural change from stage to stage. It is the shape of the 'probability curve,' that is, the curve which indicates the probability that anything will occur when it departs from a most probable value. The wind conditions shown in the Framheim curve are the ideal ones for Polar work, for the most probable wind is a calm, and the frequency with which higher velocities occur decreases rapidly and regularly as the velocities increase.

We will now turn to the results of a similar analysis for the winds recorded at Cape Evans. Column 4 of Table I contains the data, and they are plotted on the thick curve of Fig. 1. Here we have a curve which commences in a manner similar to that of Framheim: the most frequent winds are those with a velocity of less than 4 miles an hour, and higher winds are less

frequently met with. In .fact if one had the whole of
the Framheim curve and only the first part of that for
Cape Evans—as far as winds of 14 miles an hour—one
would say they were similar and would complete the
Cape Evans curve along the thin dotted line indicated
in the figure, making it run parallel with the other two
curves.

But that would be assuming that there was nothing
abnormal in the region in which Cape Evans was situated,
and that the winds were governed by the same laws as
at Framheim. The real curve does not follow this ideal
curve, but takes an entirely different shape. The frequency of winds greater than 15 miles an hour does not
decrease with the velocity, for all winds with velocities
between 15 miles an hour and 34 miles an hour occur
with practically the same frequency. It is not until we
reach higher velocities than 35 miles an hour that a
decrease in frequency accompanies an increase in velocity.
This shape of the curve indicates that there is some
factor affecting the winds at Cape Evans which is not
present at a normal station.

This factor is the blizzard. Superimposed upon the
normal winds are the blizzard winds having velocities
varying from 10 miles an hour up to over 60, in consequence of which high winds occur with a frequency
out of all proportion to what would have occurred if
there had been no blizzards.

Thus the shape of the wind curve for Cape Evans
shows clearly that the blizzard is an abnormal phenomenon
superposed upon the ordinary meteorological conditions,

A BLIZZARD

FIG. 2.

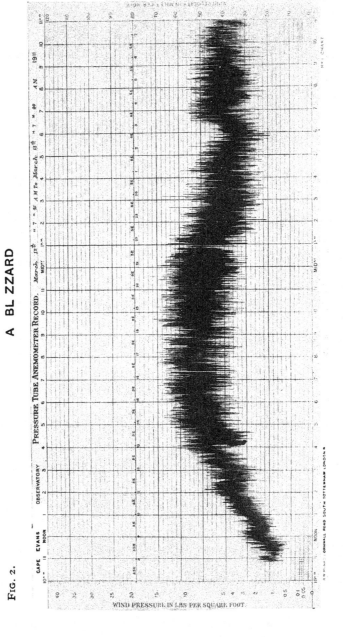

CAPE EVANS — OBSERVATORY. PRESSURE TUBE ANEMOMETER RECORD.

WIND PRESSURE IN LBS PER SQUARE FOOT.

March 12 h 1911.

and the curve for Framheim that it does not occur there.

The cause of the blizzards, their frequency, and the extent of country affected by them will be fully discussed in the scientific reports of the Expedition; here one is only interested in them in so far as they affected the fortunes of the members of the Expedition. The following table gives the number of hours blizzard winds were recorded at Cape Evans, and the mean temperature recorded while the winds were blowing:

TABLE III

Number of blizzards recorded at Cape Evans

A blizzard is taken as a southerly wind of 25 miles an hour or over.

—	No. of hours with record.	No. of hours of blizzard.	Maximum temperature during the blizzards.
February 1911			
March			
April			—
May			—
June			
July			
August			
September			
October			− 1·4
November	720		+ 9·7
December	720		+ 22·6
January 1912	744	89	+ 23·8
February			
March			

It is only necessary to study this table for a few minutes to realise the conditions which had to be faced, and it explains why the fortunes of the sledging parties were affected so largely by the weather.

With regard to the extent of the country subjected to blizzards we cannot of course be very precise. Judging from Captain Amundsen's report they did not occur at Framheim, nor on the route he took to the Pole. Very high winds were occasionally experienced at Cape Adare, but they were in no way connected with our blizzards ; as a rule when a blizzard was blowing at Cape Evans there was only a light southerly wind at Cape Adare. We know that typical blizzards were encountered at all points of Captain Scott's route as far as the Beardmore Glacier. Whether the winds met with on the Plateau were connected with blizzards on the Barrier cannot be decided until a more thorough study has been made of the meteorological records kept by the different sledging parties. From the data at present available there appears no doubt that blizzards were confined almost entirely to the western half of the Ross Barrier.

The cause of the blizzards, and why they occur only over the western half of the Barrier, are questions which cannot at present be answered with any certainty. It appears, however, that the chief factors are the following : The air over the Barrier cools down much more than the air over the Ross Sea, and in consequence there is a region of relatively low pressure over the sea. Into this region the air from the Barrier tends to move, but owing to the large deflecting force of the earth's rotation so near to

A BL ZZARD W TH GUSTS.

Fig. 3.

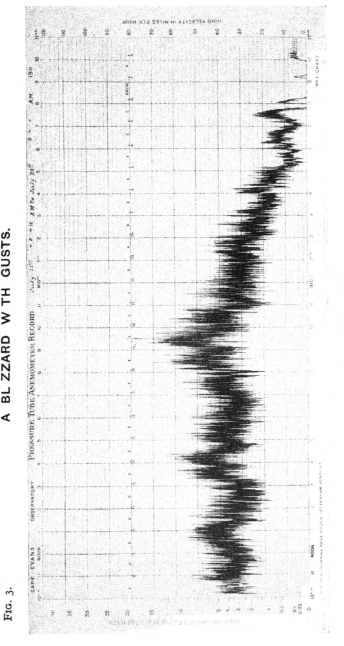

Ju y 23rd, 911.

the Pole, the air cannot move from south to north but is driven towards the west.

The western boundary of the Barrier, however, is a range of lofty mountains which stop the westerly motion entirely. In consequence the pressure distribution becomes unstable and the tension is removed by a rush of air along the Western Mountains, through McMurdo Sound out into the Ross Sea. The evidence on which this explanation is based will be given in the scientific report.

In order to give some idea of the intensity of the blizzards a few records of one of the self-registering anemometers are reproduced. These records were taken by an instrument at the hut, and as the hut had been built in the most sheltered place available the records do not give the full force of the wind. The direction of the wind has been entered on the records, and in the line below the direction the time has been shown, as the time printed on the charts was not correct.

The record for March 12, 1911, is typical of the blizzards during the first months after our arrival, when the depôts were being laid and the first ponies were lost (Fig. 2).

The record for July 23, 1911, is interesting as this was the blizzard which nearly proved fatal to Wilson's party at Cape Crozier. The important thing to notice in this record is the extreme gustiness of the wind: in the hour between 7 P.M. and 8 P.M. the wind varied in velocity between 24 and 84 miles an hour (Fig. 3).

One of the most dangerous peculiarities of the blizzards

was the suddenness with which they commenced. Three examples of the sudden setting in of blizzards are shown in Fig. 4.

The following tables contain the chief meteorological results as far as they were worked out at the time of writing. The Framheim results, taken from Amund sen's 'The South Pole,' have been included for ready reference.

Barometer

The barometer observations have been reduced to sea-level and normal temperature and gravity, except in the case of Framheim, which needs approximately ·03 inch adding to reduce to sea-level (*see* Amundsen's 'The South Pole ').

Wind

The Cape Evans wind amounts are from a continuous record by a self-recording Robinson anemometer.

The Framheim wind amounts are from observations made with a portable anemometer for a few minutes three times a day.

The Cape Adare wind was estimated on the Beaufort Scale and reduced to miles per hour by the equivalents used in the London Meteorological Office.

Maximum Wind

The maximum wind is obtained as follows :

(*a*) Cape Evans. The highest amount of wind recorded

SUDDEN COMMENCEMENTS OF BLZZARDS.

Fig.

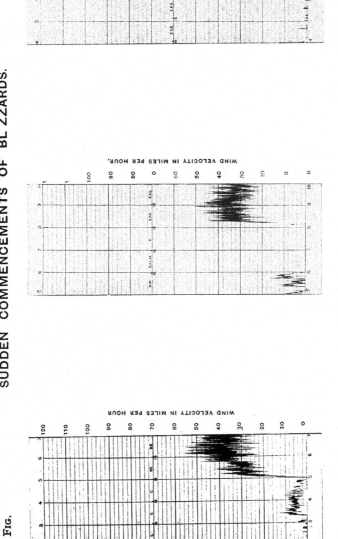

April 30th, 9.

May 1s 9.

September 1st, 9.

in a complete hour; higher winds were always recorded in gusts.

(*b*) Framheim. The highest recorded reading of the hand anemometer.

(*c*) Cape Adare. The highest Beaufort number reduced to miles per hour.

POTENTIAL GRADIENT

The values are the mean of those obtained during fine weather reduced to volts per metre over a level surface.

CAPE EVANS

.	Barometer, Inches.			Temperature, ° F:			Wind, Miles per Hour.		Potential Gradient.
1911.	Mean.	Max.	Min.	Mean.	Max.	Min.	Mean Vel.	Max. Vel.	
Feb.	29·31	29·74	28·96	18·7	33	0	23·6	61	
March	29·21	29·51	28·85	7·2	23	− 7	25·7	57	
April	29·32	29·80	28·82	− 1·1	13	−18	15·9	55	
May	29·23	29·84	28·26	−10·8	14	−29	12·0	54	
June	29·11	29·82	28·65	−13·5	17	−37	13·2	56	
July	29·08	29·55	28·52	−21·1	8	−50	18·5	66	
Aug.	29·19	29·72	28·64	−20·8	15	−42	16·7	66	
Sept.	29·16	29·85	28·29	−15·8	11	−37	14·5	57	I
Oct.	28·82	29·76	28·20	− 3·5	8	−20	17·9	59	
Nov.	29·63	30·15	28·98	+12·4	26	− 2	16·1	43	
Dec.	29·75	30·04	29·08	+22·0	32	+ 8	14·7	48	I
1912. Jan.	29·43	29·74	29·05	+21·4	39	+10	10·9	54	

FRAMHEIM

1911.	Barometer, Inches.			Temperature, ° F.			Wind, Miles per Hour.		Potential Gradient.
	Mean.	Max.	Min.	Mean.	Max.	Min.	Mean Vel.	Max. Vel.	
April	29·80	29·80	28·69	− 17·1	+ 12·2	− 54·4	7·5	35·5	
May	29·02	29·66	28·02	− 32·0	− 4·0	− 59·1	4·1	22·5	
June	28·88	29·54	28·50	− 29·5	+ 12·9	− 68·8	4·1	30·7	
July	28·86	29·51	28·24	− 33·0	+ 10·4	− 65·2	8·2	33·4	
Aug.	28·94	29·46	28·51	− 48·1	− 11·2	− 73·3	6·8	34·1	
Sept.	28·90	29·46	28·04	− 34·5	+ 15·8	− 63·4	7·5	42·3	
Oct.	28·61	29·66	28·10	− 10·6	+ 15·8	− 40·3	12·3	36·8	
Nov.	29·49	30·01	29·08	− 5·6	+ 22·7	− 18·4	8·9	40·9	
Dec.	29·66	30·14	29·20	− 20·9	+ 31·7	+ 1·8	8·2	40·9	
1912. Jan.	29·36	29·62	29·01	− 16·1	+ 27·5	+ 1·4	5·5	14·3	

CAPE ADARE

1911.	Barometer, Inches.			Temperature, ° F.			Wind, Miles per Hour.	Potential Gradient.
	Mean.	Max.	Min.	Mean.	Max.	Min.	Mean Vel.	
March	29·12	29·42	28·75		28			
April	29·25	29·79	28·61		22	−		
May	29·06	29·66	28·28		24			
June	29·11	29·70	28·63		10			
July	29·01	29·68	28·50		9			
Aug.	29·06	29·72	28·15		12			
Sept.	28·99	29·94	28·24		20			
Oct.	28·73	29·19	28·38		26			
Nov.	29·56	20·07	29·01		31	+ 5		
Dec.	29·72	20·07	29·14		39	+ 16		

D. G. LILLIE, WITH SOME OF THE SILICEOUS SPONGES OF WHICH HE SECURED
A RECORD HAUL WITH THE DREDGE

SUMMARY OF BIOLOGICAL WORK CARRIED OUT ON BOARD THE *TERRA NOVA*, 1910–1913

By D. G. LILLIE

CAPTAIN SCOTT, with his characteristic thoroughness, made it possible for scientific work to be carried out by the ship's party not only on their three summer visits to the Antarctic, but also during the two winters spent in New Zealand and on the outward and homeward voyages. As the early publication of this book makes it impossible to give any adequate account of the various biological results which may have been achieved, it is proposed to give here a brief summary of the collections brought home, together with a few notes concerning them, in order to help the general reader to form some idea of what he will find in the Biological Reports of this Expedition when they appear.

THE OUTWARD AND HOMEWARD VOYAGES

Whenever opportunities occurred on the outward and homeward voyages between England and New Zealand, tow-nets of fine mesh and of various sizes were put overboard to catch the small animals and plants which drift about in the sea and form the staple food of the whalebone whales and of many birds and fishes.

These floating organisms, which include representatives of all the larger divisions of the animal kingdom, are spoken of collectively as the plankton. On some occasions the net was towed behind the ship for about half an hour to catch the floating population of the surface waters. Sometimes the ship was kept stationary and the net sent down by a sinker to 500 fathoms or less and hauled up again; by this means samples of those forms which live below the surface were obtained.

About 70 samples of the plankton were collected. They vary greatly in size; one catch hardly covers the bottom of a half-pound honey jar, while another requires two seven-pound fruit jars to contain it.

The size of a catch of course depends upon various factors, such as the size of the net, the time it was fishing, or the amount of water passing through it, and the quantity of plankton in the sea at the place where the haul was obtained.

A small number of sea-water samples were collected from various depths by means of the Nansen-Pettersson water-bottle. These were generally taken from the areas in which plankton samples were obtained. The object of these water samples is to ascertain the salinity of the sea at different points and at different depths.

Any change in the salinity means a marked change in the character of the plankton.

The plankton catches, when sorted, will doubtless be found to contain many new genera and species to add to the list of the known forms of living things. The vertical hauls, which were generally made for quantitative purposes, will help to increase our knowledge of the relative abundance of the plankton over the oceans of the world and at different seasons of the year. Isolated observations such as these may be of small value in themselves, but every expedition which collects such data thereby adds its quota to the gradually accumulating mass of evidence and brings the time for generalisation nearer to hand. A knowledge of the relative abundance of the food supply of the ocean is not only of scientific interest but of commercial importance.

On the homeward voyage two satisfactory hauls with the trawl were obtained, one off the Falkland Islands in a depth of 125 fathoms, and the other off Rio de Janeiro in 40 fathoms. The trawl scrapes the bottom of the sea, and brings up a fair sample of whatever animals and plants it can entrap or uproot.

So little scientific trawling has been done in the Southern Hemisphere that almost every haul has a chance of containing some creature hitherto unknown from the area in which the catch was obtained.

Animals which live at the bottom of the sea are known to zoologists as the benthos.

During the outward voyage a day was spent on the island of South Trinidad by several members of the Expedition, and collections of land plants, land spiders, insects, and marine coastal animals were obtained.

The collection of plants has been examined by Dr. O. Stapf of Kew Herbarium, and found to contain some thirteen species which have not hitherto been recorded from the island. South Trinidad is a small volcanic island lying about 500 miles from the coast of Brazil, whence it has derived its scanty fauna and flora by means of such agents as winds, ocean currents, and birds. On the voyage home we actually saw one of these agencies at work. When the ship was rather more than a hundred miles from the Brazilian coast, to the southward of Trinidad, a large number of moths, belonging to about four species, were blown on board by a S.W. wind.

An up-to-date account of the fauna and flora of this island will be included in the Reports.

NEW ZEALAND

When the *Terra Nova* was engaged upon her three months' surveying in the neighbourhood of the Three Kings Islands, off the extreme north of New Zealand, some 80 samples of plankton and 32 samples of sea-water were obtained.

Seven successful trawls in depths varying from 15 to 300 fathoms yielded a good collection of benthos from this area.

During the first winter the ship's biologist spent five weeks at Mr. Cook's whaling station near the Bay of Islands in the north of New Zealand; and in the second winter, through the kindness of Mr. L. S. Hasle, four months were spent on two Norwegian floating factories which were exploiting the same waters. Three species of whalebone whales were examined and found to be identical with the three northern species—*Balænoptera Sibbaldi*, the Blue Whale; *B. borealis*, Rudolphi's Rorqual; and

Megaptera longimana, the Humpback Whale. About 30 specimens of the last species were examined. An embryo 2½ inches in length was obtained from a female humpback whale weighing about 60 tons.

While at the Bay of Islands an opportunity was taken of examining the inheritance of the pigment in several families of Maori-European half-castes. Sufficient data were collected to show that the phenomenon of Mendelian segregation evidently takes place.

Collections of fossil plants were made from several localities in the South Island of New Zealand, with a view to settling the geological age of the so-called ' glossopteris beds ' of Mt. Potts. From this material Dr. E. A. Newell Arber* has been able to show that the oldest known plant-bearing beds in New Zealand are of Rhaeto-Jurassic age.

One volume of the Reports will be devoted to a description of these fossil flora, together with the fossil plants found by the Polar Party and others in the Antarctic.

An account of some undescribed collections of New Zealand Tertiary and Mesozoic marine invertebrates is to be included in the Expedition Reports.

THE ANTARCTIC

During the three summer voyages to the Antarctic a series of qualitative and quantitative plankton samples were taken between New Zealand and McMurdo Sound, and also in different parts of the quadrant visited by the ship.

The number of plankton samples obtained was 135.

* Arber, *Proc. Roy. Soc.*, B. vol. 86, 1913; *Proc. Camb. Phil. Soc.*, vol. xvii. pt. i. 1913.

These comprise 27 collected during the first year, 48 the second year, and 60 the third year.

Also 96 samples of sea-water were obtained.

The increase in the relative size of the plankton catches as we left the warm seas around New Zealand and entered the cold waters of the far south was very marked. This increase was especially noticeable in the case of the diatoms. These minute plants became so numerous as to choke the meshes of the net after it had been fishing only five minutes. In the middle of pack ice the diatoms were much less numerous. This may have been due to the ice floes shutting out the sunlight or to an alteration in the salinity of the sea caused by the melting of the ice.

Some fifty samples of the muds and oozes from the bottom of the sea between New Zealand and the Antarctic were collected. A rough examination of some of these showed them to consist of the skeletons of diatoms and other inhabitants of the surface waters which had fallen to the bottom. These samples were obtained by letting down a weighted tube on the end of the sounding wire. The tube would sink vertically into the mud and bring up several inches of the deposit. Thus, if there were six inches of mud in the tube a sample taken from the bottom of the tube would come from about six inches below the surface of the sea floor.

In the Ross Sea it was found that many of the diatoms in a sample of mud taken from four inches below the surface of the deposit still contained their protoplasm and chlorophyll bodies. In other words, they were undecomposed.

F. DEBENHAM

When trawling in McMurdo Sound, it was a common occurrence to find that nearly half the catch consisted of dead animals.

From an examination of the summer temperatures at various depths in several parts of the Ross Sea it was found that a temperature of $+1\cdot0°$ Centigrade was hardly ever reached. The usual temperature was slightly below $0°$ Centigrade.

At these low temperatures bacterial decomposition is at a minimum, and the food supply of the ocean remains in cold storage. However, a small amount of decomposition must take place to allow of the production of nitrates for the plants.

The abundance of plankton in Antarctic waters is shown by a brownish discolouration of the sea produced by the diatoms.

Another indication is given by large numbers of whalebone whales, which feed upon the plankton.

It is true that only about three species of whalebone whales were recognised south of the pack, but the number of individuals seen daily around the ship was very great. The two commonest species seen were *Balænoptera Sibbaldi*, the Blue Whale, and *Balænoptera rostrata*, the Pike Whale.

The large schools of killer whales, *Orca gladiator*, are an indirect indication of a plenteous food supply, because they feed upon seals and penguins, which in their turn live upon the plankton.

If it was fully realised by whalers that there is a natural reason for the abundance of whales in the cold waters of

the Polar regions, they would not exploit warm seas such
as that off the north of New Zealand with a ' trying out '
plant suitable for South Georgia or the South Shetlands
and so lose large sums of money.

Fifteen rich hauls with trawl and dredge in depths
varying from 40 to 300 fathoms enabled a large collection
of the benthos to be made. A striking feature of the
marine fauna of the Antarctic is the extraordinary wealth
of individuals, while the variety of forms does not appear to
be very great. Also the large size to which some species
attain as compared with their relatives in warmer seas is
very marked.

This is, however, not the case with animals which
require carbonate of lime, for the secretion of limy
skeletons by members of the benthos seems to be at a
minimum in the cold Antarctic waters. The shells of
molluscs are small and fragile. Some sea-snails have no
lime in their shells at all.

It requires the warm tropical seas for animals with
calcareous skeletons to reach their vigorous growth.

Many of the bottom animals crawl over the sea floor
and pass the nutritious mud through their digestive organs
after the manner of earth worms; others take up a
stationary vertical position, and by means of tentacles
waft the falling diatoms into their mouths before they
have time to reach the bottom.

Almost every trawl brought up quantities of large
siliceous sponges covered with glassy spicules.

Good collections of sea-anemones, worms, urchins,
starfishes, crustacea, sea-spiders, molluscs, and fishes were

obtained. The collection of fishes has already been found to contain some new genera and several new species. There can be no doubt that many new forms will be found among the other groups.

Considerable quantities of three species of *Cephalodiscus* were obtained. These animals are of interest because they show signs of a distant relationship to the vertebrates, though their mode of life is very dissimilar. The minute individuals live together in colonies, and build up a gelatinous tree-like house.

The young forms of *Cephalodiscus* are very imperfectly known, and it is hoped that larval stages may be found among the material brought home, so that further light may be thrown upon the development of these curious animals.

In the last volume of the Biological Reports it is proposed to review the known marine benthos of the continental shelves of the globe in regard to its distribution in time and space. One of the objects of this inquiry will be to ascertain, as far as our present knowledge will permit, if there has been any tendency on the part of the benthos to originate in the Northern Hemisphere and migrate southward.

The work of Wallace on the distribution of land animals has shown that there appears to have been a tendency throughout the history of the earth for the land animals to originate in the Northern Hemisphere and gradually find their way south. The great belt of land which through long ages has almost encircled the northern half of the world seems to have been Nature's workshop for the evolution of types. These new forms spreading out from their points of origin had to find their way southward along the attenuated land areas of South America, Africa, and Australasia. Thus on account of their relative isolation these three southern continents became characterised by peculiar and in some cases comparatively primitive assemblages of animals. They became, as it were, behind the fashion. For instance, Australia to-day still has its marsupial population of kangaroos and such-like animals. In Europe marsupial types are only found as fossils, showing that they lived here millions of years ago in the Mesozoic ages of the earth's history, but have long since been exterminated and supplanted by newer types.

On account of the inadequate nature of the fauna of large parts of the Southern Hemisphere, man has had to stock these lands with northern animals.

Very few cases are known where land animals of a southern origin have advanced northwards. Whether this generalisation applies in the case of the marine benthos of the continental shelves presents an interesting field of inquiry. The collections brought home in recent years by the various Antarctic and other expeditions which have trawled in the Southern Hemisphere will, perhaps, make it possible to give some sort of answer to this question.

E. W. NELSON WITH THE NANSEN-PETERSEN INSULATED WATER-BOTTLE

MARINE BIOLOGY—WINTER QUARTERS
1911–1913
By E. W. Nelson

BEFORE the collections have been examined it is difficult
to say much about scientific results. The following is
a very brief account of the biological work undertaken
from the Cape Evans shore station during the two years
the Expedition wintered there.

In the late summer of 1911 a trip was made across
the Barne Glacier to Cape Royds.

The lakes in the vicinity of Sir Ernest Shackleton's
winter quarters were covered with only a very few inches
of ice, showing that, with the exception of Blue Lake,
they had thawed out that summer. Clear Lake was
tow-netted bv cutting a long slit in the ice and dragging
the tow-net backwards and forwards. Small catches were
obtained containing chiefly unicellular algæ and protozoa.
A few rotifers were caught, but no specimens of the blood-
red species *Philodina gregoria*, found in such quantity
by Mr. Murray, could be discovered. The masses of
filamentous algæ described by him are a constant feature
of any lake frozen or thawed. Contrary to our expecta-
tion none of the larger lakes thawed out again during our
stay.

On the return to Cape Evans an attempt was made to carry out a suggestion made by Mr. E. T. Browne. The sea was not yet frozen over, and the idea was to drop a tow-net from a kite flown out over the sea and then pull the net in to shore. A kite was made and the net dropped about 250 yards out, but unfortunately small floating ice crystals choked the net and completely spoilt the catches.

After the sea had frozen over the general winter work was commenced. A hole was cut through the ice and a wall of ice blocks built round to afford some shelter from the wind. This hole had to be cut every day, freezing during the night to as much as two feet thick.

In the spring of 1911 (September) the sea ice at this point was 8 feet 3 inches thick.

The labour entailed in keeping the holes open was considerable, and the time taken in this work very appreciably curtailed the time available for making collections.

The position chosen was about three-quarters of a mile distant from the hut in the strait between Cape Evans and Inaccessible Island, the depth at this point being 100 fathoms.

Tow-nets of various sized mesh were set at varying depths, the current under the ice being sufficiently strong to allow them to fish satisfactorily as a stationary net. Very good catches were obtained, which were brought back to the hut in Thermos flasks. These flasks proved quite invaluable, since catches could be kept in perfect condition in the lowest temperatures which otherwise would have been ruined by crystals of ice forming and spoiling all the more delicate specimens.

The physical conditions under which these drifting or plankton organisms exist is of great importance, and observations were regularly taken with this end in view.

The Expedition was fortunate in possessing some very fine reversing thermometers made by Richter of Berlin, and these were used to determine the temperature of the sea. During the winter a reversing water-bottle was used to obtain samples of sea water for analysis, but with what success cannot be ascertained until the analyses have been carried out.

During the winter only one sample could be taken each day, as the instrument had to be taken back to the hut, thawed out, and thoroughly dried.

Soundings were also taken through cracks and seals' blow-holes, and these will be plotted on the charts.

During the first year a complete record was obtained with an automatic tide-gauge constructed and looked after by Mr. Day. It might be mentioned here that the McMurdo Sound tides present some unusual features. Spring tides and neap tides are quite masked by the diurnal inequality of heights, depending on the declination of the moon. For example, with high declinations N. or S. the greatest rise and fall takes place, and there is only one high water and one low water in the twenty-four hours. But with the moon on the equinoctial there is much less rise and fall, and two high waters and two low waters are experienced.

Without entering upon any complex theory this phenomenon can be explained by the fact that with a high
southerly declination the tide that would be normally
caused by the inferior wave is so small as to be
inappreciable to ordinary observation. With the moon
at maximum northerly declination it would, of course,
be the superior wave that would not appear.   With the
moon on the equator diurnal inequality disappears, and
the two tides are experienced.

During the short summer before the work was interrupted by sledging and before the sea ice had broken
up, the air temperature was warm enough to permit
observations on the currents being taken with an Ekmann
current meter.   Series of measurements were obtained
with this instrument which should prove of great interest.

Exceptionally severe weather characterised the second
winter, and the fact that the sea ice was being constantly
blown out made marine work impossible for extended
periods.

Since a very complete tide record had been obtained
during the first year, it was decided to convert the instrument used for this purpose, of which only one was
available, into a seiche meter.   One record was obtained
and then the instrument was lost, owing to sea ice, which
past experience had led us to believe was safe, blowing
out and carrying the apparatus to sea.   Otherwise the
programme was similar to the previous year.

OUTFIT AND PREPARATION

By Commander E. R. G. R. Evans, C.B., R.N.

On September 13, 1909, Captain Scott published his plans for the British Antarctic Expedition of 1910, which he proposed to organise, equip, and lead.

His appeal to the nation, in fact to the Empire, for funds was heartily endorsed by the Press, and the first £10,000 was forthcoming by the spring of 1910. This amount was collected by Captain Scott and his *confrères* and was mainly subscribed by private individuals. The sums given varied from £1000 to 6d., coming from people in all stations of life.

This nucleus fund was obtained only after the most strenuous efforts on the part of Captain Scott, but after the first £10,000 had been raised the Government grant of £20,000 followed, and the programme of the Expedition became more and more ambitious.

Government grants were subsequently made by the Australian Commonwealth, the Dominion of New Zealand, and South Africa, and Mr. Samuel Hordern of Sydney contributed £2500 to swell the Australian contribution.

An office was taken and furnished at 36 Victoria Street, S.W., and here the preliminary organisation of the

Expedition was carried out by Captain Scott, his second-in-command, and Dr. Wilson, the Chief of the Scientific Staff.

The services of Mr. F. R. H. Drake, R.N., a Paymaster in the Royal Navy, were obtained as Secretary to the Expedition, and this capable and energetic officer made himself so invaluable that he was eventually asked to take part in the Expedition itself.* Captain Scott was determined that this Expedition should be run on business lines; Sir Edgar Speyer kindly consented to act as Honorary Treasurer, and thanks to his sound advice the finance of the Expedition was used to the best advantage.

Messrs. James Fraser & Sons acted throughout as Honorary Auditors.

Mr. George F. Wyatt was appointed business manager, and to him the Expedition owes a debt of gratitude for his expert selection of firms to supply provisions and equipment. Mr. Wyatt was a perfect encyclopædia in the matter of stores, and Captain Scott was delighted when he temporarily gave up his business in order that his whole time might be spent in assisting the Expedition.

Perhaps it would not be out of place to mention here some of the great firms who were selected to supply us with provisions. Messrs. J. S. Fry & Sons supplied our cocoa, sledging and fancy chocolate—delicious comforts, excellently packed and always in good condition.

Messrs. Huntley & Palmer: Ship's biscuit, fancy biscuit and cakes, and all the sledging biscuit which

---

* During Mr. Drake's absence on the Expedition Mr. E. G. H. Evans became (honorary) acting secretary.

stood us so well and was so conveniently packed for travelling.

Messrs. Colman of Norwich : Flour and mustard, as in the *Discovery* Expedition.

Messrs. Henry Tate & Sons : Sugar, which was in perfect condition even after three years.

Messrs. Peter Dawson, Ltd. : Whisky.

Messrs. Cooper, Cooper & Co. : 'The South Pole Tea,' which, like the cocoa, helped us to accomplish our best marches.

Messrs. Griffiths, Macalister & Co. of Liverpool supplied our tinned meats and general groceries.

Messrs. Price's Patent Candle Co., Ltd. : Candles, which were purposely made edible, though never eaten.

Messrs. John Burgess & Son, Ltd. : Pickles and condiments.

Messrs. Abram Lyle & Sons, Ltd. : Golden syrup.

Messrs. Beach & Sons, Evesham : Assorted jams.

Messrs. Frank Cooper, Oxford : Marmalade and preserved fruits.

Messrs. Gillard & Co. Ltd. : Pickles, sauces, and curried meats in tins.

The very good pemmican we used came entirely from J. D. Beauvais of Copenhagen, while Mr. Maltwood of the Liebig Co. supplied Oxo and Lemco.

Messrs. Shippams, Ltd., of Chichester supplied small potted meats and table luxuries for the outward voyage and for the base, and also delightful Christmas puddings.

Messrs. Heinz & Co. : Baked beans, tomato soups, and many relishes.

Messrs. Reckitt of Hull : Starches and cleaning materials.

Messrs. Gonzalez Byass & Co. : Port and sherry, champagne (Heidsieck).

Messrs. Simon Bros. of Northumberland Avenue : Champagne (Moet & Chandon), Courvoisier cognac, and all liqueurs. The brandy was particularly well put up in suitable bottles for sledging.

Messrs. Burroughs & Wellcome : The entire medical outfit and photographic chemicals.

The Wolsey Underwear Co. made all the underclothing, which could not be excelled.

Messrs. Mandleberg of Manchester were responsible for our windproof clothing, which was in continuous use down South, and most satisfactory ; also the tent material.

The Jaeger Co. : Boots and blankets, and all our mattresses.

Messrs. Benjamin Edgington, Ltd. : All the tents, over which they took an immense amount of trouble. The tents were made of Mandleberg material, which could not be beaten for lightness, strength, and efficiency.

In addition to the foregoing we were supplied with a rangefinder by Messrs. Barr & Stroud, standard compass and sounding machine by Messrs. Kelvin and James White, a fine player piano by the Broadwood Co., and two gramophones by the Gramophone Co., which brought a touch of home into the winter quarters of both parties, and often cheered both forecastle and wardroom of the *Terra Nova.*

Captain Scott, Lieut. Evans, and Mr. Wyatt prepared

separate provision lists and then met in committee to decide finally on the quantities and qualities of foodstuffs to be taken.

It was decided to add considerably to the kinds of stores taken on previous Expeditions, all believing in variety at the base stations. Thus, for example, we had three hundredweight of fancy chocolates for the shore parties, crystallised fruits, sweets, ginger, &c. Thanks to the magnificent generosity of the firms mentioned we practically obtained our provisions for nothing, and the packing of the stores was beyond all praise. So great was the interest taken by the employees of the provision firms that during the whole period of the Expedition we constantly came across little notes from the packers wishing us every success, &c. In two of Fry's cases were letters addressed to Captain Scott and the Second in Command, with new two-shilling pieces, to be returned if we thought fit to the packer in question, to hand down to his children, and so forth.

We were brought into close touch with the firms by visiting their works and actually seeing the goods packed in the ' Venesta ' cases, which were, if possible, of no greater gross weight than 60 lbs., to facilitate handling.

Our tobacco was presented to the Expedition by the Imperial Tobacco Company, who also gave cigars and cigarettes. They took the greatest care to preserve this very important part of our stores, and the tobacco supply was undoubtedly the best and most generous that any Expedition has had.

The above-mentioned articles form only a part of the

items of equipment necessary to a Polar Expedition with such an ambitious programme, and all this was arranged before we had collected our money or purchased a ship.

We had to obtain by purchase or otherwise ice-saws, anchors, picks and shovels, hides for soles of boots, &c., instruments of all descriptions for the various scientific purposes, lamps and lighting gear, books and mathematical tables, a library, oils and mineral grease, a colossal photographic outfit, stationery in gargantuan quantities, an efficient sledging outfit, harness and leather goods from John Leckie & Co. for our ponies and dogs, motor accessories for that part of our transport, &c., &c.

Our telescopes were presented by Lieut.-Col. J. W. Gifford of Oaklands Chard. He gave us a $3\frac{1}{4}''$ equatorial telescope for which he calculated the lenses, and also a light $1\frac{3}{4}''$ glass for the Southern Journey. Binoculars were provided by the staff.

Besides this we had great quantities of fishing gear, needles and scissors, knives, &c., from Milward's firm, and sewing machines from Singer's.

The Welsh Tin Plate and Metal Stamping Co. provided the majority of our cutlery, cooking apparatus, and mess traps free.

And then, lest anything should be forgotten, the Army and Navy catalogue was searched from cover to cover by the office staff for anything that might have been forgotten. Captain Scott *once* complained that we had forgotten to bring an article South—it was shaving soap ;

but it was produced forthwith from the 'annexe,' as we called the store outside the big hut at Cape Evans.

Captain Scott, assisted by Lieutenant Campbell and Mr. Gran, selected the sledging outfit, fur gloves, sleeping-bags, and finneskoe, and Gran personally chose every pair of ski and inspected every sledge-runner.

Mr. Meares gave us some very sound advice on the preparation of the animals' harness and accoutrements, and the credit of this part of our equipment certainly belongs to him, while Captain Oates at his own cost provided the ponies' forage from New Zealand.

A more detailed description of the outfit will subsequently be published, but the nature of this narrative does not permit one to expand on the subject of fitting out.

The choice of a ship was made on September 22, 1909, and that day arrangements were made for the purchase of the steamship *Terra Nova*, the largest and strongest of the old Scottish whalers. Thanks to Messrs. C. T. Bowring & Co., we were able to secure the ship before we had raised a tenth of the necessary funds, and she was handed over to the Expedition on November 8, in the West India Docks. The *Terra Nova* was purchased for the Expedition by Messrs. David Bruce & Sons for £12,500. This firm subsequently subscribed the amount of their commission on the transaction to the funds of the British Antarctic Expedition, and the owners (C. T. Bowring & Co.) subscribed £500 and greatly assisted Captain Scott to raise money in Liverpool for his enterprise.

The *Terra Nova* was handed over to the Second

in Command to fit out while Captain Scott busied himself more with the scientific programme and the financial side of the Expedition. She was docked by the Glengall Ironworks Co., who altered her according to the specification which had been prepared to meet the requirements of the Expedition.

We had her rigged as a barque (her original rig), and on her upper deck a large well-insulated ice-house was erected. This was to hold 150 carcases of frozen mutton, and owing to its position, free from the vicinity of iron and with a good all-round view; the top of the ice-house was selected for mounting the standard compass and the Lloyd Creak pedestal for magnetic observations. We also mounted our range-finder here.

The galley was almost rebuilt and a new stove put in.

The forecastle was comfortably fitted up with mess-tables and lockers. A lamp-room was built, with paraffin tanks to hold 200 gallons for lighting purposes, and storerooms, instrument room, and chronometer room were added.

The greatest alteration was made in the saloon, which was enlarged to accommodate twenty-four officers. This was scarcely luxurious accommodation, but it was always kept clean and the ventilation was good. Then a nice little mess was built for the warrant officers, of whom there were to be six.

Two large magazines and a clothing store were constructed in the between decks ; these particular spaces were zinc lined to prevent damp creeping in.

It was found necessary to put a new mizzenmast

into the ship, but on the whole she required alteration rather than repair.

All the blubber tanks were withdrawn and the hold spaces thoroughly cleaned and whitewashed.

A good chart-house was built above the wardroom and a large covered chart-table fitted up on the bridge.

The Glengall Co. were most anxious to meet us in everything and to push the alterations forward, and their work was efficient and not expensive.

Our original date of sailing was fixed for August 1, but by the united efforts of all concerned with the fitting out and stowing of the ship we halved the time apportioned for preparing the vessel, and the *Terra Nova* sailed on June 1.

The ship herself had to be provisioned and stored for her long voyage, and here again lists had to be prepared to meet every contingency. There were boatswain's stores, wire hawsers, canvas for sailmaking, carpenter's stores, cabin and domestic gear to be provided. The engineers had to purchase their stores together with a blacksmith's outfit. There were fireworks for signalling, whale boats and whaling gear, flags, logs, paint and tar, and a multitude of necessities to be thought of, selected, and not paid for if we could help it.

An invaluable collection of Polar literature, alike Antarctic and Arctic, was made for the Expedition by Admirals Sir Lewis Beaumont, G.C.B.; and Sir Albert Markham, K.C.B., and a beautiful library in miniature was presented to us by Mr. Reginald Smith.

When we left London at 5 P.M. on June 1 probably

the most strenuous part of the Expedition was over.
This may sound strange, but the fitting out was carried
on under such extraordinary conditions that we never
knew whether the most trivial alteration could be permitted
owing to the state of our finances.

During the year of preparation the *personnel* was
chosen. We had something like eight thousand volunteers
to select from, and, as one of the leading daily papers *
stated, 'All sorts and conditions of men seem to have
been imbued with a desire to earn Polar glory.' One
man wrote that although he was a foreigner he was quite
willing to become a British subject if Captain Scott would
find him a berth. Of the fortunate men who were finally
selected one may read elsewhere in this book, but there
were naturally very many crowded out who were fit
persons to have accompanied the Expedition.

One of these was Captain Ninnis, an enthusiast who
would have been selected had not Captain L. E. G. Oates
already been chosen. It will be remembered that he
lost his life in the Mawson Expedition after proving
himself to be eminently suitable for Polar work.

But even the eight thousand volunteers were disposed
of eventually and the appointments made. The final
selection was a happy one, and a vast amount of trouble
was taken over this important matter.

The outward voyage of the *Terra Nova* hardened
the men and taught them a good deal. Lifelong friend-
ships were commenced, and the ship routine gave great
opportunities for learning the characters and abilities

* *The Standard*, Sept. 17, 1909.

of the members and for appreciating talents peculiar to various individuals. The different parties were selected from observation made on the long outward voyage.

It only remains to acknowledge the unbounded hospitality of the Cardiff citizens, with Mr. Dan Radcliffe at their head, who docked and coaled the ship for us, gave freely in money and kind, and made their generosity so felt that Captain Scott promised that Cardiff should be the home port of the *Terra Nova.*

EPILOGUE

THE closing words of this book must be a heartfelt acknowledgment from all concerned with Scott's Last Expedition, to the Antarctic Committee which has laboured so long and so disinterestedly to further the interests of the Expedition, of those who took part in it, and of those who were left desolate by its supreme achievement. That acknowledgment is most gratefully tendered to Sir Archibald Geikie, President of the Royal Society; to Lord Strathcona, Lord Howard de Walden, Lord Goschen, Sir George Taubman Goldie, Major Leonard Darwin, and Mr. D. Radcliffe, who was invited to join at Commander Evans' request; above all, to Sir Edgar Speyer, who so ably and generously undertook the heavy duties of Hon. Treasurer; to Admiral Sir Lewis Beaumont, who gave unsparingly of his time and invaluable help; to Sir Clements Markham, the Father of Polar exploration, from whom Captain Scott assuredly drew much of his inspiration and encouragement; and to that close friend of Captain Scott, Mr. Reginald Smith, K.C. In New Zealand the interests of the Expedition were admirably represented by Mr. J. J. Kinsey, who became not merely its official representative but the trusted friend so warmly mentioned by Captain Scott and Dr. Wilson.

All the original members consented to join the Committee at Captain Scott's personal request, and their names were associated with his in the collection of funds for the equipment of the Expedition. Captain Scott himself undertook all the liabilities involved; he did not ask the Committee to share in these, albeit the Treasurer, with his characteristic generosity, gave him to understand that he would do much to see the venture through. Captain Scott, however, left a letter with Sir Lewis Beaumont giving him full authority to assume control of affairs should the ship be lost and a Relief Expedition become necessary. After Captain Scott's death the Committee translated into action Captain Scott's last appeal to the nation; the funds they raised were united with the Lord Mayor's Fund, with the further aid of the Lord Mayor, Lord Curzon of Kedleston, President of the Royal Geographical Society, the Hon. Harry Lawson, and Alderman and Sheriff Cooper; while Sir William Soulsby, Secretary to the Lord Mayor, was indefatigable over the heavy business in connection with the national fund. These funds were supplemented by a Treasury grant for the dependants of those who had lost their lives in the service of the country. Such was the response of the country and the Government to the appeal, that Captain Scott's dying wish has been amply fulfilled. The Expedition has discharged its liabilities; the dependants of the dead are well provided for; the scientific results are to be fully worked out and published under the auspices of

the British Museum. His Majesty the King received at
Buckingham Palace all the members of the Expedition
who were in the country, and conferred upon all the
Antarctic medal, while officers and men of the Royal Navy
have had special promotion ; and the Second in Command,
Commander Evans, has been given the honour of C.B. The
record is one of public munificence and personal friendship
which, could they but have known it, would have greatly
lessened the last cares of the Southern Party as they
awaited their lonely end.

APPENDIX

METEOROLOGICAL LOG

KEPT BY LIEUT. BOWERS ON THE WINTER JOURNEY. REPRODUCED FROM MR. CHERRY-GARRARD'S DIARY

The symbols used have the following meaning ·

WIND :

Beaufort Number.	Description of Wind.	Velocity, m.p.h.
0	calm	0
1 2 3	light breeze	2 5 10
4 5	moderate breeze	15 21
6 7	strong wind	27 35
8 9	gale forces	42 50
10 11	storm forces	59 68
12	hurricane	75

WEATHER :

b. blue sky   c. detached clouds
f. fog   g. gloomy
m. mist   o. overcast
s. snow

	Time.	Temperature.	Wind.	Weather.
27 June	1.15 P.M.	− 14·5 (off Glacier Tongue)	Breeze (E.) 3–4	
	6.0 P.M.		−	
	9.30 P.M.	− 15		

	Time.	Temperature.	Wind.	Weather.
28 June	7.45 A.M.	− 24·5 •		b. c.
	1.30 P.M.	− 26·5 (Hut Point)		b. c.
	8.0 P.M.	− 44·5 (Barrier)		

At Barrier edge a cold easterly air was flowing from surface on to sea ice.

	9.10 P.M.	− 47	o	b.
	Minimum	− 56·5		
29 June	9.0 A.M.	− 49	1	b. c.
	1.0 P.M.	50	1–2	b.
	7.30 P.M.	− 50·2	1	b.
	Minimum	66		
30 June	10.0 A.M.	55	o	b.
	Noon			

Enough daylight for relaying sledges. Footmarks visible in soft surface for two hours.

	2.0 P.M.	61·6	1–2	b. c
	9.0 P.M.	66	o	b.
	Minimum	− 69		
1 July	10.0 A.M.	66·6		b.
	3.0 P.M.			b.
	10.0 P.M.	− 60·5		b.
	Minimum	− 65·2		

Breeze during night, with slight drift.

2 July	10.30 A.M.	− 60·1	o	b. c.
	4.0 P.M.	− 60·5	1	b. c.

Light airs lasting till 4 P.M., when bank of fog formed over neck of peninsula. Later this dispersed to W.

	9.15 P.M.	65		b. c. m.
	Minimum	65		
3 July	11.0 A.M.	52	o	b. c.

Barrier surface featureless without sastrugi, as heavy as sand.

	5.30 P.M.	− 57·2	o	b. c.
	10.0 P.M.	− 58·2	o	b. c.
	7.30 P.M.			

Remarkably brilliant auroral display (*see* text, p. 13).

	Minimum	− 65·4		
4 July	9.30 A.M.	− 27·5	4	o. s.

Weather very thick. No march. Overcast all day, with steadily falling snow. Wind 3–4, with occasional gusts from E.N.E. to S.E. Minimum: 9.30 A.M. to 9.30 P.M., − 44·5 ; 9.30 P.M. to 9 A.M., − 54·6.

	9.30 P.M.	− 30	3	o. s.
5 July	9.0 A.M.	− 55	2	c. b.

Sky clearing ; haze over W. slopes of Erebus.

	2.0 P.M.	− 56·5	1	c. b. f.
	9.0 P.M.	− 60·1 (cloudy)		b. f.

	Time.	Temperature.	Wind.	Weather.
5 July	Minimum	− 75 3		
		6 P		
		slopes of Ere		
6 July	9.30 A.M.	− 70·2		
	9.0 A.M.	Cl		
	Noon	− 76·8 (cl		
	4 P.M.	F g y g		
		Island clea		
		b h d k		
		al p		
	5.15 P.M.	77 (care		
		− 77 5 (oth		
		(cl	c	b. m.
		minimum −		
7 July	Midnight	− 69		
		Low-lying		
	2 P.M.	68·3		
	7.30 P.M.	− 55·4		
		At 2 P.		
		scured Ross		
	Minimum			
8 July	1.15 A.M.		1	b. m. f.
	10.30 A.M.		1	
	7.15 P.M.			
	Minimum			
9 July	11 A.M.		2	
	1.30 P.M.			
			..	
	7 P.M.			
	Midnight			
		strong from S. or S.W. Noise of ice pressure in vicinity of beneath camp.		
	Minimum	− 24		

	Time.	Temperature.	Wind.	Weather.
10 July	Noon	− 24	6 to 8	o. s.
	11 P.M.		5 to 6	c. f. s.
11 July	10 A.M.	+ 7·8	5 to 9	o. s.
	Noon		5 to 7	o. s.
	8 P.M.	+ 6·8	3 to 5	o. c.
12 July	6 A.M.		10	o. g. s.
	10 A.M.	+ 2·9	3 to 5	c. s.
	0.30 P.M.		2 to 4	
	7.30 P.M.	2·8	4 to 8	
	10 P.M.		4 to 6	
13 July	4.0 A.M.	− 12·2	2	
	6.0 A.M.	18	1	
	9.10 A.M.	− 22·3	1	
	3.0 P.M.		3	
	10.0 P.M.		0	
	Minimum			

	Time.	Temperature.	Wind.	Weather.
14 July	2 A.M.			o. c.
	8 A.M.	17·4		o. c. s.
	3.20 P.M.	24·6	0–1	c. f.
	10.30 P.M.	24·5	3	o. f. s.
	Weather thick and threatening.			
	Minimum	34·5		
15 July	During night fog and snow obscured everything.			
	10.30 A.M.	19.2	3	c. f. s.
	Weather foggy, but clear sky overhead.			
	4.15 P.M.	13	4	c. f.
	8.15 P.M.	14·5	1	b. c.
	(800 feet high)			
	Midnight	− 19·2		b.
	Minimum	− 28·5		
16 July	8.45 A.M.	− 24·8	0	b.
	5.40 P.M.	− 25	3–5	c. f. b.
	Midnight	− 20·8	1	b. c.
17 July	3.0 A.M	− 23·3	0	o.
	Noon	− 19·5	3	c. m.
	6.30 P.M.	− 22·1	3	b. c.
18 July	(Unable to continue igloo.)			
	6.0 A.M.	− 27·3	4–5	b. c.
	9.0 A.M.	− 26·5	5	b. c.
	4 P.M.		4–5	b. c.
	Minimum	− 37		
19 July	3.10 A.M.	− 31·5		b. c.

	Time:	Temperature.	Wind:	Weather:
19 July	9.30 A.M.	− 33·2	0	b.
	4.30 P.M.	− 30		b. c.

(Among pressure ridges.)

20 July	3.0 A.M.	− 28·3		b. c.

(Completed igloo)

	9.0 A.M.	− 27	3	b. c.
	5.30 P.M.	− 23·3	4	b. c.
	8.0 P.M.	− 24	6	b. c.

(In pressure ridges.)
During night wind increased to 8, falling towards 6 A.M. to 5.

21 July	8.0 A.M.	20·4	3	o. c.
	Noon		2	o. m.
	7.30 P.M.	23·7	1	c. b.

Unsettled weather : pitched tent to leeward of hut.

22 July (Sat.)   *Start of blizzard :* Friday afternoon ; *Loss of tent* early morning Saturday.

3.0 A.M.   Commenced blowing heavily from S., with little drift.

6.30 A.M.   9–10   o.

Heavy drift and wind in strong gusts ; tent blown away.

A.M.   Collapse of blubber stove.

23 July 9 A.M.   All day wind blowing with almost continuous storm force—very slight lulls, followed rapidly by squalls of great violence. About noon roof carried away. Storm continued with unabated fury all day—not much drift. 11 P.M. Knoll visible. *Loss of igloo roof.*

24 July   Finding the tent.

	6.30 A.M.		2	c. b.
	10.0 A.M.		3	c. b.

From midnight squalls interspersed by short lulls to 9.

Noon   Dull, cloudy, and unsettled appearance to S. Slight to gentle breeze all day.

6.0 P.M.	12	4	c. b.

25 July   Start to return to C. Evans.

Noon   15·3 (breeze freshening)   4   o. b.

2 P.M.   Breeze freshened to fresh gale ; later to 9, and continued this for about ten hours, easing up towards morning.

	3 P.M.	− 17 (?)	8	o. c.
26 July	11 A.M.	− 21·5	2–4	b. c.

Wind fell light. Sky cleared. Among pressure ridges.

	Time.	Temperature,	Wind,	Weather.
26 July	9 P.M.	·45	o	b.
27 July	9 A.M.	−46·3	o–1	b.
	5 P.M.	−46	o	b.
	9 P.M.	−47	o	b.

At 9 A.M. clouds moving slowly over slopes of Terror from N.

	Minimum	−49·3		
28 July	8.30 A.M.	−47·2	o	b.
	3 P.M.	−40·3	o	b. c.
	8 P.M.	−38	3	b. c.
	Minimum	−46·1		
29 July	5.30 A.M.	−	o	b
	2.30 P.M.		2	b. c.
	9 P.M.		1	b. c.
	Minimum			
30 July	9 A.M.		o	b. c.
	3 P.M.		o	b. c.
	8.30 P.M.		1	b.
	Minimum			
31 July	9 A.M.		o	
	3 P.M.			

		ture.		
	10.30 P.M. (Hut Point)	−27		b. c.
	Minimum	−27·8		
1 Aug.	3.30 A.M.	−27·3	6–7	b. c.
	8 A.M.	−28	o	b. c.

During hours of daylight remarkable iridescent clouds to N.—general colours opal.

	5.30 P.M. (Glacier Tongue)	−31	1	b.

Off Inaccessible Island, northerly breeze 3, till arrived at Cape Evans.

INDEX

A

ABBOTT, G. P., P.O., (i.) 2 : accidents, (ii.) 87, 147, 148 : Erebus, ascent of, (ii.) 352 : fencing masks and foils manufactured, (ii.) 100 : Northern Party, duties, &c., with, (ii.) 78, 96 : water on the knee, (ii.) 103

Acclimatisation : dogs, (i.) 346 : men, (i.) 348, 389 : ponies, (i.) 130, 169, 238

Acetylene gas plant : carbide consumption, (i.) 272, 276

Adams Marshall Mountains, (i.) 509

Adare, Cape : geological specimens from, (ii.) 440 : height, (ii.) 112 : Northern Party's wintering place, (ii.) 89, 359 : penguin rookery, (ii.) 92 : scenery, (ii.) 92

Adélie Penguins *See* Penguins

Admiralty Bay in the Sounds, survey of, (ii.) 388

" Afterguard," keenness of—navigation studies, *App.* 19, 627 ; outward voyage, (i.) 10, 13, 14, 76, 82 ; stokehold work on homeward voyage, (ii.) 406 :—nicknames, (i.) 47, *App.* 6, 613. For particular officers, *see* their names

Age : relation to powers of endurance of cold, &c., (i.) 374 : Southern Party, (i.) 514

Ainsley, Mr., (i.) 6

Air : humidity of, measurement impossible, (i.) 291 : overlying layers, reluctance to mix, (i.) 274 : upper air currents, balloon records, (i.) 247, 250, 254, 265, 376, 380, 382, 399

Akaroa, (ii.) 387

Albatrosses, (i.) 19, *ill.* 18, (ii.) 366, 386

C

D

M

N

PRINTED BY
SPOTTISWOODE AND CO. LTD., COLCHESTER
LONDON AND ETON

9 781333 018788